S

Stone Society Book 8
By Faith Gibson

Copyright © 2016 by Faith Gibson

Published by: Bramblerose Press LLC

Editor: Jagged Rose Wordsmithing

First edition: November 2016

Cover design: Jay Aheer, Simply Defined Art

Photographer: Randy Sewell, RLS Model Images

Photography

Cover Model: Colby Dansby

ISBN: 978-1540335487

Dedication

This book is dedicated to anyone who has ever felt "less than."

Acknowledgements

Two years after book 1 came out, I am releasing Sin. When I started The Stone Society, I knew it would be a good series, but I didn't know how much I would fall in love with all my characters and the world they live in. With each new story, I have amassed new readers and new friends. My writing posse started out small, but it's grown into an amazing group of women I can't imagine not having in my life. Alex, Candy, Kendall, Jen, and Nikki, you all bring something different to the table, and I couldn't do it without your support.

To my Beta readers - Your feedback is invaluable.

My dear, precious readers, I am where I am because you continue to buy the books and leave reviews. You share this strange, new world with me. You cheer for the heroes. You boo the villains. And you always ask for more.

The wonderfully talented Jay Aheer, thank you for taking my vision and making it into art.

Randy Sewell, thank you, buddy, for such a wonderful photograph.

And as always, a major dose of appreciation goes to the man for taking this journey with me.

Prologue

Southern California
2045

"And to my niece, Raquel Taryn Cartwright, I bequeath my bar and all assets associated with it," Joel Warren, attorney and friend of Rocky's uncle, stated to the room.

Rocky squirmed in her chair as her family turned and stared her way. Uncle Ray always loved her best, and he just gave the rest of his family a double dose of *fuck you*.

"What the fuck do you know about running a bar?" Rocky's older cousin, Tommy, asked. "You're barely old enough to walk into one much less run one."

"Thomas, that's enough. My brother obviously saw something in Raquel the rest of us aren't aware of." Tommy's mom, Linda, didn't like Rocky any more than her son did, but she hated confrontation, especially in front of someone like Uncle Ray's attorney. The woman had all but offered herself to the older man, as if that would change the outcome of the will.

Mr. Warren addressed the room. "Raymond was explicit in his wishes. His body will be cremated and his ashes spread over the ocean. I will contact you when the remains are released to me, in case you would like to join me for the memorial. Now, if there's nothing further…"

Rocky got up but didn't follow the rest of her family out of the room. It was times like this when she really missed her parents. If they had still been alive, Uncle Ray wouldn't have burdened her with the bar. He'd have given it to her dad. Living with Aunt Linda had been nothing but one nightmare after another. No, living with *Tommy* had been the nightmare. He was too old to be living with his

1

mother, but Rocky doubted he'd ever get a job and move out. Not when he could sleep all day and party all night at his mom's expense.

Mr. Warren stood from his chair and came around the desk, propping against the corner. "Rocky, I know this is a lot for someone as young as you to take on, but Raymond and I discussed this on more than one occasion. He had faith in you, but more than that, he loved you like you were his own daughter. His only regret was not taking you into his home instead of letting you go live with his sister. I want you to know I'm here for you. For financial advice, legal advice, or even an ear to listen. The bar manager should be able to walk you through the day to day business, and I'll help you with the money side of things, if you need it. Speaking of money, I've also filed the necessary paperwork to transfer your inheritance into a private account. One your aunt no longer has access to. All you have to do is go to the bank and give them your signature. Ask for Mr. Dawson."

"Oh my god, thank you. I've had to beg for money for so long, I won't know how to act. This is all going to be so strange. Having control over my life. Moving from waitress to owner. I hope the others don't hate me."

"Do they hate you now?"

"No, sir. Well, there's one girl who likes to run her mouth, but I guess now I can fire her."

Mr. Warren laughed. "Just make sure it's for the right reason, dear. You don't want to start off on the wrong foot. Here are the keys to the safe deposit box and the apartment, although I would suggest having the apartment re-keyed. I don't know who had access to it, and if you're going to live there, I wouldn't want you to have any surprises. Here are the keys to his Saab. It's an older vehicle, but it should be reliable. If it isn't your style, we can sell it and get something more to your liking. Don't forget to call and get insurance in your name if you decide to keep it."

Rocky was overwhelmed. She had lived the last ten

years with only what her aunt would allow her to have. Now, she not only had her parents' insurance money, or what was left of it, but also everything Uncle Ray had left her. She was twenty-one and finally free of her family. She never had to step foot in her aunt's house again, and that was the biggest blessing out of all of this. She wouldn't have to beg for money. *Her* money. And she wouldn't have to endure another second of Tommy. *Bastard.* She would go to the bank, sign for her new account, and start fresh.

"Here's my card, dear. Please, call me day or night if you need anything. Raymond was my best friend, and I promised him I'd look after you."

"Thank you. I think I'll be okay, but it's good to know I have someone I can call if I need to." Rocky took the card and dropped it into her purse. "He talked about you all the time, you know."

Mr. Warren closed his eyes; the professional drifted away for a brief moment, and the lost lover shone through. He cleared his throat and plastered on a fake smile. "Yes, well, we were best friends for many years."

Rocky stopped at the door and started to tell her uncle's lover she knew the truth, but what would that accomplish? Nothing. She left the man to his own grief and walked out the door to her new life. She had so much to get done before her shift at the bar later that night. Except now, she didn't have to wait tables. Rocky needed to get with Bridget, the manager, and get things squared away. First things first, she needed to go shopping. Since she had access to her money, she refused to step back into the hell that had been her life. Tommy never left the house, and Rocky wouldn't chance going back for her clothes with the mood he was in.

Tommy made his presence known a few times at the bar, but Rocky had loyal employees who had her back. After the fourth time of Tommy coming in drunk and threatening her, Rocky filed an injunction against him, and he was banned from the bar. It didn't stop him from showing up on her doorstep at all hours of the night, but Rocky wasn't scared anymore. Tommy had done his worst to her many years ago. Besides, she had her uncle's nine millimeter beside the bed.

It took a while, but with Bridget's help, Rocky grabbed the reins her uncle had given her and was soon running RC's Tavern as smoothly as her uncle had. Sure, there were bumps along the way. She ended up firing the girl who'd given her grief, but she had good reason. The girl was caught stealing whiskey from the storeroom. Other than that, the employees she'd worked alongside of when her uncle was alive didn't blink an eye about Rocky taking over. She hired a new bartender to help fill in the gaps, and their team gelled.

Four months after Ray's death, Rocky was serving up drinks on a busy Saturday night. Royce, her regular bartender, had called in sick, so Rocky was doing what any good owner would do – she was working side by side with her employees. A tall, somewhat handsome man ordered a whiskey and Coke. When Rocky placed the drink in front of him, he grabbed her hand along with the tumbler. "You're the most beautiful woman I've ever seen. I know that sounds like a line, but it's the truth."

Rocky smiled, slid her hand away, and thanked the man for the compliment. She moved on down the bar to the next patron. Rocky was tall, thin, and nothing special. Her long dark hair was pulled back into a messy bun. Her T-shirt bearing the name of the bar was loose from all the hours put in learning the business and not eating like she should. The whiskey drinker was one in a long line of men who flirted with her, and being a bartender, she usually flirted back, because tips were better when the one paying thought he might have a chance at getting her phone number. At the least, she offered the men a smile and a sweet word. Something about this particular man was off.

Still, she didn't completely ignore him. He was a paying customer after all. She just didn't linger in front of him unless he was ordering another drink.

Weeks went by, and the man, Blake Stansbury, continued to come in at least twice a week, ordering whiskey and Coke. He continued paying Rocky compliments and tipping really well. One Saturday night, Rocky was tired and not on her game. When he asked if he could take her out, she gave in. "What could it hurt?" she asked herself. She placed Blake's tab in front of him and told him, "I have tomorrow night off. Meet me here at six, and I'll let you take me to dinner. But that's all."

Blake grinned, throwing cash down on top of his bill. Rocky didn't have to look at the money to know it would be double what he owed. She almost felt sorry for the guy. If he was trying to bribe her into going out with him, it was working. "If all you're offering is dinner, I expect to take you somewhere really nice, Raquel. How do you feel about Italian?"

"I can do Italian. I'll see you tomorrow." Rocky left a smirking Blake to wait on the others who didn't tip quite as well as he did. After she and her staff cleaned up and closed down the bar, Rocky made her way up the back steps to her apartment, stopping at the door. She leaned against the wall. *What are you doing, Rocky girl?* She'd vowed to never get involved with anyone, much less someone who gave her bad vibes. There was something off about Blake she couldn't put her finger on. Maybe after tomorrow night, he'd prove he was really a nice guy and she could spend some of her free time getting to know him. She would tell him she didn't want anything serious, because she didn't. She was tainted goods, and no man would want her if they ever found out the truth.

By the time six o'clock rolled around the next day, Rocky was close to having a panic attack. She had changed clothes four times. Not because she couldn't decide what to

5

wear, but because she was so strung out about going on a date. She opened her freezer and pulled out a bottle of Patron Reposado she kept for special occasions. If her first date in over a year wasn't a reason to drink, nothing was. She didn't bother with a glass. Rocky pulled the cork out of the bottle and tipped it up to her lips. Smoother than regular tequila, she took several sips before shoving the cork back in and replacing the bottle in the freezer. She took one last look in the mirror before making her way downstairs. Even though Rocky was early, Blake was already there waiting for her. He was dressed impeccably in a charcoal gray suit. His white dress shirt was unbuttoned farther than she thought appropriate for a first date, but his chest was magnificent from what she could see. The man obviously took great pains with keeping in shape. His dark hair was styled away from his face. At first glance, he looked like a mob boss.

Rocky had already told Bridget where she was going and with whom. She waved bye to her friend and took the arm Blake was offering. "Raquel, you are stunning, as always." Rocky offered a smile but didn't return the compliment. She was afraid if she opened her mouth, the tequila would come back up. She shouldn't have been surprised when a driver held open the back door to some fancy type of car. She had no idea what kind of vehicle she was getting into, but the large tips Blake had been leaving now made sense. He had money. Either that, or he'd stolen some rich old man's ride.

Thankfully, Blake didn't crowd her once they were seated. He kept his hands to himself, but he did slide his arm across the seat behind her head. She turned toward him slightly so she could keep an eye on him. "Thank you, Raquel, for accompanying me tonight. You're a hard sell, that's for sure."

"I don't date much," she offered as an explanation. Rocky wouldn't dare tell him the truth – he sort of gave her the creeps. She still didn't know why she'd agreed to the date.

"That is a shame for other men, but I am grateful you agreed to dinner. So, tell me something about you I don't already know."

This was the part Rocky hated. The *getting to know you* phase. She didn't want Blake to know anything about her other than what was on the surface.

"I hate broccoli."

Blake laughed, tipping his head back. Rocky's eyes were drawn to the corded muscles in his neck. Why did he have to be so sexy? She needed to stay alert. On her game. She could not let her guard down where he, or any man, was concerned. "I was going for something a little more personal, but that's important. Whenever I cook for you, I'll remember to omit the green stuff." His eyes twinkled with mischief. So, he planned on there being more than one date. Of course he did. A man with his money didn't take a woman out to a nice restaurant if he thought he wouldn't get a second date. "I think you are a mystery, Raquel Cartwright. One I fully intend to unravel." Rocky didn't miss the look in his eye that traveled down the length of her body. Blake intended to unravel her all right.

Dinner was more comfortable than Rocky expected. Blake kept the conversation light and chatted about himself. He owned a club, although he didn't elaborate as to what type of club it was. He was a native Californian and an only child. His parents had come from Sicily right after they were married forty years ago. Rocky tried to figure out his age without asking. He looked to be in his late twenties, but he could also be thirty-something for all she knew. At least he had money and wasn't after hers. Nobody except Mr. Warren knew exactly how much money Rocky had in the bank. Aunt Linda only knew about the insurance money, and that hadn't been a whole lot after Linda used it to "raise" Rocky.

When there was a lull in the conversation, Rocky excused herself to the restroom. When she came back, two glasses of wine were on the table. She didn't drink wine, but Blake held the glass out to her. "A toast, if you will." Rocky took the offered glass, waiting for Blake to speak. "To many more nights of getting to know you. Salute," he said, extending his glass toward her. Rocky clinked her glass to his and sipped the dark liquid. She'd never tasted a wine so sweet. She actually liked it. Blake sipped his own glass and watched her from his side of the table. As soon as she had finished all the liquid, Blake was pulling her to her feet.

"I think a nice walk in the park would be a lovely way to cap off the evening." He didn't ask her opinion, but Rocky didn't see anything wrong with a walk as long as they stayed to the lit pathways. The driver held the door open to the car once they reached the sidewalk, and Rocky began feeling the effects of the wine. Her body was warming from the inside out, but it wasn't uncomfortable. When Blake slid into the seat beside her, he sat closer than he had on the ride over. His thigh was pressed against hers, and the contact was electric. Rocky wanted him closer. Wanted him to put his hand on her bare leg and slide it up until it reached the apex. She wanted to straddle his lap and ride his dick until she screamed. These thoughts were still going through her mind when the car stopped. Blake exited the car and held out a hand. She placed hers in his and allowed him to pull her to standing. She staggered a bit, and he caught her up against his chest.

"Are you okay, Raquel? I thought with you owning the bar, you wouldn't be affected by one glass of wine."

He knew she owned the bar? They'd never discussed it. It was public record if anyone wanted to look. Or maybe he had asked one of the other employees. "Fine. I'm fine, just not used to wearing heels." That wasn't a lie. She wore comfortable shoes on a daily basis. She hadn't dressed up in over a year.

8

He was still holding her close, gazing into her eyes. At her mouth. His tongue eased out and slid over his full, lower lip, enticing her to want a taste. She unconsciously licked her own lips, and Blake took it as an invitation to kiss her. His lips brushed hers softly. Sensuously. Rocky wanted more. She was on fire, and she needed this man to ease her suffering. Her brain was telling her to stop, but her body was begging her to strip down and let him take her right there.

"Take me home," she begged. Blake didn't hesitate to give her what she wanted. As soon as the door closed and the car was back on the road, Rocky was in Blake's lap, kissing him with everything she had. It wasn't late. At least she didn't think it was, but when he walked her up the back stairs to her apartment over the bar, there were no cars in the parking lot. It took her fevered hands several tries to get the key in the lock. When she had the door opened, Blake crowded her inside, slamming the door behind them.

Rocky's body was drenched in sweat, her stomach roiling. She barely made it to the bathroom before she dropped to her knees, her head spinning. After everything in her stomach was emptied, she flushed the toilet and pulled herself up to the sink, washing her mouth out. Rocky stumbled back into her bedroom looking for Blake. She was so embarrassed. She had climbed his body like a dog in heat but had thrown up before he could even get her clothes off. It was then that Rocky noticed her clothes were already off. She grabbed her robe and pulled it on. "Blake?"

When she found he wasn't waiting in her bedroom, she padded into the small kitchen-living room combo. Everything was dark. The clock on the microwave showed it was almost six in the morning. Rocky sat down on the sofa, trying to gain her bearings. Hadn't she and Blake just come home from dinner with her begging him for sex? The last thing she remembered was coming through the door. "Shit. Shit, shit, shit!" Rocky stood quickly, her head spinning. She

9

waited until the dizziness subsided and looked around. She found a note on the table.

Raquel,

Thank you for the most wonderful evening I've had in a long time. I hope you feel better in the morning. I will call and check on you then.

Until next time,
Yours... B

The note made her feel a little better. She must have gotten sick, and like a gentleman, Blake left her alone instead of taking advantage of her. Maybe she could trust him after all.

Chapter One

Present Day
2048

Sin gripped the sword with both hands and swung it as hard as he could at Banyan, but the tall blond easily knocked it away. When he'd woken up early, Sin had been itching for a fight. He couldn't put his finger on what had him on edge, but something was eating at him. Something that had him wanting to hunt the Unholy in the light of day so he could release his pent-up frustrations while getting a workout in.

"Damn, you need to get laid."

Sin glared at Banyan, trying to gauge if the Goyle was baiting him or if he was serious.

"If I didn't know better, I'd think you're trying to take my head. Good thing you're not really focused," Banyan told him in his soft yet strong voice.

If Gargoyles could sweat, Sin would be drenched. The two of them had been going at it for hours, and Banyan looked like he had been sitting on a lounge chair sipping a cocktail. *Bastard.* Sin dropped the tip of his sword and held up his free hand in surrender. "Fuck it. I'm done."

Banyan took the sword from Sinclair and stored it along with his own in the building where the weapons were kept. When he returned, he tossed Sin a bottle of water and a towel. "Wanna talk about it?"

Sin downed the whole bottle and wiped his mouth with the towel. "You ever get in one of those moods where you want to rip someone's head off? Anyone's will do, but you don't know why?"

"Sure. We all have those days. Most of the time I know who it is I'd like to throttle, though."

11

Sin caught Banyan's grin. "Urijah still busting your chops at every turn?"

Banyan's grin turned into a full-on smile. "He's trying, but I've known the asshole long enough that I've learned how to ignore him. So, no idea what has you on edge?"

Sin sighed. "I have a feeling I do, but I do not want to put voice to it. It would make me sound like a prick."

"You're jealous." It wasn't a question. Banyan cocked his head to the side, narrowed his eyes, and continued, "I've heard tell of you marrying humans because you like the interaction, yet it's been close to a century since you last took a wife. Now, all your brothers as well as your cousins have found their mates, and you're still alone. Plus, I can't imagine it was easy having Rafael and Kaya in your home."

"Who the fuck are you? Dr. Freud?" Sin groused, but in truth, Banyan was spot-on.

"Someone who's sat on the sidelines for centuries watching and waiting for their own mate to step up to the plate."

"Yet you are so calm."

"Like I said, I've had centuries of hiding my feelings. Of putting on my game face when inside I'm dying."

Sin had a new appreciation for the Goyle, even if he did like his sports references. Sin hadn't spent much time around Banyan since the male relocated from New Orleans, but what he'd seen he liked. "Speaking of games, have you and Urijah come to any type of truce? I would rather not have to ask you to leave town when you only arrived a short while ago."

Banyan blanched but quickly recovered. "We have. He will be solely responsible for forging new weapons, and I will continue to lead training. On the days he is scheduled to spar, I will make myself scarce."

"And you are okay with that arrangement?" Sin

knew Banyan better than he did Urijah, but Rafael had brought Uri to the West Coast. Even though Rafe was his brother, Sin wouldn't go against his King's wishes no matter how close they were.

"I am. While I love working in the armory, I'm Goyle enough to step back and let Uri have his day. Besides, it gives me more time to do other things." Banyan didn't elaborate as to what those other things were, and Sin let it go. They walked together toward their vehicles. Sin had driven his Lamborghini, and Banyan had shown up on a silver Harley Street Glide. Sin was one of the few Clan members who didn't ride a motorcycle. Not that he didn't enjoy them, because he did. He preferred the smooth ride of his sleek, high-end sports car more.

"If you need me to spar, or for any other type of recreation to take your mind off things, I'm here," Banyan offered.

Sin wasn't about to touch the *other* type. It wasn't that he was opposed to sex with another male. Over the five centuries he'd been alive, Sinclair had enjoyed sex with males on occasion. Sometimes he needed to let loose, and with a Goyle, he didn't have to worry about hurting them. No, this was about not wanting to get in the middle of whatever this thing was with Banyan and Urijah. He wasn't even sure sex was what Banyan had been suggesting. Still…

"I appreciate the offer. For now, I am going to let the horses loose," he said, gesturing to his car. It was still early, and maybe a ride up the California coastline would do him good.

Banyan grinned. "I understand that. I'll catch you later." He slung a long leg over the seat of his bike and started it up.

Between the sports car and the Harley, the sounds of purring motors filled the air. Sin drank it in before throwing his car in gear and heading out. He cranked the stereo, letting the sounds of Cyanide Sweetness wash over him. Sin liked hard rock, but knowing one of their own offspring was belting out the lyrics made it even better. They had been lucky where Sixx's son was concerned. If it wasn't for his mate, Simone, they might not have found the half-blood in time. Fuck! Even Desi had found his mate, and the kid was only twenty-three. Sin was almost six hundred, and he felt as though he was destined to live out the rest of his days either fucking random people or marrying humans only to watch them eventually die.

Maybe Banyan hadn't been offering himself up for sex, but now that the seed had been planted, it was exactly what Sinclair wanted to get his mind off not having a mate. Vivian, the curvy redhead Finley brought around several times, had hinted at having a friend who was into playing. Sin turned the volume down and hit the button on the steering wheel to dial the phone. When the robotic voice asked for instructions, Sin said, "Call Finley."

A sleepy voice answered on the third ring. "Sin? You okay?"

"No. I need you to bring Vivian and her friend over."

"Now?" Finley whispered.

"Is now not a good time? I could meet you at your place," Sin offered. Having Gargoyle hearing allowed him to eavesdrop.

"Go back to sleep. It's just Sin," Fin said to whoever was in bed with him. By the sound of things, Finley got out of bed and closed the door behind him. A few seconds later, he was back. "The fucking sun's not even up, Sinclair. How about I come around tonight? You know, when normal Goyles are awake?"

Sin let out a deep sigh and ran a hand down his face. "Yeah, whatever." Frustrated, he disconnected the call. He didn't want to go home. There was nothing there for him except a lot of alcohol and his garden. The sanctuary hadn't offered any peace earlier. It was why he'd called on Banyan.

14

Now, he was even more restless, and driving around aimlessly had lost its appeal. For about five seconds, Sin considered calling Banyan and asking what exactly he had in mind earlier, but he thought of Urijah. Nope. Still not getting between the two of them. Sin had enough headaches. Deciding he needed to expound some more energy, Sin turned the car towards the gym.

Like Frey's gym back in New Atlanta, The Iron Bar was open twenty-four hours a day. Unlike Lion Hart Dojo, where several styles of martial arts as well as boxing were taught, the gym Sinclair had purchased several years ago was geared toward body-builders. There were a few cardio machines scattered throughout the large building, but for the most part, weight machines filled the space. When he bought the failing business, Sin remodeled it to fit the needs of the Gargoyles with a private area where they could work out unhindered by human eyes.

The special punching bags that filled the room were the ones Julian had designed to withstand their extra strength. Malakai Palamo had worked there for a while, but he missed the martial arts sparring and had moved to New Atlanta to help out Frey. Sin employed all Gargoyles so he didn't have to worry about any humans walking in on him while he was pounding away at the bag. He parked the Lambo in his reserved spot and headed inside. Thane Sommers, who had recently relocated from New Orleans, was manning the desk. Thane had been instrumental in helping to rescue Desi a few weeks back when he'd been kidnapped by Alistair's goons.

Whenever Sinclair thought of his uncle, his blood boiled. If it were up to him, he'd fly across the ocean to Greece and take the bastard out once and for all. Alistair had been targeting the mates of the Stone Society for months now, and Sin was tired of it. But it wasn't his call to make. Rafael was biding his time, getting the Society ready for war by training instead of meeting the Goyle head-on.

"Sin, you're here awfully early. Everything okay?"

"Couldn't sleep. Thought I would get a little workout in before too many people show up."

"Let me know if you need anything."

Sin clapped the Goyle on the shoulder and strode toward the back of the building, doing his best to keep his mind off the "anything" offer. As with Banyan, Sin was trying to keep his libido in check. The urge to fuck was growing stronger by the minute, and he was pretty sure Thane only went for females.

Sin didn't bother stopping by the office. He had males he trusted in place to run the gym. Since he was already dressed properly from sparring with Banyan, he headed straight to the private room and got down to punching and kicking. After a couple of hours of his mind refusing to close down, Sin gave up and hit the shower. As did most of the Clan in the area, Sin kept several changes of clothes in the private locker room. Whenever they hunted the Unholy, the Goyles often got bloody and needed a place they could wash up and change. It was rare they had the opportunity to fully phase when they were tracking the monsters. Maybe that was part of Sin's problem – he needed to let the beast loose.

Sin's home was located on property that backed up to the Angeles Forest, and when the moon was new, it was the perfect time to take to the skies. He had to fly low, but he was able to let his shifter come out to play. It had been over three weeks since he'd done more than allow his wings to unfurl and longer still since he'd taken anyone to his bed. The beast within was eerily quiet. When his shifter stopped chattering incessantly in his ear, that's when Sin knew something had to change.

After showering, Sin made his way toward the front of the gym. As he reached the counter, Thane was having a conversation with a human male. He was almost as tall as Sin's six-three, and he was built, so he already worked out

16

somewhere. Something about the man was off, at least to Sin's senses. His smell was masked deeply by that of a woman, and it called to Sin. He studied the human as he and Thane spoke about membership fees. Sin's shifter came to life. *Get closer. I want to smell him.*

Oh, now you want to talk. Sin did not move closer, and his shifter vibrated. *Would you fucking stop it? I'm not getting closer so we can sniff him.* Maybe the man had recently rolled out of bed with a woman. He inhaled deeply from where he was. Big mistake. Sin became light-headed. He tossed a hand up to Thane, not wanting to interrupt, and hurried out the door for fresh air. *Godsdamn, that was weird.*

The beast rumbled deep inside, but Sin ignored it. Maybe Banyan was right and Sin needed to get laid. Hopefully, Finley would bring the females over sooner rather than later, and he could slake at least some of his need.

Rocky rolled over and looked at the clock. Six a.m. was too damn early for her to be awake, but her dreams wouldn't leave her alone. She'd rather get up after three hours of sleep than to revisit the face in her nightmares. Too bad she had to see his face in her waking hours, too. Staring at the ceiling, Rocky scratched at the spot on her arm that would always haunt her, even if it wasn't bruised and begging for a needle. Rocky was at another low point in her life, but this time she'd come up with a solution that wouldn't have her dancing for money. "I'm so sorry, Uncle Ray." The tears began to fall as Rocky thought of putting the bar up for sale, but she would rather sell her uncle's legacy than sell her soul to the devil. Again.

As she wiped the tears from her eyes, Rocky's phone pinged with a text message. She rolled over and grabbed it off the nightstand. Sighing, Rocky punched in her pin and read the text from her best friend.

Got a hottie who wants to play tonight.

Rocky had seen the *hotties* Vivian hung around, and the girl could definitely pick them. The one named Finley was nothing less than a god. He was well over six feet, and his coloring was unlike anything Rocky had ever seen before. His hair was reddish brown, and his eyes were emerald green, yet his skin was tan. He had a perpetual smile on his extremely handsome face. If he wanted to play, Rocky wouldn't say no. Well, any day but today. She had too much to get done. The first thing she had to do was go see Joel Warren. She hadn't seen her uncle's partner and lawyer much over the last three years, but she wanted to get his help in putting the bar up for sale. It was going to take a lot of guts for Rocky to be honest with the man, but she owed him that much.

First, she responded to the friend who'd helped her get clean. *You know I love me some hotties, but today's a no-go. Raincheck?*

Definitely. This is one man you're gonna fall for. Guaranteed.

Not if Rocky had anything to say about it. She'd fallen for one man, and he'd nearly killed her. It was because of him she had to sell the only thing in her life that meant something. The only link she had left to the man who had loved her. Besides, even if Rocky fell for someone, she was no longer worthy to have a good man. She had nothing to offer anyone other than an abused body.

Give him a blowjob for me. Rocky didn't have to give Viv instructions on how to please a man. Having been a prostitute for a couple of years when she ran away from home at the age of seventeen, the girl knew her way around a dick. And a pussy. Viv was an equal opportunity pleaser. Ever since Vivian had taken care of Rocky and saw her through the worst days of her life, the two had been the best of friends. Rocky owed her life to the busty redhead, so when she wanted Rocky to join in her late-night trysts,

18

Rocky couldn't say no. Since she was never going to let herself get involved with any one man ever again, she had nothing against having a little fun in the sack as long as she could walk away sober at the end of the night, and Viv made sure she walked away.

She tossed her phone on the bed, padded to the kitchen, and started the coffee pot. While she waited for it to brew, she lit a cigarette and rummaged through her mail, sorting it between bills and junk. A shiny postcard caught her eye. A free week's membership at the local gym. Rocky didn't have the money for what came after the free trial, but she would love to start getting back in shape. Dancing had kept her thin body lithe, even if she'd been strung out. Now, she was just skinny. She tucked the postcard into her purse and decided to check it out before she dropped in to see Mr. Warren.

Rocky pulled back the curtain and peeked out the back window that overlooked the parking lot behind the bar. On the other side of the lot was a small park where Rocky used to like to sit and enjoy the sunshine. When more and more families began showing up, it hurt her heart too much to watch them. Growing up, Rocky had dreams of becoming a nurse and having a family of her own – the perfect husband, two kids, and a dog. Her husband was going to be tall. So tall she had to lean back to see his handsome face. They were going to have a boy and a girl, both of whom took after their father, because Rocky wasn't anything special to look at.

Her mother had been a nurse, and Rocky used to sit for hours and listen to her mom go on and on about helping people. Rocky had wanted to help people, too, but then life got in the way. Actually, it was death that got in the way. Her mother's battle with ovarian cancer had lasted a couple of years. Rocky had been young, but her mother had been truthful with her during the whole ordeal, so when her mom passed away, it hadn't been a complete shock. Her

19

father's heart attack soon after had been sudden, and Rocky figured it was because his heart was broken. Uncle Ray's passing was sudden like her father's, and he'd also died of a heart attack.

Rocky's plans to follow in her mom's footsteps were shot all to hell when her parents died and she'd had to go live with her aunt. She'd started off well with the bar, but things had taken a nosedive when she met *him*. Blake Stansbury, aka Satan, had charmed the pants off Rocky. He'd had a little help, though. First, he slipped her Rohypnol. Next, he roofied her *and* got her to snort coke. Next came the heroin. He was smooth in the way he eased her into getting hooked. It was so subtle she didn't even realize it was happening. It wasn't long until she was begging for her next fix, and Blake was just the one to supply it. If it hadn't been for Bridget being such a wonderful bar manager, RC's would have fallen apart completely. She was an excellent manager as well as friend, and the woman kept things going as long as she could. As long as Rocky wasn't taking all the profits and shooting them up in her arm.

By the time Vivian managed to get Rocky the help she needed, the damage had been done. Rocky was up to her hairline in debt, and there was no other choice but to sell. She could go back to dancing for Blake, but she would just as soon slit her wrists first. She had no idea what she was going to do for money once the bar was no longer hers, but she would figure something out. Hopefully.

Drago remained hidden in an alcove as several Unholy scanned the street. He'd spent most of the previous weeks observing the freaks trying to determine who their leader was. As of yet, he'd been unsuccessful. There was no rhyme or reason as to where and when they moved about at night. There was also no one Drago could ascertain to be in charge.

When Crane had gone rogue and kidnapped Desmond Rothchild, Drago had thought long and hard about returning to Greece, but facing the wrath of Alistair Gianopoulos was not high on his list of things to do. He preferred his head where it was – attached to his shoulders. Even though Kallisto had been released, she had yet to reach out to him. Sergei was still being held in the New Atlanta pen, so Drago decided to bide his time in the southern city in case Sergei was let go, too. Besides, with Julian Stone and Achilles monitoring security cameras for Drago's whereabouts, he didn't have many options of places to go without being identified.

When he first caught sight of the Unholy moving about, Drago got an idea of blending in with them, even though he appeared human whereas the lab experiments gone wrong did not. Now, after nearly three weeks, he was ready to use his Gargoyle strength to infiltrate the local group and take over. Once he had them under his command, he would formulate a plan to get Sergei out of prison if he wasn't released beforehand. Stepping out from under the covered alcove, Drago moved in behind the Unholy, ready to put phase one into motion.

Chapter Two

Rocky was shaking by the time she stepped into Joel Warren's office. How did she tell her uncle's partner she had squandered away his legacy? Rocky had never been more ashamed in her life.

"Rocky, how are you?" the older gentleman asked. By the bags under his eyes, Joel hadn't fared much better lately than she had.

"I've been better, but I've also been a lot worse. May we sit? I don't think I can get this out if I have to stand."

"Of course, dear." Instead of sitting behind his desk, Joel led Rocky to the small sofa that centered the far wall.

Rocky didn't know where to start so she blurted out, "I'm in trouble. Not as much trouble as I was in, but I've made some really bad choices these past three years, and I need to sell the bar. I should have come to you sooner, but I couldn't face you. I was ashamed. I *am* ashamed."

Joel didn't ask what those choices had been. "Are you certain selling is your only option?"

"That or bankruptcy, and I'd rather not have the employees go through that kind of downtime. If I sell, it will hopefully be a smooth transition between owners. That's why I'm here – I want you to draw up the paperwork and include a clause stipulating my employees retain their jobs."

Joel didn't respond straight away. He clasped his hands together with his forearms on his thighs. "Please say something," Rocky whispered.

He finally leaned back, and the tears in his eyes made Rocky feel a hundred times worse than she already did. "I failed you. I failed Ray, and I failed you." He wiped a tear away that had escaped from the corner of his eye.

"No, you didn't. I failed us all. One date with the wrong man turned into a life filled with drugs and other things I don't care to mention. This is all on me and no one else. If it wasn't for my best friend, I probably wouldn't even be here." Rocky grasped the older man's hand. "What's done can't be undone, and no amount of tears or regret will change things now. I've learned a hard lesson, but I'm clean, and I intend to stay that way. I should've come to you earlier, but I didn't. Will you help me now? Please?"

"Of course I will." Mr. Warren pulled Rocky to him in a fatherly hug. They held on to each other for a few minutes, and when they pulled back, they got down to business. Rocky stood from the sofa and opened the messenger bag she'd brought with her. She laid out the paperwork the attorney needed to help her in selling what should have been her life's work. She prayed her cousin Tommy didn't catch wind of her downfall. She wouldn't be able to stand seeing him gloat.

An hour later, Rocky walked into RC's feeling better than she had in three years. She would be the one to vet the new owner, and unless she felt good about whose hands her employees were being handed over to, she wouldn't sell. Joel had assured her he would help her stay afloat until the bar sold to the right person. She refused to take a handout but promised to pay him back with interest. Instead of going to her office, Rocky stepped behind the bar. She needed to keep busy, and slinging drinks was just the way to do it.

Sinclair leaned back in his office chair and clasped his hands behind his head as Rafael filled him in on the latest happenings in New Atlanta.

"We've beefed up security at all of our jobsites, but so far, there haven't been any incidents."

"What was the point of breaking into your office if whoever is responsible wasn't going to use the information

23

in some way against you?" Sin asked his brother.

"That's the million-dollar question. Either they're biding their time for something, or it was a diversionary tactic."

"Or a 'fuck you' to Julian from his hacker buddy."

"It seems his hacker buddy, as you put it, has disappeared. There have been no further incidents, not since Katherine Fox's life was thrown into turmoil," Rafe said. "Still, we're not letting our guard down."

"How is Julian holding up with his mate in prison?"

"About as well as any of us would be – he's not. He still won't go see her, but I'm trying to get Nikolas to help change his mind about that. He can't focus on what we need him to with her sitting there. He's spending most of his time trying to figure out how to undo everything that was put into place that landed his mate in jail."

Sin couldn't imagine what his cousin was going through. If it were his mate in jail, he'd probably be sitting in the cell with her. That or he'd break her out. "Landon Roxburgh is good with computers. If you need his assistance, let me know. I'll get him to concentrate on the things Julian should be doing so he can clear his mate's name."

"Thanks, Brother. I was going to ask if you had someone skilled enough to help. Why don't you go ahead and ask for his assistance."

"I will do that as soon as we hang up."

"Very good. Now, how are things there? Have Urijah and Banyan called a truce?"

Sin thought back to his conversation with the Goyle earlier. "Banyan says they have. I've not been called in to mediate any fights yet. Still, I have a feeling they will eventually come to blows, one way or another."

"Meaning?"

"Meaning there is pent-up sexual tension between them. If my instincts are correct, those two are mates."

"Now that's interesting. Sixx had thought Finley was the one Uri had his sights set on," Rafael said.

"He may have, but Finley is too much of a Goyle whore to only have one partner. He has slacked off his late-night activities since Uri has been in town, but he is still seeing the ladies when he can."

"Shit. I need Uri focused on weapons, not his friend's dick."

"I will do my best to keep him on task." Sin had an idea, but it could very well backfire. "How is our Prince doing?"

"Growing stronger every day. He woke me up last night kicking. Kaya's convinced he's going to be a soccer player."

Sinclair was truly happy for his brother as well as their Clan. Now that the mates were getting pregnant, the Di Pietro line as well as the Gargoyles as a whole would continue to be, even if they were half-bloods. Still, he was ready to be mated, so his happiness for his King and Queen was somewhat bittersweet. "I am sure Mother is thrilled at the prospect of becoming a grandmother again." Even though Connor wasn't Dante's biological son, Athena claimed him all the same.

"I haven't spoken to her in a while, which is odd. She was calling for regular updates. I need to reach out to her."

"Let me know when you contact her. I know she walked out on us, but she is still our mother. Anyway, give Kaya my best."

"Will do. And Sin? You will get your family, too," Rafe promised.

"I hope you are right, Brother." Sin disconnected without saying goodbye. He hated the word. Sin wasn't necessarily superstitious, but he was afraid if he said the word, it was giving the cosmos permission to take away the person he was talking to – like his father. Edmondo had been not only a great King, but also a wonderful friend to Sin and his brothers throughout the years. The last time Sin had uttered the word *goodbye* had been to his Papa right before he was slain. Maybe it *was* a little superstitious, but Sinclair refused to say it ever again.

Sin placed the call to Landon asking him to come by the next day to discuss his new role within the Clan. He would send the Goyle to New Atlanta since that's where the high-tech equipment was. Sin returned his attention to the computer. One of the things he did was to make sure all the West Coast Goyles had jobs they enjoyed. As Clan members moved around, positions came open, but not all males had the same interests.

Banyan had been in California for several months, and he was helping his Brothers in much the same way Sixx did by investing their money. It didn't take up much of his time, and he had mentioned how he would like to own a bar or restaurant like he had in New Orleans. So, Sin was keeping his eye out for businesses for sale. From what little time he'd been around Banyan, Sin gleaned from their conversations that the Goyle missed his life in the bayou. Sin visited the port city on occasion and enjoyed his time there, but he preferred the mild climate of California over the humid heat of Louisiana.

When he didn't see anything lucrative, Sin shut off the computer and went to see what delicious meal Ingrid had prepared for him and his guests. Finley liked to get right down to playing when they shared women, but Sin preferred to wine and dine them first. He was quite a bit more selective in who he allowed in his bed. If the women didn't pass muster during their initial conversations, Sin would possibly call it an early evening. Chemistry wasn't essential to fucking, but it was needed in the way he preferred to play when more than two people were involved.

Once Sin was satisfied with the menu, he excused

Ingrid to her section of the house. The human was no stranger to Sinclair and his "guests", even though it had been a while since he had invited Finley over. Sin and Lorenzo had shared women over the last thirty years, and when he moved to New Atlanta, Sin thought his threesome days were over. Color him surprised when Fin suggested a "party" soon after he arrived on the West Coast.

The only thing Sin could figure out was Lor and Finley had discussed Lorenzo's life in California, including his after-hours activities with Sin. It also surprised Sin, because Urijah was all Fin talked about. Maybe he was using the women as a way to forget his best friend, but it would be hard to forget someone who was practically living with you. Sin didn't try to figure out their relationship. He was glad Finley agreed to the night's activities, because he needed to get lost in a soft female body. Or two.

Remembering his vow to Rafael, Sin shot Urijah a text stating if he could get away from the armory later to swing by for a small get-together. Either the Goyle would join in or he'd be so pissed off he'd never speak to Sin or Finley again. If that was the case, sparring sure would be interesting from there on out.

When seven o'clock rolled around, Sin was wound up more tightly than he had been that morning. His shifter hearing alerted him to Finley's car pulling down the drive. He checked the food and champagne one more time before meeting his guests at the front door. If Fin had been alone, he'd have come around back to the pool area. Since the women were with him, Sin preferred the use of the formal entrance. Rarely did Sin allow strangers into the less formal areas of his home, and never did he allow anyone, not even Fin, into his bedroom. Besides Rafael, the only ones to have ever seen his sanctuary were his three wives. Not even Ingrid was allowed in the top floor where his bedroom was located.

Sin opened the door to Finley, Vivian, and a blonde

he'd never met. Once they were inside, Fin made the introductions. "Sin, you remember Vivian. And this beauty is Dana. Dana, my friend Sinclair."

Sin greeted each woman with a kiss to the back of her hand. "Ladies, thank you for joining us this evening. If you would follow me, my cook has prepared a special meal."

Dana's eyebrows shot up, but Vivian smirked and licked her lips. She had hinted more than once at getting in between Sin and Fin. If she and Dana impressed him during dinner, she'd finally get her chance. Finley kept the conversation going for the most part while Sinclair sat back and observed. Dana was reserved without being too quiet, and Vivian flirted shamelessly. She never let an innuendo pass by without glancing Sin's way. He had met a lot of brazen women over the years, but none so much so as the curvy redhead.

Dinner was delicious, and Dana made sure to compliment Ingrid's abilities. Vivian stated she was ready for dessert. Finley was full of talk and bluster during dinner, but in their arrangements where he and Sinclair shared women, Fin was the more submissive of the two. Theirs wasn't the type of relationship where Sin was what the BDSM world called a dominant, but he did call the shots in the bedroom, even when they were at Fin's house.

Instead of something sweet for dessert, Sin poured everyone a glass of champagne. When it came time to deliver a toast, he couldn't find the words. He was looking forward to what they had planned, but something was off. It wasn't Dana. The young woman was pretty and polite. Vivian was… Vivian. Sin didn't have a problem with her attitude. Something he couldn't lay claim to had him hesitating, if briefly. When he realized everyone was waiting for him to say something, Sin simply raised his glass and said, "Salute."

Finley frowned at him before drinking his

champagne down in one swallow. He raised his eyebrows, waiting for Sin to let him know whether they would proceed to the large guestroom, or if Finley would be taking the women home to his place. Exhaling a small sigh that was only audible to Finley's shifter hearing, Sin nodded. Fin, less enthusiastic than usual, clapped his hands together. "Ladies, if you would like to follow me..." He didn't elaborate. They both knew what was going to happen next. Sin remained in the dining room momentarily trying to figure out what the fuck was wrong with him. The women were desirable, and he'd been looking forward to being with them all day, needing the release. Something had been off with him ever since he left the gym. He finally gave up trying to figure out what was wrong and followed his guests to the large bedroom where they would play for the next hour or so.

Urijah found it odd that Sinclair sent him a text asking him to come over. He hadn't seen much of the Goyle since he began forging new swords at the armory. The two of them had sparred a couple of times, but other than that, Uri didn't see anyone other than Finley. There were some nights he didn't see his best friend. In the weeks since Sixx and Rae had found their way back to each other, Uri had done his best to stay away from their home, giving them space to become reacquainted. He either spent the night at Fin's or stayed at the armory working on weapons.

Uri wasn't stupid. He knew Finley went out on occasion for sex. He'd hoped once they spent more time together, Fin would see him as something more than a friend. Even though they shared the bed some nights for sleep, rarely did Uri get what he wanted. The few times they'd had sex had been good for Uri, but he knew it was nothing more than an orgasm for Fin. The Goyle had never been picky about who he got his rocks off with. That should have been a flashing neon sign to Uri that Fin would never return his feelings. Uri needed to face facts and accept he would never be happy. The thirty years he spent in New Orleans should have taught him that.

He was at a good stopping point, having finished several hilts that were now ready to be fitted to their blades, and decided to take Sin up on his offer. Even if he was only visiting California, Uri needed to spend time with his Clan. When he arrived at Sin's home, he spoke into the security box and drove through the gate once it opened for him. Whenever he entered one of their secure locations, Uri thought about Julian and how the Goyle was faring with his mate sitting in prison.

Finley's was the only car in the driveway, and Uri wondered just how small of a get-together Sin was having. He parked beside his best friend's SUV and got out. Whenever Uri had been to Sinclair's home, he'd been granted entrance through the back door. So, Uri headed toward the pool area and let himself into the kitchen instead of going to the front door and ringing the bell. When he didn't find anyone in that part of the house, he opened his senses. The noises that met his ears were not what he expected. At all. Sin, Finley, and two females were somewhere toward the front of the large house, and if Uri had to venture a guess as to where they were, he'd say they were in a bedroom. Had Sinclair intentionally invited Uri to join in their sexual activities? Or had he given up on Uri coming over and suggested they move the party somewhere more intimate?

Uri had never shared partners. As handsome as Sinclair was, Urijah wouldn't mind seeing the Goyle unclothed, but he wasn't sure he wanted to participate in group sex, especially when one of the participants would be Finley. Urijah had several choices. He could continue to stand in the shadows and listen. He could join them and see whether or not multiple sexual partners was to his liking. Or, he could leave. Urijah's feet remained momentarily frozen. As much as it pained him to think of Finley fucking someone else, his curiosity got the better of him.

Chapter Three

It was clear to Sinclair that Vivian and Dana had played together before. Instead of waiting for their host to give instruction as to how the night would progress and what the rules of engagement would be, if any, the two of them had stripped down to their bras and G-strings and were in the middle of the bed on their knees facing each other, kissing. Their hands were fondling whatever body part they landed on, teasing before moving on. Finley was still dressed and standing beside the bed, but the way he was stroking his cock through his pants was a clear indication he was enjoying the show.

Sin was accustomed to setting the pace, thus the reason Fin was still fully clothed. Urijah was somewhere in the house, but instead of making his presence known, he was waiting in the wings. Sin hadn't elaborated on the type of get-together he was having, but by now, the big blond should have figured it out. Sin was still unsure how to proceed where Uri was concerned, so he decided to let the Goyle make his own decision on whether to come and join in or to leave.

Turning his attention to the females, Sin forgot about everything else except what was happening in the room. Vivian reached behind Dana, unclasping her bra. She slid the tiny straps down Dana's arms and flung the garment somewhere on the other side of the bed. Dana's breasts weren't as large as Vivian's, but they were pert, and her nipples were hard peaks, begging for attention. Sin's dick stirred in his pants, and he rubbed his hand over his hard length as he watched the show. Vivian pushed Dana to her back and straddled her legs, leaning over the woman. Vivian kissed Dana deeply before licking her way down the other woman's flat stomach. Sin released his cock from his pants, but didn't remove them. He stroked his erection while Vivian nuzzled Dana's mound through the satin panties she still wore.

"That is hot," Sin said to Finley. This was the first time they'd had two women in bed together.

"It sure is," Fin replied, but he was looking at Sinclair's fist on his dick instead of the women. When Fin let his own cock free, he began sliding his hand up and down in time with Sin's fist.

"You want some of this?" Sin asked, daring the other Goyle to play in a way they never had. He was taunting Urijah more than anything, enticing him to join in the fun. He never expected Fin to take him up on his offer.

"Fuck, yeah," Finley said, dropping to his knees in front of Sin. In one slick movement, Finley swallowed Sin's cock down his throat. Sin couldn't stop the moan that escaped his throat as the other male sucked and licked better than he'd had in a long time. Sin reached out with his enhanced hearing, searching for Urijah. He had moved closer, but he still hadn't joined them. The women stopped what they were doing long enough to enjoy the show Finley was putting on. Sin split his attention between the Goyle on his knees and the one who was now inching toward the bedroom. The door was open far enough that Uri could see what was going on. When Uri was visible, Sin turned his attention to the females.

"Take your panties off. Now," Sin instructed. He was ready to sink his throbbing cock into a slick, warm pussy. He was enjoying Finley's mouth, but he wanted to feel softness underneath him. Sin grabbed hold of Finley's hair and fucked his mouth while the women finished removing the rest of their underclothes. Fin was stroking his own cock in time with Sin's thrusts, moaning around the thick head as it struck the back of his throat. Sin called on his shifter's resolve to keep from coming. It had been a long time since he'd been with another male, and he'd forgotten how skilled they could be.

Sin wasn't the only one affected by Finley's oral skills. Uri's breathing had become heavier, but at the same time his mood was growing darker. Sin pulled his dick out of Finley's mouth and ordered, "On the bed." Fin's eyes were hooded as he stood and removed his clothes. Fin lay down next to Vivian, but waited until Sin chose the woman he desired most.

Sin knew Vivian wanted him; she'd made it clear all night during dinner, but Sin turned his attention to Dana. After he shed his own clothes, Sin stepped to the other side where the blonde was waiting. Even though Gargoyles were immune to human diseases, he opened the drawer of the side table and grabbed a condom, rolling it down the length of his thick cock. That way he wouldn't have to have a conversation regarding their safety. He didn't give Dana warning, nor did he offer her any foreplay. Sin climbed on top of her, parted her legs with his powerful thighs, and slid his cock home in one thrust. She arched her back and let out a soft groan, her fingernails trying to dig into the flesh of Sin's legs. Sin placed one of her legs over his shoulder, nipping the inside of her knee with his teeth as he continued stroking her core with his dick.

Fin pushed Vivian onto her back, but he didn't immediately start fucking her. He nuzzled her large breasts, licking and sucking her nipples. Fin dipped his hand between her legs, sliding his fingers in and out of her wet pussy. This was the part Sin enjoyed. He liked watching Fin bring their female to the brink of orgasm only to pull away, edging her over and over until she was begging.

Since he had his own female, Sin focused his attention on her. Dana's eyes were glazed over from the fullness of Sin's prick stroking her insides. Hitting her special spot that would end in an electrifying orgasm when he decided it was time. Having learned the female body over the last five hundred years, Sin could bring a woman to the edge as well, but he wasn't as tormenting as Finley. Sin didn't need Dana to beg him verbally. Her muscles tightened around his cock, but he wasn't ready to come yet. He pulled out and slid down her body, meeting her wet pussy lips with his mouth. It never ceased to amaze him how different each woman tasted. Dana was sweet, like her disposition. She was one of the quietest lovers he'd ever encountered, but he wasn't complaining. Finley and Vivian were making more noise than a couple of porn stars in a bad triple X film.

The one noise Sinclair had been waiting on finally sounded in the back of the house. The door leading to the patio closed, and soon after, Uri's car started and pulled out of the drive. If Finley heard it, he didn't let on. Sin hoped he hadn't totally screwed up by inviting Uri over, but like Rafe said, the Goyle needed to focus on something other than his best friend's cock.

Sin returned all his attention to the female he was feasting on. He sucked on her clit and flicked it with his tongue. Dana had already been on the brink of coming, and as soon as Sin dipped a couple of fingers into her core finding the spot just inside, she came apart on his mouth. He lapped up all her sweet juices before moving back up her body, sliding his throbbing cock into her wetness.

Finley and Vivian had finished round one and had moved on to sixty-nine. Sin was angled so he could enjoy the show while fucking Dana. The sight of Vivian's full lips around Finley's dick was revving Sin's motor, and he was ready for his release. He amped up his thrusts while bringing his partner to the brink of another orgasm. This time when Dana's muscles clamped down on Sin's dick, he didn't pull out. He moved in and out faster, chasing his own orgasm. When he'd had sex with his wives, he only held back a fraction. He allowed his fangs to drop although he kept them hidden so as not to scare the humans. With Dana, he didn't allow the beast inside close enough to the surface

35

to risk it. One day, Sin wanted to be able to share what he was with a female. He was ready to find his mate so he could unfurl his wings and let the beast have at their mate. Until then, his orgasms would have to be sub-par.

When Sin was no longer coming, he held onto the condom as he pulled out of the pretty girl lying beneath him. He didn't kiss her or offer sweet words. He hadn't kissed a woman since his last wife passed away almost a hundred years earlier. Dana was nothing more to him than a way to get off. Finley was supposed to make that clear before they agreed to come over. Sin was past the point of marrying random humans for no other reason than to have companionship. Now that his brothers and cousins had all found their mates, he was holding out hope the Fates would finally allow him to find the one he would spend the rest of his long life with.

Since Finley and Vivian were still going at it, Sinclair told Dana, "You can stay and join them, or you can come with me for a drink. I'm fine with whatever you decide."

Dana smiled and said, "I'll stay here." The woman slid across the bed where she helped Vivian work Finley's cock and balls. So much for worrying about her feelings. After disposing of the condom in the bathroom and washing up, Sin pulled his pants on while his guests continued to pleasure each other. Vivian and Dana had swapped places, and when Sin reached down for his shirt and shoes, Vivian leaned over, running her long fingernail down his bare arm. "Sure you don't want to play some more?" she purred.

"I'm sure, but you three stay as long as you like." Sin gave her a weak smile as he slid his arms in his shirt, not bothering to button it. He padded barefoot to the back part of the house where he could be alone with his thoughts. As much as he'd been looking forward to their night, the thought of finding his mate had left him wanting something... more.

He dropped his shoes by the liquor cabinet. After

pouring a tumbler full of Scotch, Sin lit a cigar and let his mind drift to Urijah. Now that it was all said and done, he felt like a dick for inviting the Goyle over. He made his way outside to sit on the patio. The moon was reflecting on the water in the pool, and Sin let out a deep sigh. He'd felt off since leaving the gym, and he still didn't feel like himself. Sex hadn't calmed him like it usually did.

Sin stuck the tip of the cigar in his mouth and rolled it around. He inhaled right as his cell phone rang. He wasn't in the mood to talk to anyone, but the caller I.D. showed it was Julian. His cousin rarely called unless it was important.

"Jules, is everything okay?" Sin asked instead of saying hello.

"Not really. Rafe said you have a guy who's good with computers."

"Landon Roxburgh. He is coming by tomorrow."

"Can you get him out here as soon as possible? Fuck, Cousin. I'm losing my godsdamn mind here. Nik's doing all he can, but he isn't as adept as I need someone to be. Lorenzo does his part, too. It's just I need someone as good as I am."

"Have you been to see your mate lately?" Sin asked. Having Katherine Fox sitting in the Pen, even if Gregor was keeping her in a special room, had to be taking its toll.

"What does that have to do with computers?"

"Nothing, but it has everything to do with why you are so overwhelmed. Now, have you been to see her?"

"No, but I'm going to have to soon. My shifter is ripping my insides apart, and I can't avoid it any longer. I just don't know what I'm going to say to her."

"How about the truth? If you are absolutely certain she is your mate, you could start with the truth and go from there. If she accepts you for what you are, you can visit with her and soothe the beast."

"I'm trying to protect her and us. If the Feds find out she's connected to me, they'll start digging, and I can't have that."

"Julian, you are smarter than the federal government. You are smarter than anyone I know with the exception of Jonas, and even then, I am not so sure."

"If this were six months ago, I wouldn't argue with you, but ever since..."

"Stop it. Do not let this mystery hacker get you down. Let me send Landon to you, and together, you can figure out what is going on. With the exception of helping Nik and Sophia in Egypt, you have not taken a break in a long fucking time. Your brain has to be on overload. Go see Katherine. Tell her the truth, and let her ease you and your shifter."

"Maybe you're right. I'll think about it. Do you think you can get Landon here tomorrow?"

"I will call him right now, but go ahead and get the jet headed this way. I will text you with his plans when I know something definitive. And Jules? It is going to be okay. I have faith in you."

"Thanks, Sin." Julian hung up knowing Sin wouldn't say goodbye.

It was a five-hour flight from New Atlanta to the small airport in New Burbank. If Landon was agreeable, he could be on the East Coast by the time the sun rose. Sin pulled up the Goyle's number in his contact list and hit send.

"Hello?"

"Hello, Landon. Sinclair calling. I apologize for interrupting your evening, but instead of meeting tomorrow, I would like to do it tonight if you're not busy. Is that a problem?"

"Not at all. Do you still want me to come to your place?"

Sin had no idea how long his guests planned on hanging around, and even though he wasn't ashamed of his and Finley's lifestyle, he didn't want everyone knowing his business. "No, I'll come to you. Let's find somewhere to get a drink and talk."

"There's a small bar about halfway between us called RC's. I'll text you the address."

"Sounds good. I will see you there." After disconnecting, Sin downed his Scotch and crushed out his cigar while pulling RC's up on his phone. It was a small dive in an out-of-the-way location. He stood from the patio chair and buttoned his shirt before going inside for his shoes. He let out a whistle that sounded like a bird call. Within a few minutes, Finley was jogging into the kitchen in nothing but his boxer briefs. "Something has come up, and I need to leave. Ingrid is in her wing, but I would still prefer if you and the women stayed in the front of the house."

"Anything I can do?" Finley asked, pushing down on his still-erect cock.

"I need to meet with Landon. Julian is not handling Katherine being locked up very well, and we need Landon to go help with the technology side of things. I will catch up with you later. Go enjoy the girls."

Finley stepped closer before he whispered, "You didn't play long. Did you not like Dana?"

"She was perfectly acceptable, Fin. I've just felt off all day. It will pass."

Fin narrowed his eyes, trying to gauge whether Sin was telling the truth. He ran a hand through his hair and said, "We'll call it a night, and I'll talk to you tomorrow."

"If that is what you want, but really, you do not have to leave on my account. Whenever you do, though, please lock the front door on your way out."

"Will do, Brother." Fin clapped Sin on the shoulder and turned to go back to the bedroom.

Sin tracked Finley, admiring the Goyle's physique. He was still shocked by the blowjob, but if he was honest with himself, Sin had thoroughly enjoyed having Fin's mouth on him. Shaking the image from his mind, Sin tucked his shirttail into his pants. He was overdressed for the bar where he was meeting Landon, but he wasn't in the mood to change into jeans.

Sinclair slipped his feet into his Italian loafers and headed for the garage. Instead of driving the Lambo to the out-of-the-way bar, he opted for his Lexus. It was less conspicuous and less likely to get tampered with. When he arrived at the small tavern, Sin was surprised at how crowded it was for a Tuesday night. He didn't see Landon's car, so he went inside and found a seat at a high top towards the back of the room. As he sat down, the nauseous feeling he'd had earlier returned, only this time it was worse. Sin was pretty sure his mate was somewhere in the bar.

Drago phased, spreading his wings wide behind him as his claws and fangs also made an appearance. The Unholy weren't surprised to see him in his Gargoyle state considering they fought the Stone Society. New Atlanta wasn't as good a place for phasing as Greece was. The state was full of people who owned cell phones with those nasty cameras on them. Greece wasn't backwards by any means, but the islands were much less populated than New Atlanta was. When the world fell apart some thirty years ago, the islands weren't affected nearly as much as the United States had been. And considering New Atlanta had been the site of the initial bombing, it was hit harder than most anywhere else in the world. Now, Georgia was thriving almost as well as it had been before the bombs.

It was almost enough for him to rethink his decision to take over the Unholy. Almost. Drago had no way of contacting Kallisto without Achilles finding him, and he didn't trust the mystery Goyle to keep his whereabouts a secret from Alistair. For the time being, Drago would continue with his plan to lead the monsters and build an army he could hopefully use against the Stone Society, should it come to that.

The handful of Unholy who'd thought to test him had learned quickly that even though he was one male, he was still stronger, more powerful, and faster than ten of them. "Clean that up," he instructed to the two closest to him. *That* was four of their Unholy brethren who were now lying dead on the ground at their feet. The two looked at each other. One of them shrugged and began dragging two of the dead out of the room. "Anyone else want to test me?" Drago asked the others who were standing around staring at him.

Chapter Four

Sin knew the others had felt sick upon coming in contact with their mates, but what was he going to do? Walk around the room accosting each patron until he found the one who made him want to vomit?

His shifter felt it too. *There is that smell again. Is the human male here?*

Before he could answer, a young human came to wait on him. "Name's Derek. What can I get you?"

"I'll take whatever ale you have on tap." He preferred liquor, but he doubted a bar of this caliber would have the expensive Scotch he drank at home.

"You got it. Would you like a menu, or are you just drinking?"

"Just drinking."

"No problem. I'll go put your drink order in at the bar." Derek's smile was forced and his heartbeat erratic. Sin had that effect on most everyone. He was a large male, and dressed as he was, he didn't fit in. While Derek had been talking, Sin's shifter had been berating him mentally.

Get up and find him.

I'm pretty sure our mate is not going to be a him. Landon's here. Settle the fuck down so I can discuss business. His shifter left him alone, but he wasn't happy about it. He continued to grumble in Sin's head, making it hard to concentrate.

Landon strolled up to the table as the waiter returned with his beer. "Landon, what would you like to drink?"

"Whatever he's having," Landon told Derek as he took the stool across from Sin. Even with the loud voices, they would be able to hear each other without yelling.

When Landon was seated, Sin didn't make the Goyle wait. "Thank you for meeting me. I mentioned on the phone we are in need of your computer skills. Julian is overwhelmed with his mate having been arrested. He is trying to keep the Clan safe while figuring out how Katherine was framed." Sin stopped talking when Derek came back to the table.

"Will there be anything else?"

"No, thank you," Sin told him. When the waiter was out of earshot, Sin continued. "I know you relocated to California recently, but we need you to head to New Atlanta and help man the computers."

"No problem. When do you want me to leave?"

"Can you be ready in about 5 hours? The Clan jet is already in the air headed this way."

"Absolutely. As a matter of fact, I'm looking forward to it. I'm ready for a challenge. I've been bored lately. It's why I moved."

"I don't think you will have that problem any longer. There is a lot going on behind the scenes we have kept quiet." Sin filled Landon in on the hacker and what he'd done to sabotage Julian at every turn. "Maybe between the two of you, you can find out who he is and take him down."

Landon chugged his beer and wiped his mouth with the back of his hand. When Derek noticed the empty glass, he returned, and this time Landon ordered two shots of Patron. Sin still had half a glass of his ale left, so he told the waiter he was fine. He was anything but fine considering the way his stomach was roiling, but he couldn't pinpoint the reason.

"Hey, are you okay?" Landon asked.

"Not really. I've felt off all day. When the others have found their mates, the feeling they've described is the same thing I've been subjected to all day. My mate could be in this room, or she could have been here earlier. I am going to take a walk to the restroom and see if it gets worse." Sin left Landon at the table and headed to the rear of the building. The feeling worsened as he passed by the bar. Sin

43

took a good look at everyone sitting there, but nobody stood out to him. After taking a piss and washing his hands, Sin splashed water on his face. As he was drying off, female voices drifted through from the next room. He didn't intend to eavesdrop, but the conversation called for it.

"There's no easy way to say this, so I'm just going to spit it out. I've decided to sell the bar. Instead of struggling to make ends meet and cutting hours, I'm going to bring in someone who can make this place what it was three years ago."

"What about the rest of us?"

"I have a stipulation in the contract stating all of you are to retain your jobs. I will be meeting with the prospective buyers myself, and I'd like you to sit in on the meetings with anyone I feel might be well-suited. I want you to be comfortable with the new owner."

"Isn't there any other way?"

"Yes, but I refuse to go back to that life."

Sinclair was looking to buy, and this woman was looking to sell. He liked the atmosphere, and the little tavern had potential. He would pay more attention to his surroundings when he returned to his seat. The feeling in his gut wasn't better, and on his way back from the bathroom, Sin noticed the man who'd been at the gym earlier. No fucking way was his mate a male. Something had to be going on, or the fates were fucking with him.

As soon as he got back to their table, Sin grabbed one of the small glasses of tequila and knocked it back. He motioned for Derek, and when the young man finally got there after stopping to check on several other guests, Sin pulled a hundred out of his wallet and said, "Keep them coming." He would have asked for the bottle, but he knew that was against the rules, so he would order them one at a time. The clear liquor might not ease his nausea, but it would help take his mind off of it.

"Anything?" Landon asked when they were alone.

Sin shook his head no. He wouldn't admit a male was causing his unease, not until he got to the bottom of what was going on. "So, tell me where all you have been and what you have done." Sin wanted to learn more about the Goyle he was sending to help not only his cousin, but their Clan. Landon did as Sin asked, and by the time the bottle of Patron was empty and the bar was closing down, Sinclair felt good about the male he was entrusting with the Clan's secrets. He did not, however, have a lock on whoever was making him feel sick at his stomach.

Rocky had been behind the bar for less than an hour when Blake showed up, so she ended up spending the night locked in her office, hoping the bastard would finally get the hint and leave. Instead, he nursed a drink until it was watered down then ordered another. He wasn't breaking any laws or harassing anyone, so they couldn't kick him out. As she hid herself away, Rocky debated on gathering her employees together after the bar closed for a short meeting but decided against it. She would tell Bridget first when they were alone since the woman had the most to lose. Together, they would have a mandatory staff meeting when all the employees were present. Rocky had never felt hate in her heart until now. Now, she hated Blake Stansbury with every fiber of her being for getting her hooked on drugs. She hated herself almost as much for not listening to her gut instinct when he continued to ask her out.

Bridget was the only one of her workers who knew the extent of her drug use. Rocky had confided in her manager when she'd gone into rehab. She had turned the business over to Bridget, and they'd told everyone else she was going away on an extended vacation. If any of her employees had realized her "vacation" saved her life, no one let on. The only thing Bridget wasn't aware of was what Rocky had done to keep the bar afloat while being entrenched in her drug-induced stupor. Blake's business

45

had turned out to be a strip club. When Rocky needed more drugs, Blake convinced her to dance in exchange for her next fix. He'd paid for her to have breast surgery, saying she'd make double the tips with larger tits. Now, every time she caught sight of herself in the mirror naked, she wanted to cut her boobs open and remove the liquid bags.

Every piece of clothing she'd bought with her dancing money had been donated to charity. All her wigs and costumes were still at the club as far as she knew. The last time she walked out of the club, Rocky had done so with nothing but her street clothes. Somehow, Vivian had found a way into the back of the building after one of Rocky's numbers and practically dragged her out the back door. Vivian hadn't let Rocky go home, despite her protests. On the long drive to the out-of-town rehab clinic, Vivian convinced her to get clean and forget about Blake. Rocky still to this day didn't remember what her best friend said to convince her to go, but she would forever be grateful to Vivian for saving her life.

Blake had come calling regularly while Rocky was in rehab. For months after Rocky got straightened out, the man made himself a fixture at her bar. He didn't cause trouble, so she couldn't file a restraining order, but he made her uncomfortable. Gone were the large tips, and in their place were notes of regret. Sweet words of love. Rocky didn't buy into it. She knew the only thing he missed about her was the money she'd made him. She might have been high when she took to the stage, but if there was one thing Rocky was good at, it was making grown men lose their shit merely by taking her clothes off. After she got her boob job, Rocky raked in enough tips to live off of for months, but somehow, Blake managed to take most of it from her, saying she owed him.

It took every bit of nerve she could muster, but whenever Blake came into RC's, Rocky ignored him. The more she ignored him, the less often he came around. For about a year, Rocky thought she was free from him. Then, for whatever reason, Blake started coming in RC's again. Tonight was one of those nights, and Rocky opted to hide out instead of having to deal with him.

When Bridget came into the office to take her break, Rocky asked her to close the door.

"This can't be good. We never have closed door chats."

Rocky crushed out the cigarette she'd been smoking and smiled at her friend, doing her best not to cry. "It is and it isn't. I'm sorry to do this on your break, but I need to talk to you. You have been the best manager I could have ever had to run RC's. You've also been an invaluable friend. There's no easy way to say this, so I'm just going to spit it out. I've decided to sell the bar. Instead of struggling to make ends meet and cutting hours, I'm going to bring in someone who can make this place what it was three years ago."

Bridget's face didn't offer any clues as to how she felt when she asked, "What about the rest of us?"

"I have a stipulation in the contract stating all of you are to retain your jobs. I will be meeting with the prospective buyers myself, and I'd like you to sit in on the meetings with anyone I feel might be well-suited. I want you to be comfortable with the new owner."

"Isn't there any other way?"

"Yes, but I refuse to go back to that life." Rocky didn't tell Bridget what that life had been, and the woman didn't pry.

"I love this bar. It's been my home for almost ten years. Your uncle gave me a chance when I was barely out of college. I've never thought about going somewhere else," Bridget told her.

"And you won't have to. I promise you I won't allow some douchebag to come in and take over." Rocky would take Joel up on his offer of a loan so she could keep her promise. "I want to call everyone in before the listing goes live. I don't want them to think I'm hiding anything."

"Okay. I'll schedule a meeting Friday morning an hour before we open. That'll give us enough time to break the news and answer any questions they may have," Bridget said.

As soon as Bridget was out the door, the tears Rocky had been fighting couldn't be held back any longer. She should have known the woman would have her back. Bridget had been a good friend these last three years, and Rocky owed almost as much to her as she did Vivian. Thinking of her best friend, Rocky couldn't wait to hear the details of her wild night with Finley. Usually when they played, it was only three of them. She was curious as to how it worked with four – *if* Vivian invited someone else.

Rocky dried her tears, and made sure everyone was gone before she let herself up to her apartment. Before she'd so carelessly given all her money to Blake, Rocky had dipped into her savings and had the apartment stairs enclosed so she could access them from inside the bar, and no unwanted visitors could surprise her from the outside. She could still come in from behind the building, but she liked knowing she didn't have to. When she reached the top of the stairs, her cell phone rang. Thinking it was Vivian, she answered without looking. "So, how was your night?"

A familiar voice answered, and chill bumps formed on Rocky's arms. "It would have been better if my girl hadn't avoided me for three hours."

After all this time, Blake still considered Rocky his. "How did you get this number?" She had blocked him several times and even got a new phone. He never failed to find out what it was. The only people she gave it to were Bridget and Vivian, and she was pretty sure neither woman would share the number with the man who ruined her life.

"Oh, my sweet Raquel. You should know by now I always get what I want." His voice made her want to throw up. It was the same, sugary tone he used to woo her in the beginning. It might have worked back then, but it sure as hell didn't work now.

Without responding, Rocky hung up and immediately blocked him from calling back. She let out a long sigh and tossed her phone on the counter. It slid off and hit the floor on the other side. Thank goodness she'd been smart enough to purchase a protective case. She couldn't afford a new phone right now. She retrieved the wayward phone and placed it gently on the counter. Blake's words haunted her, bringing back memories of him *getting what he wanted*. He wanted her. He'd made that clear from the first time he took her out, and he never let her forget she belonged to him. Even now.

Earlier when she'd gone to the gym, Rocky had gotten nervous waiting on someone to come talk to her. Several men glanced her way, and Rocky didn't like being the object of their attention. While she was standing there, she noticed there were self-defense classes offered along with the other fitness sessions. Now that Blake was coming around again, and a lot more often, Rocky either needed to enroll in the classes or learn to shoot her gun. Maybe both. There was no way in hell she would succumb to him willingly. Not this time. Instead of waiting around, Rocky picked up several flyers and decided to go back the next day.

Urijah needed to fly. He needed to let his beast loose before his emotions got the better of him. Seeing Finley on his knees sucking Sin's cock had infuriated him. Seeing Sin's long, veiny dick slide in and out of Fin's mouth excited him. He didn't understand how he could be so godsdamn angry and so fucking hard at the same time. For a split second he thought about joining them. Wasn't that why Sinclair invited him over in the first place? Hell, he didn't know *why* Sin had asked him to come over. But there was no way he was joining in as a third wheel. Or a fifth, considering there had been two females there.

When he realized the needle was pushing one-eighty, Uri slowed the vehicle to an almost normal speed of one hundred and hit the call button on his steering wheel. He knew this was a mistake, but he needed information.

"Urijah, to what do I owe this pleasure?" Banyan's slick voice echoed throughout the vehicle. His cock automatically came back to life. His shifter stirred inside, the same way it had for the last eight hundred years. Every single time he was around Banyan. Motherfucker. Yeah, this was a bad idea.

"I need to know where I can go to fly that I won't be seen."

"The training area is secure, but you would need to stay below the trees."

"I'm thinking of somewhere more wide open. I need…" Uri stopped himself before he divulged too much information. Not that Banyan didn't already know what Uri needed. Or wanted. The Goyle could read him like an open fucking book from a thousand miles away.

"The desert is where I go when I need to fly off some tension. Driving the speed limit, you can get to Joshua Tree in about two hours. Knowing how you drive? Less than sixty minutes." Banyan's tone wasn't smug, just honest. "Want me to go with?"

"No!" Uri took a deep breath. "No, thank you. I need to get rid of tension, not add to it. I appreciate the information." He disconnected the call but not before a chuckle reached his ear. *Bastard.* Uri refused to dwell on the male any more than he already did. Urijah had left Banyan behind in New Orleans. He should have known the Goyle would find him again. *Actually, you found him.* That much was true. Banyan had kept his distance as promised. He moved to the West Coast while Urijah took up residence on the East Coast. It was Uri who had come to California to work. In the weeks Uri had been there, Banyan hadn't sought him out. Not once. Banyan didn't miss any opportunity to fuck with him, but he only did it when Uri contacted him. *Fucker.*

Uri pulled over to the side of the road so he could input the destination into his GPS. The hour-long drive would do him good, but not as much good as taking to the air. Maybe phasing would calm both his libido as well as his anger. Then what? He would go back to the house he was sharing with Finley, only to be reminded of the scene that played out on a continuous loop in his brain. Maybe it was time to move back in with Sixx. No, he and Desirae were getting to know one another, and Desi and Simone had moved into the guest house. All around him, Goyles were having sex.

Uri's shifter, who rarely spoke to him, decided it was time for a chat. ***You could always call...***

No! We are not going there. Ever again.

He's our mate.

He will never be my mate.

Stubborn fucker. The beast within was angry. Angrier than Urijah had encountered in a long time.

Let's go fly. It'll make us both feel better. Uri didn't wait for an answer. He knew his beast was ready to fight, and that never turned out well. He pulled back onto the road and, with the radio blaring, headed east.

Chapter Five

Julian paced back and forth behind the bank of computer monitors that were currently the bane of his existence. Sin was right; until Julian went and spoke with Katherine, he'd never be able to concentrate. He *needed* to concentrate. Julian had to find a way to get the Feds off his mate's back. They were already pissed she'd been moved to the Pen. They were looking at the evidence they had against her, but the last he'd heard from both Dane and Victoria, his mate was really close to being taken into Federal custody. He couldn't allow that. At least with her being with Gregor, they could keep her comfortable. She had asked Isabelle a million questions, but Izzy hadn't told her anything other than they were doing this for her own safety.

Julian had to go see her. Whether or not he told her the truth remained to be seen. But he had to lay eyes on the petite redhead and soon. Julian had already looked through the archives on the Goyle Sinclair was sending to help. From what Julian could tell, he was good at what he did. For all their sakes, Julian hoped so. Someone needed to protect the Stone Society from the hackers of the world, and currently, that someone wasn't him.

"Jules, go home. Or better yet, go to the godsdamn Pen. You're making me dizzy." Nikolas walked into the room, stopping in front of him.

"What are you doing here? You should be home with Sophia."

"Sophia is fine. She's with her grandmother. I'm here for the night, so you go. Go to your mate."

Julian ran a hand through his already disheveled hair. "Yeah. Okay."

"And for the gods' sake, go home and take a shower before you do. You look like hell."

Leave it to his brother to be honest. But Nik was right. When was the last time he'd showered? Saturday? Sunday? Fuck. He couldn't remember.

"Thanks, Nik. I'll be back as soon as I can."

"No. You'll be back when you've taken care of business." Nik pulled him into a tight embrace. "I've got this."

Julian clapped Nik on the back and left the room before his brother could see the wet in his eyes. For a badass Gargoyle, Julian felt like a failure. He needed to get his shit under control and fast before Rafael fired him and sent him packing. Julian slid into the seat of his Corvette. Driving had always been fun for him. Now, like everything else, it felt like a chore. He drove home on auto-pilot, showered and dressed, and then drove south to the New Atlanta Penitentiary.

Mentally, Julian had gone over different scenarios when seeing his mate, trying to come up with the best way to handle what was happening with her. *Tell her the truth.* Sinclair had said as much. So had everyone else. She was his mate, and as such, he needed to trust she would accept him and their Clan. Julian wanted to tell Katherine everything, but with the Feds getting more adamant every day about jurisdiction, the less she knew about the Clan the better. The way things stood now, she only knew what Dane and Gregor had told her, which wasn't much. Dane informed her she was being moved to the Pen for her safety. She was clearly upset and just as mystified as to why the Federal government would have found weapons in a house she'd never even laid eyes on. Julian knew why, but he was having a hard time making it go away.

As he was pulling down the long drive that led to the prison, Julian's phone rang. "Gregor, I'm pulling up to the Pen now."

"You better hurry, Brother. The Feds are on their way to get Katherine. It seems Victoria has stalled them as long as possible."

"Godsdamnit!" Julian gassed the accelerator even though he was less than one hundred yards from the building. He slid to a stop, barely taking time to put the car in park before he was out and running toward the back door.

"Come on, I'll show you where she is," Gregor said as soon as Julian entered the building. Neither one said a word until they reached a door not far from Gregor's office and Isabelle's clinic. "She's in here," Gregor said, placing his I.D. badge in front of the security scanner. The indicator flashed green, and Gregor pressed the handle down, pulling the door toward him.

Julian stepped into the small room and froze as he took in the still body of his mate. The door closing roused her, and sleepy green eyes met his. "Julian?" Katherine sat up and brushed her long red hair away from her face. "What are you doing here?"

It took everything within Julian not to pick her up and run away with her. That would cause nothing but trouble for both of them. "I'm contemplating a prison break, truth be told." His beast was clawing at him from the inside, berating him to do just that. "I should have come before now, but I didn't know exactly what to say. Katherine, I have so much to tell you. So much I should have already told you, but now we're out of time. We've kept you here as long as the Feds will allow. They're on their way to get you, I'm afraid."

"Julian, you have to believe me. I don't know anything about weapons or computers," she said as she stood from her bed, wrapping her arms around herself. Katherine was a petite woman, but in the dimness of the room, she seemed even smaller.

"I know you don't, Sweetheart. I've been working nonstop since you were arrested trying to figure this mess out." Julian took a step closer. The mate bond was too

54

strong to ignore. Katherine must have felt it. She inched closer to him as well. "I'm so sorry this happened to you. It's all my fault."

"Julian, I don't understand. What are you talking about? I'm not complaining that you're here, but *why* are you here?

"It's complicated, and I don't have time to explain it to you now. I should have told you as soon as I knew, but I was trying to protect you."

"Knew what?" she asked, the confusion etched on her face. "Protect me from who?"

"They're here. We need to move Miss Fox into a regular cell," Gregor announced from beyond the door, loud enough for them both to hear.

Julian sighed and did what he'd wanted to do for months. He closed the distance between them and pulled his mate against his body. Instead of wrapping her in both his arms, he placed one hand on the small of her back, holding her against him, and he used his free hand to tip her chin up so he could drink her in for the short time they had together. What a fucking fool he'd been for staying away. Katherine wrapped her arms around his back, fisting his shirt. "I don't understand any of this," she admitted.

"I know you don't, and I'm so sorry, but I promise you, I will not stop until I find a way to clear your name," Julian vowed as he placed a kiss on the side of Katherine's mouth. "We have to put you in a regular cell now so the agents don't realize we were playing favorites."

"Why were you playing favorites?" she asked, her eyes searching his for the truth.

Julian brushed the back of his hand down her beautiful face. Even void of make-up, she was stunning. "Because you belong to me, Sweetheart. After I prove your innocence, I'll tell you everything, but know this Kat – you are mine." Julian pressed their lips together, but he didn't kiss her softly. He slanted his mouth over hers and kissed her like he would never see her again. When Julian pulled back, they were both breathing heavily. The door behind him opened, and he knew he was out of time. He kissed her forehead softly before lacing their fingers together. Gregor led them to the wing where the women prisoners were held. The first cell had been cleared out so Katherine didn't have to walk past anyone.

"Julian?" Katherine whispered, uncertainty shining in her eyes.

"Don't say anything to the Feds. Tell them you have a lawyer, and without her present you don't have to talk. I vow to you, Katherine Annalise Fox, on everything holy, I *will* set you free. Never doubt my words." Julian kissed the inside of both her wrists before releasing her and stepping back so Gregor could close the cell door. Julian placed his hand on the window briefly before stalking off. He couldn't stand to see her so lost and alone. He knew Gregor was behind him, but he didn't stop walking until he was outside. His beast was ripping at him, and Julian knew he had to find somewhere to phase before he completely lost his mind.

"Jules, wait."

"I can't, Gregor. I have to get out of here. Please call Victoria and let her know what's going on."

"Already on it."

"Thank you. I need to know where they're taking her."

"I'll see what I can find out." Gregor closed the distance and gripped Julian behind his neck. "We'll figure this out."

Julian's throat was too tight to speak, so he merely nodded. Gregor released his hold, and Julian angled himself into his car. As fast as the Vette would take him, he headed to Gregor's house. It was the closest home to the Pen, and he needed to take to the air as soon as possible.

Sinclair returned home to a quiet house. Ingrid was in her wing, but other than her, the house was empty. Sin was glad. His mind was a blur as the last several hours replayed over and over. He needed to apologize to Urijah. The Goyle had come to California to forge weapons for the Clan, a task of utmost importance at the moment. Now, instead of helping Uri's mindset, Sin was pretty sure he'd only made things worse by inviting him over. The sex hadn't been as fulfilling as Sin hoped, and he blamed that on Urijah being in the house. Sin had been more focused on how the other Goyle was feeling than what was going on in the bedroom. The blame didn't lie with Uri, though. It was on Sin.

The sick feeling he had at the bar wasn't helping his attitude, either. There was no fucking way his mate was a male. He'd had sex with males, but that was nothing more than scratching an itch. He loved females. Loved their soft bodies. The curves. The silkiness of their skin. The way their hair smelled like flowers. If the fates had deemed a male to be his mate, he would go without. He wasn't opposed to a little fun with a male every so often, but he didn't want one as a full-time companion. And wouldn't that be the biggest *fuck you* to his malehood. Sinclair Stone, lover of women, husband to several, alone without a mate for the rest of his long, immortal life.

After changing out of his dress clothes, Sin chose an unopened bottle of whiskey from the cabinet and headed outside. He knew better than to try to sleep with his mind churning. Being secluded in the hills, the lights from the city below didn't detract from the night sky. The only light was coming from inside the swimming pool, and he dimmed those on his way out the door. When he was alone, Sin preferred the dark. He enjoyed scanning the skies, picking out the constellations, something he and Rafael had done as boys. They would wait until the house was quiet and make their way outside. When they were young, the world was different. No electricity meant no lights everywhere getting in the way of the most beautiful lights there were – the moon and stars.

Gargoyles could take to the skies without fear of being seen. They could fly whenever they wanted, letting their shifters come out daily. As time went on and technology changed, the beast inside was deprived more often than not of its freedom. Sin missed those simple days. Even with their father being King of their Clan, life was good. If good old Uncle Alistair had wanted to fuck with them back then, he'd have had to send in a group of Gargoyles to do it, not use a computer hacker to fuck with everyone's lives.

Landon had assured Sin he would do his best to help Julian any way he could. Landon had explained extensively his experience with computers. What he hadn't elaborated on was how smart he was. Sin appreciated the Goyle being humble. He'd found more often than not when someone had to brag about themselves, they weren't as good or as smart as they thought they were. Julian was a genius, but not once had his cousin boasted about it. If anything, the opposite was true. Now that he'd run up against someone challenging, Jules was feeling less smart than he truly was.

Sin poured another glass of whiskey and lit a cigar. Red glowed against the inky dark as he inhaled. Ice tinkling against the glass accompanied the nocturnal creatures' natural cadences, and Sin closed his eyes. Thankful his shifter was letting him enjoy the night in peace, Sin did his best to calm his mind. Frey had taught him long ago how to meditate, and he used those techniques now to find some semblance of peace.

The conversation he'd overheard at the bar came back to Sin. Other than the nausea, Sin had enjoyed the small tavern. It might not be a good fit for Banyan, but if the money was right, Sin didn't see a reason not to invest in the place. After he checked it out, he would take Banyan there and get his feel for it. The Goyle had owned his own place for a long time, and he had a good head for business. Even if he didn't want it for himself, he could give Sin an insight on whether or not it was a good investment.

When his cellphone pinged with an incoming message from Landon stating he was aboard the Clan's jet, Sin realized how long he'd been sitting outside. In a couple of hours the sun would be coming up, and he had business to tend to. If Ingrid wouldn't chastise him for it, he'd go to sleep on one of the patio lounge chairs. She knew Gargoyles could go without sleep, but the human in her liked to mother him. So instead of worrying the woman any more than he already did, Sin got up and headed for his bedroom. The large room on the top floor was his sanctuary, but the longer he went without his mate, the less like a haven it felt. Sin had allowed his last wife to decorate it the way she wanted, but as soon as she passed away, he changed it to a more utilitarian look. He didn't want his mate, if and when he ever found her, to feel like she was competing with a ghost from his past.

While meditating, Sin concluded there had to be another reason for his feeling nauseous around the man at the bar. He just didn't know what the reason was. Yet. He was bound and determined to figure it out, though. Sin shed his clothes, tossing them into the chute that dropped to the laundry room on the first floor, and stepped into the massive tile shower. As much as he abhorred the bright lights that kept him from seeing the stars clearly, Sin appreciated the modern showers with unlimited hot water. He didn't hurry to bathe. Instead, he stood with his hands braced against the wall and allowed the rain showerhead to beat down on his shoulders.

His hair cascaded around his face. With it long, he and Rafael could pass for twins. Sin rather enjoyed looking like his older brother, and if he ever needed to stand in for him, he could. The need had never arisen, but with Alistair causing chaos for the Clan, Sinclair would gladly take his brother's place if and when the time came. He would put his life on the line so Rafael would be protected. Now that Rafe was going to be a father, it was even more imperative he stay safe.

Sin finished bathing and dried off. When he turned down the covers on his massive bed, he slid beneath the heavenly coolness of the cotton sheets caressing his bare skin. The blackout curtains assured he wouldn't be bothered should he want to sleep past the sunrise. Closing his eyes, Sin once again used meditation to calm his mind so he could go to sleep.

"Have you located Drago?"

Kallisto did her best not to flinch at the harsh tone of her father's words. "No, sir." She didn't elaborate. The Goyle had gone off the grid, and she didn't want to risk anymore of her father's Clan to go look for him.

"Achilles is in the wind. I need someone who is skilled with computers to take his place. That is your assignment. I don't care what it costs. I want the best there is, even if that means you find a human."

"Yes, sir." Kallisto had already been looking for a replacement. Considering her father remained holed up in the compound for months on end, he needed someone competent to conduct aspects of his business via electronic means.

"I will be moving to Ithaca and calling in most of the Clan. I am going to amp up our military training. You are to stay here. Once you find someone skilled at technology, they are to move into the compound with you. It is your duty to monitor their progress, and it is also on you to keep them here at all times. I won't have another Achilles on my hands."

"Yes, sir," Kallisto responded meekly. She had known coming back to Greece wouldn't be easy, but the wrath she'd endured at her father's hands had been like nothing she could have imagined. The scars on her body were a constant reminder of what he was capable of. No longer was she the beautiful young woman who'd held her head high. Now, she was the marred young woman who had prayed for death. Never in her life had she regretted any decision. She couldn't say that any longer. The fact her father was going to live on the larger island was a blessing. Kallisto would be free to roam the villa without fear of being attacked. She would be able to sit in the garden and enjoy the sunshine on her face. She would be free from fear as long as Alistair wasn't around.

"You have one week to find someone. I have a plan I need put into motion and one week is already too long to wait. Don't let me down again." Alistair didn't spare his daughter another glance before he strode out of the room. Kallisto understood why he was angry. She had failed him. Her brother had failed him, and now, Theron was dead. Kallisto walked over to the open door of the balcony and looked down at her brother's grave. Theron might not have been the level of evil Alistair was, but he would have taken over eventually. Now, Alistair was scrambling to find a right hand. With Achilles going off the grid and several of the Gargoyles recently disappearing from the city, Alistair was not only livid, but he was paranoid about whom he could and couldn't trust. With Kallisto and Sergei failing in their last assignment, he no longer trusted her. She would once again have to prove her abilities and loyalty to him. She would find the best computer expert in the world, and she would ensure her father never felt the need to strike her again. Because she knew, if there ever was a next time, it would be the last.

Chapter Six

Rocky woke to the sound of her cell phone ringing. She squinted one eye toward the clock and groaned. For the second morning in a row, she'd awakened before noon, and she didn't like it. She grabbed her phone, praying it wasn't Blake. Seeing it was Joel, she quickly answered before it had time to go to voicemail.

"Hello?"

"Good morning, Rocky. I'm sorry to call so early, but we have an interested buyer for the bar."

"So soon?" Rocky sat up and pushed her hair out of her face.

"It surprised me too considering I only called the broker half an hour ago. Whoever it is would like to meet with you this afternoon."

Rocky hadn't told the team she was selling. She thought Friday would give her plenty of time to tell them before anyone inquired. "Uh... Yeah, I guess that's okay."

"Is there a problem with today? I can reschedule for tomorrow if necessary."

"I had wanted to tell all the employees before I met with someone. I don't want them to find out this way. Can you please put the person off until tomorrow? That way I can gather my team together today and let them know what's going on."

"Of course. Would you like me to be there with you tomorrow?" Joel offered.

Rocky smiled to herself. Her uncle's partner was a sweet man. "I appreciate that, but this is a preliminary showing. If and when I have someone ready to sign on the dotted line, that's when I'll need you with me."

"Of course, dear. Whatever you want. I will call the broker and set up a meeting for tomorrow."

"Thank you, Mr. Warren."

"Anything for you, Rocky. I'll call you when I have the exact time."

"Sounds good. Talk to you then." The line went dead, and Rocky flung herself backwards on the bed, staring at the ceiling. The sadness crept its way into her heart. This was really happening. She crossed her arm over her eyes and gave herself a moment to let it all sink in. Rocky knew it was the best thing to do for everyone involved; still, she couldn't help but regret it had to happen. If only…

Rocky needed to call Bridget, but it was too early. She would wait a while, but not too long. She wanted to give her friend plenty of time to call the troops together. Knowing she wouldn't be able to sleep with the thought of selling the bar going through her brain, Rocky rolled out of bed.

She'd forgotten to set the coffee pot when she got home, so Rocky fixed it to brew while she was in the shower. She couldn't function without her caffeine. She kept soda in the refrigerator for emergencies, but she preferred to hold a mug of the hot java so she could enjoy the aroma as well as the taste. As soon as she was out of the shower, she poured her first cup of coffee and sipped it while she untangled the mess that was her hair. After that was taken care of, Rocky left it hanging around her shoulders to air dry. She sat down at the small table that doubled as a desk, lit a cigarette, and clicked away on her laptop. Rocky wanted to check about going into nursing school. To see what her options were with regards to grants and loans. After two cups of coffee and three cigarettes, Rocky had most of the information she needed. Since she didn't have any college credits, Rocky would have to take some required courses before she could register in the local nursing program. That was the bad news. The good news was the quarterly payments weren't as outrageous as she'd thought they would be. Plus, they offered scholarships.

When she deemed it was late enough to call, Rocky phoned Bridget and told her about the prospective buyer and asked if she would gather the employees together that afternoon instead of Friday. If they couldn't make it, she'd call them personally and tell them over the phone, even though she hated the idea. Bridget promised she'd get everyone together, and as she hung up the phone, Rocky's doorbell rang. She unlocked her door and headed downstairs to see who was calling so early. When she looked through the peephole, she was relieved to see it was Vivian. She unlocked the metal door and smiled at her disheveled friend. "Looks like you just rolled out of bed."

Vivian was grinning even though she waved her hand in the air. "Oh, you know me. Why call it an early night when you can enjoy a fine male specimen for hours on end? Please tell me you have coffee."

"I have coffee."

"I love you even more than I already did," Vivian cooed as she followed Rocky up the stairs.

"Don't keep me waiting. I know you're here to gloat, so go ahead. Get on with it," Rocky teased as she poured her best friend a strong black cup of joe.

"I'm telling you, Rocky, I've been with some mighty fine men over the years, but Finley and his friends are like gods. I told you about the one who calls himself Sixx, and the hateful one who makes Thor look like a pimply-face teenager. But the one last night?" Vivian fanned herself with her free hand. "Girl, he was something else. Sinclair is his name. He's tall, and he is built, but not too bulky. Just enough to make you want to run your tongue over the grooves between his abs. And his V? It pointed down to the finest cock I've ever seen. His hair is long and dark, and his eyes are black. He looks Italian but not in the 'My name is Guido, gold chain wearing, mob goon' kind of way. More like the 'he's going to be the best lover you ever had' kind of way. Sinclair is a broody sort, but not so much it's a turn off.

Everything the man does is with purpose. The way he speaks. The words he chooses. The way he studies you." Vivian shivered.

"Wow. I think you're in love with him. So? He's hot. How was he in the sack?" Rocky sipped her coffee while studying her friend.

Something was off, and Vivian's next words explained what it was. Without looking at Rocky, Vivian said, "I wouldn't know. Everything was going great. We had a nice dinner with champagne before heading to the bedroom. I'm pretty sure it was a guest room, because there was no sign of anyone living in it. Anyway, Dana and I... I asked Dana to go since you couldn't... Dana and I got down to business while waiting on the men to join us. Before they did, though, Sin – that's what Finley calls Sinclair – Sin sort of issued Fin a challenge, and Finley accepted. While Dana and I were kissing, Fin dropped to his knees and swallowed Sin's fat cock down his throat. I've seen men go at it before, but seriously, I was jealous at the way Fin could deep throat his friend. It was ah-ma-zing. Sin looked shocked at first, but Finley got in the groove."

"And? What happened next? Don't tell me the guys fucked each other and left you and Dana to your own devices. Or did you not pull out the toys?"

"Uh huh. Before he could shoot his wad into Fin's mouth, Sin pulled out and ordered Finley to get on the bed. He chose Dana to play with instead of all of us taking turns. He fucked her well and good, her words, and then he left the room. I asked him to stay, but he seemed distant after he got his nut. I almost had my feelings hurt, but Finley more than made up for it. He played with both of us for a little while before he abruptly left the room. When he returned, Fin informed us we needed to take things back to either my place or Dana's. We went to Dana's since it was closer where we spent the rest of the night tangled in a three-way heap."

65

"So, Mr. Tall and Broody likes blondes." Rocky wasn't dissing Vivian; she was merely making an observation.

"That or he prefers the silent type. I could tell during dinner he was more drawn to Dana than me, but whatever. I got what I wanted, and it was heaven with a capital H. Even watching Sin was hotter than a lot of sex I've had. I am telling you, Rocky girl, you have got to get your hands on Sinclair. And your mouth. And your pussy. I'd be more than happy to watch him in action again."

Rocky laughed at her friend. "I'm glad you enjoyed yourself. And if he's as fine as you say he is, I wouldn't mind playing. But that's all it will be. I learned my lesson about trusting a man. Speaking of Satan, I spent last night in my office hiding from Blake."

"You're shitting me."

"Nope. After I went to see my lawyer, I decided a little bartending would be good for the soul, but as soon as Blake entered the room, I stayed away doing paperwork all night."

"Why did you see your lawyer? Everything okay?" Vivian got up from the table and refilled her cup. "You need me to top you off?"

Rocky held out her cup while Vivian filled it to the rim. "I'm selling RC's."

"You're what?" Vivian shrieked.

"I'm selling the bar."

"I heard you the first time, but what I meant was *why* are you selling? That's your Uncle Ray's legacy. Your legacy now."

"Not much of a legacy if I can't pay the bills. Mr. Warren said he'd float me a loan if I needed one, and if I don't sell soon, I may have to take him up on the offer." Vivian started to interrupt, and Rocky knew what she was going to say. She held up her hand. "No, Viv. I love you, but no. I think it's time I let someone else have it who can do it justice."

"What are you going to do after you sell it? You want to come work at the airport?"

"I'm thinking about going into nursing."

Vivian stared at Rocky for a beat before she responded. "Does all this have anything to do with dickhead coming around again?"

"No. Yes. I don't know. I thought if I ignored him long enough, he'd keep away. He called me last night."

"How the fuck did he get your number?"

Rocky sighed and leaned back in her chair, cupping her mug in both hands. "That's a good question. When I asked him, he said he always gets what he wants. Viv, he's not done with me. I'm going to take a self-defense class down at the gym. I need to be able to protect myself in case…" Rocky couldn't finish her sentence. Thinking about Blake made her sick to her stomach.

"You need to get a restraining order."

"A piece of paper isn't going to keep him away from me. Guys like him don't give two shits about restraining orders."

"See, this is why you need a *friend* like Sinclair. He'd squish Blake like a bug."

Rocky rolled her eyes. She knew Vivian wouldn't leave her alone until she'd at least met the man. "I'll be his *friend*, but that's as far as it goes. Besides, he might like Dana and not want to play with anyone else."

"From what Finley said, Sinclair's not the settling down type. He has a huge home up in the hills next to the Angeles Forest. He drives a Lamborghini. Why would he want to settle down when he can have his pick of women?"

Rocky wasn't about to hurt Vivian's feelings by saying if that were true, why would he want to play with Vivian and her friends? Vivian was a knock-out, no doubt about it. But she was also a little rough around the edges. Maybe this Sinclair liked his women experienced. Whatever

67

the reason, she would definitely like to see this "god", as Vivian put it. She wasn't above having sex with someone that hot.

Her best friend rose from the table and rummaged through Rocky's cabinets. She pulled out a box of instant macaroni and cheese. "Want some?" she asked. Neither one of them ate what most people would consider normal food for breakfast. Rocky picked up the habit when she was living with her aunt after her dad died. Linda couldn't cook worth a crap, so she bought instant everything. Since Rocky didn't like oatmeal, and Tommy refused to share the cereal, Rocky started eating rice and mac-n-cheese for breakfast. When she moved out, the habit stuck. Vivian didn't care what you fed her as long as you fed her.

"Yeah, I'll take a pack. Throw some tuna in mine, if you don't care." She needed the protein. Hell, she needed all the necessary nutrients for her to be healthy, but Rocky didn't eat like she should, and she rarely remembered to take her vitamins. Besides that, she refused to go to the doctor. The last time Rocky did, she'd received some bad news that rocked her world. *Fucking Tommy.*

When the noodles were nuked, Vivian divvied up the one can of tuna into the bowls, added the cheese powder and stirred. She set Rocky's in front of her, and the two women ate in mostly silence. The only sound was the spoons scraping the bottom of the bowls. Vivian retrieved the empties and rinsed them out before putting them in the dishwasher. She leaned against the counter and crossed her arms over her large breasts. "I'm worried about Blake."

"I am, too, honestly. It's another reason I think selling the bar is a good idea. If he realizes I'm not there twenty-four, seven, maybe he'll give up."

"Why don't you move in with me? At least for a little while?"

"I may have to do that. If the new owner won't let me continue to rent this place, I'll need somewhere to crash until I figure something out."

Vivian pushed away from the counter and stood behind Rocky. Vivian bent over, wrapping her arms around Rocky's shoulder. She kissed her on the cheek. "You've always got a place with me, babe."

"I know, and I love you for it." For that and for so much more. Rocky would never be able to repay Viv for everything she'd already done.

"All righty. I'm going to go home and get some sleep before work."

"Since when do you work during the week?" Rocky asked.

"Since Jocelyn got pregnant and can't stop throwing up."

"Jocelyn's pregnant? How'd that happen?" Rocky knew *how* it happened, but the woman in question was a lesbian.

"It seems her lesbianism isn't one-hundred-percent tried and true. She shagged an Air Journey pilot on one of his layovers." Vivian had been a waitress at RC's when Rocky started working there. It was how they met. When Vivian was offered a weekend only job at one of the restaurants in LAX making more in tips in three days than she did in two weeks at the little out-of-the-way tavern, she jumped at the chance.

"Huh." Rocky shrugged and pushed back from the table. "You never know about people."

"No, but I know all about you. You take care of yourself, and for Christ's sake, be careful."

"I will. Love you, Viv."

"Love you right back." Vivian pulled Rocky in for a hug and gave her another kiss on the cheek.

Rocky followed her downstairs to make sure the outer door was locked up tight behind her best friend. Rocky leaned against the door and stared at the back entrance to RC's. Selling was going to break her heart, but in her heart, she knew it was the right thing to do.

It took him longer than expected, but Sinclair finally found the listing for RC's. He called the broker and asked to meet with the owner that afternoon. When the woman returned his call, she informed him the current owner needed an extra day before she could meet with him. Sin was eager to talk to the woman, but if she couldn't meet, she couldn't, so he scheduled an appointment for the following day. After thinking about it, he decided to visit the little bar again, giving it another once-over, hopefully without feeling sick. He needed to find Uri and apologize, so Sin decided to invite the Goyle to meet him at RC's for a drink.

He tried Uri's number, but it went to voicemail. Sin didn't leave a message, opting to call again later. After making the call, Sin dressed in workout clothes and headed to the training field. When he arrived, the males who were already there were in deep discussion. The word Unholy was being thrown around. When he stepped up beside the group, Banyan handed him his sword and said, "Seems the Unholy are stirring."

Being the West Coast leader, Sin liked to be in the know on all happenings regarding their Clan. "Would somebody care to be a little more specific?" he asked as he eyed each of them.

Thane spoke up. "Sorry, Sinclair. I should have called you, but we were patrolling late into the morning hours. We actually came straight here from dealing with the bastards."

When Sin took in the males before him, he realized most of them were bloody. He raised his eyebrows, and Thane continued. "Last night was different. They were fighting with a purpose. They were spread out around the city instead of staying in a large pack. I called in

70

reinforcements to help contain them all. We managed to round up most of them, but a few slipped through. The main thing you need to know is there were rumblings of a new leader. I couldn't get a name out of any of them. While they know there is someone trying to take over, they don't know who it is."

"That cannot be good. If the Unholy are actually listening to and obeying someone, whoever it is must be powerful. Banyan, double-up on patrols. Scatter the Clan throughout the city until we can get a name. Add me to the rotation. This is important."

"Yes, sir," Banyan said, inclining his head.

"Okay then, let's get busy." Sin normally sparred with Banyan, but he chose to let someone else train with the Norseman. Each of them needed to be challenged to the best of their abilities, and no one was better suited for that than Banyan. Except maybe Urijah. Sin hadn't seen the two males go at it, but he knew if they ever did, it would be a sight to behold.

Three hours later, they called it a morning. Sin was excited about hunting Unholy. He hadn't patrolled in a long time. Rafael preferred he remain on the sidelines considering he was next in line to the throne. When Sin called him a hypocrite, Rafael had laughed. It was necessary to keep tabs on the mutants, but it was also exhilarating. The Goyles on the East Coast had it better in that they could fly more easily than those on the West Coast. New Atlanta had been hit harder during the explosions that rocked the world, and even though they had rebuilt the city, it was still less inhabited than the cities in California.

If he wasn't needed to rule the West, Sinclair would move to the inner states where the most damage had been done. The giant fissure that separated the country had left many of those states uninhabitable. Sin would love to take over a couple thousand acres and build a house out in the middle of nowhere so he could take to the skies whenever he felt like it. Being second-in-command of the Stone Society meant he would stay where he was needed most. For now, that was California.

Chapter Seven

Rocky confirmed with Bridget everyone would be at the bar an hour before they were scheduled to open. Most bars opened early, before noon, but RC's had always opened later since they didn't have a large lunch crowd. The location was out of the way, and most people who frequented the small establishment came there for that reason. It was smaller and more intimate. The new owner might decide to change that. There was plenty of room to expand the kitchen and serve more than bar food, but Rocky had kept it simple, the way Uncle Ray had. There were several other businesses in the area, but they weren't in a strip mall. The building sat off by itself, which Rocky had thought was appealing. That was until Blake.

Even with the park across the street behind the building, it wasn't the most secure place, so whenever Rocky left, she made sure she looked around before going to her car. She kept mace on her keychain and had it ready to use should she need it. Rocky beeped the locks on the car and hurried from the back door to her vehicle, sliding in and slamming the door closed. She reengaged the locks before she put the key in the ignition. Anyone who saw her would think she was paranoid, and they would be correct. She'd lived through the nightmare Blake Stansbury had brought on, and she prayed to all deities who would listen that she never had to endure anything like it ever again.

Being strung out on drugs was alluring to those who wanted to forget about their lives. Rocky had just started living her life when Blake got her hooked. She hadn't wanted to forget anything except the things he did to her when she was too doped up to fight. Rocky had basically lived in a zombie trance for over a year. She still had no idea how she managed to keep the bar from going under. *You didn't. Bridget did.* Rocky smiled when she thought of her friend. Bridget was one of the good ones. Steady. Strong. Bridget would never succumb to the likes of Blake Stansbury.

When Rocky arrived at the gym, she made sure she had the free week offer in her purse before she went inside. The guy behind the counter was tall and fit, reminding her of Vivian's description of Finley's friends. *They're like gods.* The man in front of her definitely fit the bill. The nervous butterflies she had from running to her car had turned into flutterings of a different kind. Rarely did a man affect her, but he was no mere man. When she realized she was staring and he was smirking, Rocky lowered her eyes and pulled the flyer out of her purse, handing it over. "I want to sign up for self-defense classes."

The smile drained from the man's gorgeous face. "Is someone hurting you, Chère?" he demanded in a deep cadence that sounded Cajun. If Rocky said yes, she had no doubt this guy would find the culprit and beat him within an inch of his life.

"No, nothing like that," she reassured him. "I tend bar, and sometimes I have to walk to my car alone. I want to be able to protect myself. Just in case."

The smile returned to his tan face, and he said, "Well, in that case, let's get you signed up. Oui?"

"Oui," Rocky responded, smiling back at his infectious visage.

"Remy Doucet, at your service," he drawled, holding out his large hand.

"Rocky Cartwright." She tentatively placed her small hand in his. Instead of shaking, Remy pulled her hand to his mouth and kissed her knuckles. The heat rose in her cheeks. If that had been Blake, she'd have wanted to wash her hand immediately, but Rocky felt nothing negative coming from the guy standing behind the counter. Strangely, she felt safe. Maybe it had been his attitude when she first walked in, or

74

maybe it was wishful thinking on her part. What girl didn't dream of a knight in shining armor riding in to save the day? Or sweep her off her feet. *Rocky girl, you're losing it.*

Rocky had dressed in workout clothes, but after the paperwork was filled out, Remy informed her the women's classes were on Tuesday, Thursday, and Saturday. "Can you come back tomorrow, Chère?"

"I can, thank you." Rocky was a little disappointed, but it gave her something to look forward to the following day. Remembering the meeting at the bar with the potential buyer, she checked the schedule for the classes. She could come to the early one and still have plenty of time to get home and cleaned up before she met with them.

"Let me walk you to your car, oui?" Remy offered, following her out the door. Rocky smiled up at him and nodded. Now that he was next to her, she realized exactly how large he was. He dwarfed Rocky, but she still didn't feel intimidated. When she got to her car, he waited until she was safely inside before he returned to the building. Maybe chivalry wasn't dead after all.

Instead of driving straight home, Rocky turned her car toward the beach. It wasn't often she allowed herself the freedom to stray far from home. Locking herself away in her tiny apartment or the bar was her self-imposed penance for the bad choices she'd made. Sure, she was now clean from drugs, but she still felt dirty on the inside. It was another reason she would never let a man get close to her emotionally. How could she in good conscious give herself to a decent man when she wasn't good? Wasn't whole?

After parking in the public lot, Rocky put her cell phone and lighter in the zip pocket of her workout pants and shoved her small purse under the seat. She took one cigarette from the pack, because if she took any more, she'd end up smoking them all. Locking her car, Rocky kept her mace ready and walked down the wooden planks leading to the beach. Being March, it was practically deserted. The cool breeze off the ocean tossed her long hair about her shoulders, but Rocky didn't try to contain it. She walked toward the ocean, making sure to stay far enough back the surf didn't get on her tennis shoes. She might be giving herself the pleasure of seeing the waves roll in, but she wouldn't go as far as putting her bare feet in the sand or the surf. That was too much of a good thing, and she didn't deserve anything good. Rocky had already used up her allotment of good when Vivian saved her from herself.

Laughter caught her attention, and Rocky turned her head toward the sound. Two couples were walking toward her along the water's edge. The men favored so much they had to be brothers. One was fit and had tattoos covering most of his upper body. The other was built like Remy, and his arms were bare. Neither one was wearing a shirt, which seemed odd to Rocky. They looked familiar to her for some reason. Their women were both beautiful, and by the way they couldn't keep their eyes off their men, obviously in love. As they passed by, they all spoke to Rocky and smiled. She couldn't imagine finding a man who would make her blissfully happy. Rocky was envious, but she knew it was her own fault she'd never find a love like the kind these people had.

Rocky returned her attention to the waves and did her best not to let the tears fall.

She failed.

Miserably.

The waves coupled with her sobs drowned out any other noise around her until the one sound she hated more than anything else reached her ears. "Hello, Raquel."

Landon Roxburgh was a godsend. Julian had turned the Goyle loose after about an hour of showing him around the Clan computer system, and the male had already found a couple of backdoor entryways his hacker nemesis had managed to find. Landon closed the portals and put even more elaborate security protocols in place. Julian silently berated himself for not finding those. His head wasn't in the game, and since the Feds had Katherine, his lack of attention to detail was only getting worse. He had been torn between figuring out how to clear Katherine's name and keeping the Clan secure. Now, Landon could help with the Clan while Julian focused on his mate.

Landon had managed to put Sixx's plan in motion with regards to finding their hacker. If the culprit was paying attention, he would more than likely win the contest. Whether he or she came forward to claim the job offer was another matter altogether. Having accomplished the test, Landon began helping Julian hack into the FBI's system. The Goyle was confident he'd be able to figure out what they had done with Katherine as well as help Julian fix the damning evidence against her.

"Is there anything else I can help with?" Landon asked.

"Yes. Figure out who's been hacking our system. I never thought I'd admit this, but he's smarter than I am. At this point, I'm hoping you are as well. I need to figure out how to undo the damage he's done to my mate."

"I'll do what I can, Julian." Landon turned to the computers and began typing faster than even Julian could. Julian left the Goyle to whatever it was he was doing and sat down at one of the monitors. While he was typing, he called Gregor to find out if the Feds had mentioned where they were taking Katherine.

A pissed off Gregor said, "Not only did they not tell me where they were taking her, they wouldn't speak to me at all. They acted like I was a pile of shit they had stepped in and proceeded to march Katherine out the door without so much as a thank you or a kiss my ass. Talk about a chip on their shoulder. These guys are out to prove something. But why they insist on using Katherine to prove their point is beyond me."

"We need to find a way to infiltrate their ranks, Brother. I talked to Nikolas, and as far as our records show, we have no Clan members within the FBI."

"I'll have Tessa call her father. Maybe Xavier has a contact we aren't aware of."

Julian sighed. "I would appreciate it. Not knowing what is going on with my mate is far worse than watching her from afar, especially now that I've promised to clear her name."

"Like I told you before, Jules, we will get her away from them. One way or another."

Julian thanked Gregor and hung up. He agreed with his cousin. One way or another. No matter what it took, he would free his mate, even if he had to do it illegally.

Rocky's head lolled to the side. She was unable to hold it upright. Her tongue felt as though it was swollen, making it hard to swallow. *Damn you, Blake. No, damn you, Rocky. You let your guard down, and now he has you again.* The tears rolled down her cheeks, but her arms were filled with lead, and she couldn't lift them to wipe her face. She had no idea how long she'd been out of it. Rocky tried to look around, but it was dark wherever she was. Rocky couldn't tell if she was sitting on something soft or hard. Whatever Blake had given her was different than anything he'd injected her with before.

The drug coursing through Rocky's veins was nothing she would ever have paid money for. Or danced for. Or fucked for. This was something that made her want to cut her veins open so the blood would drain out, taking the poison with it. While she was lying there, Rocky thought about her short life. Twenty-four years old and she'd wasted

78

everything. All for a fucking man. After what her cousin Tommy had put her through, Rocky knew she would never find anyone who'd want her. Good men didn't want spoiled goods. But Blake had come along, and for a split second, she'd let herself think maybe, just maybe, she had a chance at happiness. Love wasn't in the cards for a girl like Rocky. Neither was happiness.

Rocky had done her best to make a go of the bar, but she wasn't smart enough to bring it back from the low she'd helped it to sink. She'd given up on thinking about love. She smiled when she bartended but never let herself study the men too closely. The couples on the beach flashed through her mind, and the ache in her chest tightened to an unbearable level. Why couldn't the man she fell for have been one of the good guys? Why couldn't she have met Remy instead of Blake? Too tired to try to fight it, Rocky closed her eyes and begged for death.

Her prayers went unanswered, and Rocky was aware of her body being moved. She didn't open her eyes, because she didn't want Blake to realize she was awake. At least she assumed it was Blake. If only she could stop her breathing, he might think he killed her. An ungodly amount of cologne was present on the man's skin, making Rocky's nose itch. She didn't recognize the scent, but Blake could have changed fragrances in the last year. Rocky inhaled and did her best to hold her breath until the urge passed. Blake laid her down on something, and this time she could tell the surface was hard, like a table.

He began humming an unfamiliar tune, and that in itself was enough to make Rocky want to scratch his eyeballs out. It was something he did when he ignored her pleas for mercy. The only time he'd ever backed off was on the days she was supposed to dance. Fridays and Saturdays had been Rocky's only brief respite from needing her fix. Those two days Blake fed her just enough of whatever concoction he came up with to keep her strung out while awake enough to give the patrons a good show.

Blake pushed her hair away from her face before bending over and pressing their lips together. Rocky managed not to flinch and give her state of wakefulness away. "I told you I always get what I want, Raquel. I've given you time to come to your senses, but I'm tired of waiting. You belong to me. You've had long enough of a reprieve." His hand left her face and skimmed down her body. Her limbs were still heavy, but the weight of his hand was evident as he continued lower until he got to the juncture between her legs.

Rocky wanted to scream. She wanted to cry out for help, but she knew none was available. She'd been there before. Why the man insisted on drugging her for sex had been a mystery in the beginning, but now, she knew it would be a cold day in hell before she let him get anywhere near her body without being drugged. It was useless to try to fight him, so Rocky continued faking. If he decided to have his way with her, it would hopefully be quick and painless. Blake's cell phone pinged. He let out a curse, and instead of continuing his perusal of her body, Blake stuck a needle in her arm, plunging yet more drugs into her system.

"Sleep, my Raquel."

Rocky fought the drugs as long as she could. She recognized the room Blake was keeping her in was the basement at the club. If she could just get her cell phone. Her arms were growing heavier by the second, but she managed to figure out her phone was still in the pocket of her yoga pants. She felt it vibrate against her leg, but she couldn't make her arms work. Good. Someone was looking for her. If she missed the meeting and didn't show up for work, Bridget would start to worry about her and call someone. Vivian. Bridget would call Vivian.

Instead of going to the gym after sparring, Sin returned home. He continued to feel off, even though the feeling wasn't nausea. Something was nagging at him. Something he'd never encountered before in his long life. Sin always prided himself on being the steady one. As steady as Rafael. He loved life. Loved to laugh. Loved to love. Maybe that was it. He was missing out on the love of a woman, and with his brothers and cousins finding their mates, he was jealous.

As soon as he pulled in the driveway and parked, Sin made his way to the garden at the back of the swimming pool. Lush greenery surrounded a stone pathway which meandered back and forth forming an infinity symbol. Several benches were hidden among the foliage where one could sit and enjoy the serenity the garden offered. Sin stopped at one of the benches and sat down, stretching his arms along the back of the seat. He closed his eyes and cleared his mind. Using the techniques Frey had taught him many years ago, Sin compartmentalized all noise and pushed all thoughts away until he found the one sound that brought him the most peace.

The multitude of birds that made his garden home sang to each other. He had practiced until he could mimic each individual species' particular tone. He envied the birds because they were free to fly whenever and wherever they felt like it. Often Sin wondered what the world would be like if the humans were aware of the Gargoyles' existence, and they were free to fly whenever they wanted. Rafael, ever the voice of reason, reminded him it would be chaos. The government would try to either rule them differently, or worse, lock them up as they did the Unholy when they were successful in catching one.

Hiding their true nature was necessary, but it was still something they all fought with from time to time. With Sin's shifter becoming more restless with each day that passed, he was having a harder time than usual. Maybe the nausea meant his mate was closer than he realized.

The peacefulness Sin finally felt was interrupted by Rafael's ringtone coming through the phone. Sin leaned his head back and looked up. Had it been anyone other than Rafael, he would probably have let it go to voicemail.

"Rafe?"

"Hey, Brother. I wanted to let you know what I found out from Xavier. He spoke to his father, and William was confident those on the Elder Council would be split when it came to trying to overthrow Alistair, since I don't have definitive proof he is behind the trouble with our mates. William feels most assured Alistair will throw Kallisto under the bus and claim his own innocence. Then there are those who didn't agree with him when he urged Jonas's clan to ostracize him, and it might not take much for them to side with us."

"Kallisto is back in Greece, so we cannot make her talk. Sergei isn't necessarily a credible witness since he is human. So, how do we get proof?"

"Find the hacker and make him talk."

"That is easier said than done, Brother. Julian is having a hard enough time keeping the hacker out of our system." Sinclair was confident Landon would be able to help secure the system, but if Julian hadn't been able to locate the hacker before...

"Truth, but Sixx came up with an idea we feel could lure the hacker out into the open, so to speak. It is one of the things we are going to have Landon focusing on." Rafael explained the idea of issuing a challenge and setting up a fake system. Whoever could infiltrate the system fastest would win a million dollars.

"What if the one we are after doesn't need the money?"

"We're hoping the bragging rights will entice him or her."

"You think the culprit could be a woman?" Sin

82

asked.

"I've met some intelligent women over the years."

"I have as well, but I was thinking about the fact whoever is behind this could possibly be responsible for Katherine Fox's predicament."

"You don't think women are capable of evil? Look at Kallisto Verga. That bitch kidnapped Connor and killed Isabelle's friend," Rafael seethed.

"You have a point. Speaking of Kallisto, any movement there?"

"She hasn't left the compound, but word is Alistair left earlier this morning. We're waiting to find out where he's going. I'm going to let Julian and Landon do their best to track down the mystery hacker. If they can do that, maybe we can convince them they're working for the wrong team. If not, we'll plan accordingly."

Sinclair didn't have to ask what the plan entailed. The Clan was preparing for war.

Chapter Eight

Sin gave up on meditating after talking with his brother. He stepped into the pool house and changed out of his clothes into a pair of swim trunks. If Ingrid hadn't been there, he'd have gone commando, but he didn't want to give the older woman a heart-attack. After swimming laps for about an hour, Sin dried off and headed inside to find something to eat. Normally, he'd have eaten whatever leftovers were in the fridge, but he and Finley had taken care of everything Ingrid had prepared the night before. Actually, Finley had eaten everything. The Goyle could put away some food. Sinclair had no problem with the way Fin ate. Since he didn't have his own cook, he often came over and ate Sin's leftovers.

Maybe since Uri was staying with Fin, he was getting decent meals. If Uri wasn't any better of a cook than Finley was, they were probably living on takeout. Thinking about Uri, Sin tried his number again. If Uri was with Finley when Sin called, he'd invite them both so things wouldn't seem so awkward. Sin also wanted to see how Uri and Banyan were getting along, so he made that phone call as well. Since they still had time to kill, Sinclair invited Banyan over to hang out until later.

Sin showered and dressed, opting for casual. He debated briefly about shaving his beard but thought better of it. He hated shaving every day. As he was walking toward the kitchen, the motor of Banyan's car sounded in the driveway. Sin grabbed the whiskey and a couple of cigars and headed to the patio.

Driving out to the desert and letting his shifter loose

had been a good decision. Urijah returned early that morning to an empty house, knowing who Finley had spent the night with. He decided not to ruin his friendship with Fin by being a little bitch about it. It took a while, but Uri realized Finley was going to be Finley, and he was never going to see Uri the way he wanted to be seen. When Uri left that morning to go to the armory, Finley still hadn't returned. He was a big Goyle, and Urijah had to let him go. Urijah had thought about getting his own place, but he was almost finished with his assignment. It would be stupid to rent a house for a few days, so Uri decided to suck it up and deal.

When he entered Fin's home that evening, Uri went in search of his friend. He found Finley sprawled out on the sofa, flipping channels on the television. Finley had obviously taken a shower, because he smelled like his bodywash. When Finley moved to the West Coast, Uri had bought a bottle of the stuff so he could remember what Fin smelled like.

"Finally," Fin said when Uri sat down on the sofa next to him. Fin tossed him a controller and brought their favorite game up on the screen. He didn't ask how Uri's day was. Didn't tell him what he'd been doing all day. They weren't involved intimately, so Finley didn't share with Uri the way a partner would. Uri should have been used to it, but he still wanted the domesticity that came with having a mate. *We have a mate.* Uri's shifter never let him forget there was someone else out there besides Finley. Uri ignored the shifter and concentrated on the game.

Normally Uri loved playing games, but he was nervous about the night before. He'd wondered all day whether or not Finley had known Uri was being a voyeur. If he had, Fin didn't mention it. He treated Uri the same as he always did when they were going head to head. Finley was competitive, and he did anything he could to distract Uri into screwing up.

85

They were deep into a game when Uri's phone rang. Finley paused their video game so he could answer it. It was Sinclair. If Finley hadn't been sitting there, Uri would let it go to voicemail. He wasn't ready to talk to Sin, but he couldn't ignore him without explaining why to Finley. "Hello?" Urijah answered.

"There is this little bar not too far from here I want to check out. Can you and Fin put down the video games long enough to go do something a little more grown up?" Sinclair asked. Uri noticed Sinclair had yet to tone down his formal way of speaking, even after almost six hundred years.

Uri didn't need to repeat the question for Fin. He was sitting next to him on the sofa, his controller idle on his lap.

"Why? Do you need chaperones?" Fin asked as he stood. He strode to the entertainment console and turned the game off. He was obviously on board with going out. Urijah had hoped he would at least have Fin to himself for one last night before he went back home.

"No, smartass. I want your opinions on the bar. I am thinking about buying it."

Uri wasn't ready to face Sinclair. The Goyle had to have known he'd shown up at his home. Sighing to himself, he said, "Text me the address, and we'll meet you there."

"Coming to you now." Sin disconnected without saying goodbye. For some reason, the Goyle never signed off on his phone calls. They all had their quirks, so Uri went with it.

"You okay with going? I know you're not big into the bar scene," Fin asked him.

"Yeah. You're probably getting tired of me anyway."

"Nah. Give me another couple of weeks, and I'll be hiding from you."

Urijah laughed, but he really didn't find the comment funny. He had a feeling Finley was already tired of spending every night on the sofa playing video games with him. Last night was proof. What Uri didn't understand was why he was so hung up on Finley. They were compatible in every way that mattered between friends, and when they did get around to having sex, it was good. But Uri knew Finley didn't want him the same way.

When Sixx asked if they were mates, Uri assured him they were not. He knew for a fact they weren't, but it didn't make him want Finley any less. Uri was attracted to him, but the deep longing the others spoke of when referring to their mates wasn't present. At least not with Finley. Uri knew the truth deep down, but he couldn't allow his shifter to get riled up, so he refused to think about someone else.

Uri offered to drive since his SUV was sitting in the driveway. He preferred to drive anyway. He was all about being in control, and lately, he'd felt anything but. The drive was comfortable as it usually was. Finley loved to sing, and Uri loved to listen to his friend. Even though he wasn't good at it, Finley belted out the songs and kept Uri entertained. The closer they got to their destination, the more confused Uri became. When Sinclair invited them out for drinks, Uri had expected to head toward the city. Instead, they were heading away from it. "Do you know where we're going?" he asked Fin.

"Nope. But with Sinclair, you can never tell. One night we're wearing dress clothes and sipping champagne. The next, we're in shorts and flip flops drinking beer at a beach bonfire. The male is all over the place when it comes to nightly entertainment." Uri knew the previous night had been filled with champagne. He'd seen the empty bottles.

When they pulled into the parking lot in front of the building Sinclair had sent the address for, Uri was pretty sure they wouldn't be ordering Dom Pérignon. "What the hell?" he muttered. There was no valet parking. The bar could only be described as a dive. There were quite a few vehicles lined up along the front of the building. Uri looked around for Sin's Lamborghini, praying the male had enough sense to drive something else. As a Gargoyle, Uri wasn't scared, but he didn't take the area for the safest place either.

As the two of them made their way inside, Uri's shifter eyesight quickly adjusted to the dim lights. The place was larger than it looked from the outside. There was a long bar along the back wall of the room. Booths and high tops made up the right side of the building, while the left was filled with pool tables, dart boards, and an old-fashioned juke box. The middle of the room was open. Uri assumed it was the dance floor.

A low whistle caught their attention. Sinclair was shooting pool. With Banyan. "What the fuck?" The Goyle smirked at Urijah, his shifter hearing allowing him to catch what Uri had said. The atmosphere grew thick, almost suffocating. Uri felt like the room was closing in on him. Sin had invited Uri over to witness his best friend with someone else, and now he had invited the one male Uri avoided at all costs to have drinks with them. Was Sinclair trying to piss him off?

Finley walked up to Banyan, shaking his hand. *He* obviously had no quarrel with the other male. Then again, he didn't know him the way Uri did. *Fuck it. Keep your head down and your eyes to yourself. Do not let him bait you.* Urijah followed his best friend over to where Sin and Banyan were in the middle of a game and halfway through a pitcher of beer.

Fin sidled up to the table, eyeing the number of solids versus stripes. "Wow. I don't think I've ever seen a game so evenly matched."

Sinclair downed the last of his beer and refilled his glass. "Banyan is not bad. I hear Uri is pretty good, too."

Finley laughed, because he knew the truth. The only person better at pool he'd seen was Tessa. Gregor's mate could run the table before even the Gargoyles could blink. "I'm not bad," Uri replied, grinning at Sin.

"It really doesn't matter who's *not bad*. Uri's on my team," Fin declared. "Do we have a waitress, or do I need to go to the bar?" he asked, looking around.

"The bartender is doing double duty since it is slow. You will probably be served faster if you go to her," Sin informed him as he set up his next shot. Urijah hadn't seen Sin play, but he and Banyan had gone head to head in the past. In more ways than one. Sin sank two balls in a row, but didn't leave himself set up for the third. Instead of taking a shit shot, he played defense and left the cue ball in a bad spot for Banyan. The big blond took his time, observing where his balls were on the table. He leaned over his stick, but before he took his shot, he winked at Uri. He pulled his stick back and tapped the cue ball. Barely missing Sin's nine ball, it struck his own thirteen with just enough force to knock it in the pocket.

"Fucking lucky shot!" Sin declared, laughing.

Banyan grinned. "Looks like Uri's my lucky charm." He rounded the table to set up for his next shot, ignoring the scowl on Uri's face.

Uri tried distracting the male. "Shouldn't you be patrolling?"

Knocking the eleven in, Banyan asked, "Shouldn't you be at the armory?"

Urijah waited until Banyan was about to hit the cue ball and said, "I have been all day, making the swords you were supposed to pick up this afternoon." Banyan missed the shot and glared at Uri.

"I did pick them up. *After* you left so I wouldn't run into you. Isn't that what you wanted?"

Ignoring the undercurrent between Uri and Banyan, Sin laughed. "Lucky charm, huh? Maybe he is mine." Sin proceeded to run the table. When he sank the eight ball in the called pocket, he asked, "Partners now?"

Urijah nodded. He was looking forward to this. He and Finley were a hard pair to beat. "Yes, and like Fin said, he and I are a team." Urijah racked the balls for the next game while he waited on Fin to get back with the beer.

They started off betting a hundred bucks per game. By the time Banyan had lost a thousand, he was ready to up the ante. "One game. Just you and me," he propositioned Uri in his low, sexy voice. It had always unsettled Uri.

"What is the wager?" Urijah asked, but should have known better.

"Loser cooks for the winner."

"I've eaten your cooking. I think I'll pass," Uri huffed. Banyan was actually a fabulous cook and had taught Uri everything he knew.

"I tell you what. If I win, you cook for me. If you win, you can choose anything you want as your prize." Banyan loved baiting Uri. He always had. It was one of the reasons Urijah wanted nothing to do with him. He had his friendship with Finley, and that was all he needed. Not someone like Banyan who didn't know when to quit. Or how to take no for an answer.

Forgetting they had an audience, Uri told him, "You know my cooking sucks. It hasn't improved in the last thirty years."

"I'll take my chances." Banyan's expression let Uri know he was referring to more than food.

"It's your stomach. Break 'em." Urijah grabbed the chalk from the table and twisted it on the end of his cue. Sinclair and Finley were eyeing him and Banyan curiously. *Well, fuck.* Being around the other Goyle made Urijah forget his surroundings. Made him forget why Uri did his best to stay away from the other male. Uri chose to ignore their questioning looks. Sin, he wasn't worried about, but Fin would surely question him on the ride home. As long as they had been friends, Urijah had never spoken of his time in New Orleans.

Urijah didn't want to cook for , so he concentrated on every shot, making sure to leave the cue ball set up for the next. Shot after shot, he sank his balls into the pocket he called. When it got down to the eight ball, Banyan did his best to distract Uri. He stood next to him leaving barely any space between them. He leaned over and whispered in Uri's ear, "You've always been good with balls. And holes."

Luckily, the shot was a straight one. One Uri could have made with his eyes closed, because Banyan's hot breath on his ear was enough to jolt even the most stoic of Goyles. Sin and Finley were clapping and grinning until Sin grabbed his stomach and moaned. Finley gripped his bicep asking if he was okay. While Sin was feeling sick, a familiar voice reached Urijah's ears. He looked around the room to see who was there. Several more people had entered the bar since he and Finley had. He had been so focused on the game that he hadn't been paying attention to the other patrons. All the booths and tables were full, as were the seats at the bar. A couple of girls were dancing together, one a redhead who looked too familiar.

Uri forgot all about his past with Banyan and Sinclair's sudden stomach ailment. *Vivian* was dancing with a brunette, and by dancing he meant they were practically holding each other up. Vivian did not look happy. Luckily, Finley was focused on Sinclair and not the redhead.

The brunette didn't look coherent. He reached out with his senses to listen in on their conversation. "Dammit, Rocky! Girl, you need to fucking focus."

"'s not my fault. I was sitting on the beach, and he showed up. Can't. Stand. Up." The brunette hadn't been wrong. She slid out of Vivian's arms and crumpled in a heap. Without thinking, Uri rushed to the female's side and lifted her from the floor.

"Follow me," Vivian said. Uri carried the unresponsive brunette to a small office in the back of the building immediately past the restrooms. He laid her down on a worn-out, leather sofa that was full of bare spots. "Jesus fucking Christ, Rocky. I swear..." Vivian closed her mouth when she noticed Urijah. "You. What are you doing here?"

"He's with me," Finley said from the doorway. "Viv, what's going on?"

"She's been drugged."

"Call an ambulance," Uri instructed. While he let Finley hash things out with the redhead, he reached out with his senses and checked the female over internally as best he could. Fin and Vivian were now out in the hall trying to calm another female voice.

The brunette slurred, "No, no hos...pit...al."

"What can I do to help?" Banyan asked, squatting down at Uri's knees. "How bad is she?"

"Please call an ambulance. Her heart rate is slowing."

"Rocky? Rocky!" the bartender yelled, running into the now crowded office. "Oh, God! Is she dead?" The other woman was growing more hysterical by the minute.

"Finley, a little assistance please." Urijah needed to keep an eye on Rocky. She hadn't passed out, and she was doing her best to argue even though she was weak. Banyan was calling for help. Sinclair hadn't made an appearance, so that left Finley. When his friend appeared in the doorway, Uri pointed to the bartender. "Please take her out of here. Find Sinclair and shut the bar down. I'll pay for any open tabs. I need it fucking quiet in here."

Finley wrapped his arm around the bartender and did as Urijah asked. Banyan knelt back down beside Urijah, their knees touching. Fuck, Urijah couldn't breathe. With his phone to his ear, Banyan told whoever was on the other end of the line as much as he knew. "Do you know what she took?" Uri asked Vivian.

"Not take..." the woman on the sofa said before her head rolled the side.

"She said she was drugged. If that's the case, whatever he gave her was some bad shit," Vivian said.

"He who?" Banyan asked as he hung up.

"Her ex. He got her hooked once before, but she's been clean for almost a year. He's a real piece of shit, and if I get my hands on the bastard..."

Uri had not liked Vivian when he first met the redhead, but the way she was being protective of her friend said something about the woman. This obviously wasn't the first time she'd taken care of her friend.

"Viv, who are you going to put your hands on?" Finley asked when he stuck his head in the room.

"Her ex." Vivian squatted next to Rocky's head and stroked her hair back. "It's gonna be okay, Rocky girl. We've been through worse," she whispered, probably only loud enough for Rocky to hear, but with his shifter hearing, Uri caught her words.

"The ambulance is here," Banyan said. He placed his hand on Uri's shoulder and gave him a squeeze. "I'm going to go show them where we are." Banyan left the room, and Uri closed his eyes. *Bastard.* His body betrayed him, again, from just one touch.

"I don't hear the ambulance," Vivian said, frowning when the sirens finally were audible to her human ears.

Uri twisted so he could adjust his cock which was painfully pushing against his zipper. Thankfully, Vivian was still focused on her friend's face. The front door opened, and the paramedics were wheeling the stretcher in. Urijah stood so he could give them some room, pulling Vivian along with him. "Let's give them some space."

"Who?" she asked. Uri pointed to the door as soon as the first EMT came through. She frowned again, but he ignored her.

"So nobody knows what she took?" one EMT asked as he began working on Rocky.

"She didn't take anything. She was given something. You need to call that bastard Blake Stansbury and ask him what it was. He's the one who did this to her," Vivian protested.

"Did you see him give it to her?"

"No, but they have a history," Vivian tried to explain.

"So she's used before?" the EMT continued.

Urijah interrupted them. "Sir, her pulse is fading. If you would, please tend to the girl, and we'll answer your questions when you get her stable," Urijah stood to his full height, and the EMT bristled but got busy checking Rocky's vitals. Speaking into the two-way radio on his shoulder, he reported her information to the hospital after he and the other EMT got Rocky situated on the stretcher.

"One of you can ride with us," the first responder said. Urijah gestured for Vivian to be the one, but before she could climb into the back of the ambulance, he pulled her aside.

"Don't give them any damning information. Just tell them you don't know specifics. I'll have someone waiting on her when you get to the hospital." Vivian nodded and hoisted herself up inside the transport.

Chapter Nine

Urijah looked around for Sinclair. Instead, he found Finley and Banyan. "Where's Sin?" he asked.

Finley answered, "He went on home. Said he didn't feel good."

"Didn't feel good. We don't..."

"...get sick. I know. Either he's found his mate, or something else is going on with him," Finley said.

"I was going to get him to call Dr. Mercato and have him meet Vivian and the girl at the hospital. I don't like the fact she was drugged. I'd rather have one of ours on this so we can keep tabs on her," Uri told Finley. He'd yet to look at Banyan.

"I've already called the doctor. Bridget's waiting inside for you to settle all the tabs. If you want to handle that, I'm going to head on over to the hospital and wait with Viv."

"Yeah, okay." Uri turned toward the door, and when Banyan followed, Uri stopped. "What are you doing?"

"Going with you."

"I can handle this, B." *Fuck. Why'd you go and do that?* Using his shortened nickname was not going to get the Goyle to leave him alone. Not that Banyan was actually bothering him.

"I know you can, but I was hoping you'd give me a ride. I left my car at Sinclair's."

"What were you doing at Sinclair's?" Uri's mind went back to the night before when Finley was on his knees in front of Sin. Surely he and Banyan weren't hooking up too.

Banyan leaned in and whispered against Uri's ear, "Jealous, lover?"

"Not on your fucking life, Sorensen." Uri brushed

past his ma... past Banyan and went to settle the tab. The employees were gathered around whispering to one another instead of cleaning like they probably should have been doing. He found the bartender and tossed a credit card on the bar. "Double the total, and add thirty percent for tips," he instructed.

The bartender's eyes grew huge, but it was only right they be compensated appropriately since he was the one who wanted the bar closed down. "I bet your girlfriend loves you to pieces," the woman fished as she scooped the credit card off the bar.

Uri didn't bother commenting, but Banyan didn't let it go. "No, but his boyfriend sure does," he said, giving the woman a knowing look. Uri glared at Banyan, but the Goyle's smirk grew into a full-on smile right before he winked.

The bartender returned with the credit card and receipt for Uri to sign. "So, Rocky's your friend?" he asked while he scribbled his name on the dotted line.

"Yeah, but she's more than that. She owns this place."

Banyan took a few steps closer to Uri and propped an elbow on the bar. "The owner, huh? I heard she was looking to sell."

The bartender leaned closer and whispered, "She was supposed to be here before everyone's shift started to tell them she's selling. When she didn't show, I got worried."

Banyan asked, "Is she also the manager?"

"No, that'd be me. I do double duty most nights when we're busy."

Banyan eyed the woman for a moment. Instead of responding to her comment, he told her, "They're taking Rocky to New Angeles Medical, if you want to go check on her after you get things tidied up here."

"If you don't mind me asking, who are you guys,

and why are you taking such an interest in Rocky and RC's? I've never even seen you in here. Well, except for your other friend. The one who bolted. He was in here last night."

Banyan looked to Uri for help. Urijah shrugged. "Because Rocky is a friend of Vivian's who is a friend of Finley's. We take care of our own."

"Oh. Okay. Well, thank you for the generous tip. You sure you bat for the other team?" Bridget asked, eyeing both men. Urijah ignored the woman's flirting and once again glared at Banyan.

"You just can't leave shit alone, can you?" Uri asked before striding toward the door. Banyan was at his back within two steps.

"Not when it comes to you, I can't."

As soon as he was outside, Uri stopped, turning abruptly. Banyan grabbed Uri's biceps trying to halt his forward progress, putting them chest to chest. Eye to eye. Lips to plump, totally kissable lips. Uri's beast was gearing up for a fight. The shifter wanted him to put his arms around Banyan and pull him closer. Taste his lips like he had so many times before. Lick his... Uri pulled away from Banyan and crossed his arms over his chest. It was his go-to stance when he wanted to keep from grabbing Banyan and doing what the shifter wanted. Banyan knew this, but he didn't call him on it.

"Sorry. I promise to behave, *if* you'll give me a ride to Sin's," Banyan conceded, holding his hands up.

Once again, images from the previous night came roaring back. Uri did his best to keep the jealousy at bay. If he wasn't careful, Banyan would pick up on it and think Urijah was jealous over him instead of Finley. "Get in the fucking car," he instructed. Gods help him get through one car ride with this male at his side.

97

Sinclair was getting tired of the nauseous feeling, but he was also tired of running. Every time he'd felt the strange sensation, the same man had been around. First at the gym, second sitting at the bar, and then earlier that evening, the man had been outside the bar smoking a cigarette. Sin hadn't stuck around to make conversation with the man. There had to be some other explanation as to what was going on with him. If this shit persisted, he was going to go visit Dr. Mercato. If he couldn't help, Sin was going to call Dominic and have Lilly make a potion for him.

He hated bailing on Banyan, but he could grab a ride home with Fin and Uri. The two blond Norsemen had been flirting the whole time they were playing pool. Banyan had enjoyed the shit out of it, if the permanent grin etched to his face had been any indication. Urijah? Not so much. Sin would love to find out what their story was, because there most definitely *was* a story there. Sin also needed to find out what all the commotion had been right after he felt sick. The good thing about the night was Banyan had been able to visit the bar and give Sinclair his opinion on it before Sin met with the owner the next day. If Banyan didn't like the place, there was no reason to meet with the woman. Sin assumed RC's was named after the current owner, one Rocky Carmichael. Banyan had been interested, so Sin was going to go ahead with the meeting.

Wanting to be alone, Sin had called ahead and asked Ingrid to retire to her wing for the evening. The woman wasn't a nuisance, but when Sin got in his moods, he didn't want to talk to or be bothered by anyone, Ingrid included. The only time he'd ever been soothed by another was when he'd been married, and even then, he'd had to tamp down the urge to send his wife away. Sin had a feeling he was a flawed Goyle in need of therapy deeper than meditation.

He went straight upstairs to the top floor of his home and stripped down to his underwear. Sin paced the floor, trying to get rid of some pent-up frustration. He was irritated because he was having what were more than likely the stirrings of being around his mate and had no clue as to who it could be. He wasn't positive that's what was wrong with him, and *that* was why he was so agitated. Because he didn't know for sure. The more he paced, the antsier he became. Sin dropped to the floor and did push-ups. When he lost count at over one thousand, he rolled over to his back and did sit-ups. He then went to the far side of the room where there was little furniture and did a handstand. With his feet resting against the wall, Sin did another set of push-ups.

A car in the driveway caught Sin's attention. He dropped his feet to the floor and strode over to the window. Sin pulled the curtain back and remained in the shadows as Urijah drove slowly up the driveway. Sin moved to the window that faced the back of the house so he could observe Uri. Either the Goyle was dropping Banyan off to get his car, or he'd come to talk about the night before. Sinclair still hadn't apologized to Uri. Maybe he didn't need to. The male had seemed okay with Sin while they were shooting pool. Then again, he'd been distracted by Banyan.

Urijah parked his car but left it running. It wasn't long before the passenger door opened and Banyan stepped out. He leaned down into the car and said something to Uri. Banyan closed the door and watched until Uri was out of sight. Banyan's body language spoke volumes to Sinclair. He might appear to be the laid-back Goyle with no problems, but the look on his face as he watched Uri drive off said something else completely.

Wanting to have a chat, Sin opened the window and called down to Banyan. "You want a drink?"

Banyan shoved his keys in his front pocket. "Yes, thanks." He headed toward the patio, and Sinclair slid his jeans and shirt back on before making his way downstairs. Their conversation before they went to the bar had been light and not about anything specific. Sinclair was ready to find out a little more about the Goyle and his relationship with Uri.

Sin met Banyan on the patio with the same bottle of whiskey they'd been drinking earlier and two more cigars. Banyan was sitting in one of the lounge chairs, rubbing his eyes. "Everything okay?" Sin asked.

"Sure. If by okay you mean going ten rounds with my beast on the drive back from the bar. I don't know how much longer I can stand it."

"Uri is your mate, isn't he?" Sin held out a glass of liquor.

Banyan scrubbed his hands down his face before he took the proffered glass. "Yes. But Uri hates me and has vowed to never let me get close to him again."

"I take it your time in New Orleans wasn't all beads and parades?"

"It wasn't all bad. As long as I kept my distance." Banyan downed the whiskey in one long gulp, and Sin poured it full again. He set the bottle between them on a small, glass table.

"Cigar?" Sin asked.

"Thanks. Maybe I can choke my beast with the smoke."

Sinclair knew the feeling. His own shifter had been quiet since he returned from the bar. While they had been at RC's, that was a different story altogether. "I understand. Mine fought me every step of the way until I got home. So, how do you know Uri is your mate?"

"Because he's the only male or female I can't resist. Over the years I've watched mates together. Seen the need. The want. The jealousy. I feel every bit of it when I'm near him. When we were young males, I didn't realize why I was reacting to my best friend the way I was. He would get mad when I approached him about it. Uri has spent his life running from *us,* and I've chased him all over the godsdamned world. After New Orleans, I gave up."

100

"What happened in New Orleans?"

"He tried to take my head."

"You're joking."

"I wish I were. I was trying to make him jealous, and it obviously worked. Too well. I decided after that to stop making a fool of myself. I resigned myself to the fact I would be alone forever."

"And now?"

"And now he still hates me. He made it clear he wants nothing to do with me." Banyan inhaled on the cigar he'd been holding. Sin waited for him to exhale. Banyan had either swallowed the smoke, or he truly was trying to choke out his beast.

"I saw the way he looked at you tonight. He did not look like a male who hated you. He looked like a male who wanted to throw you down on the pool table and fuck your brains out."

Banyan finally expelled the smoke and shook his head. "You're wrong. He knows he can have me. Three little words, and I'm his. But he will never say he wants me. So, I'm biding my time until he returns to New Atlanta. Now, enough about me. What about you?"

Sin knew the conversation would eventually circle around to him, but he didn't have an answer. "No idea. I've encountered what the others who have found their mates have described feeling, but I have yet to figure out exactly who is causing the disturbance within. There has been a male present all three times, but I am certain it is a coincidence."

"How can you be so sure? I mean, you have been with males, right?"

Sinclair thought back to the night before and how Finley had sucked his cock. "Yes, but not often, and it has always been when a female was around. Don't get me wrong. I have nothing against males being together, but I prefer the softer sex. If I find out the fates have decided a

101

male is for me, I will remain without a mate. I can no longer stomach watching a human wither away into old age when there's nothing I can do to stop it."

"I can understand that. I've held out for so long praying to the gods Uri would come around, but I'm ready to move on with my life. Once he's finished with the weapons, he'll move back east, and I can get back to forgetting about him."

Sinclair doubted Banyan would be able to forget Uri. Not if they were truly mates.

"I appreciate the whiskey and the cigar, but all this talk of Uri is making me want to punch someone. I'm going to go mope in the privacy of my own home." Banyan set the glass on the table. "Oh, I meant to tell you. The owner of RC's came in while you were leaving. She was in pretty bad shape, so you may have to wait a day or two before you can meet with her."

"What was wrong with her?"

"According to her friend, the woman's ex-boyfriend drugged her. She was losing consciousness when the paramedics arrived."

"I can see why the douche is an ex if he is drugging her. Who is with her now?"

"Her friend rode in the ambulance with her, and Finley followed them to the hospital. He called Dr. Mercato to meet them there. Better to have someone we know calling the shots."

"Why is Fin getting involved?"

"Because he knows the girls. At least the friend who brought the owner in. Curvy redhead. Vivian or something like that."

Sin was surprised he hadn't noticed them when they came in the bar, but he had been dealing with his own problems at the time. "I will call Fin and check in."

"Sounds good, and thanks again for the company."

Sin stood and embraced the male. Banyan was tense,

102

and Sin understood his need to be alone. "Take care, Brother. I will talk to you soon."

Banyan clapped Sin on the back before heading to his auto. Sin didn't bother watching the other male walk away. He sat back down and refilled his glass. Sin thought he had it bad not knowing who his mate was or if he had, in fact, met his mate. He couldn't imagine what it would be like to know who your mate was only to have them reject you. That would suck.

Sin pulled out his phone and sent Finley a text since hospitals frowned upon phones being used inside. *How's the female?*

It took several minutes for Fin to respond. *She was roofied by her ex.*

Have the cops been there?

Yes. I called in one of ours. After what Vivian told me about the ex, I didn't want to take any chances. He's still waiting for her to come around.

Sin wanted to hear the whole story. *Call me when you can.*

Will do.

Something about the whole situation nagged at Sin. For some reason, he felt the need to get involved even though he didn't know the female. It could be because she was a friend of Vivian's, but deep down, he knew it was more than that.

A couple of hours later, Finley called and filled Sin on everything he knew, which wasn't a lot. Finley had called in Everett Murdock, a cop who was also one of the Clan. Rett was one of the best detectives Sinclair had ever met, and the male was overly protective of all females. If anyone could get the evidence needed to put this piece of shit behind bars, it would be Rett.

"I'm going to keep watch overnight, and tomorrow I'll make sure she gets home safely. If I can, I'm going to talk her into coming home with me where I know she'll be safe,"

Finley told him.

"What will Uri think about having another house guest?" Sin asked before he thought better of it.

"Considering it's my house, he shouldn't have a problem with it. Besides, our duty is to protect humans, especially the weaker ones. And Rocky is pretty weak right now. I hate a bastard who would take advantage of someone the way he did her. He didn't just roofie her. The concoction he shot into her veins contained traces of heroin," Finley seethed.

"Easy, Brother. Let Rett do his job, and she will be out of your hair before you know it."

"Trust me, it's not a hardship. This girl is beautiful."

"Even more so than Dana?" Sin had thought the blonde was a knock-out, but she wasn't his type. He wasn't sure what his type was any more, but he knew she wasn't it.

"There's something about her. Maybe it's because she's a victim and my heart is being pulled toward her, but yeah, she's special."

"But not your mate?" Sin prodded.

"No, nothing like that. I can't put my finger on it, but it's there."

"Well, you go stand watch, and if you need anything, don't hesitate to call me. I doubt I will get much sleep tonight."

"Will do. Later."

The phone disconnected leaving Sin alone again. He wondered what Finley found so interesting about Rocky Carmichael. If the woman recovered quickly, he'd get to find out for himself when he met with her about the bar. Now, he was actually looking forward to it.

Chapter Ten

When Rocky came to, she was coherent enough to tell Vivian and Finley what happened before Vivian found her sitting on the sidewalk beside the door to RC's. Rocky explained going to the beach, waking up in the club, Blake injecting her with something, and Vivian finding her. At first, Rocky was on the defensive, but Vivian assured her she believed what happened. What they couldn't understand was why Blake had dropped her off at the bar instead of taking her back to the beach or keeping her locked in the club.

Rocky was still woozy, but she had enough sense about her to talk to the doctor as well as the cop. She was thankful Vivian was there with her to act as a buffer if she needed one, but for some reason, they were nice to her. She was pretty sure it had something to do with Finley. She could understand a cop being built like an MMA fighter, but the doctor? If she hadn't sworn off men the rest of her life, Rocky might have given the man her phone number. He was just as hot as the cop and Finley. It was like everyone in the man's life had to meet a certain criteria or they weren't allowed in the club. Not only were they nice to look at, they were just plain nice.

The cop – Rocky couldn't remember his name – said he'd look into it. He and Finley stepped out into the hallway where Rocky couldn't hear them. The reality of the last twenty-four hours came rushing back. Rocky wanted to scream. She wanted to cry. But mostly, she wanted to find Blake Stansbury and rip his eyes right out of his head and shove them up his ass.

Vivian squeezed her hand, getting Rocky's attention. "Stop it," Vivian chastised. "Whatever is going through your head, let it go. Now that Finley and his friends know about Blake, you'll be safe."

"How do you know? Other than being your friend, I'm nothing to Finley or the cop except a former junkie."

"Former is the operative word here, Rocky girl. I have faith they will prove Blake did this to you. Right now, it's your word against his, but Finley is determined to make Blake pay."

"Why?" Rocky wanted to believe there were good men in the world, but men like Blake gave them all a bad name as far as she was concerned.

"I'm not questioning why; I'm just glad he is. When he saw you passed out on the couch in your office, Finley was upset. So was Urijah, the one I met a few weeks ago who I said puts Thor to shame. I've never seen someone so angry on behalf of someone they barely know, but let me tell you, Urijah was *pissed*. I didn't like him much after our first meeting, but now, he's sliding over into the okay column."

"Was he the big blond who was carrying me, or did I dream that?"

"That was him. And there was another blond with them. I don't know what it is about Finley and his friends, but there's not one in the bunch I wouldn't let eat crackers in my bed."

"I was thinking the same thing. Not the cracker part, but how they all have this alpha thing going on. It's like they all were bred from the same gene pool. I usually prefer men with dark hair, but Finley's hot," Rocky whispered in case he was listening.

"That he is. Now, why don't you try to get some rest?"

"I will, but you need to go on home."

Vivian shook her head. "I'm not leaving you here alone."

"Rocky's right. It's late, and you need to go get some rest. I'll be here until the doctor says she can go home,"

Finley said when he came back into the room.

Rocky didn't know Finley all that well, but the more he was around, the more she liked him, even though she didn't understand why he was there for her. "You both can go home and get some rest. I'll be fine."

"No way. I'm not leaving you alone where that motherfucker can get his hands on you. I'll be posted outside in the hallway. Nobody you don't want in here gets in," Finley declared, his arms folded over his massive chest.

Vivian cocked an eyebrow. Rocky knew that look. Vivian was getting turned on at the he-man behavior. Rocky wasn't turned on, but she could appreciate a guy who acted like a real man. Not since her father was alive had she witnessed a man go on the defensive for a woman. It softened her stance against men.

Well, not *all* men.

Vivian agreed to go home and told Rocky she'd come see her the next day.

True to his word, Finley guarded the door all night. The only one to come in the room other than nurses had been Dr. Mercato, and seeing him dressed in street clothes, Rocky had a feeling he was only there to see her. After explaining how he had detoxed her system, the doctor signed the release papers, and Rocky was more than ready to get out of there. She was not ready to go home, though.

"I need to call someone to come get me since my car is still at the beach," Rocky told the doctor.

"I'm driving you," Finley stated like there was no argument to be made on her part. "If you don't feel up to driving your car, I can have a friend retrieve your vehicle and bring it to you. Also, if you insist on going home, there will be someone watching your place. You won't know they're around, so you won't feel crowded, but I do want you to feel safe until we can get Stansbury behind bars where he belongs."

Rocky realized her mouth was hanging open, so she

closed it, but she was still taken aback at the way Finley was commanding control over her life. No, not her life, but her safety. "My purse is in my car, but I have no idea where my keys are." Right before she passed out, Blake had returned to the room in the basement and pulled Rocky's phone out of her pocket, smashing it to pieces.

"Your keys are in your office at the bar. Bridget locked them in your desk."

"I probably need to stop by the business office on the way out. They don't have my insurance information."

"All of that's been taken care of. Now, I'm going to step outside so you can get dressed. If you need help, I'll gather one of the nurses to come assist you."

Vivian must have taken care of the paperwork. She didn't have Rocky's insurance info, but she did know most everything else the hospital would've needed to know. "Thank you, Finley. If you'll get me home, I can see to getting my car."

Finley merely nodded and stepped out into the hallway, closing the door behind him. *Wow.* No wonder Vivian had latched on to the man. He was a keeper – for Vivian. Rocky slid off the bed and walked to the closet where her clothes had been stashed. She'd been up a couple of times during the night to pee, so she knew she was able to dress herself. Once she'd changed clothes, Rocky brushed her teeth using the flimsy hospital issue toothbrush, and she combed out the tangles as best she could with her fingers. Her face had been streaked with make-up, but she'd removed it the first time she glanced at herself in the mirror during one of her bathroom outings the night before. When she was back in the room, she called for Finley. "I'm ready."

When Finley came back into the room, he was accompanied by a nurse pushing a wheelchair. Rocky knew it was hospital procedure to roll all patients to the front door, so she sat down without making a fuss. Neither she nor Finley talked while the nurse pushed the chair. When they reached the front door, a black SUV was waiting for them. Finley opened the passenger door and helped Rocky get in. The man who'd been driving inclined his head to Finley before striding off across the parking lot.

Once Finley was seated, he put the vehicle in drive and pulled away from the curb. "Are you hungry? I know you haven't eaten anything since yesterday."

Rocky still felt a little queasy, but she was hungry and knew it was better to have something on her stomach. "I can fix something when I get home." What she really wanted was a cigarette. She knew they were bad for her, but it was a habit she'd taken up when she was under the influence. It was a weak replacement for when she needed a fix but couldn't get her hands on one.

Finley glanced at her sideways but didn't respond. He turned the radio on, keeping the volume low. "Do you want to tell me about Blake?" he asked, keeping his eyes on the road.

Rocky sighed. She didn't like to talk about the dark days, especially to someone like Finley. He'd probably think she deserved what she got for being so stupid.

"I won't judge you, Rocky. I've done some less than stellar things in my life. I just want to know who and what we're up against."

Rocky turned in the seat to face Finley. "We? Why are you so willing to help me?"

"I don't like men like Stansbury. He gives the rest of us a bad name. Besides, you're friends with Vivian, so I consider you my friend as well."

"But you don't know me."

"Then help me change that. I know Vivian invited you over to Sinclair's, but you had prior business to tend to. If you had been free, you and I would have gotten to know each other on a whole other level already. Since that didn't happen, I'd like to get to know you as a friend."

Rocky hadn't thought about that. He was right. If she

hadn't gone to meet Joel, she would know all about the man sitting next to her, at least in the physical sense. "Take me to breakfast, and I'll tell you what you want to know." She wasn't ready to go home to an empty apartment, and if the man wanted to get to know her, she'd need lots of coffee to get through the roughest parts.

"Deal." Finley turned away from the restaurants and headed to a secluded area. When he pulled up to a gated residence, she began to get worried. Finley spoke something in a language she couldn't understand into the security box, and the gate swung open. Before he drove farther into the driveway, he turned to her. "Relax. This is my home, and I vow to you on all that is holy no harm will come to you while you are with me."

Instead of pulling into the garage, Finley parked beside another SUV at the side of his massive home. "Ah, good. Uri's still here."

Finley came around and helped Rocky out of the tall vehicle and held her hand as he walked her toward a door on the side of the house. Before they got there, the door opened, and the tall blond who'd carried Rocky the night before stood filling the frame. Finley smiled up at the blond. "I'm glad you're still here. I'm going to make Rocky some breakfast. Would you like some?"

Urijah backed up allowing them entrance. "That'd be great, but let me cook so we don't poison the girl," he said, narrowing his eyes at Finley. Vivian had been right; the man was less than friendly. "Rocky, how are you feeling?" he asked, smiling, and his countenance changed instantly. Maybe it was Finley he had a problem with.

"I'd feel better if I had about five cups of coffee in me. And a cigarette. I don't suppose either of you smoke?"

Uri shook his head. "No smokes, but I do have coffee ready. How do you take it?"

"Just cream, please."

Urijah turned and gracefully strode across the

110

kitchen to pour her some coffee. Finley held out a chair, and she sat down at a large table. When Finley approached Uri, he pressed himself to the man and leaned in against his ear. "Thank you for last night. I'll pay you back."

Uri leaned his head against Finley's for a beat before turning to look at him. "It's not necessary."

Rocky had no idea what they were talking about, but the way they interacted was almost intimate. Uri's disposition flip-flopped making Rocky wonder what exactly was going on with him. Urijah walked over to the refrigerator and pushed the button that dropped ice cubes. When one fell down, he caught it and slipped it into her coffee. "Now you won't burn your mouth," he said as he set the big mug in front of her.

"Thank you," she replied. Who were these guys, and where had they been when she met Blake? She'd bet her last dime they knew Remy from the gym.

"Rocky was going to tell me about Stansbury. If you don't mind, Rocky, I'd like for Uri to hear this, too. I'm not trying to embarrass you, but like I said before, the more we know about the bastard, the easier it will be to get him off the streets."

It was going to be hard enough to tell Finley, but if they could keep her safe, she figured she might as well include Uri in the conversation. While Urijah cooked breakfast, Rocky told them both about how she met Blake, how he got her hooked on drugs, and about Vivian finding her and getting her the help she needed.

"I'm not judging you. I just don't understand how you couldn't know he was drugging you," Uri stated.

"He eased me into it. The doses in the beginning were miniscule enough to make me question myself. Besides, whatever concoction he'd come up with made me feel good, unlike whatever he dosed me with this time. The first few times we were together, he roofied me. I didn't realize it until it was too late. After that, he gave me shit that had me soaring. I never wanted to come down. But I would, and he'd be right there to make me fly again. After a while, I couldn't afford to pay him for the drugs *and* keep the bar going, so he convinced me to dance for him at the club. Not bragging, but I made him a lot of money, yet I hardly saw any of it. Blake took most of it as payment for keeping me high. Eventually, I stopped showing up at RC's. Bridget confided in Vivian what was happening. Or should I say what wasn't happening. Vivian found me at Blake's club one night and dragged my ass to rehab. I've been clean ever since. Until last night."

"Do you feel you will relapse now that you've had drugs in your system again?" Urijah asked as he put a plate of eggs, bacon, and an English muffin in front of her.

"No. I will lock myself away before I let that happen. I will never go back to that life. Not knowing where you are half the time coupled with not having control over yourself is no way to live. I'd rather be dead."

Both men stared at Rocky, but she ignored their shocked faces and dug into her food. Uri refilled her coffee before he sat down to eat. "May I suggest until Blake is taken into custody you stay somewhere other than your apartment?" Uri said.

"I won't run from him," she vowed.

"It's not running, love. It's staying safe," Finley countered. "I can go grab some of your things and bring them back here." Rocky didn't miss the look Urijah gave Finley. He wasn't as eager to have her move in as Finley was.

"I don't want to intrude on the two of you. Besides, I have to go back. I have a meeting with a potential buyer for the bar."

Finley smiled. "It just so happens we know who you're meeting with. We could invite him to join us here. He's already been to the bar a couple of times, so it isn't necessary to meet with him there."

Rocky bit off a piece of her bacon and chewed. The smart thing to do would be to stay away from the apartment until Blake was arrested, but she didn't know these men. Not really. Uri was definitely against the idea if his body language was an indication, although his words said differently.

"It will only be for a couple of days. I'm sure Officer Murdock will have the evidence he needs quickly," Urijah added with a smile. God, the man was beautiful. Rocky tore her gaze away from his crystal blue eyes and picked up her muffin.

"If you don't trust us, I could invite Vivian to stay here with you," Finley said. Rocky was almost certain Urijah growled at the suggestion. Maybe it had been his stomach, but she didn't think so. He abruptly stood from the table and took his empty plate to the dishwasher. He downed the rest of his coffee and put the mug on the top rack.

"I do apologize, Rocky, but I must get to work. Fin, if you need me, you know where to find me." Uri disappeared into another part of the house and was gone. Finley leaned back and slung an arm over the back of the chair, staring down the hallway where Uri had gone.

Rocky finished her breakfast while trying to decide what to do. She still needed to meet with her employees, but at this point, she wasn't ready to go back home. She could call Bridget and explain what happened. She owed her manager that much. Rocky needed to call Vivian and get her take on staying with Finley since she was bed buddies with him. If Vivian thought it was safe, Rocky would take him up on his offer. "Before I say yes, I'd like to make a couple of phone calls, but I'll need to borrow a phone. Blake trashed mine."

"I'll show you to a spare room. Feel free to make yourself at home, and you can use my phone." Finley stood and gestured to the same hallway Urijah had disappeared down. Rocky followed Finley and stepped into a bedroom that was larger than her whole apartment. She'd like to know what Finley did for a living that afforded him a home so large, but she wasn't going to be rude and ask. She'd wait and find out from Vivian later.

Of course Vivian was on board with Rocky staying with Finley. Not only would she be safer there, but it gave Vivian an excuse to visit the man's home. Vivian had the day off, so she agreed to stop by the apartment and grab some of Rocky's clothes as well as her toiletries and a pack of cigarettes. Rocky would have to wait until Bridget showed up at the bar to get her keys, and then she would have Finley take her to get her car. After assuring Vivian for the hundredth time she was fine, Rocky returned to the kitchen and handed Finley his phone. When she went to get her car, she would go to the cell phone store. She had insurance on her phone, but she didn't know if it covered lunatics.

"So, what's the verdict?" Finley asked.

"Vivian is going to stop by the apartment and gather some of my things. I'll stay here, but not long. I refuse to be an imposition."

"Trust me, love. You're no imposition. It'll be nice to have a woman around. Uri's my best friend, but there's only so much testosterone one home can take after a while," he said, grinning. "And now since that's settled, I'll call Sinclair and have him meet us here this afternoon."

"Sinclair? Isn't he the friend who you and Vivian visited the other night?" Rocky wasn't ready to have sex. She didn't know if she'd be ready for a while. The doctor had swabbed her for evidence of rape, but the test had come back negative. Whatever Blake had been playing at, it hadn't been sex, or he would have taken the opportunity while she was drugged.

"Yes, and he's also the one who is interested in RC's."

"But I hadn't put the bar up for sale then."

"I'm not sure I follow," Finley said, frowning.

"I thought you invited me so I would feel obligated." Rocky was confused. Maybe she had the timeline wrong. Her brain was still a little foggy.

"Not at all. You were invited for a good time, nothing more. I didn't even know he was looking into purchasing a business until last night. I will invite Sin here to discuss the bar, nothing more. I promise."

Sin. If he was as hot as Vivian had described, Rocky wasn't sure she was ready to meet with the man, but business was business. "Yeah, okay. But can you ask him to wait until after I've had a chance to shower? I don't want him seeing me like this," she said, gesturing down her body. She was wearing the workout clothes she'd worn to the beach, and her face was void of make-up.

"There's nothing wrong with the way you look, Rocky. But yes, I'll ask him to drop by around one. Will that work?"

"Sure." Rocky knew there wasn't enough time in the day to make herself truly presentable to men like Finley and Sinclair, but there was only so much she had to work with.

"Excellent. Now, let me show you around. I want you to make yourself at home while you're staying here."

Rocky didn't plan on staying but a couple of days. There's no way she'd allow herself to get comfortable in a home like Finley's. She didn't belong there, but she honestly didn't know if she belonged anywhere.

115

Chapter Eleven

Sinclair was anxious about meeting Rocky. The woman had been through a traumatic experience, and he didn't want to add to her suffering by discussing her bar. Finley had already filled Sin in on everything Rocky had told him and Uri about her past. He now knew why she was selling RC's, and it didn't sit well with Sin. He had called in several Goyles to help Rett with investigating Blake Stansbury. Scum like him didn't belong on the street, and Sin would make sure he didn't stay there much longer. After he hung up with Finley, Sin called Banyan. Since Landon had gone to help Julian, Banyan was the next best Goyle to do a little digging into Blake's life.

The other reason he was anxious was because Rocky was supposed to have been with Vivian instead of Dana. Had she not been busy, Sinclair would have had sex with the woman. That would have been awkward when it came to discussing the bar. Sin never mixed business with pleasure. He'd learned over the years it was best to keep the two separate. From what Finley told him, Raquel Cartwright was pretty, but she needed to put on some weight. Then again, Finley preferred his women curvy. Sin had never discriminated. He loved women of all shapes and sizes. It was what was in their heart that mattered most to him.

His wives had been as different as night and day in the looks department, but they all had the one thing that drew Sin to a female – inner beauty. But now, it didn't matter what someone looked like. Sin would either accept who the fates had chosen to be his mate, or he would live the rest of his life having unfulfilling hook-ups.

Fin had asked Sin to wait until one to show up. He was getting antsy, so he decided to drive by the armory and see how Uri was doing since it was on his way. He told

Ingrid he'd see her later and made his way to the garage where he slid into the low seat of his Lambo. He turned the music up and rolled the windows down. His long hair was flying in the wind, so at the first stop sign he came to, he found a band and tied his hair back at his nape. Sin changed his appearance often. Sometimes he wore a beard, sometimes a goatee. Right now, he sported a short beard, since he wasn't a fan of shaving. His hair had been long for some time. He usually kept it that way in case he ever needed to impersonate Rafael. He could shave if he needed to.

When he arrived at the armory, he was surprised to not find Uri's vehicle there. Sin got out of the car anyway and walked to the door. He tried the knob, but it was locked. Sin reached out with his shifter hearing, but there was no noise coming from inside. He could have let himself in, but there was nothing inside he needed to see. Since Uri wasn't there, Sin decided to head on over to Fin's, even if he would be early.

When he got there, he noticed a couple of strange cars in the driveway. Sin assumed one belonged to Rocky, the other was more than likely Vivian's, since Finley mentioned the woman might be there. He had made it clear to Fin he was only there to discuss the bar with Rocky, not pile up in the bed for a repeat of Tuesday night. He let himself in the side door as he did anytime he visited. The kitchen was empty, but voices sounded from farther inside the home. He followed the voices and wound up in the door of one of the bedrooms. Fin was on the bed. Vivian was situated between him and a brunette whom Sin assumed was Rocky. They had their clothes on, and it appeared they were relaxing together.

The sick feeling he'd had before came rushing back, almost knocking him to his knees. Was it possible Rocky was the cause of his unease? She had been at the bar the night he felt ill. When he grabbed the door frame to keep himself upright, Finley asked, "Sin? Are you okay?"

"Fine," he ground out. "I need you and Vivian to leave. Now."

Finley stood, pulling Vivian with him. Rocky remained where she was, staring at Sin. Finley held out his hand to Rocky. "We should probably take this meeting somewhere less cozy. How about my office?"

"Out. Now!" Sinclair growled. Rocky scooted to the far side of the bed, looking to Vivian and Finley for help.

"Brother? You need to calm down."

"And you need to get out of here so I can talk to Rocky. I have a funny feeling, if you know what I mean," he whispered.

"Come on, Viv. Let's give Sinclair time to talk privately with Rocky."

"I'm not leaving her alone with him if he's going to be violent," Vivian said, arms crossed over her ample breasts.

"I apologize if I came on strong, but I sincerely need to speak with Miss Cartwright alone. Vivian, I vow I will not harm her."

"She'll be fine." Finley pulled a hesitant Vivian from the room, and Sinclair shut the door behind them.

Sin took a moment to study the female sitting on the bed before him. Her long brown hair was pulled over one shoulder in a messy ponytail. Her eyes were a deep sapphire that sparkled even in the dim lighting of the bedroom. They were mesmerizing. Her face was glowing with a touch of make-up, and her lips were full. Plump. Kissable. Finley had been wrong about her. She wasn't pretty; she was exquisite. She was on the thin side, but that didn't matter to Sin.

When she crossed her arms over her chest, Sin found his voice. "I am sorry if I frightened you, Rocky. I just want to talk business, and I'd rather we do that in private." He inhaled deeply and had to grab hold of the wall to keep from going to his knees. "May I ask you a question?"

Rocky was on the bed with her knees pulled up to her chest. Her eyes were wide, but she nodded.

"Have you ever been in Iron Bars, the gym down in New Pasadena?"

"Yes. I went in to sign up for self-defense classes. Guess that free pass isn't going to do me any good now," she mumbled.

"Thank the gods." The man being in the gym and the bar had been a coincidence. Now he understood the need to get involved with her. Subconsciously, he must have known she was his mate. Sin stepped toward the bed, and Rocky scooted farther back, if that was possible. "I promise I will not hurt you. I just want to look at you."

"Why? What do my looks have to do with whether you buy the bar or not?"

"Absolutely nothing. I am purchasing the bar, so you can stop worrying about that. It's just..." Sinclair wanted to climb on the bed beside the female and merely bask in the scent that was drawing him to her. His beast was berating him to do more than lie there.

"Now hold on a second. I didn't say I'd sell to you. I have a staff of friends I need to look out for, and you might not be the right person to take over RC's."

"I won't be taking over. A friend of mine will. I believe you have already met him. Banyan was one of the males who looked after you when you were drugged. He owned an establishment much like yours down in New Orleans, and he misses it. He is looking to get back into the mix, if you will."

Rocky grimaced when Sin mentioned being drugged, but she quickly recovered. "In that case, I will need to meet with him. So will the manager, Bridget. If you've done your due diligence, you're aware there's a clause stating all employees retain their jobs."

"I am well aware of the conditions of the sale. I

119

promise you, nothing will change except for who pays the bills, unless Banyan decides to upgrade the kitchen so the bar will serve more than grill food."

Rocky's hands relaxed from around her legs, and it was all Sin could do to keep from grabbing her and ripping her clothes off.

"Raquel..."

"Don't call me that!" she snapped.

"But it is your name, is it not?"

"Yes, but someone from my past chose to call me that, and I hate it. And him."

"Ah, the bastard Blake Stansbury. I understand now. Please accept my apology. Rest assured we are doing everything we can to get him behind bars quickly."

"Finley told you?" Rocky went from mad to livid.

"Finley and I are like family. We have a large group of males who we consider brothers. Think of us as a clan of sorts. We watch out for each other, and when one of our friends is in need of assistance, we are there for them as well. You are one of us now."

"Why? You just met me, and you only fucked Vivian once. Are you in some kind of cult? Do you think we belong to you now?" Rocky slid from the bed, clearly agitated. She began pacing the floor on the other side of the room, and without thinking, Sin went to her. He stopped her steps by grabbing her arms. Rocky squirmed, trying to get away from him. "Let go of me!"

"Everything okay in there?" Finley asked from the other side of the house.

"Fine. We are fine." Sin let go of her arms, but his beast decided to protest.

She is our mate. We need to bed her.

She is not willing. You need to chill the fuck out.

I will not wait long. You need to tell her the truth.

When the time is right. Now shut up. I need to concentrate on her.

120

The shifter quietened, but he continued to push at Sin's mind.

"For the record, I didn't fuck Vivian. And no, I don't think I own you."

Yes, we do.

Shut up!

"We are a caring, tightknit family who looks out for those we consider our friends. I am sorry if I've upset you. Maybe it is best if we go into Finley's office and discuss the terms of the sale."

"I don't want to sell the bar to you. I would like for you to leave."

"Excuse me? I have money. You need money. Banyan will make an excellent owner."

"If Banyan's the owner, why are you putting up the money?"

"I'm not. I am brokering the deal for him since he is busy."

"I've already told you, if he's going to be the owner, I'll need to meet him."

"That can be arranged. I will call him now, and he can stop by here." Sinclair absolutely did not want Banyan anywhere near Rocky. Sure, he was fated to be Uri's mate, but the male was gorgeous. In fact, Sin didn't want anyone near Rocky. He wanted to kidnap her, take her far away, and make love to her until she submitted herself to him.

"Whatever. Now, if you'll excuse me, I'd like to go see Vivian."

"Rocky..."

"What? Until you get this Banyan over here, you and I have nothing to discuss."

Sinclair was losing her. Hell, he'd never had her. But he knew beyond a shadow of a doubt she was his mate. This wasn't going to be easy. "I understand, and again, I apologize for upsetting you." Sin left the room and went in search of Vivian. He found her sitting on Finley's lap in the

121

den. Fin's hand was precariously close to being inside of the woman instead of resting on her thigh. Sin cleared his throat.

Finley stood, depositing Vivian on the sofa. "Everything okay?"

"Vivian, she wishes to see you." Sin waited until the redhead was down the hallway. "Fucking hell, Brother. She is my mate."

"I had a feeling that might be the case the way you demanded Vivian and I leave the room."

"I went about things the wrong way, and now she wants nothing to do with me."

"Give her time, Sin. Rocky's had a rough twenty-four hours. Hell, man. She's had a rough three years. The one male she allowed into her life royally fucked her over."

"This does not bode well for me."

"You need to give her time. Let her get to know you. You'll win her over."

"I hope you are right. It is hard going through life thinking you will never find your mate. It is harder finding her and thinking you will never have her." Sin walked over to the liquor cabinet and poured a tall glassful of Scotch. He drank it all down and poured another. It was times like this when he wished Gargoyles could get drunk.

"I need to call Banyan. She wants to talk to him since he is going to be the owner."

"Now that you know she's your mate, have you considered letting her keep the place?"

"Absolutely not. No mate of mine is going to work in a place such as that."

"Wow, I didn't realize you were such a snob."

Sin jerked his head around to Finley. "I am not a snob. But I am fully capable of taking care of a female. She will not have to work if she ever allows me to get close to her."

"She won't have to, but she might want to. Kaya

refused to give up being a cop until she got pregnant. Abbi still teaches. Sophia still works, even if it's helping Nikolas combine the archives of the Gargoyles and the half-bloods. Trevor goes to the morgue every day, and he's studying to take over for Dante. Isabelle goes to the..."

"All right, all right. I get it. I will talk to her about it. Let her know she has options. But one of those options is not slinging drinks all night at a bar where her ex has access to her. If you will excuse me, I need to get Banyan over here." Sin left Finley standing in the den and walked outside. It wasn't that he didn't want Fin to hear his conversation; he wanted to get some fresh air. If only he could phase and take to the skies.

Rocky wanted a cigarette and a shot of tequila. No, she wanted the whole damn bottle. When Vivian had described Sinclair, she'd fallen miles short of how handsome the man was. It had been all Rocky could do to pay attention to what he was saying. The need to reach out and touch him to see if he was real had been overwhelming. The way her body reacted to him as soon as he opened his mouth to speak had been unlike anything Rocky had ever experienced. It was better than any high Blake had given her, and it was worse than coming down had ever been. Something about Sinclair called to Rocky, and she wanted no part of it.

She was positive he had that effect on all women. How could he not? His dark hair hung across his shoulders, and his eyes... Damn those eyes had burned a hole right through to her soul. The way he looked at her had her panties getting wet. She couldn't imagine what would happen if he touched her. Yes, she could; she'd go up in fucking flames. And that wouldn't do. She'd been burned by Blake, and he hadn't been anywhere near as good-looking as Sinclair Stone.

Vivian came through the door asking, "What the hell happened in here?"

"You didn't tell me he's a jerk," Rocky blurted. He hadn't actually been rude, but her self-defenses were coming to the forefront.

"Tell me what happened," Vivian urged as she came around and sat down on the bed beside Rocky.

"He said he's buying the bar."

"And? Isn't that a good thing?"

"No, it's not. He's not actually buying it. He's brokering the deal for Banyan."

"Uri's friend?"

"Yes."

Vivian frowned. "What else happened?"

"What do you mean?" Rocky slid back until she was once again sitting against the headboard with her arms wrapped around her knees.

"I mean, when he came to find me, he looked… devastated."

"He's probably not used to being turned down."

"He asked you out?"

"What? Of course not. Have you seen him? Scratch that. You've seen him. *All* of him. Damn, where did these guys come from?"

"I told you he was hot," Vivian smirked.

"Viv, hot comes nowhere close to what he is. But it doesn't matter. He's him, and I'm…"

"Stop it, Raquel Cartwright. I will not listen to you put yourself down. You are beautiful." Vivian pushed Rocky's hair back behind her ear and touched her cheek. "Absolutely beautiful," she whispered. Vivian often gave Rocky looks that let her know she was interested in being more than friends, but that was a line Rocky refused to cross with her best friend. Vivian pulled her hand back and said,

"The look on that man's face spoke volumes. He was truly upset."

"I have no idea why. I simply told him I wanted to speak with Banyan since he would be purchasing the bar and thus in charge of my employees. I won't sell to the first person strictly because they have money. And what is it with Finley and his friends 'having our backs'? I mean, chivalry's great and all, but they take it to extremes."

"You're just used to dickheads like Blake and Tommy. These guys are the real deal, Rocky girl. They know how to treat a woman."

Rocky had told Vivian that Tommy was mean to her, but she'd never told her best friend the whole truth. "I'm glad... for you. I'm not looking for a good man, Viv. I'm not looking for any kind of man. Never again will I trust another one as long as I live."

"Ahem." Rocky hadn't heard Finley come into the room. By the look on his face, he'd been standing there a while. "I'm sorry to disturb you. Banyan will be here in five minutes. I thought you might want to come into the office where you could conduct your business." He didn't wait to see if she followed. He left them alone to finish their conversation.

"I'm going to go smoke before Banyan gets here. I need something to take the edge off." And by edge, she meant Sinclair. Her body was still buzzing from being around him.

"I'll go with you," Vivian offered.

"I appreciate it, but I'd like to be alone for a few minutes." Rocky wasn't trying to be rude, but Vivian was so awestruck with these men that she wasn't able to offer an unbiased opinion. Rocky found the cigarettes Vivian had bought on the way to Finley's and took the whole pack with her. Instead of going toward the office, she headed the other direction. She found the back door which led to a small balcony overlooking the patio below. It wasn't until after she lit up that she noticed Sinclair leaning his elbows against the railing, head bowed.

As if he knew she was there, he turned his head in her direction, his eyes never wavering from hers. Rocky felt as though he was undressing her with just a look, even though the look wasn't sleazy. It was possessive. Wanting. A shiver ran down her spine, but she couldn't divert her gaze. The pull was too great. Never in her life had Rocky felt something so strong. Not even the urge to shoot up had been as compelling as the need to go to him and give herself over to him. The cigarette she'd just lit remained untouched, the ashes growing longer as the fire eased its way toward the filter. Sinclair tilted his head to the side and said, "Banyan's here." Only then did he turn away from her. Rocky took a shaky drag on what little was left of the cigarette before snuffing it out on the bottom of her tennis shoe.

Chapter Twelve

Rocky made her way back to the bathroom attached to the bedroom she was using and tossed the butt in the toilet, flushing it away. She washed her hands and gargled some mouthwash before going in search of the others. Finley's house was large, but not so much so that she got lost. As she padded down the staircase, male voices echoed down the hallway where she remembered his office to be. When she stepped into the room, the three men stopped talking. Banyan inclined his head to Rocky and did some weird thing where he made a fist and placed it over his chest.

"Rocky, I'd like to introduce you to Banyan Sorensen. Banyan, Raq... Rocky Cartwright." Sinclair caught himself before he used her real name. This was the first time Rocky had been standing close to Sinclair, so it was only then she realized how large of a man he was. Rocky was rather tall for a woman, but he had a good five or six inches on her. Ignoring the urge to stand next to Sinclair, Rocky stepped farther into the room and held her hand out to the tall blond. Banyan glanced at Sinclair before he took her hand. Something unspoken passed between the males, and Banyan briefly gripped her hand before backing away.

"Rocky, thank you for meeting with me so soon after your incident. How are you feeling?" Banyan asked, in a soft yet firm voice that belied his looks.

"Better. Thank you for helping get me to the hospital."

"Please, it's my honor to be of assistance. Would you care to have a seat so we can get down to business?" Banyan gestured to the chairs across from the large desk. Rocky sat down, and Banyan took the seat behind the desk. Sinclair stepped to the side of the room and leaned against the wall.

Finley excused himself and took Vivian's hand, leading her away. The door shut behind them, and the room closed in on her. She'd never been alone with two men such as these, and it made her uncomfortable. She sat on her hands to keep them from shaking.

Banyan leaned back in Finley's chair and crossed a booted foot over his knee. "I understand the terms of the sale, and I'm agreeable to them all. The only question is whether or not you deem me worthy of leading your crew."

Rocky felt Sinclair's eyes on her, but she didn't look his way. She cleared her throat, and said, "I would like for you to meet with the manager, Bridget. She's the one you'll be working closely with. If it wasn't for her..."

Banyan held up his hand. "There's no need to explain. You went through a rough patch, but now you're here, putting your life back together. I commend you for your strength."

Rocky didn't know what to say. Did every one of Finley's friends know about her past?

"I'm sorry if I upset you," Banyan added. He glanced at Sinclair before continuing. "As Sin told you earlier, we're a tightknit group. We protect those around us who we feel need it. We do not see you as weak, per se, but Blake Stansbury is a credible threat. Sin has brought several of us into the fold and explained the situation. Rest assured your past was only shared so those of us looking into the situation would know who and what we are dealing with. We like you, Miss Cartwright, and we hope you'll be in our lives for many years to come. Now, back to the bar; when would be a good time for me to visit with Miss Jones?"

Rocky was flabbergasted. Banyan had just spoken basically the same words Sinclair had earlier, only she didn't find herself getting defensive. She rather liked the blond, but not for any reason other than he seemed nice. Sinclair had yet to speak, and Rocky still refused to look his way. Oh, she wanted to. She wanted to know if his stare would affect her the same way it had outside. Hell, just him being in the same room was enough to make her skin crawl and not in a creepy way. She itched to reach out to him. Pull his head down so she could taste his lips and see if they were as soft as they looked. How could such a large man whose features were hard and chiseled have lips that appeared to be made from velvet?

"Rocky?" Banyan said softly. She had been looking at him but not *looking* at him. More like through him.

"I'll need to call Bridget and see what's convenient for her. I still haven't spoken to the other employees, so I'll want to do that first."

"That's understandable. If Bridget approves of me taking over, I would appreciate it if you would stay on for a while."

Sinclair had remained silent until Banyan made that request. He didn't protest verbally, but a low growl rumbled in his chest. Somehow, Rocky felt the vibration in her own body. She did look at him then, and his gaze was predatory. She swallowed hard, wanting to sink back in the chair. Rocky absolutely had no problem helping acquaint Banyan with the bar and her bookkeeping process, but she also had a feeling Sinclair didn't want them together.

"Sin, Brother." Banyan got Sinclair's attention, and again, something silent passed between them. Sin pushed away from the wall and left the room.

"What was that about?" Rocky whispered.

Banyan's eyes were bright with mirth, and his lip curled on one side. "It was me reminding Sinclair I am spoken for."

"I bet your girlfriend's beautiful."

"She is a he, and he is the most exquisite of any creature on this earth." Banyan's bright smile turned sad. There was a story there, but Rocky wasn't one to pry. Of course his boyfriend would be gorgeous. Banyan Sorensen was one of the most delicious men Rocky had ever seen, in real life or otherwise. As hot as he was, she wasn't drawn to him the way she was Sinclair, and that was a problem.

"I understand Sinclair is brokering the deal, but I would like to ask that going forward, I only deal with you." The less Rocky was around Sinclair, the less she would be tempted to do something stupid.

"I'm not sure..." Banyan was interrupted by a loud roar and a door slamming. Banyan briefly closed his eyes, seemingly trying to regain his composure. When he opened them, he continued, "I'm not sure that's a good idea, Miss Cartwright. Sinclair is sort of my legal advisor, and as well-versed in business transactions as I am, I would prefer he be present with any and all dealings you and I might have."

Rocky knew she was being railroaded, but she didn't understand why. Why was it so important Sinclair be around? The sooner Banyan met with Bridget, the sooner Rocky could get the paperwork done and get on with her life. One that didn't include Sinclair Stone.

"Fine. I'll call Bridget and set up a meeting. Will you wait here?"

"Of course." Banyan stood when Rocky did, his impeccable manners shining through.

Rocky left the office in search of Finley and Vivian. She needed to borrow a cell phone to call her manager. She found the two of them in a large den, side-by-side on a leather sofa playing a video game. Vivian obviously sucked at it, because every few seconds, Finley would set his controller down and point out the buttons Vivian needed to push. Jealousy eased its way through Rocky's core. She had never sat next to a man doing something as mundane yet fun as playing video games. She'd never sat curled up next to the man she was dating watching a movie and eating popcorn. Other than the couple of times Blake had taken her to dinner, Rocky had never been on a proper date.

"Rocky?" Finley spoke softly, bringing her back to the present.

"I need to borrow your phone again." After Banyan left, Rocky was going to go buy her own phone.

"Sure thing, love." He pulled his phone out of his pocket and handed it over. Rocky excused herself and headed to her bedroom.

After talking with Bridget, Rocky returned Finley's phone to him and headed back toward the office. The windows in Finley's house were floor to ceiling on the front and back of the house, affording a breathtaking view of green foliage, color flowers, and every now and then, various species of birds. The view currently taking Rocky's breath was Sinclair. The man had stripped his shirt off and was hanging from a tree branch doing pull-ups. Rocky was mesmerized. How the hell had he reached the branch without a ladder? She stopped counting at a hundred and merely enjoyed the view. Like earlier on the patio, Sinclair's eyes found hers. He stopped pulling himself up and hung there, staring.

"There you are..." Banyan said as he stepped up behind her. She was grateful to the man for interrupting, because she was only confusing the situation for Sinclair. She couldn't stare longingly at him only to push him away. "I'll be in the office," Banyan added and walked away. Rocky turned to follow but not before Sinclair dropped to the ground.

Rocky gasped, afraid Sinclair was falling, but he landed on the balls of his feet as easily as a cat would. Instead of returning his gaze to her, he picked his shirt off the ground and tugged it over his head. Sinclair disappeared around the corner of the house, and Rocky remembered what she was supposed to be doing. When she entered the office, Banyan turned from the window he'd been looking out.

"Were you able to set up a meeting?"

"Yes. I'm going to the bar tomorrow afternoon to speak with the employees, but Bridget would rather meet with you tonight. Can you meet us there around six? The bar doesn't start getting crowded until after eight, so you will have plenty of time to talk."

"It will be my pleasure. Sinclair and I can drive you there, if you like."

"That's not necessary since I have my car back. Besides, I need to run some errands beforehand."

Banyan cocked his head to the side as if listening to something Rocky couldn't hear. His eyes met hers and he said, "Very well. I do appreciate you taking the time this afternoon to talk with me. Until this evening..." Banyan bowed his head and left the room. He had some strange behaviors and talked rather proper, but she liked him. She was sure Bridget would, too. Things were looking up, and in just a few days, Rocky might be on her way to a new life.

As she passed the den on her way to the bedroom, Sinclair's voice called to her even though he wasn't speaking to her. His voice was deep, yet soothing. She passed by the door but stopped and leaned against the wall so she could listen to the conversation. However, the voices ceased, and Rocky was afraid they'd noticed her when she walked past, so she pushed away from the wall and continued down the hallway. She didn't want Sinclair to catch her again, and she was certain he would. It was like he had a homing device where she was concerned.

Rocky had promised Finley she would stay at his home for a few days, and she would be crazy not to keep her promise. His house was a mansion compared to the cracker box she lived in. Why not take advantage of the luxuries his house afforded? His fridge was stocked with actual breakfast items, not instant macaroni and cheese. The bathroom off her bedroom was heaven with a waterfall showerhead hanging in the middle of the large walk-in space. The view was spectacular with its manicured lawn boasting all sorts of trees and plants instead of overlooking a parking lot. The only thing missing was a swimming pool.

Yeah, she would be more than happy to stay there, pretending she was on a semi-vacation while Finley and his friends investigated Blake.

She still didn't understand their reasoning for them taking her into their fold even though they had all explained it to her, but the more she thought about it, the more she appreciated knowing someone was looking out for her. Other than Joel, it had been a long time since a man had her best interests at heart. She would take their generosity while it lasted, and then she would move on with her life and get reacquainted with the way things really were.

Rocky changed into her work clothes. She fully intended to work the bar that evening after Banyan met with Bridget. It might be one of the last times Rocky got to sling drinks. RC's had been part of her life for so long, she would miss it when she was no longer part of it. She blinked back the tears that were forming and went into the bathroom to freshen up. Her hair was a hot mess. Having long wavy hair was a blessing most days, but some days it looked like rats had decided to take up residence there. She twisted it up into a messy bun and secured it on top of her head.

Next, she spread a little more foundation over her skin, mainly to hide the splotchiness. Before she met Blake, her skin had resembled porcelain, thanks to her mother's genes. After she'd been hooked on drugs, her face lost its smooth complexion. Before Sin showed up, she had put on foundation and mascara. Now, she ran some gloss over her lips, telling herself it wasn't in case she ran into Sin again. When she had danced at the club, Rocky had worn a lot of make-up to make her face glow in the spotlight. Now, she barely wore any, not wanting to look like the whore she'd been back then. She might not have sold her body to every man who came along, but she had sold herself to Blake for her next fix. In her eyes, it was the same thing.

Satisfied as much as she could be with the face

staring back at her, Rocky left the bathroom, grabbed her purse, and went in search of Vivian. She found her friend on the same patio Sinclair had been staring at her from. Vivian was lounged on a recliner, a mixed drink in her hand. The weather wasn't warm enough for sunbathing, but it was warm enough to enjoy the outdoors. "Hey Viv, I'm going to stop and get a new cell phone before I head out to the bar. You coming by tonight?"

Vivian set her drink down and shaded her eyes. "It seems Finley has decided a night out at RC's is called for, so we both will be there. I know he's using a date with me as an excuse to watch out for Blake, but either way, I get to hang out with him all night." Vivian wiggled her eyebrows. Rocky had a feeling Viv was falling for the man. Rocky didn't blame her, though. Finley was not only gorgeous, but a sweetheart as well. She hoped her best friend wasn't getting in over her head.

"Okay, well I will see you later." Rocky bent down and kissed Vivian on the cheek. When she got to her car, she was surprised to see Sinclair waiting for her.

"I know you don't like me very much, but I do care about your safety. Please allow me to accompany you until you arrive safely at RC's. At that point, I will fade into the background, and until the meeting with Bridget, you won't know I'm around."

Rocky seriously doubted his last statement. Her body was hyperaware of Sinclair. "Suit yourself," she responded and climbed in her old car. When Sinclair lowered himself into a high-dollar sports car, Rocky could only stare. Vivian had said he drove a Lamborghini, but seeing him get behind the wheel of the shiny automobile was still a little shocking. She doubted he'd won it in a poker game from a mobster. Soon after she started seeing Blake, she found out how he "inherited" his Rolls Royce. She'd overheard a conversation he had with one of his bouncers, and it made her hesitant to believe anything else the man said. She should have listened to her gut. If she had, she never would have gotten strung out on drugs.

Rocky backed her car up until she was facing out and drove down the long driveway. Finley didn't live in a highly populated area, but it was easy to navigate her way back to the main part of the city. Rocky kept her eyes on the rearview mirror as much as she did the road in front of her. Having Sinclair following her was nerve-wracking, but it was better than going out into the world alone where Blake could come at her again. Trying not to think about Sinclair and what he did to her, Rocky turned the radio up and let the music keep her mind occupied.

Alistair was planning to go to war with Rafael, and Kallisto had a feeling her father was in for a surprise. Now that the Stone Clan was finding their mates in humans, they had much more to live for than they had previously. They would stop at nothing to protect their families and their homes.

Kallisto had pretended to lock herself in her office until her father left the compound. Only when he took off for Ithaca did she dare to come out and walk freely throughout the large villa. When she wasn't eavesdropping on Alistair's plans for war, she had been scouring the Internet for a replacement for Achilles, but finding an expert hacker was easier said than done. Most hackers didn't put out online resumes for fear of being tagged by the government. What Kallisto did find was a contest of sorts calling for hackers to "break the code." The first one to break through the security walls set up by the gaming company running the contest would be offered a substantial reward. Kallisto was doing her best to find out all she could about the contest. If she could get her hands on the winner, she would offer them double what the company was. The only trouble was Alistair had given her one week to find Achilles' replacement.

As for her plan for helping Sergei, Kallisto chose two Gargoyles she knew she could trust. It was amazing how loyal they were to her when they knew how Alistair felt about humans. Kallisto had to be careful, though. She'd known Crane would go rogue, and she warned Sergei about the Goyle. He hadn't listened, and now The Stone Society had Crane, and Sergei was in prison. She doubted she'd ever see either one of them again. If she could only get word to Drago, she'd have an ally in the States. Since Kallisto couldn't risk returning to the States, she had no other choice but to call in a couple of Goyles to go in her place. She prayed they would do what they were supposed to and not let her down.

Julian was barely containing the beast. He had yet to find out where Katherine was being held, and he was ready to rip someone's head off. If it wasn't for Landon keeping things going, Rafael would have probably locked Julian in the Pen until he could get his shit together. Then again, Rafe had watched as his mate was taken from him. Kaya had been kidnapped by Vincent Alexander instead of the federal government. Julian almost wished he were going up against an insane Gargoyle. At least then he would be on more even ground.

The more Julian dug into Katherine's background, the more red flags arose. He had only scratched the surface into her past before he hit a roadblock. Landon was working on getting past that hurdle and deeper into the false codes and documents the hacker had fabricated. If Landon managed to figure this shit out, Julian was going to step down from his position and hand it over to the other Goyle. He was going to hide Katherine far away from society

where she would never be subjected to this type of torment
again. If he only knew what she was going through.

Chapter Thirteen

Katherine gasped for breath when the butch of a woman pulled her head out of the toilet. She had long since given up on hope Julian would get her out of the hell she was currently in. Katherine had seen a lot of shit in her time as a reporter, but she'd only heard of the types of torture she'd already endured. She was certain there was more to come. If only she were guilty, she could tell them what they wanted to know. Since she'd been framed, they were going to kill her and still have no information.

"The sooner you tell the truth, the sooner this will all stop," the woman said against Kat's ear.

"Just go ahead and kill me. I can't tell you what I don't know." Kat gasped in a breath as her head was shoved under water. She didn't fight it. The harder she fought the more oxygen she craved. She squeezed her eyes shut and thought about the kiss. The soul-shattering kiss Julian gave right after he called her Kat. Nobody called her that, not even her parents. Coming from him, she liked it. Ever since he'd talked to her at the diner a couple of months back, Katherine couldn't keep her mind on anything else. Not her work, not the man she was supposed to be dating, not the same page she'd read a hundred times before giving up. *You are mine.* Julian had claimed her, but he'd also promised to clear her name. If he didn't hurry, it wouldn't matter because she'd be dead at the hands of the U.S. Government.

Sinclair was trying his best to understand where Rocky was coming from. She'd been through the ringer as far as Blake Stansbury was concerned. Still, it didn't do his heart good to hear her speak the way she did. What if he couldn't convince her to change her mind?

You must convince her. She is our mate.

She's been hurt.

You cannot give up. We are Gargoyle, and we are *strong.*

Strong has nothing to do with it. I can't very well *manhandle her into wanting us.*

No, but you could kiss her.

Rocky pulled her old Saab into the parking lot of the same cell phone store where Sin bought the Clan's phones. He parked in a spot close to her and got out of his car. He did not follow her in the store. Instead, he leaned his butt against the hood of his car and waited. For the foreseeable future, Sin needed to drive his sedan instead of the Lambo. It wasn't conducive to hiding out or tailing someone. Not that Rocky didn't know he was following her.

As for kissing Rocky, he and the beast were on the same page. He wanted to kiss her. Hold her. Feel her skin against his. Maybe he should kiss her and let her feel the mate pull. It would be cheating, but when it came to convincing Rocky he wasn't like Blake, he might have to resort to nefarious tactics.

Sin reached out with his shifter hearing to listen in on Rocky's conversation with the clerk. When she began explaining that she didn't need an expensive smart phone, Sin pushed away from the car and went inside the store. It was probably going to piss her off, but his mate was not going to settle for some cheap phone when she could have the best. He strode up to her, pulled her to his side, and said, "Hi, honey. Sorry I am late." He kissed her on the temple before turning his attention to the salesman. "My girlfriend would like the newest model smartphone."

Rocky tried to interject, but Sin twisted her body so she was facing him. He leaned down and placed a soft kiss on her lips. "Only the best for my girl," he whispered against her mouth. He banded his arm around her waist so she couldn't go anywhere even though she was squirming against him. The salesman was still standing there, and Sin raised his eyebrows at the man. When the clerk disappeared into the back of the store, Sin leaned his bearded cheek against Rocky's smooth one and rubbed. "Please indulge me in this one thing, beautiful girl."

"Why is me having an expensive phone I don't need important to you?" Rocky asked. She had stopped trying to get out of his embrace, but she had yet to touch him.

Sin had never been one for public displays of affection, but he couldn't help himself where his mate was concerned. He didn't have to tip her chin up, because she was glaring at him. Her sapphire eyes were bright with disdain. Sin leaned closer and whispered into her ear, "Everything about you is important to me. You have bewitched me with your beauty and have beguiled me with your stern countenance. Your strength makes me want to applaud you." Sin kissed the shell of her ear, and Rocky shivered. "I want to wrap you in my arms and hold you close. I want to kiss your pink lips until I can no longer breathe. I need to feel your skin against mine as I take your body to heights you never thought possible."

Rocky closed her eyes, and Sin continued, not caring that people were watching them. "Most of all, beautiful girl, I want to show you I am a real man who will treat you the way a woman should be treated. With respect. Gentleness. Caring. Love. I want you to know what it feels like to be cherished." Sin pressed his lips to hers again, keeping it chaste. He would wait until they were alone to show her what a real kiss was.

The salesman returned with a phone, and Sin pulled back only far enough to address the man. "Put it on my account."

"Yes, Mr. Stone. Will there be anything else?"

"No, thank you."

Rocky's eyes were still guarded, but her body had

relaxed, and her hands were on his chest. Sin wanted to throw her over his shoulder and take her to his home, never letting her go. But he knew he had to tread carefully, even with the little progress he'd just made. The clerk returned with the phone in a bag, and Sin took it from him. He linked his fingers through hers and led her out of the store. Once they had reached her car, Rocky snapped out of her trance, trying to jerk her hand away from him. Sin let go so she wouldn't hurt herself.

Rocky whirled around on him and put her finger in his face. "All right, Captain Caveman, you got what you wanted. The only reason I didn't bust your balls back there is because I didn't want to make a scene. From now on, keep your fucking hands off me."

Sin grabbed the finger and brought her hand to his chest. "No can do, beautiful girl. I meant what I said. I am going to prove to you what a good man is."

"Why?"

"Because your soul calls to mine, Raquel." When Sin used her real name, she flinched. "I will call you Raquel until you forget the man who made you hate your beautiful name." Sin pressed his body against hers, securing Rocky's body against her car. His dick had been hard ever since he first stepped foot into her bedroom at Finley's. "I know you feel it. The inexplicable force drawing us together. You want to touch me. You want to kiss me. You are afraid of giving yourself over to me because you do not know me. I want to change that. I will give you all the time in the world until you give me a chance to show you what it is like to be with someone good."

"And what if I don't want that? What if I want to simply fuck you and Finley every once in a while? What if I don't want to know the good side of you, only the naked side?" Rocky was turned on, but mentioning Finley had been as effective as a bucket of ice.

"There will be no sharing, Raquel. Once you and I

141

become intimate, there will be no need to invite anyone into our bed."

"You're such a hypocrite. If I hadn't gone to meet with my lawyer on Tuesday, you and I would have already been intimate, and Viv and Finley would have been right there with us."

"I can assure you, if you had shown up instead of the blonde, the night would have turned out much differently. Finley and Vivian would have found their way back to Finley's home before the clothes came off."

"Why? You fucked Dana with them in the room. Is it because you're ashamed of my body? You don't want anyone to see how damn skinny I am?"

Sin growled low and deep. Rocky tried to shrink away from him until he explained, "You are never to speak ill of yourself again. Do you hear me? You are the most beautiful woman in the world. I am drawn to you in a way I hope to someday explain to you. Until then, rest assured all trysts are in the past. I will not be sharing my bed with Finley or anyone else. Only you. If I have to wait years until you come around, I will keep myself from all others."

Rocky may or may not believe him, but he was tired of talking. Sin slanted his mouth over hers and licked at her lips. He thought she was going to refuse, but Rocky finally opened up, and he plunged his tongue into her heat. With one hand, Sin loosened Rocky's hair, letting it fall around her shoulders. He fisted a handful and deepened the kiss, making love to her mouth the way he wanted to do to her body. Rocky grabbed his hips and writhed against him. When someone let out a wolf whistle, Sin remembered they weren't alone. He grabbed her hand and pulled her toward his car. There was no way he was letting her get away now.

"What are you doing?" she asked as he opened the passenger side door to his car.

"I am getting started showing you how good you can feel."

"No, you aren't. I have to get to the bar."

"Not until six. I promise to have you there on time." Sin nudged Rocky, and she slid down into the low seat on a huff. When Sin was seated, he said, "Please put your seatbelt on." Sin didn't wait for the buckle to click into place before he was tearing out of the parking lot. His home was too far away to have her back to RC's on time, so he made his way to the penthouse.

"Kidnapping me is not the way to make me like you," Rocky huffed.

"No, but ravishing your body might be a good start," he responded.

Rocky turned her attention to the interior of the car. Most people had never seen a Lamborghini up close, much less ridden in one. Sin left her to her perusal and turned into the parking lot of the hotel where he often conducted business meetings. He pulled up to the curb and, once he was out of the vehicle, tossed the valet his keys.

"Mr. Stone," the young man greeted him.

"Jeffrey, how are you today?" Sin asked as he opened the door for Rocky. He held his hand out to her, and she reluctantly allowed him to help her from the car.

"Fine, sir. Thank you for asking."

Sin handed him a twenty before leading Rocky inside. He bypassed the front desk since he paid monthly for the penthouse suite. He had never brought a woman to the hotel, so he knew the clerks at the front desk were probably already gossiping, but he couldn't care less. The most important thing was getting his mate upstairs and naked. Rocky remained quiet until they stepped into the elevator. Once the doors were closed, she started in on him.

"If you think taking me upstairs and fucking me is going to–"

Sin grabbed Rocky's hair and pulled her head back so her neck was exposed. He kissed her hard to shut her up. Sin's dick was ready to burst out of his pants, and by the way Rocky's heart was beating, she wasn't immune to his kiss, either. When she began breathing hard through her nose, he let her up for air, only to trail his tongue down the curve of her jaw. Sin realized the elevator wasn't moving. He'd been so caught up in his mate he'd forgotten to press the button. He pulled his wallet from his pocket, removed the key card he needed to reach his private floor, and swiped it in front of the sensor.

"I guess you come here a lot if you have your own key." Rocky's mood had cooled off instantly. Sin was having nothing to do with it. He pulled her against him again and brushed her hair back from her beautiful face.

"I have a suite I use for business. I have never brought a woman here for any reason. I doubt if you believe me, but it's the truth."

"Are you always so proper?"

"Does it bother you?" Over the years, Sin had not adapted to the less formal way of speaking. He had never felt the need, but if Rocky didn't like it, maybe he could try to change.

"It doesn't bother me, but you sound stiff. Stuffy."

The elevator door opened directly into the foyer of his apartment. Rocky didn't move to get out as she took in their surroundings. When he procured the suite, Sin redecorated it to suit his needs. To the right was a hallway leading to the two bedrooms. Directly in front of them was a long conference table that seated twenty. To the left was a full kitchen and living area. A set of double doors opened off the living area onto a large balcony equipped with a patio set and six chairs. With the hotel being situated as it was, the balcony was hidden by a group of trees. While it wasn't the best scenario, if he or the other Gargoyles needed to take flight, they could without the probability of being seen. But that was only on a moonless night.

"Would you care for something to drink?"

"Do I have a choice?" Rocky asked as she stepped

into the room, tossing her purse on the table. Sin handed her the bag containing her new phone so she could activate it.

"Of course. You are not my prisoner, Raquel. I only brought you here so we could spend some quality time together. While I would love nothing more than to rip your clothes off and take you right there against the wall, I will n... I won't be so brutish. Unless you want me to be."

Rocky swallowed hard, her eyes dilating with lust. Yes, she wanted him. Maybe she needed a little coaxing. "Or would you rather I push you over the arm of the sofa and have my way with you from behind? Slide my hard cock into your pretty little pucker? Maybe drop to my knees in front of you and tease your clit with my tongue? Would you like to straddle my lap and ride me while I twist and suck your nipples? What would please you, Raquel? Because I am willing to give you anything your heart, and pussy, desires."

"Anything?" she asked, her chest rising and falling faster than it had been.

"Within my power, yes."

Rocky set the bag down next to her purse and toed off her shoes. She pulled her shirt over her head, exposing a lacy black bra. Her breasts were larger than average, and by the placement of them on her chest, Sin knew she'd had them enhanced. He preferred the natural look and feel, even if they were smaller. Maybe he could convince her one day she didn't need implants to be beautiful. Rocky unbuttoned her jeans, pulled the zipper down, and pushed her pants to the floor. She kicked out of them and was standing before him in matching lace panties.

"What is it you want from me?" he asked, his eyes continuing to take in all her beauty.

"Kiss me."

"Excuse me?" She'd removed her clothes for a kiss?

"You said anything, and I want to be kissed. Is that a problem?"

If Sin didn't feel Rocky was his mate, then yes, it would be a problem. Since he had no doubt of their bond, he would give her what she wanted.

"Absolutely not." Sin stepped toward her and placed his hands on her jaws, caressing her cheeks with his thumbs. He leaned down, slanting his mouth over hers. He kept the touch gentle. Tentative. Testing her lips and relishing the taste. Sin pulled back so he could see her eyes, but they were closed, so he kissed her again, this time with more pressure. Rocky's lips parted slightly, and Sin teased her with his tongue. She opened farther, meeting his tongue with hers. If Sin didn't know better, Rocky was either shy or wasn't exactly sure of herself. He planned to keep the kiss gentle, but Rocky deepened the movements and moaned.

Sin allowed his female to lead the mating of their mouths, and before long, she was grabbing at his clothes, trying to pull him closer. His already hard cock was straining against his pants, and his beast was getting agitated.

Fuck her now!

I'm getting there. Shut up.

"Turn around," he instructed. Rocky did as he bade, showing off her toned ass cheeks, which were peeking out from beneath the lace edges. Sin placed his hands on her thin waist. It was taking every bit of his strength not to rip her panties off and shove his hard cock into her slick core. He knew she was wet for him. The evidence was seeping through her panties. Sin slid his hands around to her stomach and up to her breasts, cupping and squeezing them together. As nice as her bra was, it was in his way. Sin preferred skin on skin action. He dipped his right hand into the left cup, cradling her breast in his hand. Massaging. Kneading. Twisting her nipple until she leaned back against his body and moaned. He lowered his left hand, sliding it between her panties and skin, not stopping until he reached the tiny nub he would soon have in his mouth. Sin loved eating pussy, and he knew his mate's essence would be the sweetest he'd ever tasted.

Sin continued his torture of Rocky's body with his hands while his lips found her neck. His fangs itched to slide forth from his gums and sink into the skin on her shoulder. His claws were tingling to break through so they could rip the lace from her body. His cock was pulsing behind his zipper, and if he didn't free it soon, he was afraid it would never recover. "What do you want, beautiful girl?" Sin whispered against her ear as his hands continued to pleasure her.

Rocky wrapped her arms around Sin's neck and rocked her lower body forward, trying to get more friction where she needed his fingers. He would gladly give her what she needed, but he wanted her to ask for it. "Anything you want, Raquel. Just ask, and it's yours."

"Make me forget. Fuck me until I don't know my own name," she begged, still squirming against his hand.

That he could do. He removed his hands from her underwear and scooped her into his arms. Rocky let out a squeal but held on tight as Sin strode down the hallway into the bedroom he'd only used a couple of times to rest. When they reached the bed, Sin set her on her feet. Rocky had asked for a fucking, but Sin was going to make love to her. He was going to torment his mate until she didn't know her name, but by the gods, she'd be screaming his.

Sin slipped his shirt over his head, and Rocky's eyes drifted to his chest. He slid his feet out of his shoes while he unbuttoned and unzipped his pants. Rocky's eyes moved to his hands, and he didn't make her wait to find out what was hiding beneath. His cock jerked free of his underwear as he pushed them down his legs. He pulled his socks off and tossed them to the side. While Rocky gave his body a once-over, Sin stepped closer to her and unclasped her bra, releasing her breasts.

When Rocky's hand circled his dick, Sin almost

came. He knew when he got her alone things would be intense, but just the feel of his mate's hand touching him was almost more than he could stand. Sin picked Rocky up and laid her on the bed, pushing her legs apart. He ripped the lace from her body and wasted no time in getting his mouth on her wetness. He lapped at Rocky's lips, savoring the sweet juice escaping her core for him. Rocky grabbed onto his long hair and pulled, trying to get him closer to her pussy, if that was possible. He sucked her nub between his lips, nipping at it with his teeth before licking at her wetness again.

Wanting to see more of her, Sin pushed Rocky's legs toward her chest, and she gripped them, holding herself open to him. He dipped his tongue down to her pucker and licked the sweet, pink hole before trailing up to her clit. He did that several times, and each time her moans got louder. She released one of her legs and fisted his hair. The tingle in his scalp traveled down to his cock, and Sin had to concentrate on not rubbing his erection against the bed. He needed friction, but he was going to get it from the inside of his mate's pussy. Or her ass, if she'd let him.

"Sin..." Rocky husked as she pushed her pussy against his face. He focused on her clit while he inserted a couple of fingers into her core. He worked her body over, taking her to the brink of orgasm and pulling back. "Sinclair, please," she begged. Sin loved hearing his name roll off her tongue, but it was too soft a tone. He wanted everyone in the hotel to know who was fucking his female. Sin increased the speed of his fingers, coaxing and teasing while his tongue worked on her clit. When Rocky's breathing grew faster, Sin didn't make her wait any longer. He removed his fingers and grabbed a nipple, twisting at the same time he bit her nub. Rocky screamed out, but it wasn't his name like he'd hoped.

Sin crawled up his mate's body, not giving her time to come down from her high. He stuck his fingers into her

148

mouth, letting her get a taste of her sweetness. Rocky's eyes widened at the first taste, but she sucked them clean. As he slanted his mouth over hers, Sin slid his aching cock home in the slick heat of Rocky's pussy. When his balls were against her ass, he held still, allowing her to get acclimated to his size. Sin was a large man all over, and he didn't know how long it had been since Rocky had fucked someone. He didn't want to think about it, so he put it out of his mind and began moving his hips back and forth. Slowly. Languidly. As he made love to his mate, Sin kept his eyes locked on hers. This was their first coming together, and he didn't want to miss one second of it.

Chapter Fourteen

Sin must have drugged her. It was the only explanation as to why Rocky was in bed with him in the middle of the afternoon. Granted, the things he was doing to her body had Rocky flying high, but she had sworn she would stay away from the man. For some inexplicable reason, she couldn't. She told her brain she was going to get away from him as soon as they got out of the phone store, but Rocky had allowed Sin to put her in his car and drive her to a hotel. Not just any hotel, either. The Ritz Pasadena was one of the swankiest hotels in the city, and Sin had his own fucking penthouse.

Now, here she was, staring into the darkest eyes she'd ever seen while he made love to her. There was no other way to put it. They weren't fucking. Sin's huge body was moving slowly above hers, his cock caressing her pussy. He wasn't talking dirty. As a matter of fact, Sin wasn't talking at all. He was using his massive body to say what he wanted to. Rocky's hands were roaming all over his skin, imprinting each dip and plane of his abs into her brain. His back flexed as she skimmed her fingertips lower until she grabbed the tight globes of his ass. Sin's hair was falling around his face, mingling with the whiskers of his beard. Rocky had never been a fan of facial hair, but the way Sin's whiskers rubbed against her skin sent tingles to all parts of her body. It might have had nothing to do with the whiskers and everything to do with the man.

Rocky never thought she would ever be touched so gently by anyone. Never imagined anyone would consider her to be worthy of such tenderness. Yet here she was, lost in the mystery of Sinclair Stone. Instead of thinking too hard on the whys, Rocky let herself feel. She licked her lips and pulled Sin's face down for a kiss. She had found out earlier his lips were indeed as soft as they looked. Her tongue sought his as soon as their lips met. Sin made love to her mouth with the same gentle strokes he was making with his cock.

Rocky hadn't been with many men, but Sin was by far the largest of those she had. Even with his large size, it felt as if they were made for each other. Maybe that was wishful thinking on her part. *Stop it.* Rocky would not allow herself to get caught up in this man. Being here with him in his penthouse was a one-time deal. He would get what he wanted and toss her to the side for another conquest. Finley had said Sinclair wasn't looking to settle down, and she sure as shit wasn't looking for a relationship. Maybe if he found her appealing, he would offer to fuck her again in the future. Rocky wouldn't be opposed to that, because the man knew his way around a woman's body.

Sin pulled away from the kiss. "Where are you?" he asked, his eyes serious.

"Right here with you," she reassured him. Rocky had noticed Sin and his friends were observant when it came to body language and moods. She had to keep her focus on him, or he might not want a repeat performance.

"Good." Sin dipped his head down and licked at her neck. She had hated when Blake had licked her. She'd equated him to a dog when he'd done it, but somehow, Sin made it sexy. Everything the man did was sexy. With purpose. Rocky had never had an orgasm during sex. As far as she knew, she'd never gotten off one single time when she'd been with Blake. She wouldn't even think about what Tommy had done to her. Sin had wrung a release out of her quickly and easily, and her body was amping up for number two. Sin's cock was hitting something deep inside that was sending sparks of electricity through her core.

"Sin," she husked as she arched her back, trying to get him deeper.

"Yes, beautiful girl?" Sin kissed her lips again, only

this time it was barely a touch.

"I'm close." Rocky wrapped her legs around his waist and dug her heels into his butt. She was probably hurting him, but she needed him to fuck her. Hard. "Harder. Oh, god, I need it deep," she groaned.

Sin rose up on his knees, placing her legs over his shoulders. "Hold on, beautiful," he instructed. Rocky grabbed hold of the comforter as Sin gave her what she asked for. His hips pistoned into her pussy, his balls slapping against her ass. He never took his eyes off hers as he fucked harder the way she wanted. The deeper he went, the more intense the sensation inside.

"Oh, god." Rocky squeezed her eyes shut as her pussy clamped down with the hardest orgasm of her life. She'd known if he ever got his hands on her, she would incinerate. Rocky's body was on fire. A raging inferno no amount of water would extinguish. She screamed out Sin's name among some expletives that had probably never been strung together before. Sin bottomed out one last time and held her thighs tightly as he spilled his seed deep inside of her, muttering something in a language she didn't understand. As explosive as his release had been, Sin's face wasn't scrunched up in pain. If anything, he looked at peace. Rocky took the opportunity to study the man who'd made love to her. He was nothing short of breathtaking, especially when he opened his eyes and regarded her with something that looked a whole lot like love. *Stop it. You're seeing things that aren't there. You just met the man, for crying out loud.*

Sin kissed the inside of both knees before releasing her legs and slowly slid his still hard cock out of her dripping hole. She should have been freaking out because he hadn't used a condom, but Rocky couldn't get pregnant, and she knew she was clean. She had regular check-ups whenever she and Vivian played around, and the last time had been over six months ago. If Sin wasn't clean, it would be something else she deserved for her past sins.

Instead of rolling off the bed and putting his clothes on, Sin pulled Rocky to him, settling her in the safety of his arm. She laid her head on his shoulder and swirled her fingers through the dark hair on his chest. Vibrations coming from his chest tickled her ear, and she realized he was humming. Sin pulled her arm across his body and stroked her skin, up and down from her wrist to her shoulder. He peppered kisses on her hair and forehead then resumed his humming. There was only one word Rocky could think of as to the way she was feeling – content. It was stranger to her than any other emotion there was, because Rocky couldn't remember ever being content.

"Thank you," Sin whispered against her cheek.

Rocky wasn't sure how to respond. Why was he thanking her? It was just sex. *Liar.* That's all it could be. Sinclair was obviously a wealthy, probably important man, and she was nobody. Whatever misguided reason he had for her being there, she'd have to make sure it never happened again. She'd thought maybe they could get together for a quick fuck, but Rocky knew it would never be something so meaningless. At least not to her. She'd get her hopes up that maybe the universe had forgiven her for her past and decided she deserved a little happiness. She knew that was never going to happen, so she pulled away from him and said, "You're welcome, but I need to get cleaned up and get over to the bar." She didn't bother kissing him. She rolled off the bed and grabbed her underwear, rushing into the bathroom and closing the door behind her.

Rocky leaned against the counter and took in her appearance. Damn, she looked well and truly fucked. Her hair was a mess and her mascara was smudged under her eyes. She finger-combed her hair the best she could until she could find the band Sin had removed earlier. She wet a washcloth with warm water. She unsmudged the mascara before wiping off the jizz running down her legs. Rocky tossed the cloth onto the floor and pulled on her bra. The panties were ruined, so she'd have to go commando. Rocky opened the door and screamed. Sin was standing there, propped against the doorframe.

Instead of moving out of her way, he pulled her flush to his body and kissed her. This was unlike any of the other times he'd kissed her. Gone was the soft caress. Nowhere to be found was the mating of their tongues. This was as possessive a move as she'd ever known. Blake Stansbury had nothing on Sinclair Stone when it came to claiming what was his. When Sin released her, Rocky was breathless. And scared. She wasn't afraid Sin would physically harm her. She was scared shitless he would steal something precious from her. Rocky had locked her heart away a long time ago, but now, standing in front of this man, she was afraid Sin might have found the key.

Sin felt it the moment Rocky pulled away emotionally. It was seconds before she physically rolled away and shut herself in the bathroom. He closed his eyes and reached out to gauge her emotions. When he felt her heartrate gaining instead of slowing, he rolled off the bed and waited outside the door. He had tried to show her with his body what she was probably afraid to hear. He was not going to let her run from him.

When Rocky finally opened the door, Sin didn't give her time to think. He grabbed her up and kissed her. He was staking his claim whether she knew it or not. One hand slid into her long hair, cradling her head, while the other held firmly to one of her cheeks. Rocky was thin, but her dancing days had done wonders for her ass. If she didn't have to get to the bar, Sin would have dipped his hand into her jeans and stroked her wetness. When he released her mouth, he said, "I owe you a pair of panties."

154

Rocky laughed. "Yes, you do. You should also let me drive your car as penance for stealing me away."

Sin couldn't get enough of his mate. He wanted to take her home and hide out from the rest of the world. But he also wanted to show her off. The need to stake his claim on her publicly was akin to a dog pissing on a tree, marking his territory. "I'll let you drive on one condition." Sin had never let anyone drive his Lambo.

"Yeah? What's that?"

"You drive straight to the bar. I will have someone pick your car up later and bring it to you."

"Deal," Rocky agreed quickly. It was obvious she want to drive his car badly. He had been ready for her to put up a fight, but was thrilled when she didn't. "I don't plan on going anywhere else, so it won't be a hardship."

"What about later? You agreed to stay with Finley until Stansbury is caught." The thought of her spending one more night at Finley's was eating away at Sinclair. He thought about taking her to his home anyway, but it would probably undo every bit of progress he'd made.

"I can hitch a ride back with him and Vivian."

Sin decided then he would be inviting Finley and Vivian over, but not for the same reason he had before. He would do it to get Rocky into his home, and whether the other couple stayed was up to them. "Let me get cleaned up then we will hit the road." Rocky moved out of the doorway, and Sin took the fastest shower of his life. He almost expected Rocky to slip out of the penthouse while he was getting dressed, but he found her tinkering with her new phone. "Ready?" he asked.

Rocky nodded and dropped the phone into her purse. She put the packaging into the bag and carried it with her. Since the phone now belonged to the Clan, Sinclair would always have access to her whereabouts. If Blake somehow managed to get his hands on Rocky again, Sin would be able to track her down. If Blake somehow managed to get by the Gargoyles, it would be the last thing he ever did once Sin found him.

When the elevator opened, Rocky stepped in first, and Sin didn't allow her much personal space. He took her free hand in his, laced their fingers together, and kissed her knuckles. He didn't miss the sigh she expelled afterwards. When they reached the bottom floor, he continued to hold her hand as he led her outside. He had called the valet while getting dressed, and the Lambo was at the curb waiting for them. Sin walked with Rocky to the driver's side and held the door open for her. "You're really going to let me drive?" she asked incredulously.

"I told you, anything your heart desires, beautiful girl. All you have to do is ask." Sin placed a sweet kiss on her parted lips and nudged her toward the car. When Rocky slid in, Sin strode around the car and joined her. Sin pushed the button to turn the car off so he could give Rocky instructions regarding the controls.

"Push this button to start or stop the engine. Your seat controls are beside you." Sin waited while Rocky adjusted the seat closer to the steering wheel. "When you start the car, it will automatically be in Strada or street mode. Since this is your first time driving, we will take the back roads and let you get used to the power. Once you h... you've driven her a few times, we will get you out on the freeway where you can turn her loose. Don't worry about the rest of the controls; we'll go over those later. All I ask is you take it easy until you get a feel for the power."

"What if I wreck?" Rocky asked, licking her lips. She was visibly nervous yet excited.

"I have insurance. Now, let's get going, shall we?" Sin couldn't wait for Rocky to feel the six hundred horses in the engine behind them.

Rocky started the car and pulled on the right paddle shifter to get the car moving. She eased away from the curb and navigated the parking lot like a pro. Sin didn't have to give her directions. Rocky was familiar with the area and took the back roads like he requested. When she'd driven a couple of miles, Rocky relaxed back into the seat, her face an ear-to-ear smile. Sin couldn't take his eyes off her. The pure joy at driving his car was pouring off his female in waves. He would buy Rocky her own sports car if it made her this happy.

No, you won't. You aren't letting her out of our sight.

You're right. She can drive me around everywhere I go.

Rocky giggled when she took a corner a little fast, and Sin couldn't help but grin. He understood what she was feeling. "You're doing well, beautiful girl. If you want to shift gears, put it in manual, hit the sport button and let her fly." Sin trusted Rocky to know her limits, and he wasn't disappointed. While she took some corners faster than he thought she would, she drove the car like she'd done it a hundred times. As they neared the bar, she put it back in Strada and slowed to a boring speed. Instead of parking in the front of the bar, she drove around back and parked in her reserved spot, well away from any other car.

"Can't have her getting scratched, now can we?" Rocky asked as she hit the off button. Her face was flushed, and she gave Sinclair a huge smile.

"No, we cannot".

Rocky cut her eyes to him, but he couldn't help the way he spoke. He was making a conscious effort, though. "Where'd you learn to drive like that?" he asked, not able to tear his gaze away from her mouth.

Rocky shrugged. "My Saab may be old, but it's fun to drive. I've put a lot of miles on her since my uncle gave her to me."

Sin reached out for her hand and kissed her knuckles again before linking their fingers. "Well, color me impressed. You can drive her any time you want."

"Really?"

"Yes, really. Now, let's get you inside so you aren't late." Sin kissed her hand again and hurried around to open the door and help Rocky out of the car. The back door of the bar opened, and one of the workers came outside carrying a garbage bag. He froze when he saw the two of them, but he couldn't take his eyes of the car.

"Holy shit, Boss." The man dropped the garbage and circled the car, whistling low. "You sure do know how to pick 'em," he muttered.

"Pick what, James?" Rocky demanded. Her happy mood was quickly dissipating.

"Nothing. I, uh, the garbage..." James grabbed the plastic bag and rushed away from them.

"Jerk," Rocky murmured, but Sin heard her.

Sin didn't want to cause a scene, but he also wanted to comfort his female. Instead of holding her hand like he was itching to do, he placed his hand on the small of her back and walked close behind as they entered the door James had exited. Sinclair noticed another door and asked, "Where does that door go?"

"To my apartment. Before I spent all my money on drugs, I had the good sense to enclose the back door leading upstairs. That way I can get home from inside the bar without having to go outside."

Sinclair was happy to know this, but if he had his way, she wouldn't be living over the bar much longer. When they entered her small office, Sin thought back to the first time he'd heard her voice coming from this room. He'd assumed his feelings were coming from the man sitting at the bar. Now he knew differently. Rocky locked her purse away in her desk and stopped in front of him. "Thank you for... letting me drive your car." She kept her hands to herself, and if the mate bond was calling to her as strongly as it was to Sin, she was dying to touch him.

In one quick move, Sin whirled Rocky around against the door, closing it in the process. He crowded his body against hers and leaned down for a kiss. He wasn't going to let her forget the afternoon they'd shared just because she feared her past. Sin was going to constantly remind her he was different. Rocky opened for him and their tongues melded together in perfect harmony. Sin slid a hand up her side, resting it on the outer curve of her breast. One day, when they knew each other better, he hoped to talk her into having the implants removed.

Rocky's hands caressed Sin's face, her thumbs smoothing down his beard. Instead of pulling away like he'd feared, she tried to get closer. Rocky rose on her tiptoes, pressing their bodies tighter together. His cock was hard and had been since he'd admired her driving skills, but now, it was aching. If that was going to be the way of things from having a mate, Sin wouldn't complain as long as he was able to sate his need with his female's body. He trailed his lips over her cheek, down to her ear, farther down her shoulder, sucking at the skin. One day, hopefully soon, he would sink his fangs into that same skin and seal their bond.

"Sin..." Rocky's plea was breathless. "I have to meet with Bridget," she reminded him.

Sin was loath to release her, but he didn't want to give her any reason to ever be mad at him. "I know, beautiful girl, but I cannot get enough of you."

The doorknob turned, but whoever was trying to get in met with resistance since Sin still had Rocky trapped. "Rocky? You in there?"

"Yes, Bridget." Rocky pushed on Sin's chest, and he backed up so she could open the door. If the manager noticed Rocky's kiss-swollen lips, she didn't say anything about it.

"Are we meeting with Banyan back here?" Bridget asked, eyeing Sinclair.

"Yes. Is he here?" Rocky asked, putting some distance between her and Sin. She walked behind her desk and sat down.

"Yes, I'll go get him." Bridget looked up at Sin again before going to get Banyan.

Banyan and Bridget entered the office, and Sin and Banyan shook hands. "Brother, you're looking... well," Banyan smirked.

Sin cocked an eyebrow at him but didn't tell him he was absolutely correct. He walked over to the front of the desk and sat on the far edge. It put him close to his mate but far enough out of the way he shouldn't be *in* the way. Banyan and Bridget sat down on the sofa, and the meeting began.

Chapter Fifteen

Alistair had always ruled with an iron sword, and his Clan was used to it. However, the group of Gargoyles assembled at his compound in Ithaca was not the males he remembered. Had it been so long since he'd made an appearance they'd forgotten who was in charge? Theron had been responsible for keeping their army battle ready, but he was gone, and Alistair was having a hard time finding someone worthy of taking his son's place.

Standing on the balcony overlooking the training field, Alistair asked, "Who amongst you is the strongest, most feared Goyle?"

The males looked around at each other, shrugging, seeming to discuss the matter. Alistair felt as though he was dealing with a bunch of newbies. "It shouldn't be that hard of a question. If I were to come down and challenge you all, who do you feel would be able to take my head?" At his question, the ranks fell back, and one male was left standing. The male was a large Goyle Alistair had never seen before. "What is your name?"

"Darian Lindbergh, Your Highness."

"Darian, are you capable of taking my head?"

"I have trained with the sword for over six hundred years, and I am competent, so yes, Your Highness, I could take your head."

"Would you like to prove your abilities in front of your Clan?" Alistair tested.

"No, Your Highness. I would never wish any harm upon you, even during a sparring exercise."

"And what if I demanded you to fight me to the death?"

"I would obey your command, but I would make it known to all who would witness our combat I was doing so under your orders, not at my own free will."

"Is there any other who feels they are better than Darian?" Alistair waited while the males murmured to one another.

"Darian Lindbergh, in light of recent events, I am in need of a second-in-command. Unless one of your Brothers wishes to challenge you, the title is now yours. Meet me in my office in three hours. Until that time, you will lead the Clan in the first of your daily training exercises. War is imminent, and you must be prepared."

"Yes, Your Highness." Darian bowed low before turning to his men and shouting orders.

Alistair remained on the balcony as the males got into formation and began sparring. Darian moved through the ranks, stopping every now and then to give pointers. Overall, Alistair was pleased with what he saw. Being Greeks, his Clansmen would have all been raised on the sword from the time they shifted regardless of whether there was threat of war or not.

As he studied his new commander, Alistair's mind drifted as it always did to his sister and her offspring. The family who should be down below fighting for the Greeks. Instead, his sister had shamed the family and married a godsdamned Italian. Every time he thought of Athena, he wanted to behead the bitch. One day. For now, he would use her as the perfect bait to lure his nephew to him. Targeting the mates hadn't met with the result Alistair had hoped for. Holding Athena hostage would bring Rafael riding in on his white horse to save the day, and that's when Alistair would kill two Gargoyles with one sword. Mother and son. At last, he would have his revenge on the bitch.

A knock on his door took his attention away from his army and toward something else. Someone else. He opened the door to his bedroom and smiled. "Hello, Athena."

His sister couldn't speak plainly since she'd been gagged, but the threat was obvious.

"Now, now, Sister. Do you really think you and your bastard son are any match for me?" he taunted. The Gargoyle holding his sister tightened his grip as she tried to lunge at him. Alistair laughed and jerked his head to the hallway. Athena was hauled off to a room he'd prepared especially for her.

Rocky sat back and let Bridget interview Banyan since she would be the one working with him. With Sinclair sitting so close to her, Rocky couldn't keep her focus on the conversation. Several times she thought of asking him to leave, but then she remembered driving his car. Who in their right mind let someone they didn't know drive a two-hundred-thousand-dollar sports car? Sinclair Stone, that's who. When Rocky thought back to the penthouse, she really couldn't say Sinclair didn't know her. He knew her on a most intimate level. The man was as talented with his tongue as he was his beautiful, veiny dick.

Sin growled low in his throat, and Rocky snapped her eyes up to his. His nostrils were flaring, and he was looking at her like he wanted a repeat performance. Banyan laughed and asked, "Do we need to take a short break?" Bridget was looking at all of them like she'd missed out on a joke.

"No need, Brother. I'm going to check the perimeter," Sin said as he stood from the desk. He left the room without as much as a glance at Rocky. What the hell was his problem? And check the perimeter? What did that even mean? Rocky leaned back in her chair and focused on Banyan and Bridget. After thirty minutes, Sin still hadn't returned, but Bridget had asked Banyan to excuse the women while they talked it over.

"I think he's perfect, but ultimately it's your decision," Rocky said as soon as the door closed.

"He would be perfect if he wasn't gay, but yes, I think he'll make a wonderful boss. He has lots of great ideas, *and* he has plenty of money to spend on a new kitchen. What I want to know is what's up with you and Mr. Broody? I thought he was going to fuck you right there on your desk."

"What? Nothing's up with us. He's brokering Banyan's deal."

"Right. Then what did I walk in on earlier?" Bridget asked accusingly.

"He was kissing me. But that's all it is, Bridget. There's nothing between us other than a physical connection. You know my history with men, and I do not care for a repeat."

"I think you're going to have a hard time convincing him of that. He couldn't keep his eyes off you."

"Whatever. Do you want me to tell Banyan the bar is his?"

Bridget rose from the sofa and came around to where Rocky was sitting. She leaned against the desk with tears in her eyes. "If this is our only option, then yes. Please tell me you won't disappear on me, though."

"I won't disappear on you. I've decided to study nursing, so I will be scarce, but not invisible. Besides, Banyan agreed to let me stay in the apartment, so I'll be right here if you need me." Rocky stood and pulled her friend in for a hug. The tears she thought would form were surprisingly absent. The proverbial weight lifted from Rocky's shoulders. Her friends would all keep their jobs, and RC's would get the facelift it deserved. "Let's go find Banyan and give him the good news."

When Rocky opened the door, Sinclair was leaning against the opposite wall, both his arms and feet crossed. He did not look happy, but Rocky wasn't going to let his mood sway hers. "We have a deal," she said to him. When he didn't acknowledge her words, she did a mental eye roll and turned toward the seating area to find Banyan. A large hand gripped her bicep, and she was pulled to Sinclair's chest.

Instead of speaking, Sin crushed their mouths together, pulling her lower body to his. This was the same possessive kiss he'd given her earlier. The kind that left her breathless. Bridget sighed as she scooted around them, leaving them alone in the hallway. Sin pulled her chin up so he had her undivided attention. "Come home with me tonight. Please," Sin requested. It was hard for Rocky to think clearly when she was this close to him. It was hard to think at all.

"Sinclair…"

"Raquel, please. I didn't get enough of you this afternoon. I want to be able to take my time with you. After you speak with Banyan, I want to treat you to dinner. My cook is preparing a meal as we speak, and I would hate for Ingrid's hard work to go to waste. She lives with me, so you don't have to worry about being alone in the house with me."

Vivian had told Rocky how good Ingrid's cooking was, and knowing her best friend had been in Sin's house without her had the green-eyed monster rising up. She knew it wasn't Vivian's fault, nor had Sin had sex with Vivian, but Rocky was feeling a little possessive when it came to Sinclair Stone. She didn't understand it. She could say there was nothing more than a physical attachment to the man, but she would be lying. After less than eight hours, Rocky was falling for Sin, and there was nothing she could do about it. She knew she was making the second biggest mistake of her life, but she said, "Okay."

"Okay?" Sin narrowed his eyes. "Just like that… okay?"

"Yep. Now, let's go talk to Banyan so we can get out of here." Rocky pulled his face down and brushed a soft kiss across his lips before linking their fingers together. Hand-in-hand, they made their way to the front of the bar and found Banyan and Bridget sitting together at a high top.

Banyan glanced at their joined hands and smiled. "I see you've calmed down," he said to Sinclair.

"I hear congratulations are in order, Brother. You are the new owner of RC's," Sin replied.

Rocky took the seat next to Bridget and said, "I'd like to tell the employees tomorrow. Would you meet me here so I can introduce you to them?"

"I'd be glad to," Banyan replied. "Bridget, would you please bring a bottle of your finest whiskey so I might propose a toast?"

"Be right back," she said and left to go retrieve the liquor and four glasses. When she returned, she said, "Normally I don't drink on the job, just so you know."

"I'm not a hard ass, Miss Jones. As long as you maintain a professional demeanor, having a drink during your shift with a patron will not be frowned upon. It's a great way to build rapport." Instead of allowing Bridget to serve them, Banyan poured a healthy amount into all four glasses and distributed them. "Here is to new friends, new family, and a beautiful future." The four of them clinked their glasses together and sipped their drinks.

Bridget finished hers quickly, and said, "Thank you, Banyan. I need to get to work now." The man inclined his head to her, but didn't watch her walk away. Bridget was a beautiful woman who had a body most men drooled over. He was definitely gay, but Rocky had no problem with that. Thinking of him with another man reminded Rocky of Finley sucking Sinclair's cock. She had to wonder if Sin was bisexual or if it had been a one-time deal. She planned on asking him when they were alone.

"Banyan, if you will excuse us, Ingrid is cooking, and I don't want her to have to keep the food warming."

"Of course. You two enjoy your evening. Rocky, what time would you like to meet tomorrow?"

"How about three? That will give the employees time to ask questions before they start their shift."

"Excellent. I will see you then. Sin, I'll see you later as well?" Banyan asked, raising his eyebrows. An unspoken question passed between the two of them, and Rocky was curious as to what was going on.

"I apologize, Brother. My mind has been preoccupied. I will make it up to you."

Banyan grinned and glanced at Rocky. "I completely understand."

"Thank you. Rocky, are you ready?" Sin stood from the stool and held his hand out to her. She allowed him to help her down even though she didn't need it.

"Good night, Banyan. I'll see you tomorrow." In response, Banyan did that fisting his chest thing and inclined his head to her before returning to his bottle of whiskey.

"My things are still at Finley's. I need to run upstairs and grab a change of clothes. I mean..." Rocky assumed Sin wanted her to spend the night. Maybe he only wanted dinner and a good fuck before he took her home.

"I would be most appreciative if you would pack all the clothes you have and bring them with you. I have a feeling it is going to take more than one night to get my fill of you," Sin whispered in her ear. As they made their way to the back of the bar where the door to her apartment was, a familiar face passed them coming out of the women's restroom. The woman knocked shoulders with Rocky, not bothering to apologize.

"Hey, watch where you're going," she said to the woman's back. The woman turned around and glared at Rocky. It was Shelby, the employee Rocky had fired as soon as she took over RC's. Rocky hadn't seen her around since then, so she was surprised to see her now. Sin turned to follow the woman, but Rocky pulled on his hand. "She's not worth it. Come on, we don't want to keep Ingrid waiting."

167

"Do you know her?"

"She's an ex-employee. I had to fire her right after RC's became mine."

"Does she come in here often? I'll give Banyan a heads-up."

"This is the first time I've seen her in three years. It's probably nothing."

"If you are sure." Sin was still staring where Shelby had been moments before.

"I'm sure," Rocky said, even though she wasn't. Ever since Blake had conned Rocky into believing he was interested in her for a relationship, Rocky had stopped giving anyone the benefit of the doubt. Everyone had a motive, and more often than not, it was nefarious. Everyone except Sinclair. For some reason, Rocky trusted the man not to hurt her.

Something about Sin called to her on a level deep within her soul. She didn't understand why someone like him would be interested in someone like her, but stranger things had happened. Her mother had been a beautiful woman and had been madly in love with Rocky's father even though he wasn't a handsome man. Her father was short and round with thinning hair. Her mother was outgoing and spontaneous where her father was quiet and introverted, but he loved her mother with every fiber of his being and made sure she knew it every single day.

If her parents, as different as they were, could make it work, it was possible Sin actually saw something in Rocky, even if she didn't see it in herself. She was going to keep her heart guarded and take whatever this was between them one day at a time. When Sin found out the truth about her past or when he got tired of her and kicked her to the curb, she would have the great sex to look back on. Besides, now that she no longer had to worry about RC's, she could get on with her new life of studying nursing. She wouldn't have too much time to worry about Sin.

168

Sin followed Rocky upstairs and waited, taking in her small apartment, while she packed her clothes. She didn't pack them all like he'd asked, but she did plan on spending more than one night with him. She found a spare toothbrush and an unopened tube of deodorant.

The glass of whiskey downstairs had taken the edge off Rocky's nerves. Not caring what Sinclair thought, she placed her bag on the floor by the door before going to the freezer and pulling out her stash of Patron. "Drink?" she asked when he stepped closer to her. Rocky took a swig and held the bottle out to him. He took a sip of the smooth liquid and, taking the cork from her hand, replaced it and put the bottle back in the freezer.

"Do you drink a lot?" he asked.

"Does it matter?"

"Yes, beautiful girl, it does. If you drink often, there's a reason for it. You are either celebrating life or trying to hide from it. I want to help you celebrate. I also want you sober when I make love to you. I want you to remember every single moment you and I spend together." Sin took her hands and placed them on his chest. His heartbeat was strong beneath her fingertips. "I vow to you I will do everything within my power to make your days going forward memorable. I will do my best to help you forget the bad from your past. As long as you allow, I will be by your side making your days the best they can possibly be."

That was the most beautiful thing Rocky had ever heard. Even her father, as mushy as he'd been, had never spoken such powerful things to her mother. Not that she'd heard, anyway. Rocky blinked back the tears threatening to fall, but she failed. Sin caught each one as it rolled down her cheek with his thumbs. When they finally stopped falling, he gently kissed the wetness underneath her eyes. "I vow you will only cry happy tears, too," he whispered before he pressed their lips together.

Rocky's body was ready for Sin to make love to her,

169

but he pulled away. "I do not wish to keep Ingrid waiting. There will be plenty of time after dinner for us to continue getting to know one another." Sin grabbed Rocky's bag from the floor and held open the door for her. She didn't know how far it was to Sin's home, and she hoped it wasn't far. She didn't know how much longer she could hold out.

Chapter Sixteen

Rafael waited patiently while Willow finished her phone call. His assistant had been different lately. He was pretty sure it had something to do with Mason, or the lack of her seeing Mason. The young Gargoyle was remaining firm about not asking Willow out until he was a little older, thus he was staying away from her as much as possible lest his beast take over. Rafe knew Willow was going through a type of withdrawal. Once a Goyle and their mate met, it was nearly impossible to think about anything else until the bond was sealed. Rafael thought of Willow as a daughter, and he was going to do something Kaya had begged him to weeks ago. He was going to intervene and tell Willow the truth.

As soon as she hung up, Rafael said, "I know it's late, but there is something I need to discuss with you. As soon as Kaya arrives, please lock the doors and accompany her to my office." Rafael knew he sounded cryptic, but he wouldn't divulge any information until he knew the office was secure.

"Am I in trouble?" Willow asked.

"Of course not. Kaya should be in the parking lot, so please do as I asked."

"Yes, sir."

Rafael made his way to the bank of windows in his office. New Atlanta was bustling with rush hour traffic. Humans trying to get home after a long day's work. His city was getting back on its feet, and new buildings were going up everywhere. Most of them were being built by Stone, Incorporated.

His cell phone rang, and he hesitated answering until he saw who it was. "Xavier, what can I do for you?" Rafael asked the Italian King who happened to be Tessa's

171

father.

"Have you heard from your mother?"

"Not for several days. Why? Has something happened?"

"I'm not sure. She and I were supposed to meet yesterday to discuss your uncle. She didn't show up, and when I called Donovan, his phone had been disconnected. I reached out to the twins, but neither one of them have seen your mother in a couple of weeks. They are looking everywhere Athena would have gone."

"It isn't like her to miss a meeting, and she hasn't called to check on Kaya, either. Do you think Alistair has her?"

"It's possible. I'm going to give Carter and Hunter one more day. If they haven't located her, we might have to do something drastic. The reason Donovan's phone was cut off is the Goyle has immersed himself into Alistair's world. He's cut off all communication with his Clan so there won't be any chance of him getting caught. However, if we cannot locate your mother, we may have to find a way to get a message to him."

Kaya and Willow entered the office and he held up one finger. "I have something personal I need to tend to at the moment, but please keep me posted. I will send Sinclair abroad if need be."

"Let's hope it doesn't come to that."

"Yes, let's." Rafael hung up and pulled a waiting Kaya to him. "Bella Mia," he whispered against her lips. He bent over and kissed her stomach as he always did. "How's my little Prince?" he asked.

"Ready to play, as always." Kaya didn't sit in one of the chairs across from his desk. Instead, she took a seat on the sofa. "Willow, please join me," she said and patted the seat beside her. Willow looked between them before she sat down.

"Willow, as I said before, you are not in trouble. But,

I do have something I need to discuss with you. One reason I asked Kaya to be present is so she can assure you what I tell you is the truth. When I finish, you will better understand why Mason has been acting odd as of late."

"The truth about what? Is Mason sick?"

"No, nothing like that. First off, I need for you to promise that what I tell you stays between us. Once I tell you, you will understand why this is so important. I'm trusting you with something few humans know."

"Humans? Rafael, what are you talking about?" Willow frowned.

"Promise me, Willow."

"I promise," she whispered.

"Now, let me start at the beginning..."

When Rocky told Bridget there was nothing between her and Sin, the beast wanted to kick the door in and prove to her she was wrong, but Sin had the good sense to bide his time. He needed to take things slow with Rocky and show her how good things could be. Now that he had his mate in his home, their home, he sorely wished he hadn't invited Finley and the two females to join him Tuesday. Hindsight, as they say, was twenty-twenty, but it didn't make him feel less guilty about having sex with Dana.

In all the years Ingrid had been serving Sin, not once had he introduced her to a woman he allowed in his home. He always asked her to remain in her wing of the house while he entertained guests. The last time he'd taken a wife was years before Ingrid was born. Tonight, he had introduced the two most important women in his life to one another. He didn't ask Ingrid to leave them alone, but she did after making sure they had everything they needed. As she left the kitchen, Ingrid had pulled Sin's face down so she could kiss his cheek, something she'd never done in all the years she'd been serving him.

Instead of eating in the large dining room, Sin and Rocky sat at the island in the kitchen and helped themselves buffet style from the dishes Ingrid had left on the stove. Sin didn't want to overwhelm Rocky or make her feel like he put on airs. Sure, he loved entertaining, and when the Clan gathered, he allowed Ingrid to go all out. Sin wanted to ease Rocky into his life. For now, they were enjoying a delicious meal, a bottle of wine, and good conversation. At least he hoped they were. Rocky had indulged him with tales from her childhood up until the point her parents had died within months of one another. After that, Rocky refused to say anything other than she'd gone to live with her aunt.

Sin knew there was much Rocky wasn't telling him, so he decided to have Banyan do some digging into the aunt's personal life. Sin had no trouble seeking retribution on Rocky's behalf for any harm that might have befallen her. He was supposed to protect humans, but he wasn't quite as noble as Rafael. There was a reason Rafe had been born three years earlier than Sin. Rafe was fit to be King whereas Sin probably was not. Rafe made sure a human deserved the punishment he or she received.

As soon as he had enough dirt on Blake Stansbury, Sin was going to bury the human up to his neck in the Mojave Desert and let the buzzards have at him. A slow, painful death would give the bastard time to reflect on what he'd done to Rocky. Blake was one of the reason's Rocky was guarded and only wanted a man for sex. She hadn't admitted as much, but he'd eavesdropped on her enough to know it was how she felt. Sin had his work cut out for him. The one good thing about her being his mate was the bond was helping to draw her to him. Rocky no doubt felt the same pull Sin did, thus she wanted him sexually. There was so much more to being mates than sex, and it was the other parts Sin had to work on.

When Rocky shut down and refused to talk about

174

her past, Sin had picked up the conversation, telling her about his brothers and cousins. He couldn't wait for the day he could admit to her he was a Gargoyle and she was to be his for a long time to come.

"Rafael and Kaya are expecting their first child in August, and Nikolas and Sophia are due in September." Sin was excited at the prospect of more children being added to the Clan. Connor, Dante's adopted son, was mostly human, and they didn't know if he'd phase into a half-blood or not since Isabelle was a half-blood herself. "What about you? Do you ever think about having children?"

Rocky stopped eating and began pushing her food around with her fork. She wouldn't meet his eyes. "I can't have kids," she whispered, the pain strong as she admitted the truth. Sin wanted to hit something. Not because he would never sire a child but because Rocky would never be a mother. Sin took her hand in his and kissed her knuckles.

"That's a shame, beautiful girl, because together, you and I would make beautiful babies," he said and winked, trying to lighten the mood. "If down the road, you desire to be a mother, you can always adopt."

"Nobody would let an ex-junkie adopt a baby, Sin." She dropped her fork and chugged all the wine in her glass. She picked up the bottle to refill it, but Sin took it away from her.

"Hey, look at me." When she gave him her undivided attention, he said, "I promised to give you everything your heart desires. If you desire children, I will give you a houseful. If you haven't noticed, I have money. More than our great-grandchildren would ever be able to spend. I am not trying to buy your affection, Raquel, but I am offering you the world. Whatever it is, great or small, it is yours."

"What do you do for a living?" Rocky asked, pulling her hand away from his and reaching for the wine bottle again. This time, Sin didn't keep her from it. The

175

conversation had taken a turn, and she probably needed the alcohol to help with her pain.

"Real estate investments. Our family is rather large, and our resources are vast. We've been buying up properties since the world fell apart. When island resorts closed down due to lack of tourism, our family began buying them up for pennies on the dollar. Have you traveled much?"

"I've never been out of the state of California. My mom worked long shifts at the hospital so my father could do what he loved. He didn't make much money teaching, so we rarely had time or money to go anywhere for vacation."

"The love in your voice when you speak of your parents is wonderful, Raquel. I lost my father a long time ago, so I know the hurt you feel."

Sin had put his phone on silent, and it was currently vibrating in his pocket. He removed it to see who was calling. "Rocky, I apologize, but I need to take this call."

"Do you want me to leave the room?"

"Of course not. Please, finish your dinner before it gets cold," he urged as he swiped his thumb over the screen. "Rafe, is everything okay?"

"I'm not sure. Xavier called, and Mother is missing."

"Missing? Is he sure?"

"Pretty damn sure. She missed a meeting with him yesterday, and neither Carter nor Hunter has spoken to her since week before last. I may need you to fly to Greece and see what you can find out. I would go myself, but I'd rather not leave Kaya behind, and I won't put her anywhere near our uncle."

"Of course you are not going. It's been years since Alistair has seen either one of us. I will need to shave my beard, but he will never know the difference if it comes down to a face-to-face." Rocky reached up and caressed Sin's beard, frowning. He knew she liked his whiskers, because she was constantly stroking his jaw, but family duty came first, and he could always grow them back.

"Thank you, Brother. I hope it doesn't come down to that, but I wanted you to be prepared, just in case."

"I will be ready. Anything else I need to know?" Sin was ready to get off the phone and back to his mate, but Rafe's voice held a bit of nervousness to it.

"I told Willow the truth of us. Now she understands why Mason has been acting so funny."

"Did you tell her his age?"

"I may have fudged a little there. He's going to go for my head as it is. I couldn't very well tell his mate he's only sixteen."

"How did she take it?" Sin wondered how Rocky would take it when he told her the truth.

"Like all human mates have so far; she was skeptical until I phased. Now she thinks it's the coolest thing ever, and she's excited to get Mason alone to see his fangs."

Sin laughed, and Rocky's eyes grew wide. He kept the smile on his face when she grinned at him. "I would say I'd like to be a fly on the wall, but even I am not that much of a voyeur." Sin winked at Rocky and placed his hand over hers that was still stroking his beard. "Keep me posted, Brother. If there is nothing else…"

"You sound different, Sinclair. Should I ask?"

'No, you shouldn't, but know I am having a most wonderful evening."

"I'll leave you to her, and. I'll call you tomorrow."

Rafe disconnected the call, and Sin placed the phone back in his pocket. "That was Rafael. It seems our mother cannot be found. If she isn't located in the next couple of days, I will probably have to take an impromptu trip."

"What's this nonsense about you shaving your beard?"

"Rafael is rather important, sort of like a King, if you will. He and I can pass for twins even though he is three years older. Whenever there is a crisis, I pose as him to keep him safe."

"I thought he was an architect?"

"He is, but he is so much more than that. There is a lot about my family I haven't told you. Maybe one day soon, you will trust I am not going to hurt you, and you will give us a chance at a future. When that happens, I will tell you all about my family."

"Does your family include Finley and Banyan?"

"Yes, though not by blood. And before you ask again, no we are not a cult. We are a Brotherhood that goes back many centuries."

"Like the Masons?"

"Something like that. We aren't a religious sect, but a clan who has vowed to protect hum– those who cannot protect themselves. Now, if you are finished eating, I would like to show you the rest of the house." They put their plates in the dishwasher but left the food on the stove. As Sin had explained to Ingrid, once they were finished eating, he intended to show Rocky his bedroom. That in itself had been all the woman needed to hear to know Rocky was special. Before he got that far, though, Sin took Rocky outside to the garden. The sun had set a couple of hours earlier, but the lights along the pathway automatically illuminated the way as Sin and Rocky walked past.

Rocky took her time enjoying the serenity the garden offered, taking in the twinkling lights strewn throughout the trees. Sin had thought Rafael was crazy when he suggested the lights, but after he saw them lit up in the dark, it was nothing short of magical. Seeing the wonderment on Rocky's face had been worth it. As they moved farther into the garden, Rocky reached for Sin's hand. They walked in silence until they had completed the loop. "I've never seen anything like this. If I lived here, I'd want to set up a hammock between the trees so I could stare at the lights all night long." Sin made a mental note to purchase a hammock.

He prayed to the gods his mother was located unharmed, not only for her sake, but for his as well. Sinclair had only just found his mate, and he was not ready to leave her behind, even if it was only for a short trip. "I rather enjoy the peace it brings. This, along with the top floor of the house, is my sanctuary. I have not shown you the top floor, because there is something I need to ask before I take you up there." Sin pulled Rocky to him and tilted her chin up. "Are you willing to give me the opportunity to show you how good we can be together?"

"What does that have to do with the top floor? Is it a sex room or something?"

"No, it isn't a sex room; it is my bedroom. Other than my wife who died a long time ago, no woman has been allowed on the top floor. Not even Ingrid."

"You were married?" Rocky tried to pull away.

Sin tightened his grip. "Yes, but as I said, she passed away many years ago. I will not keep my past from you, Raquel. Once you and I become better acquainted, you will learn everything there is to know about me. But I am willing to show you my sanctuary if you are willing to give us a chance."

Rocky frowned, and Sin could see the wheels turning. She had yet to ask many personal questions, and before now, he'd wished she had. At least then he would have known she was interested in him in a way that wasn't only physical. Now, the questions would more than likely require him to lie, or at the least, skirt the truth, and he didn't want that with her.

"If you prefer, we can relax in the den and watch a movie. I will not pressure you, Rocky. I want you to be sure as to your intentions with me before I share that part of myself with you. If sex is what you are after, we can retire to one of the bedrooms downstairs. You've already seen they are spacious and comfortable. Your choice, beautiful girl."

179

Chapter Seventeen

Rocky had never been so unsure about anything in her life. Even when Uncle Ray died and left her the bar, she had Joel and Bridget to lean on, guiding her through the first few weeks. Sinclair was asking her to make a life-altering decision on a dime. He'd shocked the shit out of her when he admitted he'd been married before. If the woman had still been alive, Rocky would have bolted. There was no way she would risk the ex-wife coming back into the picture. Sin must have an enormous capacity to love if he was willing to get involved with someone else. Then again, he did say it was a long time ago.

The way he talked about his family, hell the way he talked period, was different. His brother was likened to a king, and his friends were his brothers. It now made sense why they were all testosterone-laden men. Rocky was curious about Sin and this brotherhood, but he wasn't going to divulge any information if this was merely the two of them getting together for sex every once in a while.

If she gave in to him, Rocky would be dropping the wall she had so carefully constructed around her heart. She was certainly curious about the top floor. If no one had ever seen it, no one had been deemed worthy. What did he see in her he deemed worthy? *He doesn't know the truth. The real you.* Sin had agreed to tell her the truth about him and his family if she gave him the chance at a future, but what happened when she told him the truth about herself? Would he turn her away, or would he be mad as hell on her behalf? Time to find out.

"Before I give you an answer, I need to tell you more about my past. After you hear what happened, you might rescind your offer."

"Nothing you say will change the way I feel about

you."

"You've known me less than ten hours. That's hardly time to forge honest feelings about someone, especially when you don't know all their sins."

"Then confess your sins so I may offer absolution," Sin said. "Tell me, Raquel; tell me the worst of your past." In the soft glow of the twinkling lights, Sinclair was asking her to bare her soul. Asking her to put voice to words no one – not even Vivian – had heard.

Rocky took Sin's hand and led him to a darker part of the garden. If she was going to do this, she didn't want to be able to see the disdain on his face. She tried to pull her hand away, but Sin held on tighter. Rocky sighed and began, "I've already told you I went to live with my aunt when my father died. What I didn't tell you was about my cousin, Tommy. He's a few years older than me and as useless as ice cubes to an Eskimo. He's one of those losers who lives in the basement of his mother's home, watches porn all day, and steals money to go to strip clubs." Rocky paused, gathering her nerves.

Sin squeezed her hand, so she continued. "The first time it happened, I was asleep. Aunt Linda was working late, and Tommy came to my room. I was only thirteen. He put duct tape over my mouth so I couldn't scream. He tied my arms to the headboard. I kicked and kicked, but he was too strong." Rocky was now whispering, but it was the only way she could get it out.

"You do not have to tell me the rest, Sweetheart. I can imagine what came next." Sin was vibrating. Rocky could feel the way his body was shaking.

"I do have to. You need to know how bad it got so you'll know I'm not worthy of someone like you. He ruined me, Sin. At first he used his body, and I stopped fighting him, hoping he would take what he wanted and leave me alone. When that made him mad, he began using items to do the job. He raped me with anything he could shove

181

inside me, the worst being a broken off broom handle. He's the reason I can't have babies. I tried to tell Aunt Linda, but she called me a liar. I was fucking thirteen for Christ's sake! When she found me in the bathtub bleeding, she said I was just having a bad period. When the bleeding wouldn't stop, she still refused to take me to the hospital."

Sin pulled away and stalked up the path until he was no longer in sight. An anguished cry ripped through the darkness, and Rocky dropped to her knees. She prayed his anger wasn't aimed at her, because Rocky would never live through the rest of the story if it was. She wrapped her arms around her waist and rocked back and forth. Admitting what Tommy did to her was bringing the pain back to the surface. After several minutes had passed, Sin returned. He picked Rocky up off the ground and carried her into the house.

Sin bypassed the kitchen and took a staircase he hadn't shown her. When he reached the top, he opened the door into his private bedroom and took her directly to the bed. Sin stretched out beside her and pulled her into his arms. He didn't say a word, but he didn't have to. The tears rolling down his face said it all. He rocked her in his arms and whispered, "I'm sorry. I'm so sorry." Rocky had told him the worst of it. Sin now knew she was damaged goods, and he hadn't kicked her out. Hadn't told her how shameful she was or how dirty he found her. Her own tears blended with his, and they stayed wrapped in each other's arms until she fell asleep.

Rocky woke up screaming. A large body was holding her down, and she knew Tommy had found her. "Shh, baby, it's me, Sin. Shh," he whispered against her ear. When she gained her bearings, she realized he wasn't holding her down but simply holding her. She was fully dressed save her shoes, and Sin had been holding her all this time.

"Sorry," she muttered.

182

"No need to apologize. Bad dream?"

"Sort of. I need to pee," she said, and he loosened the hold he had around her. Rocky sat up on the side of the massive bed and looked around. There were several closed doors in the sparsely furnished room.

"The door to your left," Sin offered.

"Thanks." Rocky dropped to the floor and padded to the bathroom. She flipped on the light and paused as she took in the tile room that was almost as large as her apartment. Inside the bathroom were two doors, and she assumed one of them was hiding the toilet.

"The door to the right," Sin called from the bed.

After she relieved her bladder, Rocky washed her hands and took in her appearance in the mirror. She cringed upon seeing the mascara she'd put on the day before had smeared under her eyes from the crying she'd done before she fell asleep. She found a washcloth and washed her face. When Rocky took stock of the items on the counter, she found that all the items were hers and not just the spare toothbrush she'd brought from home. The toiletries she'd had at Finley's were lined up along the vanity.

"Sin? Where did my stuff come from?" she asked, looking around the bathroom door at him. Sin was stretched out on his back with his arm cradling his head.

Turning to look her way, he said, "I had Finley drop it off."

"In the middle of the night?"

"He was out and about anyway."

Finley's house wasn't close to Sin's, so she hoped he hadn't made a special trip just to bring her stuff. And in the middle of the night at that. Before returning to bed, Rocky brushed her teeth. Her hair was going to get messed up again, so she didn't bother trying to fix it.

"What was he doing out so late?"

"Patrolling."

"He's a cop?" Even though she'd wondered, Rocky

183

had never asked what kind of job he had.

"Of a fashion. Now, come here to me," Sin said as he rolled over on his side. Rocky slid in beside him, and he snugged her closer to him. He teased her lips with his tongue, and she opened for him. Her body was ready, but it seemed to stay ready whenever he was around. Her panties were wet, and her nipples ached to be touched.

"Do you like my boobs?" she blurted.

Sin lifted her shirt over her head and tossed it to the floor. He urged her to lie on her back and focused on her breasts. When he met her gaze, he was honest. "I prefer real ones, but if you like yours the way they are, I'm not going to complain as long as I get to touch and taste them." He proved his point by licking a nipple and sucking it into his mouth. Rocky's body arched off the bed.

As Sin took turns tormenting each hard peak, Rocky asked, "So, it wouldn't bother you if I had the implants removed?"

Sin nuzzled the side of a breast before kissing his way down her stomach. "Not at all. As a matter of fact, I will pay for it if you have it done."

"That's not why I was asking. I don't want your money, Sin."

"I know, but I am still willing to pay, because honestly? I would prefer if they were natural."

So much for Blake's theory all men liked big, fake tits.

"Sin?"

"Yes, beautiful girl?" he asked as he pushed her panties down her legs. She'd removed her jeans in the bathroom and left them there hoping he'd get the hint she was ready to get naked.

"Will you fu… make love to me now?" Rocky was never going to get used to the fact Sinclair wanted to make love to her. Never once had he said he wanted to fuck her.

"After I get a taste of your sweet pussy." Sin situated

himself between her legs and took his time getting her off. Knowing how good it would be when he slid inside her, Rocky enjoyed the teasing and licking. Sin brought her to the edge over and over, and when she begged him to let her come, he didn't hesitate to give her what she wanted. Like the day before, he didn't wait for her to finish coming down before he was stripping his clothes off. Unlike the day before, Sin rolled to his back and lifted Rocky so she was straddling his waist. She took his cock in hand and directed it to her slick opening.

Rocky slowly lowered herself, knowing as large as he was, it would hurt if she went too fast. When she bottomed out, Sin grabbed her hips. He didn't direct her movements, but he did squeeze her to get her attention. "Ride me, beautiful girl. Use me to make yourself feel good." Placing her hands on his chest, Rocky did as he instructed and rode his cock just as slowly as he'd made love to her at his penthouse. She rocked back and forth, sliding his dick along her clit, enjoying the friction inside and out. Sin's hands left her hips and found her breasts. He twisted her nipples, pulling them harder with each moan she released.

As her orgasm closed in on her, Rocky increased the pace, and Sin flipped her to her back, taking over. Rocky pressed her heels into the bed, meeting each thrust. Harder and harder, Sin sank his cock into her body. A low growl came from deep within Sin, reverberating throughout Rocky's body. If she didn't know better, she would have thought an animal was in the room. Sin's eyes darkened, and he dropped down onto his forearms. Rocky's body shuddered, and she once again arched her back as she spasmed inside. Calling out Sin's name, Rocky almost blacked out. The intensity with which she came overtook her senses, and she gasped for breath. Sin yelled out as his release filled her up. It was the second time they'd gone without a condom. He now knew she couldn't get pregnant, but she had to wonder if he'd used protection with Dana.

Before she could ponder that further, sharp teeth scraped along the skin at her neck. Her body jerked and another orgasm followed the first one. Or maybe it was the aftershock from the first just now reaching her core. Whatever it was had Rocky flying. She felt as if she could levitate above their bodies. When Sin's cock stopped pulsing inside her pussy, he dropped his head and licked her shoulder. Again with the licking. That time hadn't been to seduce her. It was more like he was cleaning her. Maybe he'd drawn blood with his teeth and was removing the evidence.

When Rocky teased, "My very own vampire," Sin's body tensed. She turned her face so she could see his, but he kept his head turned away from her.

"Vampires are a myth," he muttered. Sin kissed her shoulder, but instead of snuggling like he'd done the day before, he rolled off the bed and headed to the bathroom, closing the door and shutting her out.

Sin retracted his fangs and prayed to the gods Rocky was so caught up in her orgasm she didn't realize what he'd done. He licked the blood from her neck and got his beast under control. He'd been so close to biting her instead of merely scraping his teeth long her skin. He waited for his mate to freak out over what happened, but she teased him about being a vampire. If she only knew. Rocky tried to look at him, but he didn't want her to see the dread. He slipped out of her body, and like a coward, rushed into the bathroom, closing the door. He stared at his reflection and was relieved to see he had returned to normal except for the drop of blood at the corner of his mouth. He licked the sweet nectar and savored the taste on his tongue. If Rocky ever agreed to the mate bond, Sin would have to be careful when he sank his fangs into her neck. She tasted too good.

Instead of hiding out, Sin wet a washcloth and returned to the bed. He sat down next to Rocky's hip and wiped his essence from between her legs. "I am clean. I've never had sex without a condom until you."

"What about with your wife?" she asked.

Sin couldn't tell her the truth. Not yet. "No, I didn't use protection with her, but like you, she couldn't get pregnant." It was only because she wasn't his mate. Physically, she was in perfect health, unlike Rocky.

"And you were okay with that?"

"Raquel, I did not marry my wife so she would bear my children. I married her because I enjoyed the time we spent together. Besides, I was not ready for kids back then."

"And now you are?"

Sin tossed the washcloth toward the bathroom and pulled Rocky into his arms. "Whether or not I have children is yet to be seen. If they are biologically mine or if they are adopted, I will still love them with everything I have. The fact you cannot have children doesn't lessen the feelings growing inside of me. I am telling you, beautiful girl, I have no doubt you and I can have a wonderful future together. For now, let's take it one day at a time, and if you get tired of me, you can leave whenever you like. All I ask is you give me – give *us* – a chance."

"Why did Finley tell Vivian you aren't the settling down type?"

"So neither she nor her friends would get the wrong idea about what it was we were doing in the bedroom."

"But I was supposed to be the one to show up, not Dana."

"As I already told you, all bets would have been off. There is something special about you, something I cannot get enough of. Something I refuse to let go of. I want nothing more than to settle down, but only with the right woman. You are that woman, Raquel. So, what do you say?"

"I still don't understand it."

"But?"

"But yes, I will give us a chance, against my better judgment."

Sin scooted back so he was leaning against the headboard. Rocky draped her naked body across his, and he willed the beast to be quiet. When he left the bed earlier to call Finley, he had a heated discussion inside his head about why he couldn't lock their mate away and fuck Rocky senseless for the next week.

Sin felt as though they'd crossed a major hurdle when Rocky told him the truth of her past. That was another reason he'd left her alone in his bed. *Their* bed. He called Banyan and told him to make Tommy Cartwright another priority. Sin was going to cut off the man's dick and shove it down his throat. Then he was going to bury him in the desert right alongside Blake Stansbury. He reached deep inside and calmed his mood so Rocky would calm also. He'd noticed their link was strong even though they hadn't completed the mate bond. When she was upset, he felt it as strongly as she did and vice versa. His breathing evened out, and Rocky's breaths matched his, eventually allowing her to fall back to sleep.

Sin remained stone still during the night, holding his mate and watching her sleep in his arms. He had silenced his phone so it wouldn't bother her, but the vibration of a message sounded against the night stand. When Sin saw it was Rafe, he blew out a sigh and read the text. He did not want to travel to Greece now he'd met Rocky, but it was his duty to his King and Clan to do whatever was needed. He would ask Banyan and Finley to keep an eye on Rocky while he was gone.

Keeping his ears open for when Rocky awoke, Sin packed his bags and called the two males to come over to his house. They were drinking coffee and talking about what dirt Banyan had uncovered on Blake Stansbury. The

188

human had been close to bankruptcy around the same time he met Rocky, but soon after, he'd managed to bounce back. The club's bank records showed an increase in income, and Banyan attributed it to Rocky dancing. "If you give those girls enough money, they'll spill their guts. It took me several lap dances, but I found out Rocky was the star when she was on stage."

Sin didn't want to hear about his mate taking her clothes off for other males, but he needed to know the truth.

"Before Rocky, the club was practically empty, even on the weekends. Once she took to the stage, the seats began filling, and Stansbury was back in the black. When I asked about the drugs, the girls all said it was a perk of working for Blake. None of them complained about the way they were treated. Since Rocky quit, things have declined once more. I'd say it's why the man is targeting her again. If he can get her hooked, she'll come crawling back to him for her next fix, and he can convince her to dance for him."

"We all know that will never happen. What about her cousin? Anything on him yet?" Sin asked. Of the two males in Rocky's life, Tommy Cartwright was the worse of the two evils since he'd forced himself on an innocent young girl.

"He frequents Stansbury's club two or three times a week. His financials are almost non-existent. He still lives with his mother who works two jobs, so it would make sense he's either taking money from his mother, or she's enabling his habits, neither scenario good. He amasses an enormous Internet porn bill, but his mother pays that off at the end of each month. Either she's that stupid, or he has something on her. I showed the girls Tommy's picture, and they all knew him. His girlfriend has danced there on and off. I got her name and checked her out, but she's as much of a loser as Tommy is. The one thing I wanted to bring to your attention is she used to work at RC's. She was fired soon after Rocky took over the bar."

189

"Do you happen to have a photo of the woman?" Sin had a sinking suspicion as to who she was.

"Yes." Banyan flipped through the folder in front of him and pulled out a scanned photo of the woman's driver's license. "Shelby Billings."

"Motherfucker. She was in the bar last night. She literally ran into Rocky as she was coming out of the restroom. Banyan, I'm beginning to think there is a connection between her, Tommy, and Blake. Rocky told me how her cousin lost his shit when the bar went to her instead of him. See if you can find the connection. How is Uri coming along with the weapons? If he is close to finished, I would like for him to take over training so you can concentrate on this."

Finley spoke up. "He mentioned last night while we were patrolling that he was on the final batch. He should be finished by the end of today."

"Did he mention going back home afterwards? Because we could really use his help for a few more days. At least until I can get back from Greece."

"He did, actually. He was planning on flying home Sunday."

Sin didn't miss the change in Banyan's demeanor at the news Urijah was leaving. "I will call him and request he stay. Finley, since Rocky is familiar with you, I would ask you allow her to stay at your home until my return. I would appreciate if Vivian is there as well. Banyan, you can help keep an eye on her by requesting she assist you with the bar. I want someone with her around the clock until we figure out Stansbury's angle."

"Are you going to be the one to tell her she will have constant babysitters?" Finley asked.

"Of course, but I will put it a little more delicately than that. Now, I am going to call Urijah, and then I am going to wake my mate so we can... talk."

Both Banyan and Finley laughed, but they didn't

make any smartass remarks. Sin left them in the kitchen, and he stepped outside onto the patio to call Uri. Once he heard Sin's reasoning, he readily agreed to remain on the West Coast until Sin could return from Greece. As soon as he hung up, Sin headed upstairs to wake Rocky. He was going to use their mate bond to get her to agree with constant protection. He was also going to make love to her right up until the time he had to leave for the airport.

Chapter Eighteen

"Where's all your stuff?" Rocky asked while Sinclair wrapped her in a fluffy black towel. He had woken her up when he slid his cock home and made love to her. After he'd made sure they both were sated, he'd picked her up and carried her to the shower where they had sex against the tile wall. Rocky didn't weigh much more than a hundred pounds, but Sin held her up as if she were weightless. Where he'd been slow and gentle in the bed, Sin had taken her hard and fast in the shower. It was almost urgent. Ever since he'd woken her, he'd seemed different. A little distant. Not with her, but about something else.

"What stuff?" Sin asked when he grabbed his own towel off the shelf.

"Your personal things. I would never have known this was your bedroom if you hadn't told me it was."

"I have a room downstairs I use if I want to sleep. Rarely do I come up here."

"Why not?" Rocky was pushing, but if she was going to learn anything about this man, she was going to have to ask. He was forthcoming with some information, but Rocky felt he was keeping so much from her. He'd said he would tell her everything, but only if they had a future.

"I've reserved this room for my partner. As I told you before, nobody has been up here since my wife died. If and when you decide to join me as a life partner, this will be our bedroom, and you will decorate it however you wish. Until then, it will remain as it is. Decorations do not interest me with regards to this room; it is what happens in here I am more concerned about."

Rocky began combing the tangles out of her damp hair while Sin brushed his teeth. Never had she shared a bathroom with a man, and this little bit of domestication had her heart pumping and her brain taking a step back. She wanted to believe that even after the truth of her past was out in the open someone could still find something about her redeemable, but Rocky was a realist. If the only two men in her past had taught her anything, it was that she had nothing to offer other than her body.

She had made good grades in high school, but that was because she spent as much time after school in the library as possible so she wouldn't have to go home and face Tommy. At the time, she thought her grades would allow her to go to college, but when she graduated high school, her aunt refused to give Rocky any money for tuition. Rocky didn't think to tell her uncle what was going on, so she went to work at the bar, trying to work and save money so she could eventually move out on her own.

Sin caught Rocky's reflection in the mirror and winked at her, dragging her away from her maudlin thoughts. If this wasn't where he normally took a shower, at some point he'd brought his toiletries upstairs. Everything he did was with such intensity, and she couldn't keep her eyes off him. After he spit the foam from his mouth and rinsed, Sin opened a drawer and pulled out a can of shaving cream and a razor.

"What are you doing?" Rocky asked, grabbing his hand. "You're not really going to shave your beard, are you?"

"For now, yes. On this trip, I will be impersonating my brother, and he doesn't have a beard. I will grow it back as soon as I return."

"When are you leaving?" Rocky knew it was soon, but his answer was unexpected.

"In half an hour." Sinclair used an electric trimmer to remove the whiskers she couldn't keep her fingers out of. She watched sadly as the dark hair fell into the sink. Rocky picked up some of it and rubbed it between her thumb and fingers. When all that was left was a thin layer of stubble,

Sin added shaving cream to his face and began swiping it with a razor. "I hate to leave you like this, Raquel, but it is only for a couple of days. Three at the most. While I am gone, I want you to stay close to Banyan while at the bar and Finley afterwards. I need to know you are safe, or I won't be able to concentrate on finding my mother. I will be worried about you. Will you do that for me, beautiful girl?" he implored.

Sin's face became smoother with each swipe of the razor. He rinsed the blade under the water and stroked downward. Swipe, rinse, repeat. In less than two minutes, the beard she loved so much was gone, but the face reflecting back from the mirror took her breath away. "Rocky... baby?" Sin said to her in the mirror.

"Huh? Yeah, sure. Stay with my babysitters. Got it."

"Try to think of them as your security detail. In essence, I am the vice president to Rafael's president, and therefore you would be the second lady with Kaya being first. For all intents and purposes, you are my partner; therefore, you are as important to our family as any other female. We take our family seriously, Raquel, and every one of my Brothers will protect you with their life. That's how important you are, whether you realize it or not."

"Wow," Rocky whispered. This shit was crazy. Second lady? Rocky Cartwright, former junky stripper, was now considered somebody. "Huh," she muttered. She would never be able to wrap her head around that, especially since she'd only met Sinclair the day before. A few days ago, she was supposed to visit his home with her best friend to fuck him. Now, she'd bypassed the fucking and gone to practically being engaged. Sinclair hadn't mentioned marriage, but he was asking her to be his life partner, so they might as well be.

"Rocky?" Sin had wiped the shaving cream from his face. Rocky reached up and ran both her hands along his smooth skin. The stubble underneath the surface was so

194

dark she knew he'd have to shave constantly to keep the sexy shadow from reappearing. Instead of answering him, Rocky pulled his face down to hers so she could kiss him. Sinclair had the sweetest kisses when he wanted, but he also had ones that would incinerate her panties without even using tongue. The man did things to her body she couldn't comprehend.

"I promise to stay safe, but can't I go with you?" Rocky didn't know if they were to a point in their relationship, however quickly it had started, that she should be asking for such things, but she wouldn't mind going overseas.

"It is going to be dangerous, and like I said, I need to focus on my mother."

"Are you the mob? I mean, the way you speak of *family* and the *brotherhood*, it sounds like it. Your older brother is *like a king,* and your mother's been kidnapped. I think I saw this in a mafia movie."

Sin pulled her to him and wrapped his arms around her waist, laughing. "No, we aren't the mob. I promise I will explain everything soon. For now, I need you to trust me."

"I guess." Rocky didn't have a choice. While he was gone, she would ask Banyan questions while she was at the bar with him. She'd drill Finley, too. And with Sin out of the country, Rocky would have time away from him to breathe. And think. She could really think about the last twenty-four hours and decide if she was ready to commit to someone after such a short time. "Can I stay here instead of spending the night at Finley's? Isn't it safe here?"

"If you would prefer to stay here, I can ask Finley to stay here with you while I am away. You and Ingrid could get to know one another. Wait, on second thought, she would probably tell you too many stories about me."

"In that case, I definitely want to stay here," Rocky teased. Who better to know this man's secrets than his housekeeper who'd been with him over the last several years?

Sin kissed her again. "Whatever you wish, beautiful girl, I will make it happen. Would you like to drive me to the airport?"

"I thought I couldn't be unsupervised?"

"Finley will be following you, but I thought you might like to have a little freedom in the Lambo."

"You'd trust me with your car?" Rocky knew she was dreaming, because there was no way in hell a normal man would allow his girlfriend to drive a dream car.

"You are a good driver, baby. Just don't wreck. I need you safe, not in the hospital with a concussion. Or worse."

"What about luggage? The trunk is teeny in that thing."

"It will hold a small bag, and that is all I'm going to need. I refuse to stay away from you that long. I am going to get in, find my mother, and get out."

Rocky knew at any moment she was going to wake up from this craziness, and she'd be back in her normal, shitty life. Sin left the bathroom and put on some clothes he must have gotten while he was downstairs, because the closet attached to his bedroom was empty. He'd said she could decorate the room however she wanted if they became partners. After living in her small apartment for the last three years and the tiny bedroom at Aunt Linda's ten years before that, she couldn't imagine something as magnificent as Sin's home being hers. Technically, it wouldn't be hers, but she'd have all the amenities at her disposal. The walk-in closet. A swimming pool and garden to relax in. A gate with a state-of-the-art security system. Ingrid to cook her meals and clean up after her. Nope, that's where she drew the line. She couldn't allow someone to clean for her.

"I can't put this off any longer, beautiful girl. I have to go." Sin held out his hand, and Rocky took it, allowing him to lead her downstairs. When they reached the kitchen, Finley and Banyan were standing over Ingrid, who was cooking something on the stove.

"Sin, you better give Ingrid a raise, or I'm going to take her home with me," Finley joked. "Have you tasted this sauce?" He made a show of licking his lips. Sin rolled his eyes, and Ingrid beamed.

"I will make a deal with you. If you stay here with Rocky while I am out of town, I will make sure you have all the sauce your heart desires."

Finley's face fell immediately. "Stay here. With Rocky." He backed up a few steps and crossed his arms over his chest. "Brother…"

"It is what Rocky wants," Sinclair interrupted.

"If it's a problem, I can stay at Finley's," she said, hoping to diffuse the situation, whatever it was. There was some undercurrent, and even though it was unspoken, Rocky felt it all the same.

"No, it's no problem, if Sinclair's quite positive."

Banyan, who'd been quiet until then, said, "She'll be with me most of the evening at the bar anyway, so between the two of us, she'll be quite safe."

Ingrid had returned to stirring the sauce. If she thought the conversation odd, she didn't let on. If she'd been in Sinclair's employ long, she was probably used to these types of things.

"I am quite positive. Now, if you will follow us to the airport, Rocky's going to drive me there and then return here until it is time for her and Banyan to go to RC's."

"Okay then," Finley said, not meeting her eyes.

Rocky wasn't ready for Sin to go, but she was eager to drive her man to the airport. *Not your man. Not yet.*

Finley followed behind as Rocky navigated the way to the smaller airport in New Burbank. It never dawned on Rocky that Sin would be taking a private jet, so when he directed her away from the commercial departure lane, she was surprised. "The family has its own jet. We have the need to fly often, so it is cheaper to have our own than fly commercial. When you and I go on vacation, we will have all the privacy we need when flying."

Rocky had to admit she was excited about the prospect of going on a vacation. And in an airplane? Maybe he'd take her somewhere exotic. Someplace she'd only ever seen on television. Maybe when he found his mother, he would return to Greece and take Rocky with him so she could see the crystal waters and amazing architecture. *Slow your roll, Rocky girl. You aren't a couple yet.*

Saying goodbye took a few minutes, but the pilot informed Sin they needed to get a move on so they didn't lose their place in the take-off schedule. Rocky got back in the car, but she waited until the smaller plane was in the air before she drove away. Right as she pushed the button to start the engine, her phone pinged with an incoming text. When she saw it was from Sinclair, a grin spread across her face.

Miss you already, beautiful girl.

Rocky missed him too, but instead of responding in kind, she typed out *Be safe and hurry home.*

Once back on the road, she was nervous about driving a high-dollar car without the owner beside her. Sin had let her drive on the freeway on the way to the airport, and it was actually less exciting than taking the curvier backroads. Still, she took the path of least resistance back to Sin's home. Finley remained behind her, but never crowded her. When they reached the driveway, Rocky pulled up to the security box, but Sin hadn't given her a password. She rolled the window down and stuck her head out. "What's the passcode?" she asked Finley.

He jumped out of his vehicle and jogged up to where she was idling. He grinned at her and said, "Sin is one lucky motherfucker." The gate began opening, and Finley returned to his car. She parked the Lambo in the garage where it had been before they left. By the time she was out of the car, Finley was waiting for her.

"Would you care to explain the passcode?" she asked as he opened the door for her.

"It's voice activated. I could have said 'Rocky is a beautiful woman' and it would have opened all the same."

Rocky wanted to talk to Finley alone, but he continued on in the house and headed for the kitchen where Banyan was sitting in front of a laptop. He glanced up, bowed his head to Rocky, and said, "Ingrid left a tasty meal in the oven heating. If you're hungry, I can fix you a plate."

Rocky looked behind her, but Finley had his head in the refrigerator.

"I am hungry, but I'll be glad to serve myself. Just tell me where the plates are."

Banyan stood and said, "They're in the cabinet on the far side of the stove."

While she was looking for a plate, she asked, "Are either of you going to join me?"

Banyan said, "I've already eaten. Fin, you hungry, Brother?"

"I'm always hungry. Rocky, what would you like to drink? There's water, juice, and beer, but I'm going to have some of Ingrid's sweet tea."

"I'll try some of that, please."

"You won't be disappointed. One day when I mentioned how much I missed having sweetened iced tea, Ingrid called Priscilla and got the recipe. Now she makes it all the time," he said.

"Who's Priscilla?" she asked, trying to ignore the fact that these men were offering to wait on her.

"Rafael's housekeeper. Man, can she cook. Don't get me wrong; Ingrid's a wonderful cook, but Priscilla would put out a spread every Sunday at family day. As the males began finding their ma... their significant others, the family grew, and so did the feast she would put together. I've thought about flying back just to eat her cookies." Finley had a jug of tea in one hand and a smile on his face. He poured a tall glassful and set it in front of where Rocky was still standing. "Banyan?"

"Absolutely. I got used to drinking it sweet when I lived in New Orleans. Now I can't drink it any other way."

Rocky had heard of the legendary sweet tea in books and on television, but she'd never tried it. She usually drank water since it was free. She took a sip and moaned. Both men jerked their heads to her, and she apologized. "Sorry, but this stuff's good."

She put the tea on the table and returned to the stove. Rocky wasn't sure what she was putting on her plate. It was some kind of chicken dish, but it smelled heavenly. She scooped out a serving and handed it to Finley. Instead of joining Rocky and Banyan at the table, he leaned his butt against the counter, eating standing up. Between bites, he asked Banyan, "Did you find anything else while we were gone?"

Banyan shook his head. "Not much. I'm going to have to do some recon later. Rocky, do you need to run any errands before we head to the bar? I'd like to get over there before the employees arrive so you can show me around uninterrupted."

"No, I'm good. Everything I need is here."

"Take your time eating. I need to make a couple of phone calls." Banyan stood and closed his laptop. He stretched, and his shirt rode up his stomach, showing the V which pointed to where she was sure a nice cock would be. Not that she was thinking about Banyan's dick, but she was pretty sure all the "brothers" in Sin's family were genetically enhanced somehow.

"I meant to ask Sin, but I forgot. Is Remy Doucet down at the gym in your little brotherhood?"

Finley and Banyan looked at each other, but it was Fin who answered. "He is. Why? Did he bother you?"

"On the contrary. He was an absolute gentleman. Walked me to my car and everything."

Fin cocked an eyebrow. "Would you like to expound on the *everything* part?"

"He was nice to me without knowing me. I'm not used to men being nice. Is it some kind of code you guys have?"

"We do have a code, Rocky. We protect those who cannot protect themselves, and those who are unaware they need protecting in the first place."

"So you're not the mafia."

Banyan laughed softly, but Finley let out a belly laugh. "Definitely not the mob. We're tougher than they are," Fin said with a wink. Rocky laughed with them, but Finley quickly turned away. "I, uh… need to…" He grabbed his glass of tea and disappeared with it and his plate.

"Did I do something wrong?" Rocky asked Banyan.

"No, love. Part of our code is we protect the mates of each of our Brothers, and we never cross any type of line that would hurt the other or upset him. Finley is a flirt, and as such sometimes forgets himself. With Sinclair out of town and you under our watch, Finley doesn't want to betray Sin's trust by flirting with you, no matter how innocent his intention."

"Is that why he was freaking out when Sin asked him to stay here with me?"

"Yes. Sinclair must trust Finley implicitly where you are concerned."

"Why did you use the word mate? That's an odd term for wives."

Banyan looked at the ceiling briefly before meeting her eyes. "Not all of our Brothers are married to their women. Partner is another term we use interchangeably for those who remain unmarried, but mate is the word most often associated with the one the cosmos has chosen for us."

"The cosmos, huh? You said your boyfriend doesn't

201

want you. Is he not the mate the cosmos chose for you?"

"He is, but sadly, he wants nothing to do with me. Now, if you'll excuse me..."

"Right, your phone calls." Rocky smiled, and Banyan inclined his head to her before leaving her alone in the kitchen. Rocky was stuffed, but she couldn't stop eating the chicken. She couldn't remember the last time she'd had such wonderful food. Her aunt had been a terrible cook, and Rocky had never really learned. Maybe she would ask Ingrid to teach her. *You're getting ahead of yourself again.* That she was.

With Sin out of the country, Rocky was supposed to be weighing the pros and cons of getting involved with someone so quickly. Again. So far, all the arguments were in the pro column other than the time factor. Rocky took the last bite of chicken and rose to rinse her plate off. After she placed the empty dish and glass in the dishwasher, she leaned against the counter and took in her surroundings. The view out the window was inviting. Sin's home was surrounded by greenery, and Rocky tried to imagine living in such a place, but she honestly couldn't. She still didn't understand what he saw in her. He could have any woman he wanted, but according to Sin, he wanted her.

Rocky pushed away from the counter and stepped out the back door. Her phone pinged with a text. She grinned, fully expecting it to be from Sin, but when she realized it was from Bridget, her happiness waned a bit.

Still on for this afternoon with the talk?

Yes. Banyan and I will be leaving soon. He wants a quiet walkthrough.

Do you want me there?

Rocky didn't want Bridget to feel obligated to come in early, but she would be the one working with Banyan. *Totally up to you.*

Bridget responded a few seconds later. *I'd like that. See you soon.*

"Here you are," Banyan said from behind her. Rocky jumped and grabbed her chest.

"God, you scared me." She stuck her phone in her pocket while her breathing slowed down. "You guys are too quiet." Sin was just as quiet entering a room, but with him, she always felt his presence. It was as though the two of them were connected mentally somehow.

"I apologize. You must have been deep in concentration with whomever you were texting."

"Bridget. She wants to meet us at RC's if that's okay with you."

"Of course. Are you ready to go?"

"Yes. Let me grab my purse." Rocky hurried and retrieved her purse from the kitchen and met Banyan outside. "Am I driving or riding with you?"

"Which would make you more comfortable?" Banyan asked, keeping his distance. Must be that code thing these guys had going on. The only thing Rocky didn't understand was why Finley and Sinclair had shared women if they had a code.

"I don't mind riding with you. Taking two cars is foolish since we're going to the same place."

"It would be a waste of gas, but your comfort is of more importance."

"I'll be fine riding with you."

"Excellent. Shall we?" Banyan gestured to where his car was parked. Rocky was eager to spend some quality time with the man and possibly pick his brain about Sinclair.

Chapter Nineteen

Rocky climbed into the seat of Banyan's SUV as he held the door for her. When he slid inside and was seated, he put the key in the ignition and started the motor. Before he pulled out of the driveway, he said "I need to ask you a rather personal question. You don't have to answer if you don't want to, and I apologize in advance if I upset you."

Rocky thought he was going to ask her about her relationship with Sin. She was wrong. "Ask your question."

Banyan waited until he'd navigated onto the roadway before asking, "Do you think your cousin Tommy is capable of something as atrocious as child molestation?"

"What?" Rocky whispered. How could Banyan possibly know about that?

"Sin tasked me with looking into his past. What I've uncovered so far has led me to believe your cousin is one sick and twisted sonofabitch. Pardon my language."

"I've called him worse, so no apology necessary."

"I take it your relationship was strained when you lived under the same roof?"

"You could say that." Rocky didn't know Banyan well enough to trust him, but Sinclair did. He trusted the man to not only keep Rocky safe but to also look into the men in her past. "And to answer your question, yes, I think he's capable." Rocky kept her eyes focused on the road in front of them, but she could see Banyan watching her out of the corner of her eye.

"Thank you," Banyan responded softly.

Rocky hated thinking about her years spent suffering at the hands of her cousin, so she did her best to think of something happier. Like Sin. It had only been few hours since his flight left, but she was empty without him. How was that even possible? "Can I ask you something?" Rocky didn't know if he would answer, but she needed to ask anyway.

"Yes."

"Do you believe it's possible for two people to feel a deep connection after just meeting? I'm not talking about love at first sight. I doubt I'd even know what love felt like if it smacked me upside the head. I'm talking about a deep-rooted tether that has you thinking about someone constantly."

"Yes, I do," Banyan answered immediately. "There are those people who are meant to be together, and no amount of fighting it will matter."

"What about you? You mentioned your mate didn't want you. Do you still feel the pull to be with him?"

"Every single minute of every single hour. And when he's around? It's the worst kind of feeling in the world not to be able to pull him into my arms and hold him. Kiss him."

"I'm sorry. I really don't understand this thing between Sin and me. He can have anyone he wants."

"Can he?" Banyan asked as he turned the motor off. Rocky had been so caught up in her thoughts she hadn't realized they'd arrived at the bar.

"Can he what?"

"Have anyone he wants? He wants you, Rocky. Can he have you? I know it's been a fast twenty-four hours, but I promise you this; Sinclair Stone is serious about a relationship with you. He will move heaven and earth to make you happy. To keep you safe. To make you his."

"I... I'm pretty sure I don't have a choice." Rocky let it go and got out of the car. As Banyan met her at the front door, Rocky fished her keys out of her purse. "I guess I should give you the key," she said after she turned it in the lock and opened the door. Rocky froze, and Banyan all but ran in to her. "What the fuck?" she muttered. The inside of the bar was wrecked. Tables and chairs were splintered into

205

fragments. The bottles of liquor once lining the shelves behind the bar were smashed to pieces. The mirror behind the shelves was spider-webbed.

When Rocky tried to step farther into the room, Banyan grabbed her arm and shook his head, placing his finger over his lips. Rocky remained still and silent while Banyan stared off into space. He released her arm, and said, "I'm going to call the police. Please don't touch anything." Rocky stood where she was, not able to comprehend what she was seeing. Never in all the years she'd worked at or owned RC's had there been a break-in. Since Banyan had signed the papers stating the bar was his, this was technically his mess, but it didn't hurt her heart any less.

"What the fuck?" Bridget screeched as she entered through the back hallway. She turned around in circles as she took in the damage. "Rocky, are you okay? What the hell happened?"

"I'm fine. It was like this when we got here. Don't touch anything. Banyan's on the phone with the cops now."

"The safe!" Bridget exclaimed and took off toward the office. Rocky followed her and stopped Bridget from touching anything.

"Wait, Bridget." They both took a good look around at the mess in the office. The items she kept on top of the desk were now strewn across the floor. The sofa cushions were slashed, the stuffing having been pulled out. The supply cabinet doors were open and the contents in disarray.

When Banyan caught up to them, Bridget said, "At least they didn't get the money."

"How do you know?" Banyan asked, looking around at the mess.

"Because the garbage can is still where it should be," Bridget said, pointing to the metal bin next to the desk. "The safe is underneath those floorboards. If whoever did this knew where the safe was, they would have moved the trashcan, which would have triggered the alarm. Since neither one of us got a call in the middle of the night, the money's still there."

"Why didn't the alarm go off when things were being broken in the bar?" Banyan asked.

Rocky stared at her feet. This was on her. Banyan's bar had been trashed and the culprits got away because Rocky had let the security invoice lapse one too many times, and the alarms had been disabled.

"Rocky?" Bridget took her hand. "Please tell me the alarms still work."

Rocky couldn't hold back the tears. She was so ashamed. She had been making one stupid choice after another ever since she said yes to a date with Blake, and now someone else was paying for it. "I'm sorry, Banyan," she whispered.

"It's okay. I have insurance, and I was going to remodel anyway."

Rocky looked up to see if he was serious. He reached out to touch her face but pulled away before they made contact. "The thing that pisses me off is no one except the three of us knows the bar is mine. This was done to you, Rocky. This chaos was directed at *you*, and I vow I will find whoever is responsible and make them pay." Banyan cocked his head to the side and said, "Rett's here."

Banyan left the women alone in the office, and Bridget pulled Rocky into a hug. She allowed the woman to hold her briefly before she walked away. This was Rocky's fault, and she didn't deserve compassion or concern. Rocky pulled a cigarette out of her purse and lit it. Bridget frowned but didn't say anything. As she inhaled deeply, it dawned on her this was the first cigarette she'd had since meeting Sin. Now, she wanted to smoke the whole pack.

"Miss Cartwright, Miss Jones," the policemen said as he entered the office, tipping his hat to them. Rocky crushed the cigarette out on the bottom of her shoe and shoved the butt in her pocket. She wiped the tears from her face, not caring if the cop was waiting on her to acknowledge him. When she first met him in the hospital, Rocky figured Rett was part of the brotherhood since he had the same look about him. Focused. Intense. Now she was sure. "I wanted to question you both before I called in the crime scene analysis unit." Rett allowed them to sit down on the torn up sofa as he asked them the standard questions about if they had any suspects, whether they thought an employee would have done this, or if they had any enemies. "The back door was jimmied open, Rocky. I want you to make sure your apartment is intact before we go any further."

Rocky hadn't even thought about her apartment. She remained seated, because she didn't know if she would be able to stay calm if her apartment looked as bad as the bar. "Do you want me to go look?" Banyan asked.

Rocky nodded. She pulled the ring of keys out of her purse, found the one that unlocked her doors, and handed it over. "This opens both doors," she muttered. Bridget remained by her side, and Rett continued to ask questions. When Banyan returned, his face said it all. "Oh, god." Rocky buried her face in her hands, and the tears began falling again. How she wished Sinclair was there with her. She needed his strong arms around her, but he was somewhere over the Atlantic Ocean.

Rocky was numb by the time the bar had been combed over for fingerprints and other clues as to who might have broken in. With the amount of people who came and went at any given time, it would be nearly impossible to find whoever was responsible since Rocky didn't have working security cameras. As the employees arrived for their meeting, each one was asked where they'd been between the time the bar closed and when Rocky had found the mess. She had explained to Rett she knew none of the employees would have done this. Not to her but especially not to Bridget. They all needed the money, and with the bar closed, they'd be out of work.

Banyan had taken the opportunity to introduce himself as the new owner. The immediate reactions had been less than stellar, but when Banyan explained they would all be receiving a paycheck while the bar was being put back together, that went a long way to win him over to their side. A couple of the guys offered to stay and help clean up after CSU released the bar to them.

Instead of sitting on her ass feeling sorry for herself, Rocky dusted herself off and pitched in with the clean-up. Banyan said it wasn't necessary, because he would hire a crew to come in and clean, but Rocky wasn't having it. This was her mess, and she was going to do her part, however small it was. Bridget had been right about the money. The safe was untouched under the floorboards, and that was the only saving grace Rocky could find in all the rubble.

Over the next couple of hours, she and the others got into a groove. The men cleared out the tables and chairs while Rocky swept up broken glass behind the bar. Bridget had taken the office and was doing her best to salvage the paperwork. The more broken glass she cleaned, the heavier her heart became. Deciding to take a break, Rocky headed out back so she could grab a cigarette. Stepping out the back door where the employee smoke area was, she lit up before pulling her cell phone out of her pocket to see if Sin had texted. He hadn't, but he was on a plane, and even though Rocky had never flown before, she was pretty sure you weren't supposed to use cell phones on a flight.

Taking a long pull, Rocky allowed the smoke to hang in her throat a few seconds before blowing the excess smoke into the air. She was leaning against the brick of the building, her hair catching in the roughness. While she smoked, she pulled her hair free only to lean back and get it caught again. The slight tug on her scalp was a needed distraction from what was going on inside the building. When the ember had almost reached the filter, Rocky took one more drag and deposited the butt into the tall outdoor ashtray.

As she turned around to head inside, someone ran into her, knocking her phone to the ground. When she noticed who it was, Rocky asked, "What are you doing here?" Shelby Billings. Again. Something about her being behind the building during the day set off an alarm inside Rocky's head. She tried to step around the woman, but Shelby blocked her path.

"Get out of my way," Rocky demanded, but Shelby smiled at her. A sting pinched Rocky's neck, and she slapped her hand over the spot. She tried to turn around, but before she could see who was behind her, Rocky slipped to the ground.

"Hurry up," Shelby seethed at whoever was helping her. Rocky's body was already going numb. She tried to get up, but someone grabbed her under her armpits and dragged her behind the Dumpster. Rocky's efforts to get away were hampered by someone holding her down while the other person jabbed a needle into the bend of her arm. The fluid filling her veins soon turned to fire, but she was helpless to do anything about it.

Right before Rocky lost all consciousness, pain shot through her wrist. The sting from the sharp blade was muted by the warmth of the blood trickling down her arms. Soon after, the same feeling in her other arm registered in her brain. No! She didn't want to die. Not now. A knife was placed into her palm and her fingers wrapped around the hilt. She blinked her eyes, begging them to stay open. When the person responsible came into view, Rocky screamed, but it was only inside her head.

Sin was ready to jump out of the airplane and fly beside it. His beast had been restless ever since he'd left

Rocky at the airport. Sin had a good feeling about Rocky agreeing to be his mate, but he still wanted to take things slow and give her time to decide he was one of the good guys. It was hard to focus his attention on the information he'd received from Xavier. At this point in the game, Sin was sure he wouldn't be returning with his mother. Donovan had managed to get word to X that Athena was being held in Alistair's compound on Ithaca, the same place Donovan had managed to infiltrate with none of Alistair's Goyles catching on. That was the good news. The bad news was the compound was the training ground for Alistair's army, and Sinclair wouldn't be able to get anywhere close to his mother.

After talking it over with Rafael and Frey, it was decided Sin would make his presence on the island known. He would stay long enough for Alistair to get wind of "Rafael" being there. As soon as that was accomplished, Sin would return home where they would plan their next course of action. Xavier had reached out to the twins, and the two had agreed to meet with Sin as soon as he arrived. Even though Sin would love nothing more than to stay on a yacht at the marina Hunter was currently living in, he felt it would be more suited to Rafael's tastes to find a secluded villa. Alistair's compound was on the north side of the island, therefore Sin would stay on the south, as far away from the Greek King as possible. Sin wasn't there to confront his uncle, merely to make a showing so word would get back to Alistair.

As much as Sin wanted to rescue their mother, this plan – get in and get out – was better suited to Sin's life at the moment. He was ready to be home with Rocky where he could spend time with her. Now that Banyan owned the bar, she would be free of her responsibility and could do whatever it was she wanted. She had mentioned studying nursing, and if that's what she wanted, Sin would help her get her degree. Finley had helped him to understand how females didn't want to sit at home and do nothing. They were used to being out in the world, making a difference. Whatever his mate wanted, he would see to it she got it. One of the things at the forefront of his mind was the fact Rocky couldn't have children. He did his best to put the reason why in the far reaches of his brain and focus on their options.

Sinclair hadn't given much thought to having a family over the years since the females of his kind had become close to extinct. Sin had long ago given up any idea of having sons of his own to continue the Di Pietro lineage. Now that he'd found his mate, the idea was still no good to him. He would have to watch his brothers raise their own sons and daughters while waiting for the day to see if they would transition into half-bloods or remain fully human. Even if he and Rocky adopted, the children would never become shifters. Sin didn't understand why the fates chose the way they did, but there was a reason they'd chosen Rocky for Sinclair. Something besides her outer beauty. Rocky was young and had been through so much in her twenty-four years. If anything, his mate was strong, and Sin respected the hell out of her for coming through the other side of such adversity. Maybe the fates saw something in him Rocky needed, and not the other way around.

Less than halfway into his fifteen-hour flight, unease settled in Sin's gut. Getting more restless by the minute, his beast stopped rumbling and spoke.

Something is terribly wrong.

I feel it too.

We must go back.

We don't know Rocky's in trouble.

Yes, we do.

Sin had vowed to give Rocky some space. She needed time to think about all he'd told her, even though it hadn't been much. For the security of the Clan, Sinclair wasn't going to tell Rocky the truth until she agreed to a relationship. That might not be fair, but it's the way it had to be. Still, the bad feeling deep inside continued to grow stronger the longer he ignored it. When he couldn't stand it any longer, Sin pulled out his cell phone and tapped out a text. *How's it going, beautiful girl?*

Almost immediately he received her reply. *Everything's good. Kinda busy. Chat later.*

Sin was happy Rocky responded, and he left her alone since she and Banyan were probably busy with the bar. He settled back into his chair, and the beast settled down in his head. As Sin stared out the window at the clouds, he began planning his next trip – the one he would take with Rocky, anywhere in the world she wanted to go.

Chapter Twenty

After Banyan helped Bridget get all the paperwork picked up, they began going over the accounts. Rocky had a good system in place, and he wouldn't change anything about it. He didn't see the need to fix something that wasn't broken. At least the internal workings of the bar weren't. The outer shell had been torn apart, and he vowed to find the culprit. This act of vandalism had been aimed at Rocky, and he would bring them to justice, one way or another.

Banyan hadn't seen Rocky in quite a while. The last time he'd checked on her, she'd been behind the bar, cleaning up broken glass. "Let's take a break," he told Bridget. Banyan reached out with his enhanced hearing when he didn't immediately see Rocky anywhere. The women's restroom door was open, and the small room was empty. "Have either of you seen Rocky?" he asked the two employees who were hauling the broken chairs outside. They both responded they hadn't, and Banyan began to get worried. "Rocky?" he called out. When he received no answer, he took the steps to her apartment two at a time. It, too, was empty of its occupant. Banyan practically jumped down the stairs, and by this time, Bridget had caught on to Rocky's disappearance and was yelling for her friend.

Banyan took off out the back door calling her name. When he received no answer, he reached out with all his Gargoyle senses. There was no sound out of the ordinary, but the one thing he did notice caused his heart to stop. The coppery scent of blood wafted to him, and Banyan ran the short distance to the Dumpster. There on the ground was Rocky, knife in her hand, and puddles of blood beneath both wrists. "Oh, Fuck. Rocky, what did you do? Bridget, call an ambulance," Banyan pled when the woman walked up behind him.

"Rocky!" Bridget cried, dropping to her knees.

"Bridget, call a godsdamned ambulance," Banyan yelled. Bridget snapped her head to him, but his tone broke her out of her shock, and she pulled her cell phone out of her back pocket, making the call. Banyan already knew there was a pulse, but it was fading fast. He stripped his shirt over his head, tore it into long pieces, and tied the strips around each of Rocky's wrists. "Don't you die on me, Raquel. Sin will have my head if you do." Once he had her wrists secured, Banyan called Dr. Mercato and told him what was going on. Rocky had lost too much blood, and Sin was across the pond on a business trip in Rafael's place. With Bridget standing so close, Banyan couldn't come out and say what he needed to, but the doctor understood Banyan's meaning.

"We'll do all we can to save her, Banyan. I suggest you get a hold of Sinclair and get him home. The King will understand. I'll meet you at the ER."

Banyan immediately called Sin's phone, but it went to voicemail. He checked the time, and Sin would still be in the air with probably five more hours left in the flight. If he couldn't get hold of him before he landed, it would be late the next day before he could get back home. They didn't have that kind of time. Rocky was fading fast. Banyan called Finley and told him what was going on. He asked him to continue trying to get in touch with Sin and to also call Rafael and fill him in. They had to let Sinclair know about his mate. It was imperative.

While they waited for the paramedics, Bridget sat on the ground beside Rocky, holding one of her bandaged hands. "Why would she do this? I mean, I know shit's bad with the break-in and all, but it wasn't *that* bad." Tears streamed down the woman's face, and Banyan didn't know how to comfort her. He was thinking the same thing. She had been visibly upset when they walked into the bar and found it vandalized, but it was Banyan's trouble now, not hers. She had spent the night with Sinclair, and when they were together in the kitchen that morning, it was clear on her face she was feeling the pull of the mate bond.

Banyan had been told part of Rocky's past, and he admired the young woman for coming through the other side. He couldn't say she was unscathed, but Rocky was still standing. Still, Banyan had only just met the woman and didn't truly know the faces of her demons. Sin told Banyan and Finley that Rocky had confided in him, so maybe Sin knew her secrets. Still, he refused to believe things were so bad she would take her own life. He stood from where he was crouched, and Banyan called Rett. He wanted the cop to go over every inch of the area outside to make sure there hadn't been someone there to help Rocky slit her wrists.

Once the paramedics arrived and had her loaded, Banyan rode in the ambulance with Rocky, because if she flatlined, he was going to do something really stupid like cut open a vein and drip his Original blood into her mouth. It had worked with Desi, even though it had been mixed with Simone's blood, but there was no way he was letting Rocky die on his watch. If that happened, he would have two choices. He could die at the hands of Sinclair or move far away from the Goyle. Neither appealed to him.

Dr. Mercato was waiting at the emergency room as promised. He called out instructions to the staff, and Rocky was rolled away to a private room. Banyan was taken to a room close by where a tech set him up to remove some of his blood. John explained how Banyan and Rocky were the same type, and his staff didn't question his authority. If they happened to test either one of them, they'd see he had lied. As soon as the tech had drawn a pint, she took it to the doctor, who immediately began the transfusion himself. Banyan stood right inside the door, staying out of the way. Rarely did he pray, but standing there helpless, he sent up a request to the gods they keep her alive at least until Sinclair could return home. Banyan had no doubt the despair

Sinclair would succumb to if she were to die while he was away.

Dr. Mercato excused the nurse so he could speak with Banyan privately. "Miss Cartwright's blood is laced with drugs. I can smell it. I have drawn some and will test it myself. I need to know what she's fighting so I'll know how to treat her."

Banyan grabbed his neck and rubbed. This was getting worse, and he was going to have to face Sinclair and admit he let both Sin and Rocky down.

"I know that look, Brother, but you cannot beat yourself up over this."

"I don't have to. Sin will do that for me."

"No, he won't. I've known Sinclair for many years. He's a good male."

"But this is his mate, John. He trusted me to watch out for her, and I didn't. She's fighting for her life because of my carelessness."

"Nothing I say is going to make you feel better, so I'll leave you to your self-loathing, but know this; I'm not going to let her die. I'll do whatever is necessary to keep her alive and see that she recovers fully." John clapped him on the shoulder and turned his attention to his patient. Banyan walked to the other side of the bed and picked up Rocky's hand. He stayed there, by her side, until Vivian arrived. He left Rocky with her best friend, and Banyan made the call he dreaded.

Finley was torn between sitting at the hospital and helping Rett find the ones responsible for Rocky's condition. He and Banyan had promised to protect Rocky in Sin's absence, and they'd failed. Fin should have gone with them to the bar to be an extra set of eyes. Instead, he had gone to spar with Urijah and the others. Uri had called stating they

217

were a male short, so Fin had jumped at the chance to get in some physical activity. He had left Rocky's security in Banyan's hands, and now she was fighting for her life. Not that Finley was blaming Banyan. On the contrary; Fin was blaming himself.

He had freaked out that morning when Sinclair asked Finley to stay with Rocky at Sin's home. It wasn't that Finley didn't trust himself around Rocky. Knowing she was Sin's mate was all he needed to keep his hands off her. But just a few nights ago they were supposed to have had sex. If Rocky's schedule had been different, he would have taken her and Vivian to Sinclair's home instead of Dana. Fin was attracted to Rocky before he knew she was Sin's mate, and even now, having that knowledge, he was still attracted to her. That didn't mean he would dishonor himself by approaching Rocky in an inappropriate way, but he didn't want there to be any sort of misunderstanding where they were concerned.

He was already skating on thin ice with Banyan over Urijah. It didn't take long to figure out there was something between his best friend and Banyan the first time he saw the two of them together. It wasn't until they were shooting pool that Finley felt their connection, even if they were denying it. Uri refused to speak of the years he spent in New Orleans, but Finley knew deep down something went on between him and Banyan. The longing on Banyan's face when he stared at Uri was undeniable. It was tangible. It was heart-breaking. Fin decided then and there to keep things strictly platonic from that point on with his best friend. No way would Finley knowingly cross the line with another Gargoyle's mate.

Rett had come in the waiting room and filled Fin and the others in on what he had found at the bar. CSU had looked at the area and said it was impossible to know someone had been around Rocky at the time of her incident, but Rett had been able to detect the same scent around the

Dumpster as he had inside. "There were two distinct human scents other than Rocky's. When the cops canvased the area, a local security camera had caught the images of both a man and a woman running from that direction. Their faces weren't clear, so I've asked the lead detective to begin looking at all the cameras in the vicinity, but with it being such a secluded location, it's doubtful they'll find anything. I'm going to canvas the area one more time and talk to all the other shop owners."

"I'll go with you," Finley said.

Vivian was sitting with Rocky, and Remy was standing guard outside her door. Banyan had been pacing the hallway trying to get hold of Sin on the phone. The least Finley could do was to help Rett talk to people.

Sin's phone vibrated. He couldn't help the smile that crossed his face when he thought it would be a text from Rocky. What he found was several missed calls and about twenty text messages from various people. Before he could check them all, the flight attendant left the cockpit and stopped beside his chair. "Mr. Stone, we have an emergency." Sin rarely flew with a full crew, but it was necessary to have at least one person to assist the captain. "Yes, Andre. What is it?"

"Sir, the King called the captain when he couldn't reach you. There is an emergency back home, and we are rerouting our trip so we can get you back to New Angeles as quickly as possible."

They had stopped in London to refuel and hadn't been in the air long at all. "What is the emergency?"

"I'm sorry. I wasn't given the details."

Sin waved his apology off. "Thank you, Andre. I will call Rafael now." Before he dialed his brother's number, Sin scrolled through all the voicemails and texts to find the one

219

from Rocky.

Miss you, baby.

Rocky had yet to refer to him with a term of endearment, even though he'd used several with her. Maybe the time apart had softened her to him. Smiling to himself, Sin called Rafael.

"Sinclair..."

"Rafe, what the fuck is going on? Is Kaya okay? What is so important that we would abort rescuing Mother?"

"Sin, it's Rocky."

"Rocky? She is fine. I just received a text from her."

"No, Brother. She isn't fine. I hate to tell you this, but a lot happened after you boarded the flight. She and Banyan arrived at RC's only to find it had been vandalized."

"Was anyone hurt?" Sin interrupted, getting agitated. That wasn't an emergency. The bar was Banyan's, and he could clean up the mess.

"No, but afterwards when everyone was cleaning up, Rocky went missing. Banyan found her out back by the Dumpster. Sin, Rocky had cut her wrists."

Now Sin was getting pissed. "That is impossible, Rafe. Like I said, I received a text from her. I..."

"Sinclair, fucking listen to me. Rocky is in the hospital. Dr. Mercato has given her some of Banyan's blood hoping it will help stabilize her, but Brother, you have to know, she's barely hanging on."

The blood pounded in Sin's ears making Rafe's voice fade in and out. This was a mistake. "Hang on a second," he practically shouted at his brother. Sin checked the time stamp on the text Rocky sent. It was a little over an hour ago. "Rafe, her text was sent an hour ago. When did this happen?"

"About three hours ago. We've all been trying to reach you."

"Fuck. FUCK!" Sinclair roared. He didn't

understand how he could get a text from his mate saying she missed him if she'd tried to kill herself. "Wait, did you say she cut her wrists? Rocky wouldn't do that."

"Sin, you just met her. You don't know what she's capable of. Banyan said she was upset when she found her bar in disarray."

"It is not her bar; it's Banyan's, and I do know her, Rafe. I might have just met her, but I know her heart. She is strong, and she is a fighter. With all the shit she has been through in her short life, finding her bar vandalized would be a walk in the park compared to everything else. Don't you think it is a coincidence this happens within hours of the other? Something is off, I know it. My girl didn't do this to herself. Would you have believed Kaya capable of suicide the first day you met her?"

"No, but Kaya was chief of police. She was strong. In control. Rocky's an ex-..."

"An ex what, Rafe? An ex-junkie? A former stripper? These things are in her past. She is no longer that person. You have to believe me."

"I believe you, but we need to look at the evidence set out before us."

"I don't have to look at shit. I know my girl did not try to off herself. Now, I am going to hang up and call Julian. I need someone to trace the text coming from her godsdamn phone." Sinclair disconnected the call and dialed his cousin's number, doing his best to get his breathing as well as his ire under control. When this was all over, he and his older brother were going to have words.

"Sinclair? Landon. What can I do for you?"

"Landon, why are you answering Julian's phone?"

"He's concentrating on a lead he may have with regards to his mate."

"Good. That's good. Listen, I need you to find out where my mate's phone is. I've received a couple of texts from her, but she doesn't have her phone on her." Sin

221

rattled off the phone number.

"Got it. I'll call you back as soon as I have it."

"Call Banyan first. I am on my way back from London, and he needs this information before I do. Landon, this is top priority. Someone tried to kill my mate, and I need to know who it is."

"Sin, last we spoke you didn't have a mate."

"Things can change in the blink of an eye, Landon. Do not ever forget that." Sin thumbed off his phone and stood. He began pacing the short length of the cabin while he waited on Banyan to answer his phone.

"Sin…"

"What happened?" he asked, doing his best to keep his voice even.

"She was cleaning up behind the bar, so I sat down with Bridget to go over some paperwork. Sin, I'm so sorry."

"Stop with the apologies and tell me how she is."

"Hanging in there. Barely."

"I am on my way, but it is going to take at least nine hours to get there. I know she didn't do this to herself, Banyan."

"I believe you, Brother. Not only were her wrists cut, but John found evidence of drugs in her system. Sin, whatever she was injected with was so much worse than last time. This mixture was meant to kill her. Dr. Mercato's doing what he can. He gave her some of my blood, but it would be best if she had yours to go with it."

Sin tamped down the need to roar. "I have received a text from her phone since she was taken to the hospital. Whoever did this is stupid enough to think a text will appease me. I've sent the number to Landon. He is going to call you first when he figures out where her phone is."

"You got it. Wait, hang on a sec…" Even though Banyan covered the phone with his hand, Sin could still hear his and Rett's voices.

"Sin, Rett found something. A video camera at one

of the stores caught two people, a man and a woman, running down the alley away from the Dumpster. CSU is running their images to see if they get a match."

"Have him send the images to Landon. Julian has programs in place that are ten times faster than what the local government has access to."

"Will do. Anything else?"

"Keep my girl alive until I get there." Sin hung up and scrubbed his free hand down his face, stopping when he got to his chin. His chin that was void of the whiskers Rocky loved so much. Sin continued to pace back and forth as he fought for control over his anger. He'd left his mate in capable hands, or so he thought. Yes, he had. It wasn't their fault, not really. It was his. Sin should have taken Rocky with him and brought enough Goyles to watch over her while he was looking for his mother and pretending to be Rafael. She was his mate and his responsibility. Getting mad at Banyan and Finley wouldn't change what had happened, but it would change the way Sin handled his mate's safety going forward.

Sin stopped pacing and poured a tall glassful of some Irish whiskey Jasper had left on the jet. As he sipped the smooth liquor, Sin reflected on the other male's life. Jasper's had been colorful and full of adventure, even if some of it had been marred with a crazed Goyle stalking him over the years. Sin had no wild tales or exotic adventures. He, like Rafael, had been a good and dutiful son to their father, the King. They, along with Gregor and Dante, had spread out over the States when Rafael took their father's place. Sin wasn't complaining; he had thought his life full until now. He'd longed for a mate, but he didn't realize how empty his life had truly been before meeting Raquel. Now that he'd finally been blessed by the fates, Sin was afraid they were toying with him. He had some bad qualities, and he wasn't always the best Gargoyle, but he did try his best to honor his duty to his King, his Clan, and the humans. If Raquel didn't pull through, Sin wasn't sure he could remain the good and faithful servant. He was afraid he would lose all hope and wish to pass over to the other side, because without his mate, his life would be forfeit. For the first time in almost six hundred years, Sinclair Stone was scared.

Chapter Twenty-One

"You did what?" Blake yelled at the idiots standing before him.

"She'll live. The cuts weren't that deep, and I did them horizontally. She'll lose a little blood, and when she starts to come around, she'll need another fix. Now give me my money," Tommy said, holding out his hand.

"I told you I was handling it! That's it. I'm done listening to your bullshit. For three years you've been telling me Raquel would come around. That she would get so low she'd sign the bar right over. Well, she did. TO SOMEONE ELSE!" Blake wiped the spit off his mouth and adjusted his coat. Blake's inside man at the bar had called moments earlier to inform him Raquel had sold the bar to some big motherfucker who'd been coming into RC's the past two nights.

"You had her here, but you lost her. That's on you," Tommy said, poking Blake's chest with his finger.

"I didn't *lose* her. One of the girls followed me down to the basement. When she saw I had Rocky, she freaked. I explained that Rocky had wanted to get high, but I didn't have time to babysit, and I asked the girl to take her home," Blake countered, getting in Tommy's face.

"Yeah, well it's not my fault you had to drug the bitch to get her to fuck you. She gave it up to me for free," Tommy bragged, laughing.

The girl standing next to Tommy gasped and backed away from him. "You fucked your own cousin?"

Blake shook his head and also put a little room between himself and the other man. "Goddamn, Tommy. You're even sicker than I thought. We're done here. I don't want you coming around anymore. When the cops figure out you're the one who cut her wrists, I don't want them to

225

have any way to tie you to me."

"You forget, buddy boy, we *are* tied together. The drugs came from your club, and your fingerprints are all over the bags."

"I'll tell the cops you stole them from me."

"And you'll still go to jail for possession."

"I'd rather spend a few years behind bars for possession than murder one." Blake was pissed beyond measure, but he kept his face impassive in front of this loser. When Tommy refused to leave without the money Blake owed him, Blake pulled a 9mm out of the holster at his hip. A 9mm he'd stolen from Raquel's bedside table the last time he'd slipped unknown into her apartment.

Cocking the hammer back, Blake leveled the gun at Tommy's head. The woman continued to back up towards the door, but Blake let her go. She was too stupid to rat either one of them out. "I should shoot you for raping Raquel."

"You can't rape a willing bitch," Tommy sneered. Blake knew Tommy's taste in women ran along the young side. The side younger than legal, and he had a feeling it started while Raquel was living under the same roof. Thinking of this bastard putting his dick anywhere near Raquel had bile rising in his throat. He swallowed it down and took a step forward, putting the barrel to Tommy's forehead.

"You would do well to get out of here now, before my finger happens to slip. And Tommy? If Raquel doesn't pull through, you won't have to worry about the cops, because I'll kill you myself."

Tommy spit in Blake's face. "I'll get my money one way or another, you sorry motherfucker." The threat wasn't an idle one; Blake knew this. If the man was crazy enough to slit his cousin's wrists, he was crazy enough to come back for the money.

God, he'd been so stupid to trust the loser in the

beginning. When Blake first met Tommy, the man was coming into the strip club every night the doors were open. He was a bad tipper, but he didn't bother the dancers. He ordered the watered down Scotch and nursed one as long as he could. He was a cheap bastard. When the crowds began thinning out, Tommy asked Blake what was going on. He'd made the mistake of confiding in the man that things were going downhill fast, and if he didn't find someone new and fresh to generate more business, he'd end up closing the doors.

Tommy told Blake about his hot cousin who'd inherited their uncle's bar. A bar that was doing really well. Once Blake "got all up in that" as Tommy put it, he could wrangle the bar away from her. Tommy had also introduced Blake to the drugs. At first it was roofies, but Tommy eased him into the hard stuff much the same way Blake had eased Rocky into it, a little at a time. Blake grasped at the lure Tommy dangled above his sinking head. He took the bait, and Tommy dragged him out of the water onto the waiting shoreline, ripping the hook out of his jaw. Blake had been ready to close the club. To give up everything. But once he got a glimpse of Tommy's cousin, Blake was done for. One look at Raquel Cartwright, and Blake was heels over fucking head smitten with the raven-haired beauty, that's how much she tore him up. Blake had to have her. The girl was almost perfect. The only thing missing had been big tits, and Blake eventually convinced Raquel to have hers enhanced. *Then* she'd been fucking perfect.

Raquel hadn't wanted to go out with Blake, so when he finally convinced her to go to dinner with him, he didn't take a chance on it being a one-time deal. He slipped her a little something to make her more amenable to sex with him. He didn't give her a full dose. Not the first time. Blake eased Rocky into it so she didn't get suspicious. By the time he had her good and hooked, Raquel was willing to do anything he asked just so she could get her next fix. And by anything, he meant *anything*. Even stoned, Raquel was the best lay he'd ever had. And god-damn! Could the girl dance! She was the reason the club went from near bankruptcy to tipping the scales to the black side of the column. Yes siree, his Raquel was something else. Until that bitch Vivian came in and hauled her away.

Somehow, Blake would get Raquel back, and when he did, he'd never let her escape. Not again. He needed a plan. One that didn't involve Tommy.

"Don't move, motherfucker." Cold metal met Blake's head as a sinister voice met his ear.

That wasn't part of his plan.

Sin knew the pilot could only go so fast, but he was ready to throw the Goyle out of the cockpit and take over the controls. Not that he'd ever flown a plane before, but he could call Frey, and his cousin could talk him through it. Thinking of the large Goyle, Sin thought back to what Frey went through when Abby had almost died. Frey's pretty mate had been raped by her husband before he tossed her over a bridge. Luckily, Frey had phased and flown fast enough to catch Abby right before she hit the concrete below. Still, she had been unconscious, and had Frey not bitten her, she'd have died.

If Rocky was still unconscious when he arrived at the hospital, he was going to bite her and count on whatever it was in their saliva being enough to save her as it had Abby. Sin's phone rang, halting his pacing. When he saw his cousin's name on the caller ID, Sin prayed Julian, or Landon, had good news.

"Go ahead," he answered, since he didn't know who was calling.

"I have good news and bad news. The good news is I located Rocky's phone. Whoever took it wasn't smart enough to turn it off. I traced it to a club in New Pasadena. It's a strip club owned by Blake Stansbury. I checked it out, and it's a really shady place. The owner sells drugs out of a back room."

Sin didn't want to hear how bad the club where his mate used to dance was. "What's the bad?"

"The phone didn't remain static. After remaining still for twenty minutes, it started moving, but I lost the signal once it had gone about thirty blocks."

"Did you call Banyan?"

"Yes. Finley and Rett are headed to the club to see if they can get anything out of the owner."

"Thanks, Landon." Sin disconnected and dialed Finley.

"Sin, we're about to go in and question Stansbury," Fin said as soon as he picked up.

"Call me back as soon as you have something." Sin disconnected and sat down in one of the leather captain's chairs. Neither pacing nor drinking was doing him any good. It made the beast even more restless. Sin closed his eyes and concentrated on his mate. The other males who had found their own mates had shared stories of being able to connect with them spiritually. Since Sin had bitten Rocky, even if it hadn't been deep, he was hoping the little bit of transference was enough to bond them together. It might not work since she didn't know the significance of the bite, but he had to try.

Sin called forth all the memories he had with Rocky. There weren't many, but most of the ones he had were good ones, especially when they shared a kiss. Concentrating, as Frey had taught them all to do, Sinclair emptied his mind of everything except the feel of Rocky's lips on his. The way her tongue melded to his in the perfect slow dance. The sweet smell of her oxygen as Sin breathed her into his lungs. The way her body arched into his to get even closer.

"Rocky…"

Rocky sat at the water's edge, giggling every time a wave broke and the foam covered her feet. Her parents were lying together on a blanket, lost in each other as they always were. They didn't have a lot of time or money to go on vacations like most families, but Rocky didn't care. It was days like this she cherished. Just the three of them. Laughing and loving, even if they weren't doing anything thrilling. Rocky loved seeing her parents together. She was only ten, but she understood those silent moments the two of them shared. She wanted that for herself. One day, she would have a boyfriend who looked at her the way her dad looked at her mom. He would be tall and strong, and he would move heaven and earth for her. Words wouldn't be needed. He would be able to touch her, and she would feel the love without the words.

Something weird happened with the waves. They stopped rolling in. The water had calmed to an eerie silence, and the wind was no longer blowing. She stood to go back to her parents, but they weren't there. Rocky scanned the beach and found herself alone. "Momma! Daddy!" she yelled. Frantic, Rocky ran toward where they'd parked the car thinking they had packed up and left her there. As she struggled with the thick sand, Rocky tripped, falling to her knees.

Tears rolled down her cheeks. "Momma!" Rocky screamed again, her voice breaking on a sob.

"I'm here, Rocky." Her mother's sweet voice called to her, but Rocky couldn't see her.

"Where, Momma? Where are you? I can't see you!"

"I'm here with your father, sweet girl. We're both watching over you."

Rocky couldn't see her parents, but she wanted to.

230

She wanted to be back with them. She missed them terribly. Bad stuff happened when they weren't there to protect her. Too much bad stuff. "Here, Momma. Take my hand. I need you." Still on her knees, Rocky reached out blindly, praying her mother would latch on and pull her to where they were.

"Rocky?" Someone else called out to her, but whoever the voice belonged to was far away.

"Beautiful girl?" This time it was closer, but still faint.

Rocky looked around for the man. Why was it familiar? Why couldn't she see anyone? "Momma, help me."

"Rocky, can you hear me?" The man's voice was closer still, but this time was panicked.

"Who are you?" Rocky was confused, and she was scared. Normally she didn't mind being alone, but the stillness around her wasn't normal. The ocean was unmoving, like Poseidon himself had calmed it. There were no seagulls circling overhead looking for a crumb of food. No crabs scampering along the sand. No breeze pushing her hair around her face.

The deep voice echoed around her. "It's me, beautiful girl. Sinclair."

That name sounded familiar, but she didn't know him. "Stay away from me. I don't know you. I want my parents. I need to see them."

Something surfaced at the back of Rocky's brain. Something sinister that had the hair on her arms standing up. A man... Was he this Sinclair? She didn't think so, but she couldn't be sure. "Momma, where are you?"

"I'm here, sweet girl."

"I need you. Why can't I see you?"

"It's not time. Fight, Rocky girl. You have a lot of living left to do."

"But I'm scared."

"It's okay to be scared, but we're watching over you,

honey," her father added.

"Daddy?" Rocky wrapped her arms around her waist and sobbed harder than she could remember ever doing. She missed her father. He was the only man she'd ever been able to trust. Even Uncle Ray had left her alone with her aunt Linda and Tommy.

"I'm here, baby girl. But your mother's right; you need to fight. It's not your time."

"Rocky? Are you there, beautiful girl?" the deep voice whispered along her skin. "Please hang on, baby. I'm coming for you."

Rocky sank down deeper in the sand, burying her face against her knees. "No, please don't leave me alone with him," she silently begged her parents.

Sinclair concentrated on his mate. "*Rocky...*"

"*Who are you?*" Rocky asked. Yes! He'd made contact, but wait...

"*It's me, beautiful girl. Sinclair.*"

"*Stay away from me. I don't know you. I want my parents. I need to see them.*" But Rocky's parents were dead. Was she even talking to him?

"*Momma, where are you? I need you. Why can't I see you?*" His wasn't the only voice she was hearing. But if she could hear her parents, that mean she was worse off than anyone knew. She was closer to crossing over than they realized.

"*Raquel, it's me, Sinclair.*"

"*But I'm scared. Daddy?*"

Both her parents were reaching out for her.

"*No, you cannot go to them, Rocky! Listen to me, it's Sinclair. You are my mate. You can't leave me!*"

"*Rocky? Are you there, beautiful girl? Please hang on, baby. I'm coming for you.*"

Sin lost contact with Rocky, and he let out a roar that shook the plane. Andre immediately rushed to where Sin stood, staying far enough away where Sin couldn't reach him with his claws. Most of the employees of the Stone Society were human. Their families had been serving the Gargoyles for centuries. Andre was one of those, so he was well aware of the extra appendages the Goyles had. He also knew to keep his distance when one was upset. The man kept quiet while he waited for Sin to either phase back or turn on him. Sin calmed down and retracted both his fangs and claws.

"Sorry," Sin muttered.

"Please, do not apologize. I have a wife at home, and even though we don't have the mate bond that's present in your kind, I still feel a deep connection to her. If she were in the hospital and I were on an airplane thousands of miles away, I wouldn't be calm either."

Sinclair often forgot that those who served the Clan had families of their own. He had no doubt Andre loved his wife as much as Rafael loved Kaya. Did Sin love Rocky? He had strong feelings for her that went beyond sex, but he couldn't be sure if it was love. Not yet. That would come with time as they spent more of it together. "How is Carla?" Sin asked.

"More beautiful than ever. She's about two weeks from giving me my third son," the man beamed.

Sin wasn't aware Andre had two kids already. He felt like a dick for not taking the time to know this man who was available at the Clan's beck and call. "Andre, congratulations. Why don't you pour us both a drink and tell me about your family." Not only could Sin get to know Andre, listening to the man would help keep his mind off Rocky if only for a short while.

Even though he wasn't hungry, Sin allowed Andre to serve him dinner, but Sin had asked the flight attendant to join him instead of eating in the galley. They both talked about their families – Andre about his wife and two little boys, and Sin about him and his brothers growing up. He kept the conversation away from Rocky, and the human didn't pry. When it was closing in on midnight, Sin made his way to the cockpit to check in with the pilot. For domestic trips, the Clan employed a human, but for the international flights, they used a Gargoyle in case an emergency arose. Having to turn around at the eleven-hour mark had definitely been an emergency. Since the pilot was a Goyle, there wasn't the risk of him falling asleep from exhaustion.

Frey had recruited Bryce Stark when the two of them served in the military together. The male had been a Goyle without a country or Clan, and he'd been ecstatic to be offered both. "Everything okay now?" Bryce asked as Sin took the empty seat next to him.

"Not really, Brother. I will not be okay until I see my mate's beautiful eyes staring back into mine."

"I take it Andre's still alive back there?" Bryce asked with a smirk.

"Yes, he still has his head." Sin leaned his head back and stared out at the starless night. "I meditated the way Frey taught us, and I was able to make contact with Rocky, but she's barely hanging on. Talking to her dead parents even."

"No wonder you lost your shit. You know I'm flying as fast as this bird will take us."

"I know, and I appreciate it." Sin sat there as long as he could before his beast came alive, begging to make contact with Rocky again. Sin clapped Bryce on the shoulder and made his way to the cabin. Andre had retired to the back to give Sin some space. He took advantage of the quiet and stilled his mind, reaching out for Rocky once more.

234

Chapter Twenty-Two

Finley and Rett canvased the area around the bar as soon as they left the hospital. Unfortunately, nobody had seen or heard anything out of the ordinary, and none of the security cameras had caught the two people's faces. Banyan called and informed them Landon got a hit on Rocky's cell phone at the strip club Blake Stansbury owned. There were several cars in the parking lot, but most of those had probably been left from the night before. One car, an older model Rolls Royce that had seen better days, was parked in a reserved spot. It was well before opening time, and the place was practically empty when Rett and Fin stepped up to the front door. They found the door unlocked, and using their shifter hearing, they both reached out to see who was inside.

Music was coming from down the hallway past the stage and bar area. Laughter floated from inside the room with the music. Fin peered through the crack to find a man snorting a line of coke off a naked woman's stomach. He sprinkled some of the white powder on each of her nipples before licking it off. That might have been appealing to Finley if he did drugs, but knowing what he did about the effects they had on humans, Finley hated the stuff. Rett rolled his eyes when he caught sight of the couple, but he tilted his head toward the end of the hall, indicating they should move.

The door to what appeared to be the office was ajar, giving Rett and Finley enough room to see Blake Stansbury holding a gun and talking to himself. Rett pulled his service pistol and eased through the door, coming up behind Blake. He held the gun to the back of Blake's head and said, "Don't move, motherfucker."

Blake raised both hands, gun pointed to the ceiling.

Finley stepped in and removed the weapon from his hand. Rett twisted Blake's arms behind his back and secured them with handcuffs. When Rett turned him around, Blake seethed, "Who the fuck are you?"

"Right now, I'm the man who holds your future in his hands. You tell me what I want to know, and maybe you'll live." Rett wasn't wearing his uniform, so Blake had no idea he was a policeman.

"Fuck you," Blake spit out.

"Not my type. Now, what do you know about Raquel Cartwright?"

"She used to dance for me."

"Let me rephrase the question; what do you know about her being attacked outside her bar this afternoon, *and* the fact her cell phone was here, in your club, less than an hour ago?"

Blake's eyes enlarged for a second before he schooled his features. "I didn't have her phone."

"Then tell me who did, and tell me where to find them."

"I don't know anything about that."

Rett grabbed Blake around the neck and picked him up, feet dangling a good ten inches above the ground. "I don't think you understand what's happening here, Fuckhead. One more wrong word and I'll snap your neck as easily as a twig. You are a piece of shit motherfucker who drugs women and rapes them. You sell drugs out of this club that caters to piece of shit motherfuckers just like you. Your life means nothing to me. Now, let's try this again. What do you know about Rocky?"

"All right, all right," Blake groaned, his face turning red. Rett dropped him to his feet, and Blake managed to stay upright. He twisted his neck to work out the pain. "Raquel's cousin and his whore came by here earlier. Said he had a little chat with Raquel, but that's *all* he said. Neither one of them mentioned an attack."

"Does this cousin have a name?" Finley asked.

"Tommy. Tommy Cartwright. He lives at home with his mother."

Just as Finley turned to step out into the hallway to call Banyan, the man who'd been snorting coke burst into the office. "Blake, you okay?" Finley stepped in front of the man, not allowing him to move farther into the room. Finley wasn't the largest Gargoyle in the Clan, but he had quite a bit of size on the man before him who was obviously not thinking straight. "You better step off," he said to Finley, spewing spit and swinging his finger in front of him.

With his back to Blake and Rett, Finley dropped his fangs and hissed at the man. The guy scrambled backwards and took off down the hall. Finley followed him, but only far enough he could use the phone in private. Banyan had already been researching Rocky's cousin, so Finley called him to get more information.

"Finley, were you successful?" Banyan asked when he answered his phone.

"Stansbury says Tommy Cartwright and a woman came in earlier. The cousin mentioned having a chat with Rocky, but that's it. Stansbury claims he knows nothing, but I don't believe him. He did know Cartwright lives at home with his mother. I need that address."

"I don't have my notes with me, but I do remember the address being accessible through public records. Hang on a second."

While Banyan was looking up the address, Finley eased his way toward the front of the building where two men were having a conversation. The guy who threatened him was talking animatedly to another male about what he saw. Before Fin could do anything about them, Banyan returned to the line. "I texted the address to you. It's in the same direction Rocky's phone was traveling before we lost the signal."

"Thanks, Banyan. We will head that way now."

"What about Stansbury?"

"The club will be closed tonight, because the owner will be tied up until further notice." Finley hung up and stalked to the front of the club. "Out, now." Finley pointed to the door, and the man he'd encountered in the office grabbed his buddy and dragged him out the front door. "Hello? Anyone here?" Finley yelled. The woman who'd been serving as a cocaine tray appeared from behind the stage wearing a see-through robe.

"What can I do for you?" she purred as she walked toward him. When she was close enough, the woman ran a long fingernail down Finley's chest. He grabbed her wrist before she could go too low.

"Who's here besides you?"

"A couple of bouncers and the owner. We're not open yet, but I'm sure the boss wouldn't mind if I snuck you in a lap dance."

"Get dressed and get out of here. If there's anyone else backstage, they need to leave, too. Club's closed for the night."

"Who are you?"

"ATF. Your alcohol license has been pulled. Now go on and get out of here."

The woman took Finley at his word without asking for identification and returned the way she'd come. Once he made sure the club was clear, he locked the front door. Not that it would keep employees with a key out, but at least patrons couldn't stroll in. When Finley returned to the office, Rett wasn't there. He listened for movement and found Rett in the basement with Blake. Rett had the unconscious man secured to a pole with a rag in his mouth. "I've called for back-up. I want to get over to Cartwright's house."

Before they left, Fin found a piece of paper and wrote "Closed Until Further Notice" on it and taped it to the front door. He and Rett exited through the back and drove across town to the address Banyan had given. Tension was mounting in both Goyles as they neared Tommy's home. Finley asked Rett if he was going to do things by the book. "No, Brother. This is a mate we're talking about. I'm doing things by the Clan's book."

"Won't you get in trouble?"

"Don't much care if I do. I've been in Cali long enough that if I need to move, I can. I like it here, but I'm about ready for a change of scenery. We'll get to the bottom of what happened with Rocky. If there's fallout, I'll disappear, but not before we make this motherfucker pay for what he did to his cousin." Finley appreciated the Goyle's loyalty to Sinclair over his job.

The house Tommy lived in with his mother was rather large but also fairly rundown. This was the house Rocky grew up in after her parents died. An older model car sat in the driveway, and the house was dark. Fin and Rett parked a few houses down and walked silently to the Cartwright place. They circled the house in different directions and met on the other side.

"I have voices coming from down below," Rett said.

Rett checked the back door and found it unlocked. They eased their way inside using their shifter sight to navigate in the dark. The kitchen was cluttered. The sink was overflowing with dishes that hadn't been washed in days. Finley did his best not to gag on the smell of rotting meat coming from the garbage can. He didn't want to imagine Rocky having to live in this when she was growing up. Rett slapped his hand over his nose and shook his head. Fin followed the cop until they came to a stairway leading down to the basement. The voices downstairs were getting louder, and the woman's voice was getting higher pitched.

"Stop it, Tommy. Why don't you go fuck your cousin? Oh, that's right, you can't, because you tried to fucking kill her! I never agreed to that shit."

"I wasn't killing her; I was teaching the bitch a

lesson. Don't go getting all high and mighty on me now. You hated her just as much as I did."

"Not enough to go to jail for murder. God, you're so stupid!"

"What the fuck did you say?"

"Ow! Stop it. You're hurting me!"

Rett didn't need to hear anymore. He eased his way down the stairs quietly but quickly with Fin right behind. When they reached the bottom step, Tommy Cartwright ripped his girlfriend's shirt off as she tried to get away from him.

"You have nowhere to run, you stupid cunt," he seethed as he grabbed a handful of hair, jerking her backwards.

"Actually, she does," Rett said calmly.

Tommy whirled on them. "Who the fuck are you?" he asked while looking around.

Finley held up Tommy's pistol. "Looking for this?"

Tommy pulled Shelby to his front, using her as a shield. "I don't have any money. Here, take her," he said, pushing his girlfriend in their direction. She gasped and did her best to skirt around Finley, but he stepped in her way.

"Not so fast. Just because he's a piece of shit and treats you like one doesn't mean you're without guilt. Sit down," Fin roared. Shelby scrambled backwards to what once was an overstuffed chair. Now it was flat and covered in stains. Fin didn't want to even begin to think about what those were from.

Rett closed the distance between him and Tommy. "What did you give Rocky?"

"I don't know what you're talking about, man."

With his back to Shelby, Rett let his fangs drop. "Bull fucking shit. You just admitted to trying to teach her a lesson. I want to know what the fuck you injected into her system. You have one chance to answer, and it better be the truth, because I swear to the gods, I will gut you where you

240

fucking stand if you lie to me."

"Wha... what are you?" Tommy whispered as piss ran down his leg.

"I'm your fucking judge, jury, and executioner. Tell me what you gave her!" Rett roared.

Shelby pulled her knees to her chest, closed her eyes, and covered her ears.

"I don't know what was in it. I swear to Christ! I was doing a job for someone. He gave me the drugs, man. I swear!" Tommy was shaking and snot was rolling down his upper lip. He wiped at his nose with the back of his hand.

"Who hired you to do this job?" Finley asked. His quiet voice contradicted the anger building deep inside. His shifter was ready to tear this miscreant apart with his claws.

"Blake Stansbury. He was pissed that Rocky quit dancing. He was trying to get her hooked on drugs again so he'd have a shot at her."

"How much was he paying you?"

"Paying me?" Tommy asked, confused.

"Yeah, to drug Rocky. How much was he paying you? The way I see it, it must have been a helluva lot of money for you to hurt your own cousin. Your own family. Where I come from, family means something. Family means everything. So how much was betraying your family worth?" Rett took a step closer, pulling up to his full height. He had retracted his fangs, but when he got right up in Tommy's space, Rett let his claws loose and gripped Tommy's face. "Tell me what that was worth to you," Rett whispered. Fin made sure he was between Shelby and Rett, but even if he hadn't been shielding the Goyle, Shelby still had her face buried against her legs.

"Answer me!" Rett roared again.

"Money and women," Tommy answered.

Shelby lifted her head at his admission. "Women? You've been cheating on me?"

"You stupid bitch. I met you in a titty bar. Did you

241

honestly think you were the only one I was fucking?" The crack of Rett's fist on Tommy's face shut him up.

"I can't stay here," Shelby cried.

"You're not going anywhere until we establish your role in what happened to Rocky today. While Tommy gets his shit together, why don't you tell me what you did to Rocky and why. I don't think it was for the women."

"I swear I didn't..."

"Stop," Finley warned. "We have you on video running away from the bar. You need to think long and hard on whether or not he's worth your loyalty." Finley thumbed behind him, indicating Tommy. "Let's you and I go upstairs where we can talk in private." He wrapped his hand around her bicep and not so gently led Shelby up the stairs.

Tommy called after her, "Don't you open your fucking mou..." Another loud crack echoed up the steps.

"Sit," Finley ordered. Shelby sat down at the kitchen table, her hands clasped in front of her. "Now, if you don't want to go to jail for murder, I suggest you tell me what I want to know."

"Murder? But we didn't kill her. Tommy only cut her..." Shelby clapped a hand over her mouth when she realized what she'd said.

"Tommy only cut her what? Deep enough to make it look like suicide? Well I have news for you. He cut her deeper than that."

Shelby jumped up from her chair, but Finley growled, "Sit your ass down." The woman did as he said. "You need to listen and listen good. You need to tell me, right fucking now, every godsdamn thing you know, everything you've done, everything Tommy's said or done, *and* everything you know about Blake Stansbury. You get one shot at this, and if you lie, if you omit any pertinent information, you can kiss your freedom goodbye. Do you understand?"

242

The woman shook her head up and down, but didn't say anything. Instead, she looked toward the door leading down the steps. "Don't worry about Tommy. He won't be able to hurt you." Finley had kept his ears open for what was going on down in the basement. Tommy Cartwright was singing like the little bitch he was, spilling his guts to Rett. In the end, it wouldn't matter that Rett showed his true self to the bastard, because Sin wouldn't allow him to live… not after what he'd done to Rocky. "Now talk."

Shelby twisted her hands together as she began, "I met Tommy at the club. He was one of the regulars, even when shit got bad. He and Blake became real chummy when Tommy convinced him he had a way to keep the club going. Said he had this cousin who'd just come into some real estate. If Blake could get in with her, he could take over her bar and have another source of income. Plus he said she was a looker, and if Blake could convince her to dance, she'd be able to bring back some of the lost crowd."

"They talked about this in front of you?"

"They were doing coke shots off my tits. They either didn't think I was listening or didn't care."

"How did you play into all this?"

"I was working at RC's at the time. I wasn't making shit at the club, so I had to have steady income from somewhere."

"That doesn't explain why you'd go along with ruining someone's life."

"I didn't agree to hurting her, but the bitch fired me as soon as she took over the bar. I needed money, and Tommy wasn't providing it."

"Ah, so a little revenge on your part… It's starting to make sense. Continue."

Shelby squirmed in her chair, and Finley was getting angrier by the second. "I said continue." Fin lowered his voice allowing the shifter to seep through. It wasn't something he did often, because rarely did Finley get angry, but when he did, it wasn't something humans could handle.

The woman shook in her seat. Vibrated with fear, but she found her voice. "I- I didn't know what they had planned other than Blake was going to pursue Rocky. Tommy didn't talk about her around me after he'd mentioned her to Blake. But when he found out she'd fired me, Tommy got pissed."

"Why would he get mad that a stripper got fired?"

"He and I had started dating, and I... I was the only one with a real job. Tommy told me he worked from home, but I didn't know it was selling drugs to Blake until later. This is the first time I've been in Tommy's house, so I didn't know he lived with his mother. He always came to my apartment when he wanted... when we slept together. Blake's drug business was like the club – failing. So when he didn't have men coming in to see the dancers, Tommy didn't have anyone to sell drugs to, and neither one of them made money."

This shit was taking too long, so Finley spurred the woman along. "So Blake got Rocky hooked on drugs, convinced her to dance, and the club was back in business?"

Shelby nodded.

"Rocky left and got clean, and the club started failing again?"

She nodded again.

"Now's where I need you to explain what's gone down this week. Blake drugged Rocky and took her to the club, but for some reason he let her go. Start there."

"He was going to get her hooked again. Said that's the only way she'd dance, and he needed her up on the stage. Somehow he grabbed her and took her back to the club, and I assume that's where he drugged her. One of the other dancers found them downstairs, and instead of keeping her the way he planned, he told whoever it was that Rocky had come looking to get high. He asked her to take Rocky home for him so it didn't look as though he had anything to do with it. Tommy was getting pissed that Blake was taking too long in getting Rocky back on stage, so he decided to help out."

Finley knew the rest but he needed Shelby to admit it out loud. "I'm listening..."

"Tommy figured if he could get Rocky alone, he could haul her back to Blake already drugged. He... we were going to set off the alarm and wait on Rocky to come downstairs. When the alarm didn't go off, Tommy went inside and trashed the bar. Said it should have been his all along. When we heard the front door open, we hid outside. We didn't know she'd have someone with her. Tommy insisted we wait, and as soon as Rocky came outside to smoke, I distracted her while Tommy shot her up."

"Why cut her wrists? If he had her drugged, why go to the trouble of making it look like a suicide?"

"I... I don't know. I had no idea he was going to do that to her. The plan was to grab her and take her to the club. I swear!"

Finley placed his phone to his ear. "Did you get all that? Yes, I'm headed there now." He disconnected the call to Banyan and stood. "You're coming with me," he seethed and grabbed her by the wrist. Finley had never hurt a woman on purpose. He'd vowed to protect humans, but this one and the two men she was in bed with, so to speak, Finley couldn't care less what happened to any of them. If Sinclair didn't take care of them, Finley just might.

Chapter Twenty-Three

The unseen voices called to Rocky, twisting her in circles. Her parents were still urging her to turn back. Several different men were calling her to them. Rocky couldn't see their faces. Couldn't remember their names. She was so tired. She wanted to go to her parents. To end the turmoil. The uncertainty. The pain. Not only the physical pain, but the ache in her heart that had been there for so long. *But you felt love, too.* That was her own voice adding itself to the others.

Rocky didn't know if the love she reminded herself of was real or something she conjured in her mind because she wanted it so badly. She wanted a love like her parents had. *It was real with him.* Him who? There were faces floating around her. Most of them handsome, but a couple were faces that scared her. Faces that wanted to hurt her. No, Rocky didn't want to return only to have those faces do the bad things they'd done to her for so long.

"Hey, beautiful girl. I'm here. Please open your eyes for me." That voice was familiar, but frightening. It commanded attention. Obedience. Rocky shied away from it. Another voice blended with his, and they were talking about her. She tried to concentrate on the words, but they weren't making sense. Something warm spread through Rocky. It wasn't covering like a blanket, but a slow gentle tug at her, filling her with strength. With something else. *Hope.*

"Open your eyes, beautiful girl," the strong voice encouraged. "Rocky, baby, wake up." His strong command was filled with something else. Urgency maybe?

"Can you hear us, Rocky?" This man was softer, less demanding. He was familiar, too, but his tone was soothing. Non-threatening. Rocky turned to look for her parents, but they had already gone back to wherever they were. She was alone now just like she had been ever since they both died. *You're not alone.* No, if the voices in her head were attached to the various faces she'd seen, she wasn't alone. But were these the good guys? Or were they the ones who had hurt her. *They won't hurt you.*

Listening to her own voice, Rocky opened her eyes to find the one with the harsh voice holding her hand. "Hey, beautiful girl," he husked. His eyes were so dark. Haunted. She wanted to pull away, but she was afraid.

She felt a presence on her other side. She turned her head toward it, and the one with the softer voice said, "Welcome back."

There was an instant connection with this man. His eyes were soft and warm. She couldn't help but smile at him. Her throat was dry, and she needed water. When she asked for it, the warm man stood to get the doctor, leaving her alone with the cold man. She begged with her eyes for him not to leave, but he didn't listen. She turned to the one still sitting there, and he reached out his hand. Rocky shrank back. Not because she thought he would actually hurt her, but because she was afraid of what his touch would do to her.

Something about him called to her. He had been louder and more demanding than her parents, and he was the reason she was here and not dead. Of that she was certain. Somehow, this man had infiltrated her mind while she was asleep and begged her to hold on. What kind of magic did he possess that he could call to her on such a level? It had to be magic. Nothing else would explain it. She'd spent so much time under the influence of another man... Blake... She didn't want anyone else to have that type of control over her. No, this man... Sin... she had to keep her guard up around him.

Try as he might, Sin couldn't reach Rocky again. The closer to home he got, the more worried he became. The last time he'd meditated, he caught wisps of her essence, but he never could grab hold of her the way he had the first time. Finley called a couple of hours earlier and replayed the tape recording of Shelby's confession. Tommy's incoherent babbling to Rett had been nothing more than "the bitch deserved it". Both humans were being taken to a secure location until Sin could get there to deal with them. When Finley hung up, he'd been on his way back to the club to get a confession out of Blake Stansbury. Not that a confession would matter to Sin. Blake and Tommy had done enough damage to Rocky in the past, and Sin was going to make sure neither male could ever hurt her again. He instructed Finley to take Stansbury to the same location the others were being held. It would make dealing with them all easier when he finally got around to it. Sin put his plan in motion over the phone, and after that, all he could do was wait impatiently to reach home.

It was almost four in the afternoon when the plane touched down, and Sin barely waited for the plane to stop before he was opening the door and jumping to the ground. He didn't give two fucks if anyone saw him. He ran to his waiting car and sped off like the hounds of hell were after him. In all honesty, he was the hound, and he was bringing hell with him. At some point during the day, someone had brought the Lambo to the airport. Sin didn't know who, but he was grateful all the same. He broke every traffic law there was getting to the hospital, but the gods were with him, and the police left him alone. Sin parked his car and ran inside the building, not bothering with the elevators. When he reached the private room where his mate was, Sin slowed himself in case Rocky had woken up.

Remy Doucet was standing guard at the doorway. "Remy, thank you, Brother. I've got her now." Remy fisted his heart before taking his leave. Sin entered Rocky's room as quietly as possible. His mate was asleep in the bed. Her long hair had been plaited and hung over one shoulder. Stark, white bandages covered both wrists. Sin choked back a sob at the thought of Rocky's blood spilling out of her arms. Vivian looked up, but she didn't move from Rocky's side. "I would appreciate a little privacy," he requested.

She cocked an eyebrow at him and remained seated. "For what? You've spent one night with her, and you think that gives you some kind of right to her?"

"What is between Raquel and me is none of your business, but since you mean something to her, I will give you this much – Rocky and I are together now. She is the one I have waited for my whole life, and there is nothing or no one that will get in our way. Not even you. Now, I need to speak to Rocky in private. Either you leave, or I will have you removed."

"You can't do that. You're not family."

"I can, and I will. Trust me on this, Vivian. I have had a shitty twenty-four hours trying to get back home to her. I will not wait another second to be alone with my girl."

"What's going on?" Dr. Mercato asked, coming up behind Sin.

"He's trying to kick me out," Vivian protested.

"And he has every right to do so. Please come with me, Miss Abernathy."

Vivian's mouth dropped, but she stood and went with the doctor. Before she exited the room, she turned back to Sin. "If you hurt her, I'll break your dick."

Sin would have been amused if the situation was different. He appreciated Vivian's loyalty to her best friend, but now, he was there, and Rocky didn't need anyone else. Sin bent over and kissed Rocky on the forehead. "Hey, beautiful girl. I'm here. Please open your eyes for me."

Dr. Mercato returned to the room and closed the door. "I need your blood," he said, as he rolled a cart up beside the bed.

Sin didn't hesitate to hold out his arm. "Tell me everything, John."

"She lost a lot of blood. If Banyan hadn't found her when he did, she probably wouldn't be here with us. That coupled with the fact there was an unholy amount of drugs in her system, I'm still trying to detox her without putting her into shock. Whoever did this to her wanted her dead, I don't care what they are claiming," the doctor seethed as the blood pumped out of Sin's vein into the waiting bag. As soon as he had enough, John swapped out a bag of some type of clear fluid for Sin's blood.

"Do you think it would help if I bit her? It helped when Frey bit Abbi."

"It couldn't hurt, except it will bind you to her."

"That is not a problem. She is my mate, John. I am going to bite her anyway. I would rather she be awake and willing, but desperate times…"

"I'll leave you alone." John took the cart and left Sin alone with Rocky. His blood had only begun seeping into her system, but he was growing more and more impatient to see her eyes.

"Rocky girl, please open your eyes and look at me." Sin sat down next to his mate, holding her hand, begging her to come back to him. He pushed with his mind trying to get through to hers, but she was fighting him instead of opening herself up to him.

The clock ticked the seconds by, and the medical equipment beeped. Sin wanted to scream. The only sound he wanted to hear was eluding him. Sin leaned over, ready to bite Rocky when the door opened, and Banyan entered the room. "Sin…"

Sin sat up and sighed. "Don't, Banyan. Not now." He wasn't mad at Banyan, not really. He was mad at himself for leaving his mate behind. He'd never make that mistake again. A moan came from Rocky's direction, and Sin's breath caught in his chest.

"Rocky? Baby, wake up." Sin ran his thumb over the back of her hand, waiting – praying – she would open her eyes.

"Rocky, can you hear us?" Banyan asked as he rounded the bed and took the empty chair. Sin's beast was growing agitated with Banyan being in the room, but Sin knew the male was only trying to help. Besides, Banyan already had a mate whether they'd sealed the bond or not.

Rocky's eyes fluttered open. She blinked as she focused on Sin. "Hey, beautiful girl."

Rocky frowned and looked over at Banyan. "Welcome back," he said. Rocky smiled at Banyan, and Sinclair's heart shredded.

"Water," she whispered. Sinclair let Rocky's hand go when she pulled away from him. Instead of returning her gaze to his, she remained focused on Banyan. He stood from the chair and said, "I'll go get the doctor. He might not want you to have water yet."

Rocky nodded, and her eyes followed Banyan as he left her room. When she finally looked at Sin, Rocky frowned again. Sin reached out to touch her, but Rocky pulled away, as far as she could considering she was in a hospital bed.

"I've been so worried about you. I..."

"Miss Cartwright, it's good to see you awake." Dr. Mercato returned to the room and stepped to the other side of the bed. "Banyan tells me you want water, but we need to start off with some ice chips first." John spooned out a small amount of ice and gave it to her. Rocky let the ice melt in her mouth while the doctor checked her over. "Do you remember anything?" he asked when he finished examining her eyes.

Rocky leaned her head back against the pillow and stared at the ceiling. "The bar... It was trashed. And Banyan..." Rocky looked around the room. "Where's Banyan?"

"He had business to tend to. Now, what else do you remember?"

"I... I went out back to smoke and Shelby... She was there. Someone stuck me and... Can you go get Banyan?"

Sin and John shared a look. Sin wanted to know why the hell his mate was asking for another male. John shook his head. "Rocky, Banyan had to go check in with his boyfriend. Sinclair is here, though, and he'll take really good care of you."

"I... no, I need to talk to Banyan."

Sin stood and said, "I'll go get him." He wouldn't have left his mate, but her doctor could keep an eye on her momentarily. Sin stalked the halls until he found Banyan in the waiting room, pacing the floor. "What the fuck was that?" he asked the other Goyle.

"Sin, I swear, I don't know what's going on. The only thing I can think of is she has my blood. Maybe she recognizes me. I have been talking to her while I've watched over her. I'm familiar to her."

"And I am her godsdamned mate!" Sin roared. The nurses outside the door looked their way, but they stayed where they were. John, however, did not. He entered the room glaring at Sin.

"You need to calm your ass down. She's not going to be less scared of you with you acting like the beast you are."

"And I need my mate to recognize *me*, not him," Sin said pointing at Banyan. "Why would she fear me? Fuck! I should have bitten her when I had the chance."

"Give her time, Sinclair. Your blood will mix with Banyan's. We'll give her another pint of yours to override whatever is in his that's calling to her. *If* that's what is going on. She almost died, Sin. We don't know what that did to her psychologically. Instead of acting like a scorned lover, you have to be the brave mate she needs right now."

Sin knew John was right, but it didn't hurt any less. "I am still going to bite her," he mumbled as he left the two

252

males and returned to his mate. When he entered her room, Rocky was sitting up. The color was returning to her cheeks. When she looked up at him, Sin whispered, "Hi." He remained where he was, hands in his pockets, unsure how to proceed.

"Hi," she whispered back. Rocky cocked her head to the side, studying Sin. He let her have her fill, hoping she was remembering what had transpired between them. "How were you in my head?"

Sin wasn't sure he heard her correctly. "Pardon me?"

"You were in my head. I want to know how."

Sin took a tentative step closer but stopped. "May I?" he asked, gesturing to the chair he'd vacated only minutes before. When she nodded, Sin sat down but kept his hands to himself. It was taking everything he had to keep the beast at bay. It wanted to drop their fangs and bite her. Claim her. Sin took a deep breath. When he exhaled, he asked, "Do you remember spending time with me before... Before I had to go out of town? Do you remember any of that?"

Rocky drew her eyebrows together in deep thought. Her eyes were unfocused as she tried to remember. "There was a garden."

"Yes." Sin didn't elaborate. Somehow he knew Rocky needed to remember on her own. He wouldn't coax her.

"You're different. Didn't you have a beard?"

Sin reached up and stroked his rough jaw with his hand. "I did, but I had to shave it for my trip."

Rocky's eyes stayed on his jaw while she thought some more. "There... there was a room... an empty bedroom where..." Rocky's face flushed.

"Yes," he whispered. "Where I made love to you." He would give her that much. He wanted her to know it was love they made and not the cheap hook-up it was going to be earlier in the week. "Where I loved you, beautiful girl." Sin placed his hand on the bed beside hers but didn't touch her. He wanted so badly to lace their fingers together, to feel that connection, but he waited for her to touch him. "That is how I was able to come to you in your mind. You and I share a bond, and I was able to tap into it."

"Is it magic?" she asked.

"Not really, no. When my family meets the one person who means everything to them, they are able to communicate nonverbally." His explanation was vague, but until he was able to tell her about the Gargoyles, it would have to be enough.

Rocky slid her hand closer to Sin's but still didn't grasp his fingers. "Why did you want to bite me?"

Oh, fuck. Rocky had heard him talking to the doctor. "Because you smell so delicious. I want to sink my teeth in and taste your essence."

"That's kinda gross." Rocky slid her hand closer until their fingers were touching. Sin couldn't take it any longer. He carefully lifted her hand and kissed her knuckles. "What happens now?" she asked.

"You continue to recover. Your body has been through a traumatic ordeal, and the doctor is still trying to get all the drugs out of your bloodstream."

"I don't do drugs anymore."

"No, and it is why he wants to keep you here until he knows he has all of the poison out of your system. Once your blood is clean, you can return home."

"Where's home?"

"Wherever you want it to be." If she needed time, he'd give it to her, but he would stay close by, watching over her.

"You scare me," she whispered. If he hadn't been a shifter, he'd not have heard the truth of her words.

Sin placed his fist over his heart and said, "I vow to you, Raquel Taryn Cartwright, on everything good and holy, I will never harm you as long as we both shall live. I promise to honor, cherish, and protect you for all the days of my life." Sin bowed his head and willed the tears to stay at the back of his eyes. He'd waited so long to say those words to someone, and Rocky had no idea the depth of the pledge he'd just made to her. Even if she never agreed to be his mate, he would remain true to her as long as she lived.

"How long have I been out of it?" Rocky asked, changing the subject.

"Twenty-seven hours, thirteen minutes, give or take a few seconds."

"How do you know that?"

"Because that is how long I've been agonizing over you being hurt. But I can promise it will never happen again."

"You can't promise that," Rocky stated harshly. She tried to pull her hand away, but Sin tightened his grip enough to keep their fingers entwined.

"I can. The ones responsible for this," he motioned to her in the bed, "have been captured. We have their confessions on tape, and they will never see the light of day again." Sin was assuming Finley had Blake stashed away. He'd still not heard from the Goyle and was starting to get worried. He needed to call him again but didn't want to do it in front of Rocky.

"Will you be okay for a minute? I need to check on something."

Rocky nodded. "Yes, I'm not going anywhere." She leaned her head back and closed her eyes. Sin stared at his mate, committing every detail of her beautiful face to memory. He sent up another prayer asking the gods to heal the damage that had been inflicted. If they would heal her wounds, he'd help heal her heart. Sin nodded at the nurse on duty and headed to the private waiting room to call Finley.

"Sin..." Fin growled out as he answered.

"Finley what..."

"I lost him, Sin. Stansbury. He was gone by the time

255

I got back to the club, and now I can't find him. The fucking rookie cop who was supposed to secure the club answered a domestic dispute call instead. I've got Landon tracking Stansbury's car, but so far he hasn't been able to locate it. We've been searching for him all fucking afternoon!"

"I have to get back to Rocky. Find him," Sinclair seethed. He ran a hand through his hair and stalked back to Rocky's room. He wouldn't leave her side until the bastard was caught. As he neared the door, a man's voice came from inside his mate's room. No. No. No! He pushed open the door and froze. Stansbury stood over Rocky with a syringe in his hand, ready to plunge it into her neck. Without thinking, Sinclair phased and lunged at the human before he could accomplish what he'd come to do.

Chapter Twenty-Four

Rocky closed her eyes, finding peace in the words Sin had spoken to her. Their time together was coming back to her in bits and pieces. Dinner at his home. Her breakdown in the garden where she told him the truth of her past. Sin carrying her upstairs where he made love to her. The tender way he held her while she fell asleep. The way he asked if she would give them a chance at a future together. And his promise? It was beautifully similar to a wedding vow. The door opened, and Rocky smiled, ready to see the man who had brought joy to her life after so many years of grief. Instead of Sin's handsome face, one she never wanted to see again appeared in her room. Rocky's biggest fear was coming back to haunt her.

Blake looked like hell. Like he'd run a thousand miles with rabid dogs on his tail. His eyes were wild, and he was coming for her. "I told you, Raquel, I always get what I want. If I can't have you, no one can." Blake lunged at her with a syringe. There was nothing she could do to fend him off. Nowhere she could hide. She was stuck in a bed, and she was going to die. Rocky closed her eyes and thought of Sinclair and the future they could have had together.

The needle never touched her skin. Instead, a heavy body fell over her legs, and Rocky's eyes shot open. Something had Blake's arms twisted away from Rocky, holding the syringe in a... holy shit! Were those claws? An inhuman growl came from whatever had pulled Blake off Rocky's body. The thing not only had claws, but fangs were inches away from Blake's ear. "You'll never hurt her or anyone else again," it told Blake. The thing turned his head toward Rocky, and she gasped. That wasn't a thing; it was Sinclair. His eyes were completely black. His chest was heaving, but the longer he stared at her, the calmer he became. His eyes returned to normal, and his fangs and claws disappeared.

She must have been given some powerful drugs in her IV. Rocky's imagination wasn't good enough to conjure up the kind of beast that just saved her from certain death. "Thank you," her hallucinating self told Sinclair.

"I told you, Raquel, I would never let anything or anyone ever hurt you again." Dream Sin pulled Blake's body off her bed and shoved him hard into the wall. With one hand holding Blake, Sin pulled his phone out of his pocket with the other and called someone. "I've got him. Rocky's hospital room. That's a good fucking question; now get your ass over here and get the bastard." Sin disconnected the phone and returned it to his pocket. Blake tried to move but Sin twisted his arm higher. "If you so much as make one more twitch, I'll break your neck right here."

Sin kept a grip on Blake as he turned to her. "I need you to call the nurse, baby. Can you do that?"

Rocky stared at him. He looked like Sin. He spoke like Sin. Damn good drugs she was on. "Sure." She'd play along, and maybe when she woke up, she would find her room back to normal. Rocky found the button for the nurse. Less than a minute later, the nurse entered her room and gasped at the sight in front of her. Was the nurse on good drugs too?

"What is going on in here?"

"Go get Dr. Mercato. Now," Sinclair demanded.

The nurse didn't hesitate to obey, and Rocky could understand why. Sin's voice echoed around the room. She bet people two floors down were searching for the doctor. Rocky wanted to open her eyes. Even though her dream had turned out good in the end, she still didn't like how it started with Blake coming at her. She wanted the calm, quiet hospital room back before she had drifted off. The door opened, and her doctor rushed in. As soon as his eyes met with Sin's captor, his whole demeanor changed.

"Do you want to tell me how in the *fuck* this cretin managed to get up here? Nobody was supposed to know she was even here," Sin growled.

"I don't know, but I vow to you, Sinclair, on my honor, I will find out and make things right."

"Finley is on his way to get this fucker. I want him secured until then."

"I'll take care of it personally." The doctor took over holding Blake's arms behind his back. Before he left the room, Dr. Mercato turned to Rocky, and said, "I have failed you." His eyes were haunted, but he quickly blinked away the hurt and returned his attention to the man in his arms. "Move," he commanded, pushing Blake toward the door. Wow. Dream doctor was hot when he went all alpha.

Sin closed the door behind them and stood there with his back to Rocky. He stayed still so long she began to get worried. Worried something was wrong with him. "Sin?" He looked at her over his shoulder, but he didn't make a move toward her.

"Sin, please come over here."

"You saw that," he muttered.

"Sure, I did. It was pretty impressive, too, the way you jumped on him right before he plunged the needle in my neck. You're my hero."

Sin frowned at her. Rocky held out her hand, and Sin eased his way to the bed. Instead of taking her hand, he shoved his hands in his pockets. Rocky followed the action, and she had to admit, dream Sin filled out his jeans really well. She remembered Sin's naked body doing delicious things to her. His muscular, fit body. She was a little jealous of his jeans. She'd love to have him sliding his long, thick cock inside her wet...

"Rocky," Sin growled. He didn't hide the fact he had to adjust his hard-on behind his zipper. Huh. Dream Sin wanted her. Maybe when she woke up, real Sin would want her, too. Rocky licked her lips. Her breath had to be rank from being unconscious for so long, but this wasn't real, and she wanted a kiss. Hopefully her dream breath would be nice and minty.

Rocky crooked her finger at Sin, silently asking him to come to her. He took a step forward, but the door burst open, and Finley practically ran in. "Rocky! Oh, thank the gods."

"Way to ruin a dream," she pouted. Both men stared at her as though she'd lost her mind. Maybe she had.

Sin did close the distance then and gave her a kiss on her temple. "I will be right outside in the hall, beautiful girl. I promise I'm not going anywhere this time." He kissed her again and motioned for Finley to leave the room. Finley glanced at her and gave her a sad smile.

Well, hell. Rocky closed her eyes. It was strange having a dream with them open; then again, hallucinations came in many forms, as she well knew. She was going to give it a while and let whatever was in her IV run its course. When Rocky woke up, hopefully things would be normal again.

"What the hell happened?" Finley asked as soon as they were in the hallway.

"That is what I'd like to know. Godsdamn human found out where she was. If I hadn't hung up from talking to you when I did..." Sin didn't want to think about it. "I phased, Brother. Rocky saw my fangs and claws."

"She didn't seem too freaked out."

"That's just it. I don't think she knows what happened is real. She has some pretty bad shit running through her veins. John isn't certain of the side effects."

"You mean she might not be right in the head?"

"That is harsh, but yes. There were so many drugs

260

mixed together, it should have killed her. If they hadn't been able to inject Banyan's blood in her when they did, she would not have made it."

"What are you going to do?"

"All I can do. I am going to give her time to get better while loving her and giving her the life she deserves. Gods forbid she doesn't recover completely, I will be right there by her side making sure the life she has is full."

"Are you still going to mate with her?"

"I won't risk biting her if she isn't one hundred percent healed. I am not going to take advantage of her, but she is my mate, and I've already made my vow to her."

Finley clapped him on the shoulder and squeezed. "I'm sorry I failed you, Brother. I should have gone with Banyan instead of sparring. Somehow, I'll make it up to you both. You have my word."

Sin knew how he was going to get Finley to make it up to him, but they had more pressing things to worry about at the moment. "Go find John and get that bastard far away from here. I want the three of them tied up in the same room, and I want someone watching them around the clock." Sin told Finley his plan for the three of them, but he wouldn't carry it out yet. Not until Rocky was out of the hospital.

Vivian made her way to where they were standing. "I want to see my girl," she said.

"She is resting. Vivian, Blake Stansbury managed to get into her room, but I stopped him before he could hurt her. Rocky is going to need you to help get her through these next few days. Can I count on you?"

"Of course. He didn't..."

"No. Like I said, I got to him first. Rocky's location was supposed to be a secret. We are trying to find out how he knew where to look."

"Oh, God." Vivian put her hand over her mouth. "What if he followed me?"

261

"When would he have followed you?" Finley asked.

"I thought I saw someone who looked like him at the red light, but he took off before I got a good look at him. Sinclair..."

"Stop. It is over now. Even if he did follow you, someone should have been guarding her door. *I* should have been watching her. I stepped into the waiting room to call Finley. Now, what's done is done. Please go sit with her while Finley and I finish our discussion."

Vivian wiped the tears rolling down her cheeks. Sin was glad Rocky had someone who cared about her as much as her best friend did. Sin had fully intended to go straight back into Rocky's room, but he gave the women a little while alone, and he stood guard outside.

Rocky was restless. She knew she was safe, but in the back of her mind she still felt like Blake could walk through the door at any moment. The door opened, and Rocky held her breath until she saw it was Vivian. Rocky smiled, but the look on her best friend's face quickly had her frowning. "Viv, what's wrong?"

"If anything else happened to you, I don't know what I'd do."

"That was real?"

"What do you mean?" Vivian walked around the bed and sat down in the chair Banyan had been in when she woke up.

"I thought I might have been seeing things. I mean..." Rocky stopped. Her friend was already worried about her without Rocky adding to it by telling her she was seeing shit that wasn't really there. "Never mind. I'm safe, right?"

"Yes. I told you Sinclair Stone was someone you'd want in your corner where Blake was concerned. I was right."

"Sin... he attacked him?"

"Of course he did. You should hear him talk about you. Damn, girl. I'm almost jealous. Sin has it bad for you."

Rocky didn't know if it was the drugs or thinking about Sin, but she couldn't help as the dopey grin spread across her face. "He's... different. I think I could fall for him, if I let myself."

"Please be careful."

"Why? I thought you said he has it bad."

"He does. At least he sounds like he does. It's just... Finley told me Sin's not the settling down type."

"I asked him about that."

"You did? When?" Vivian sat up straighter in her chair.

"When he asked me to give us a chance. Viv, he took me to his bedroom."

"Sorry to burst your bubble, Rocky girl, but I've seen his bedroom."

"No, you saw *a* bedroom. I saw *the* bedroom. The one upstairs he's been saving."

"Wow, I knew your pussy was special, but damn girl!" Vivian joked.

Rocky laughed at her best friend. "And don't you forget it." Rocky beamed. Sin had made her feel special. Like she deserved to be the one to see his bedroom. "Viv, I'm scared."

"Of Sin?"

"Yes. No. I mean, I'm scared of what he makes me feel."

"What does he make you feel?"

"Hopeful. I grew up with parents who loved each other more than life. More than even me. Don't get me wrong; I know they loved me, but the love they had for each other was something that transcended time and death. I heard them. Right after... when Tommy... I heard their voices, Viv. They told me it wasn't my time." Rocky stopped talking when Vivian hiccupped. Her perfect make-up was rolling down her face along with the tears she was crying. "Shh, Viv. It's okay. I'm okay. It's just, they were perfect, and I always wanted what they had, you know? Sin makes me feel like that's possible."

Vivian grabbed a tissue off the stand next to Rocky's bed and wiped her eyes. "Now I know I'm jealous. I'm so happy for you. If anyone deserves happiness, it's you. I hope he makes you happy."

A knock on the door interrupted their girl talk. "Sorry to interrupt, but I wanted to check on my girl." Sin did more than check in. He walked right up to the bed and sat down beside Rocky's hip. He took her hand in his and kissed the inside of her wrist. Rocky wanted his kiss but on her lips.

"I need to brush my teeth," she blurted.

Sin grinned at her and leaned in and kissed her lips. "I will talk to the nurse about that," he whispered against her mouth. Rocky placed her hand on his stubbly jaw. When she noticed the bandage, she pulled back. Sin took her hand and returned it to his jaw. "I love when you touch me. It makes me feel wanted," he admitted.

How could a man like Sin not feel wanted? Hell, every woman in California who'd ever laid eyes on him had to desire him. "When I get my strength back, I'll make you feel wanted all day and all night," Rocky teased. Actually, it wasn't a tease but a promise. Whenever he was around, she couldn't get enough of him. That was another thing that worried her. She was afraid he'd get tired of her after a while.

Vivian stood and grabbed Rocky's other hand. Smiling down at her best friend, she said, "I'm going to head on home and let you get some rest. I love you, Rocky. I'll check on you tomorrow." Vivian leaned down and kissed Rocky on the forehead. "Bye, Sinclair."

They both said goodbye, and as soon as the door was closed, Rocky asked, "Was that real?"

"Was what real?"

"What I saw earlier between you and Blake. Or was I hallucinating?"

"What did you see, sweetheart?"

"Fangs. Claws. Your eyes so dark there was no white showing."

Sin stood from the bed and walked over to the window. She could take his silence as admission, but she needed him to be honest with her. She'd heard of the Unholy. Had seen photos of them. She knew there were monsters in the world, but Sin wasn't a monster. At least not to her. He had saved her life. He could have snapped Blake's neck, but he didn't.

"Sin?"

He glanced at her over his shoulder and nodded almost imperceptibly.

Rocky held out her hand and kept it there until Sin finally returned. Instead of taking her hand, he looked at it like it would bite him. "Sin, take my hand." His eyes searched hers. He must have found what he was looking for, because Sin sat on the bed next to her and took her hand.

"You wanna explain what I saw?" she asked.

"You saw me."

"I saw more than you. You promised to never hurt me, right?"

"I did."

"Then I'm okay with that."

"Rocky, there is more to me than what you saw."

"How much worse could it be?"

"Worse?" Sinclair's face blanched like she'd slapped him.

"Sorry, I didn't mean worse as in I think you're a monster. I meant worse as in scary. You have to admit those

265

claws are pretty damn scary."

"They can be. Rocky, this can wait. You've been through enough, and I want to have this conversation when you are ready to hear it."

"I'm ready now, Sin. If you still want me to give us a chance at a future, I think I deserve to know who I'm having a future with."

"Fair enough, but I would still rather have this conversation when you are better."

"What else are you keeping from me? Is there something wrong with me?"

"No, sweetheart, nothing's wrong, we just want to give you more time to heal is all."

"I appreciate that, but I also want to know about you. Sin, please."

"Do you read or watch movies?" Sin asked. He was delaying the truth, for a moment anyway.

"I haven't read in a while, but I do like to watch movies. Why?"

"Do you ever watch werewolf movies?

"Are you a werewolf?" Rocky gasped. There was no way Sin turned into a dog.

"No, nothing like that. I am a Gargoyle."

"Those little concrete critters on the tops of churches?"

"I am a primordial shapeshifter. The Gargouille date back to the birth of civilization. The name has been modernized over the years to Gargoyle. We were made to look human so we could blend in with those we were created to protect. The little stone creatures were constructed by those who were aware of us as a symbol of sanctuary. When I said there was more, I meant more than claws and fangs. I also have a set of wings that almost came out and destroyed this room when I dove on Blake."

"That was hot, by the way."

"You're not scared?"

"No. Not of you. I was scared when I thought I was going to die at his hand. Scared of not seeing your bedroom again. Scared of not getting to take a ride in an airplane before I die. Scared of not driving your Lambo, airing her out. I was scared when I first woke up, because I recognized you. My heart recognized yours, and your soul called out to mine. Hell, maybe I am hallucinating and all this is a crazy dream. But when I woke up and you were sitting in that chair, I was scared you were going to take control of my life, and I wasn't ready for that. I've lived under someone's thumb for so long, all I've promised myself is I'd never succumb to another man as long as I lived. But I realized giving in to you isn't submitting, but living. I'd rather be alive and have you call the shots than to not be alive at all."

Chapter Twenty-Five

Sin couldn't believe what Rocky was saying. When she first came to, she hadn't wanted him in the room. The wariness coming from his mate had been intense. Now, even after seeing him phase, she was singing a different tune. He had saved her life, so it was possible she was feeling thankful, and that was seeping into her other emotions. The effects of the blood loss were still being monitored by John, and he hadn't convinced Sin Rocky would recover completely. She didn't act confused, but he wanted to make sure she was mentally competent to make sound decisions before he told her about being mates.

Having her in his life would have to be enough for now. Sin planned to continue on with Rocky as if nothing had happened to slow things down. He would keep her by his side and monitor her while moving forward with their relationship. Sin still had to make the trip to Greece to locate his mother, but this time Rocky would be going with him. He would take a small army with him to protect her while he was doing his job, and after that was taken care of, Sin planned to stop off in Italy and spend time with her at Rafael's villa.

"When can I see your wings?" Rocky asked with childlike wonder. The excitement was evident in her eyes, and it warmed his heart to see, but at the same time, it worried him she wasn't thinking clearly. Shouldn't she be scared out of her mind? Or at least cautious because he was something other than human? The other mates had each taken to the truth differently, but they had all accepted it. Maybe his girl was accepting him, too.

"Soon, sweetheart. But listen, you can't tell people what I am. Do you understand? We've kept our secret this long, and it wouldn't do to have the human population knowing the truth of us. It's bad enough they have to deal with the Unholy."

"I'm not stupid. Of course I can keep your secret." Rocky tried to cross her arms over her chest, but the IV line got in the way.

"Hey, look at me. I didn't mean to imply you are. Baby, it's... You know what? Never mind. I trust you with my secret. And I am trusting you with my heart." Sin leaned over and gently pulled Rocky to him so he could kiss her.

"Toothbrush, remember?" she fussed.

"I remember. Come on, I'll help you." Sin assisted Rocky to her feet. She was weak, so he held her close but still allowed her to walk. He really wanted to carry her, but he didn't know how she'd feel about being coddled. With his free arm, he pushed the IV pole beside them and maneuvered them both into the small bathroom. Rocky placed both hands on the sink for balance, and Sin put toothpaste on the brush for her.

While Rocky brushed her teeth, Sin placed his hands on her thin waist. He planned on putting a little more meat on her bones. He didn't mind her lean frame, but she wasn't healthy in his eyes. Sin wanted his mate whole in every way, and he was going to make it his mission to see she was. After Rocky spit the foam out and rinsed her mouth, she said, "I need to pee." Sin turned her around and helped her to sit on the toilet. He hadn't realized she didn't have panties on, or he'd probably have had an even harder time keeping his hands off her. His libido had been surprisingly calm, but Sin chalked it up to her not being well. He cared more about her well-being than having sex with her.

"This is embarrassing," she muttered as she pulled some toilet paper off the roll. Sin turned his back to her so she could wipe without him looking, but he had news for her – he'd wipe her ass if she needed him to. Sin would take care of every single need Rocky had. When the toilet flushed, Sin helped Rocky to her feet, and she shuffled back to the sink to wash her hands. As he helped her get back to the bed, Sin's heart was full. Human vows said for better or worse. Sin vowed the same thing with his mate, and this was one of those worse times as far as he was concerned. Better would come when he had her naked on the beach.

When Rocky was settled in the bed, Sin sat next to her so he could hold her in his arms. Rocky nestled against his chest, her fingers playing with the strands of his long hair. He kissed her on the temple, and said, "I don't want you to ever feel embarrassed around me, beautiful girl. There is no situation I'm not willing to go through with you. Nothing you can do will change the way I feel about you. One thing I have yet to tell you about my kind is that we have one mate for life. You are my mate. It's why we feel the deep connection. You have a choice in whether you want me in your life, but if you give us a chance, I think you'll be happy you did."

"Now I'm beginning to understand."

"Understand what?"

"Your friends. The way you all talk. The odd things you do. All the men you hang around are straight out of superhero movies. I have a question. Do all of you share women?"

"No, of course not. Why would you think that?"

"Because you and Finley did. You were going to share me, right? I don't think I want you to share me with anyone."

"I explained that to you, sweetheart. I had given up hope on ever finding my mate. I had no reason to remain celibate. Now that I have you, there will never be another woman in my bed but you, and I'm sure as fuck not going to allow anyone to touch you. Man or woman."

"So you don't want Dana? Or Finley? Vivian said..."

"Forget what Vivian said. I want you and no one else. I deeply regret having Dana in my home, and Finley and I have never had any type of sex before that night. Had

270

I known about you, I would have never done anything to disrespect you and our bond. Can you forgive me?"

"There's nothing to forgive. I mean, you can have anyone you want, so…" Rocky's words faded off, and Sin pulled her chin up to look into her eyes. He reached out with his senses and found her to be upset. Her heart was racing faster than it should have been.

"Raquel, look at me." When she found his eyes, she blinked a couple of times. Sin cupped her jaw and traced her chin with his thumb. "I have the woman I want. You. I don't care how long it takes; I will make you believe my words. You are the most exquisite creature I have ever seen, and no one else will do." Sin poured his heart into his words.

Rocky settled her cheek against his shoulder. "Will you sing to me?" she asked against his neck.

"I don't sing, sweetheart."

"But you hum. Will you hum to me?" Rocky's heartbeat was slowing. His mate was falling asleep, and she wanted him to hum. It was something he'd always done without realizing it. Rafael often joked with him about it, but when they'd lost their father, Sinclair had soothed his older brother by humming some song they'd loved as young boys. With Rocky's hand playing in his hair, Sin hummed his mate to sleep.

John came in several times to check on Rocky. He changed out the bag of fluids before drawing more blood from Rocky. "There was a significant amount of heroin in the concoction her cousin injected into her body. I've been giving her small doses of methadone, and with yours and Banyan's blood transfusions, her blood is cleansing. I want all traces of narcotics out of her system before I release her, but you should be able to take her home soon."

"Thank you, John." Sin was worried about her, but the doctor explained it would take time, patience, and lots of rest for her body and mind to completely heal. Sin didn't move from his position on the bed. He'd known she was

271

close to death when he connected with her subconscious, and her words had told him she felt alone. Sin would never leave Rocky alone again. He would hold her as she slept, offering his strength and comfort as best he could. During her waking hours, Sin would make sure Rocky had someone who loved her close by at all times.

Several Goyles came in during the night to check on them both. Rafael had called, but Sin let it go to voicemail. He wasn't ready to talk to his brother. Not yet. He knew what happened wasn't Rafael's fault, but if he hadn't been asked to travel, Rocky wouldn't have been harmed. Before the sun came up, the last male he expected to see walked through the door. Urijah raised his hand then shoved both into his pockets. He padded quietly to the bed and stared at Rocky.

"Brother?" Sin asked, getting Uri's attention.

"Is she going to be okay?" Uri whispered.

"She has a long way to go, but yes. She will be fine."

"I've forged all the weapons you need. I know you asked me to stay while you went to Greece, but I feel like it's time I head home. I just came to say goodbye."

"Thank you for putting your feelings aside and staying as long as you did. Uri, I need to apologize."

"For what?"

"For asking you to come over. It was a shitty thing to do knowing how you feel about Finley."

"I was pissed, but honestly, I was also turned on. Watching you two together, that was... I have no claims on Fin, so don't worry about it."

"No, but you do have claims on Banyan. Have you told him you are leaving?"

Urijah didn't respond, and Sin had his answer. "Uri, I don't know what has happened in your past, but I do know you only get one mate. Forever is a mighty long time to refuse yours."

"I... I must go. Take care." Uri didn't wait for Sin to

272

respond. He rushed out the door and didn't look back. It wasn't any of Sin's business, but now that he had found his mate, he couldn't imagine knowing she was his and not doing everything in his power to keep her. Something bad must have happened for Uri to refuse Banyan.

Finley came in almost immediately after Urijah left. "Did you see Uri?" Sin asked.

"Yes. I'm going to miss having him around, but I also understand wanting to be home."

"Do you really think he missed New Atlanta that much? Or is he running away?"

"Both, probably. Uri's always been hard to figure out." Finley stepped over to the window and looked out. He stood there quietly for several long minutes, but Sin let him have the quiet to think about his best friend.

"What do you want to do about the girl"? Finley asked.

Sin eased out from under Rocky and made sure she was still asleep before he accompanied Finley to the hallway. They had already discussed the fate of the two males, but Sin was still trying to decide the fate of the female accomplice. She swore she didn't know her boyfriend was going to try to kill Rocky, but she had gone to the bar knowing they were going to drug her and return her to Stansbury. "I haven't decided. But I'm ready to handle the other two. I'll do that tonight while Rocky's asleep. I need you to watch over her for me."

"You'd trust me with her?"

"Is there a reason I shouldn't?"

"I let you down, Brother."

"No, I failed my mate. That is on me. Now, will you watch over Rocky while I take care of business?"

"Yes, and thank you for giving me another chance."

"I need you to do something else. I need my laptop from my office and a change of clothes. Will you bring those to me?"

"Of course." Finley fisted his heart and took off down the silent hall.

The other rooms on that end of the floor had been emptied so the Goyles could come and go freely. Sin was thankful John was not only an excellent physician but also the Chief of Staff at the hospital. He could bend the rules as they suited the Clan's needs.

Sin leaned back against the wall. Being so close to Rocky didn't allow his brain room to think about anything other than her. She was his first priority, but he was the Clan leader on the West Coast, and he had things to take care of. It was in that moment he appreciated Rafael more than he ever had. Not only did his brother have a mate, but a mate who was going to have a baby. Sin was barely holding it together after knowing his mate a few days. He couldn't imagine how protective he would be if she were pregnant with his child. It hurt his heart she couldn't have children of her own. He was going to make the man responsible for that pay dearly. Whenever Sin thought about Tommy Cartwright, his shifter came alive and demanded retribution. Sin needed to remain calm while he was with Rocky, but come that night, he was going to let the beast loose.

Urijah couldn't get out of the hospital fast enough. Sin apologized for asking him over, and Uri lied, saying it had been okay. It wasn't okay, but there was no need to add fuel to Sin's already burning fire. The Goyle had enough on his plate with his mate being in the hospital. When Uri reached the bottom step, he grabbed the door knob. Before he could twist it, the door was pushed toward him. Banyan stepped through, and Uri growled.

Banyan held up his hands. "Whoa, easy tiger." The only thing that kept Uri in check was the fact Banyan wasn't teasing him.

274

"Here's my key to the armory," Uri said, fishing the metal out of his pocket. He was going to leave it at the armory, but now he didn't have to make a special trip out there.

"You're leaving?" Banyan asked, his eyes filled with hurt. If only things could be different. Urijah couldn't get over their past together, and now that he knew Banyan came from the Original line of shifters? Things were too fucking complicated for it to ever work between them.

"Yes. I did what I was asked to do, and now I'm going home," Uri said, looking at his boots. Banyan's eyes had always given away too much, and Uri couldn't deal with the pain he saw there.

Banyan's boots came into view right before he slammed Urijah against the concrete wall. Uri opened his mouth to protest, and Banyan took advantage. He crashed his mouth to Uri's and kissed him like his life depended on it. *Oh, fuck.* If there was one thing Urijah couldn't resist, it was his mate's kisses. Banyan breathed his life force into Uri's mouth while stealing a little bit of Uri's soul in the process. He'd stolen his heart a long time ago. So long ago, in fact, Uri couldn't remember having one. Banyan's stiff cock rubbed against Uri's own hard-on, and his beast roared inside his head. Uri was too close to letting it loose. Letting it take over and do what it had wanted to ever since he arrived in California. Claim this male.

No. No! Urijah pushed Banyan off him and bent over to catch his breath. Banyan's hand branded Uri's neck. Everywhere Banyan touched him had always caught fire, but this was too much. He had to get away. "I have to go."

"Urijah," Banyan begged with one word. Uri made the mistake of looking at his mate. "I still love you," Banyan whispered. Uri's heart, the one he thought he no longer possessed, exploded within his chest. He couldn't breathe. Banyan had promised to let him go thirty years ago. Guess he'd been lying. Urijah pushed past his mate and jogged

275

until he reached the front door of the hospital. When he got outside, he ran full out to his waiting car. He couldn't get back to New Atlanta soon enough.

Drago punched the Unholy he was fighting in the jaw. The beasts he had commandeered for his army were brutes, but they had lost most of their common sense during their transition. He couldn't imagine going from human to half a shifter. And most of them had signed up for this shit on purpose. Gordon Flanagan must have been one hell of a salesman to convince an ordinary human to lie down on the table and have their brains scrambled.

Kavin and Burk, the two Goyles Kallisto sent to help him, had managed to locate him early that morning. One of his army had given up his location, thus leading him to the beat down he was giving the freak at his feet. Neither Kavin nor Burk could tell him who had ratted him out, because they all looked so similar. The two males were standing at the gate to the compound making sure no one tried to leave. If Drago was going to command this army, he was going to first command their respect.

Being able to communicate once again with Kallisto made Drago feel better about his decision to take over the Unholy in New Atlanta. Together, they could formulate a plan to get Sergei out of the pen while wreaking havoc on the Stone Society.

Chapter Twenty-Six

Rocky woke up alone in her hospital room. *So much for Sin not leaving me alone.* When she noticed a tray of food on the rolling cart, she raised her bed into a sitting position. The door to the bathroom opened, and the man she'd been silently cursing peeked around the door, smiling when he saw she was awake. "Good morning, Bella Ragazza. I hope you don't mind, but I took a quick shower." Rocky couldn't help but smile back at him even though she had no idea what he'd just said to her.

His shower was evident by the damp hair curling around the collar of his button-up shirt. Rocky loved Sin's hair. Loved running her fingers through the long locks. She understood him shaving his beard to portray his brother, but she really hoped Rafael never cut his hair. Everything Sin had told Rocky about his family had come back to her during the night. Her subconscious had helped her catch up. Her brain was foggy while she was awake, making it hard to concentrate. It bothered her thinking she might not recover completely from what Tommy did to her. Sin told her those responsible were being taken care of.

Rocky took the lid off her breakfast. Broth? Great. Her stomach growled, but she was grateful for the sustenance going into her mouth and not her arm. It meant she was getting better. Sin helped her push the tray closer so she wouldn't spill it. "Where's Tommy?" she asked

Sin handed her the spoon as he answered, "Somewhere he can't hurt you."

"Is he dead?" Rocky searched Sin's face for the truth. He told her he'd never lie to her, but what if there was something he didn't want her to know about?

"Not yet," Sin admitted. He pulled the towel from around his shoulders and hung it over the door, but he didn't come to her on the bed. Sin kept the distance between them while she slurped the broth. "I made a vow to protect you, and I intend to honor my vow."

Rocky needed him close. She needed to feel his skin on hers, even if they were holding hands or sitting next to one another. He'd explained a little of the mate pull, and she chalked her neediness up to that. Whatever the reason, she needed him. "Please come over here and sit with me."

Sin sat down in the chair next to her bed. He leaned close and settled his arm against her leg, letting his thumb graze back and forth over her skin. "This mate pull – you can't ignore it, can you?" she asked.

"No, I can't."

"Would..." Rocky cleared her throat, embarrassed at her question, but she needed to know. "Would you have found me desirable even without the mate pull?"

"Absolutely. You must see the way men look at you. The way they desire you. Please do not ever think our bond is the only reason I want you, Raquel." Sin kissed the back of her hand.

"Are you going to kill Tommy?" Rocky knew her mind was ping-ponging back and forth, but she had to ask the questions when they came to her for fear she'd forget them.

"Would it bother you if I did?"

"No," she whispered. "It wouldn't bother me if I did it either. He's a piece of shit rat bastard who doesn't deserve to live. However, if I knew he would be someone's bitch in prison, that might be just as good a punishment."

Sin barked out a short laugh. When Rocky moved the tray away from her body, Sin moved to sit next to her on the bed. She wasn't full by any means, but having been through detox before, she knew she had to start slow. Since he took up most of the space with his large frame, Sin pulled her onto his lap. "You amaze me," he said against her ear. He kissed her temple, but she wanted more. She wanted his lips on hers. His hands sliding over her skin. His cock inside her core, filling her up. "Rocky," he growled. His cock grew hard against her ass, and she wiggled letting him know she felt it.

"You are killing me, beautiful girl. I want nothing more than to sink into the sweetness of your wet heat, but we are going to have to wait until we get home."

"Then I want to go home now." Rocky turned so she could kiss him.

"Ahem." Dr. Mercato cleared his throat. "I knocked, but you didn't hear me." He didn't have the blood cart with him, so Rocky took that as a good sign. He had a metal clipboard in his hands, but he didn't look at it. Instead, he smiled at them. "I have some good news. Your blood is free from contaminants, which means you are well on your way to being back to your old self. I will release you into Sin's care, but you have to promise to take it easy for the next week."

Something passed between the doctor and Sin. Rocky knew Sin could talk to her telepathically, or at least he'd done it once. She didn't know if the Gargoyles had that ability between them. "Can you read each other's minds?" she asked.

Dr. Mercato's eyebrows shot up, and Sin laughed. "No, not like you're talking about. We have the ability to gauge moods, but unless one is our mate, we cannot communicate mind to mind. Dante and his son are the only exceptions we are aware of."

"She knows?" Dr. Mercato asked.

"Most of it. I had to come clean when I phased in front of her."

"So, you're one too? That makes sense," Rocky said. She'd already thought he was hot, but knowing he was a Gargoyle put him in the superhero column with Sin and his other friends.

"Yes, I'm one too. I hope you're okay with that."

279

"I sure am. I've encountered enough villains to last me a lifetime. I'm ready to be surrounded by the superheroes."

Both Sinclair and the doctor laughed. When the doctor sobered, he asked, "Rocky, how are you feeling? Anything going on you want to ask me about?"

"I was just thinking to myself my brain feels foggy, and I have trouble remembering certain things. Is that normal?"

"Yes. You've been through a traumatic experience. You were as close to death as one can be without actually passing over. Between the drugs you were injected with and the blood loss, some mental slowness is to be expected. That doesn't mean there's anything wrong with you or you can't live a full life. I'm saying there could be moments of non-clarity or fogginess as you called it. Try not to get frustrated with yourself. Be thankful you're alive and you have someone like Sinclair looking out for you."

"Thank you for your honesty."

"You're welcome. I've already signed your discharge papers, so whenever you're ready to go, call the nurse and she'll wheel you down."

Rocky turned to Sin. "Do I have clothes here?"

"No. I wasn't expecting you to be released today. I will call Finley and have him pick some up."

"I could call Vivian. She's supposed to come see me."

"Why don't you call Vivian and have her meet us at home later this afternoon? There is something I need to take care of tonight, so she can keep you company while I am gone. Don't worry, sweetheart. The house will be surrounded by Gargoyles, all of whom would lay down their lives for you. You never have to worry about your safety again."

Wow. Sin was taking this seriously, but Rocky was glad. At least for now. As long as Tommy and Blake were alive, she would always fear one of them coming after her. Rocky snuggled into the warmth of Sin's arms as he called Finley and asked him to bring her some clothes. When he started rattling off sizes, she pulled back and looked at him. Sin grinned and told Finley he'd see him soon.

"I don't need new clothes," Rocky fussed.

"No, but your clothes are in our bedroom, and nobody but the two of us will ever step foot in there. That is *our* room. Our sanctuary."

"Oh." A warm feeling flowed through Rocky. Something akin to love. She'd never been in love with a man before, but she'd seen it through the eyes of her parents. She was pretty sure she was seeing it in the eyes of the man holding her, too. Rocky knew it was too soon to declare her feelings, and with her brain not always clear, she was going to wait a while before she told him what she was thinking. Waiting wouldn't be bad. If anything, it would give her time for her feelings to grow and make sure Sin felt the same way.

When he held the phone out to her, Rocky took it and called Vivian, even though it was early Sunday morning, and her best friend would be asleep. "Rocky, are you okay?" Vivian asked when she picked up her phone.

"Yes, ma'am. I even get to go home today."

"Oh, honey, that's great news. Do you want to stay with me for a while?"

"No, I'm going home, Viv. Home with Sin. But I did want to ask you to stop by later. Maybe we can watch a movie and talk about your co-workers? You know, something normal."

"I'd love that. I'll call you when I get close so someone can open the gate for me."

"Sounds good. See you later." Rocky disconnected the call. "She said..."

Sin cut Rocky off. "I heard her, sweetheart."

"Oh yeah, you have that superhero hearing."

281

"Yes, and your friend talks loud," he said, grinning. He wasn't wrong.

"While we wait on Finley to bring my clothes, tell me more about being a Gargoyle. I want to know everything, like how old you are. Where you grew up. What you were like as a child."

Sin pulled her closer to him and obliged. The first thing he said was, "I was born in the little town of Otranto, Italy, in the year 1478. I am the second..."

"Hold up. My brain's foggy, but did you say 1478? Like almost six hundred years ago?"

"I did. I am five hundred seventy to be precise."

"Whoa. How long will you live?"

"Until someone removes my head from my shoulders or I will my body to pass on to the other side."

"So you're going to look the way you do now practically forever, and I'm going to grow old and gray and..."

"Stop. I told you there is more to being a Gargoyle, and there is. There is also more to being a mate. I didn't want to tell you this until you had time to get to know me, get to know us together, but here is the deal. When the day comes you decide you want me as your mate, I can make our bond permanent. When that happens, you will stop aging and will live a long life by my side."

"You mean I'll look like this forever?"

"You will look the same as you do at whatever age you are when the bond is sealed. Should you wait until you're fifty to decide, you will look fifty for the rest of your life."

"How do you seal the bond?" Rocky asked. She had never thought about living forever. Hell, she'd never thought she would make it past twenty-five, and she almost hadn't.

"I have to bite you."

Rocky gasped. "Is that why you told the doctor you

282

wanted to bite me? You wanted to seal the deal?"

"I was willing to bite you to help you heal faster. It is thought that whatever makes us Gargoyles has healing powers for our mates. It is also what stops the aging process."

"So you didn't want to seal the deal," Rocky whispered.

"I absolutely did. I do. But only when you're ready, beautiful girl. I would never make that choice for you unless it was a life or death situation, and when I said those words, I was certain that was the type of situation we were facing."

"If you bite me, you're stuck with me for eternity, right?"

"And you are stuck with me. Don't forget that point."

Rocky grinned. "That's kind of like getting pregnant on purpose. Not that I would or I could. I'm just saying..." Rocky closed her eyes and tried to imagine going through the years with Sin by her side. Watching the world slip by from decade into new decade. Century into new century. "I bet you've seen some wild stuff over the years. Going from horses and boats to cars and airplanes. The changes in clothes and the different styles of music. I want to hear all about it, Sin. I want you to share your whole life with me. Will you share your past with me?" Rocky was getting excited, but she couldn't help herself. She had a walking, talking encyclopedia at her disposal.

A knock on the door sounded, and Rocky's happiness slipped a little. She wanted to be alone with Sinclair so he could talk to her. The nurse who'd been taking care of Rocky came in. "Dr. Mercato says you're going home soon. I wanted to take your IV out and make sure you have everything you need." Sin moved away from Rocky so the nurse had room to maneuver. The gentle way the nurse handled her reminded her of her mother. Before Tommy attacked her, Rocky had planned on becoming a nurse herself, but now she wasn't so sure. If her brain didn't recover, Rocky wouldn't be able to study. To learn. She would be a threat to someone instead of being able to help them. The nurse placed a cotton ball and bandage on the entry point of the needle. "There you go. If you need anything else, just push the button." The nurse smiled and left them alone.

"Baby, what's wrong? Did she hurt you?" Sin asked as he dropped to his knees beside the bed. He brushed his thumb over her cheek. Rocky didn't realize she was crying.

"No, I'm okay. I was thinking about how I can't be a nurse now." That hurt Rocky's heart the more she thought about it.

"Who says you can't? Sweetheart, you are still healing. You need to give yourself time, okay? If you really want to be a nurse, I will help you study. Together, we will get you through your classes even if you have to take one at a time. I have already told you, whatever you want is yours. If you want the moon and stars, I will find a way to capture them for you. I might have to call Julian and get his help since he is the genius in the family."

"God, I love you," Rocky whispered. She didn't mean to say it out loud, but her emotions were getting the better of her. She'd prayed for a man as kind and loving as her father, and here he was, offering her everything her heart desired.

"I love you, too, Bella Ragazza. More than life itself." Rocky wrapped her arms around Sinclair's neck and held on to his words as well as his body.

Sin was flying high. Not literally, but when Rocky claimed to love him, it had his heart soaring. If Dr. Mercato hadn't assured him the drugs were out of her system, he would have been afraid she was still under the influence, but he was going to go with the assumption she truly loved him. The mate pull had a lot to do with it. He knew that. But her heartbeat was calm, and her eyes glistened with not only the sheen from the tears but also the truth of her words. Sin had learned a long time ago to read someone by looking in their eyes.

Rocky was all over the place with her conversation, going from one topic to the next. This could be her normal behavior. They hadn't had the opportunity to talk as much as he would have liked, so Sin didn't know if she always jumped around or if this was something new. In either case, he didn't care. She was asking questions about him and his life. Rocky wanted to know all about Sinclair, and he was going to spend the next week telling her everything she wanted to know. He knew he would have to head back to Greece sooner rather than later, but he was going to make sure his mate was well enough for the trip. Then, and only then, would he go.

Was he choosing his mate's well-being over his mother's? Absolutely, and Sin had no problem with that. Athena had abandoned her sons over two hundred years ago when their father had been slain. He knew she was grieving, but so were he and his brothers. They lost both parents the day their father lost his head. If Athena was suffering at the hands of her brother, Sin would accept that over his mate suffering any more than she already had. If that made him a bastard, so be it. No one mattered more to him than Raquel.

After they declared their feelings, Sin held Rocky in his arms while she cried herself to sleep. He assured himself they were happy tears when she wrapped her fingers in his hair and kissed his chest. Finley arrived soon after, bringing Rocky's clothes. He stood at the end of the bed, his expression somber. His sadness reached across the room. Sin didn't hold his friend responsible, but it was up to Finley to forgive himself for what happened to Rocky.

"Vivian is coming over later to sit with Rocky, and they are going to do whatever it is girls do. Watch movies. Eat popcorn. Talk about people."

Finley merely nodded, and Sin held out his hand. "Brother, come here." Fin walked to the far side of the bed, and Sin pulled him down beside him. Sin put his hand on the back of Finley's neck and pulled him forward until their foreheads were touching. "I forgive you, Brother. She is going to be fine. We are all going to be fine. You feel me?"

"I feel you," Fin whispered.

Sin kissed his friend on the forehead and released the hold he had on his neck. There was nothing romantic or sexual in the kiss. Those days were over now Sin had found his mate. "Here are my keys. If you would, pull the Lambo around to the front door while I get my girl dressed. Yeah?"

"Yeah." Finley stood and headed toward the door. With his hand on the knob, Fin turned and said, "Thank you, Brother." Sin didn't miss the tears in his friend's eyes, and that caught Sinclair in the chest. It had been an emotional few days for everyone. After tonight, they could all get back to their lives as they knew them.

Landon had proven to be more than competent when it came to securing the Clan's systems, but Julian was used to being the one all the Brothers contacted when they had a problem. It was hard turning over the controls to someone else, but at the same time, it was freeing. It was his responsibility to keep the Clan safe, but it was also his responsibility to protect his mate. Julian now knew where the Feds were keeping Katherine. He couldn't concentrate on the hacker problem and come up with a viable plan to rescue his mate at the same time.

The longer they went without a hacker getting through the system Landon had put in place, the more frustrated Julian became. Either the one who'd caused all their troubles recently had disappeared, or he wasn't interested in messing with them any longer. Several had come close to getting through the maze Landon had constructed, but none had made it through the last task. Julian should be grateful, but he wanted to know who had been the bane of his existence the last year. More than that, he wanted to know if the same person was responsible for Katherine being in prison. Julian vowed to find out who was responsible and make them pay.

Chapter Twenty-Seven

Sin got Rocky settled in the living room where she could get to the kitchen and the bathroom with ease. Had they been alone, he would have taken her to their bedroom. But Sin had things to take care of, and until he returned later, she would have to remain downstairs. If she got tired, she could sleep in the bedroom he normally slept in before he met her. He had never entertained another woman there, either, and he made sure Rocky knew it. That was the last time he wanted them to discuss discretions in his past, because that's where anything that didn't include the two of them belonged – the past.

Ingrid had cooked a simple meal including chicken noodle soup for Rocky. By the time Vivian arrived, Rocky was nestled on the end of the sofa. Sin had propped her up on plenty of pillows, and there was a blanket folded over the arm should she need it. Sinclair didn't have to explain the remote controls, because Finley was staying with the women while Sin took care of business. Banyan, Thane, Remy, and Gannon were stationed outside. They weren't standing sentry. Instead, they were sitting on the patio smoking cigars and drinking whiskey. As soon as Sin left, though, all four would be on high alert until his return.

Sin kissed Rocky and told her to have fun while he was gone. She knew without asking what he was going to do since they'd already discussed it, and his mate was okay with it. Sin hated leaving her, but taking care of Tommy and Blake was something he needed to do himself. Rett met Sinclair at the training facility where the three humans had been kept since they were picked up. They had been allowed to use the restroom when they first asked, but since they hadn't been fed or given water, all three were becoming dehydrated and didn't need the facilities.

Sin had finally decided on the best course of action for Shelby. After doing some digging, Banyan had found Shelby's family in upstate New York. Sin was putting her on an airplane. A one-way ride to the other side of the country. She was never to come back to California. Sin made it clear the woman was going to be monitored twenty-four hours a day. If she so much as thought of stepping out of line, her free pass at living would be revoked. Through tears and chattering teeth, she said she understood. Rett had seen to getting her home to pack her bag and to the airport. Now, they were left with the two males.

While Rett dragged Tommy outside, Sinclair entered the room where Blake was being held. There was dried blood under his nose and on his bottom lip. He didn't say a word as Sinclair sat down in front of him and opened a folder. Sin's beast was ready to rip into the man, but he assured his shifter he would get his vengeance later. "This is a contract stating you are selling your club to me. Here is a check for double the price of what your land and building are worth."

"Why would you want to buy a piece of shit club for that much money?" Blake asked, licking his dry lips when he caught sight of the number of zeros.

"Let's just say I have my reasons." Sin handed the paperwork and a pen over to the man who signed on the dotted line without reading the contract. He grabbed the check out of Sin's hand and folded it up before sliding it in the back pocket of his jeans. As soon as that was taken care of, Sin stood the man up and wrenched his arms behind his back, securing his hands with a zip tie.

"Ow, man. What the hell?"

"We are going for a little ride." Sin grabbed him behind the neck and shoved him toward the door. "Let's go."

"I'm not going anywhere with you. Wait... Wait!" When Blake dug his feet in, Sin picked him up and slung him over his shoulder. He strode to the waiting SUV where Rett had already deposited Tommy in the back. Sin tossed Blake down next to his friend and slammed the door on them.

"Are you driving, or am I?" Rett asked.

"You can," Sin said, climbing into the passenger seat.

From what he'd been told, Tommy and Blake had yelled at each other for hours on end, both blaming the other for their predicament. Now, they were yelling at Sin, asking where they were being taken and back to blaming the other. It was hard for either one of them to do much damage to the other considering their hands were secured behind their backs. Sin did hear a couple of "umphs" and "ows". Someone had gotten creative, probably figured out their knees still worked. Rett turned on the radio to the local hard rock station, and the sound of Cyanide Sweetness filled the interior. "Hey, isn't that Sixx's kid?" Rett asked.

"Yes. It is pretty cool having one of our own on the radio." Sin needed to check in and see how Sixx and his family were fairing. Maybe invite them over so Rocky could be around other mates. He started a text to Rocky but deleted it. He had to give her space even though he was craving to know she was okay. He refused to call Finley. The Goyle would think he didn't trust him. Instead, he sat back and watched the scenery go by. Normally, Sin loved coming out to the desert. Not only could he turn his Lambo loose, but also his shifter. It was the one safe spot he could fly without fear of anyone seeing him. On nights when the moon was new, the sky was dark as pitch. Even if humans were in the vicinity, they wouldn't be able to see him flying high above them.

It took a while to get to the secluded part of the desert, but when they arrived, Sin and Rett got out, each grabbing a shovel from the back compartment. Tommy's eyes grew wide. "Hey. What are you going to do with those? Hey. Hey!" His voice faded when Sin slammed the

290

door closed. Blake's voice added to Tommy's, but Sin ignored them both.

"Are you sure you want to be part of this? You are an officer of the law."

Rett anchored the shovel he was carrying over his shoulder. "I'm a Gargoyle first. I don't know all the details of what these two did to your mate, but I know enough to believe they deserve what's coming." Rett found a spot and began shoveling dirt. Using their shifter strength and speed, they had two deep holes dug in no time. They returned to the SUV and pulled the now kicking men out of the back and dragged them to where their new homes were.

Rett held Tommy while Sin dealt with Blake. Sin reached behind the man and pulled the check out of his back pocket. "You won't need this," Sin said, sliding the paper into his own pocket.

"Hey, man. You can't take that back. I signed the club over to you. I..." Sin slapped Blake hard across the face.

"Shut the fuck up. If you haven't realized it, this is the end of the line for you two. Neither one of you are fit to be called human. You drug women, take advantage of them. Treat them like trash when you're worse than dog shit left on a sidewalk for someone to step in. You picked on the wrong girl, though. You see, Rocky is mine, and both of you raped her."

"I didn't rape her. She begged for it, man!" Tommy yelled. Rett hit him, breaking his nose in the process. Blood ran over his lips and down his chin.

"I will get to you in a minute," Sin promised. He picked Blake up and shoved him down in one of the holes. With his hands tied behind his back, the man couldn't try to dig his way out. Sin shoveled the dirt back into the hole around him leaving only his head above ground. Blake was begging Sin to pull him out, promising God or anyone who would listen he would change his ways. Tears mixed with

291

snot as the man realized his fate. His voice faltered as it mixed with the sobs that were doing him no good. Sin turned to Tommy. "Now for you."

"No man, you got this all wrong. He did it. It was all Stansbury."

"Shut up!" Sinclair roared, his shifter voice encircling Tommy like an eerie black fog. Tommy did as commanded, and Sin closed the distance. "You raped your cousin. Not once, but numerous times. You raped a young, innocent, helpless girl. Now I am going to do the same thing to you." Tommy tried to wiggle out of Rett's hold, but the Goyle was too strong. Sin phased fully, letting the beast loose. Tommy cried out and did his best to shrink back from the monster in front of him. With Rett at his back, he had nowhere to go. Sin retracted his wings, but he used his claws to slash across Tommy's chest just deep enough for blood to pool. He then shred Tommy's jeans open, cutting a path down his thigh.

Blake's whimpering mixed with Tommy's strained voice. "Please, have mercy. I'm begging you."

"Where was your mercy when you raped Rocky? Where was your mercy when you shoved a broom handle inside her, preventing her from ever having children? Where was your mercy when she was bleeding out in the bathtub alone?" Sin shouted as he ripped Tommy's dick from his body. He held the bloody appendage in front of the man's face. Before Tommy could pass out from shock, Sin did as he said he was going to and shoved Tommy's dick down his throat. He inclined his head to Rett, and the Goyle dragged Tommy to the waiting hole next to Blake. Tommy was gagging, trying to draw in a breath. Sin had intended to hurt Tommy the same way the bastard had hurt Rocky, but he was ready to be rid of the filth he felt from being around the two of them.

Rett covered Tommy with dirt. When he finished, he told Tommy, "Like I told you in your basement,

292

I'm the judge, jury, and executioner. Neither of you will ever hurt anyone again. Death is too good for either one of you, but if you'd been sent to jail, death would have come quickly. At least this way you have plenty of time to think back on your miserable lives while the vultures peck at your eyes."

Sin removed his shredded shirt and released his wings. Rett also took off his shirt and phased next to him. The two Goyles took to the skies, letting their beasts have free rein for a while. Sin needed to get the rage out of his system before he returned home to Rocky. Never in all his life had such deep-seated malevolence gripped Sin the way it had toward the two humans below. Rett had seen to it the authorities were notified of the drugs stashed in Tommy's basement. With him gone, his mother would take the fall, and Sin prayed she got what was coming to her in prison. Those who had hurt Rocky were all taken care of. With each flap of his wings, he cleared his heart of the hatred. Purged the ire from his soul.

After about an hour, Sin and Rett found their way back to the SUV. Rett grabbed the shovels and put them in the back while Sin climbed in the passenger seat. He didn't bother looking at either human. What was done was done, and he never wanted to see their faces again.

When Rett sat down in the driver's seat, Sin turned to him. "Thank you."

"It was what they deserved. And I know if I ever need you, you'll be there for me. You're a great leader, Sin. Every one of us has your back. I hope you know that. And now, we have your mate's back, too. If you ever need me, all you have to do is call." Sin's throat was thick, and he was afraid if he looked at Rett, the tears burning the back of his eyes would fall, so he merely nodded and turned his face away from his fellow Goyle. The Stone Society was filled with Gargoyles who were loyal to the death, but hearing one express their loyalty didn't happen often. It was an unspoken vow between them.

Rett dropped Sin off at the training facility where he'd left his car. He planned to go by his apartment at the hotel and take a shower. He wanted no trace of Blake or Tommy on him when he held his mate in his arms. Instead of driving across town to the hotel, Sin used the shower there so he could get home to his mate sooner. Sin removed the check from his pocket and dumped his bloody clothes in the garbage. Sin had the signed documents, and soon, he would tear down the club and replace it with something beautiful. After he was sure he'd removed all traces of the two humans, Sin found some cut-off sweat shorts another Goyle had left behind. Sin didn't race home. He was ready to see Rocky, but adrenaline was still pumping through his veins. He needed to be calm around Rocky. At least until she'd had time to heal some more. When he arrived home, he parked the Lambo in the garage and walked around to the side of the house where his bedroom was. Opening his wings, Sin launched himself onto the balcony and entered his sanctuary to further calm down.

Sin froze when he opened the door. Rocky was in the middle of their bed, curled up on her side. Sin reached out with his senses. Finley and Vivian were downstairs. Their voices blended with those coming from the television. There was no noise on Ingrid's side of the house, but Sin felt her heartbeat and knew she was asleep. Instead of bothering with clothes, Sin slid into the bed beside his mate. His naked mate. Rocky rolled over facing him, sliding her hand around his waist and nestling into the crook of his neck. Sin wrapped her in his arms and inhaled deeply. Her bare skin had his cock hard and ready to slide inside her, but he needed to wait. Needed to give her time to make the first move when she was ready.

Rocky was safe, and now they could put her past behind them. Sin would do whatever it took to erase the bad memories by making new ones for her. If only he could fix what Tommy had done. He hadn't been lying when he told her they could adopt if she wanted babies. Sin would give her the universe. Somehow. Some way.

Rocky woke up surrounded by strong arms. She wanted to wake up this way every morning for the rest of her life, however long that may be. She'd thought of nothing other than the things Sin had told her about him being a Gargoyle and what that meant for her. She had tried to pay attention to Vivian's nonstop chatter, but she finally apologized to her best friend and excused herself to her bedroom. Their bedroom. Sin had said it was hers if she accepted him and would give them a chance. Rocky didn't hesitate to make her way upstairs instead of using his bedroom on the first floor.

Rocky wanted Sin for however long he would have her. If she accepted the mate bond, they would be together a long time. She wanted forever with him. She was still weak, but Rocky needed Sin to make love to her. To make her forget the pain of her past. At some point during the night, Rocky had found Sin's hair, and she had her hand buried in its softness. She turned it loose and slid her fingers down his chest. She paused there, making circles in the bristly hair, ghosting her fingertips over a nipple. A low rumble came from Sin's chest, bringing a grin to Rocky's face. She felt his eyes on her, but she didn't look up. She continued her perusal of his body.

Snaking her fingers over the ridges of his abs, Rocky traced the outline of the V on either side of his hips. Vivian had been correct. His V pointed to heaven. Heaven that was covered by a pair of shorts. Rocky sat up and hooked her fingers beneath the waistband. Sin pushed his lower body up so she could slide the shorts down his legs. Sin kicked the shorts off his feet, sending them flying through the air across the room. He pulled one knee toward him, but left the leg closest to her flat on the bed. Rocky enjoyed the view of a naked Sin. His veiny cock was stiff and pointed at his stomach. Rocky was on the wrong side of his body to properly stroke him, so she maneuvered herself between his legs.

Rocky grabbed Sin's long hard-on in her right hand and slid her tongue through the glistening slit. She had never given a blowjob of her own free will, but this felt right. She wanted to please Sinclair in every way possible. She had nothing to offer him other than her body, and she would make sure to offer it up as often as he needed it. When Rocky placed her lips around the fat head of Sin's cock, he groaned and pushed his hips towards her. Not hard enough to take control, but enough to let her know he was enjoying what she was doing.

When Sin covered Rocky's hand with his own, she finally found his eyes, wondering if she was doing something wrong. The lust she found in the deep, dark depths let her know she was doing something right. "Baby, you don't have to do this," he offered, but the rise and fall of his chest said he wouldn't mind at all if she continued.

Rocky squeezed his cock in her hand, and said, "I know I don't, but I want to." Sin turned loose, and she stroked the velvety skin covering his rock hard dick a couple of times, using the leaking fluid from the tip to help glide her hand up and down. Sin put his arm behind his head and closed his eyes. His other hand moved back and forth from one of his nipples to the other, his short fingernails scraping over the tiny nubs. She would have to remember he liked that. Rocky returned her mouth to his dick and slid it in as far as she could take it without gagging. She hadn't been with many men, but those she had been with weren't as blessed in the dick department as Sin was. She took her time taking him into her mouth, opening her throat a little farther on each stroke. She still had to use her hand as a barrier, but the friction of her hand and the tight heat of her mouth were working if Sin's moans were any indication.

"I'm close, baby. If you don't want me coming down your throat, I suggest you stop now."

Rocky didn't stop. She'd already had a small taste of him when she licked the tip. Now, she wanted all of him. Rocky sucked harder on the head as she pulled back before sliding her tongue down the underneath. She pulled one of his balls into her mouth and sucked, and Sin pulled his knees to his chest, giving her more room. His pucker was winking at her, enticing her to explore a little. Rocky released Sin's nut and stuck her finger in her mouth. When she pulled Sin's cock back into her mouth, Rocky slid her wet finger into his ass, finding his prostate at the same time his dick bottomed out against the back of her throat. Sin shouted her name as his ass clamped down around her finger and his seed pumped out of his dick. Without her hand as a barrier, his cock was choking her, but Rocky did her best to swallow down his release.

Sin did an ab curl and grabbed her under her arms, pulling Rocky up his body. He flipped her over to her back and angled his mouth down over hers, tasting himself on her tongue. When he broke the kiss, Sin did something that should have grossed her out completely. He wrapped his mouth around the finger that had been inside of him, flicking his tongue around the digit. His eyes were wild, and Rocky's ego swelled knowing she did that to him. "I need to be inside you, sweetheart. I need to claim you, but if you are not ready, I'll go take a shower to calm down."

"I want you, Sin. I want you to claim me as yours." Rocky swallowed hard before saying the words that would change her life forever. "I want you to bite me."

Chapter Twenty-Eight

Sin had never heard more beautiful words in all his life. He had waited almost six hundred years for his mate, and now she was accepting him and everything that went with being his, yet he was still hesitant. Rocky's mind wasn't back to where it was before Tommy tried to kill her. She might never be whole again in that regard. If she wasn't, he'd deal with it then, but now, Sin had a choice to make. He could bite her and pray she realized what she was asking for, or wait and have her change her mind because he refused her.

"Sin, I know what I want. You offered me forever, and I want that with you. Are you having second thoughts? Is it because I'm not whole?"

"No, no second thoughts." He had promised not to lie to her, but he had with those words. "Okay, maybe I was, but not for the reason you think. This is a big step, Raquel, one that cannot be undone."

"Sin, please. If you want me in your life, do it. Mark me as yours." Rocky leaned her head to one side exposing the long line of her neck.

Fucking bite her. Make her ours.

I'm getting there. Shut up.

If you don't bite her, I'll take over.

Sin's beast was strong, and he had no doubt it would do its best to take over Sin's body. Rocky didn't need that, so he pushed her legs apart and rocked his erection against her wet pussy. With her neck on display, Sin slid his cock into her tight heat. Knowing what he was about to do had him ready to explode even though he'd just had an orgasm. This wasn't about the release, though. This was him taking the final step to making Rocky his for eternity. His cock swelled inside her, filling her up. The more he rocked back and forth, the louder Rocky's moans became, the deeper her nails tried to dig into his skin, the headier her scent became as her essence slicked his cock. Rocky wrapped her legs around his waist and dug her heels into his thighs, trying to pull him farther into her body. She'd done that the last time they made love, and Sin let the move guide him. It let him know his mate could take more of him. Wanted more of him.

Sin gazed down at her, thanking the gods and the fates for bringing them together. When Rocky smiled at him through her moans, Sin knew he was going to seal the bond. He called forth his wings, and Rocky gasped. She ran her fingertips along the edge of one, and the contact was enough to drive Sin to the edge. "Rocky," he husked, dropping his fangs. Once again, Rocky cocked her head to the side exposing her neck. The electrical current running through Sin's body was more intense than anything he'd ever felt. His mate's body enveloped his dick while her soul surrounded his very existence. When Sin could no longer hold back his orgasm, he whispered, "I love you," and lowered himself so his face was buried in her neck. Sin roared as the first jet of his seed exploded inside his mate, and he sank his fangs into her shoulder.

Rocky shuddered beneath him as her own orgasm blended with his. When Sin's fangs bit into her skin, Rocky latched onto Sin's shoulder, biting and sucking as hard as she could. Sin released his mouth and licked at the blood, but his mate continued to suck on his skin as she writhed beneath him. Sin retracted his wings, but he didn't pull out. He continued to stroke her core with his semi-hard cock which was coming back to life even after two orgasms. Rocky was crazed with lust, and Sin allowed his mate to use his body. When she finally pulled her mouth away from his shoulder, she grabbed the back of his head and crashed their mouths together. Rocky sucked hard on his tongue, fucking it the same way he was rolling his hips. He knew in his heart they were making love, but damn if they weren't fucking too. The love was there between them, but the lust was taking over, and Sin was ready to go with it.

His mate would be sore after he got through with her, but she had all the time in the world to heal. For now, he would give her what she wanted. What she needed. And by the way she was trying to climb his body, Rocky needed it hard and fast. Sin flipped Rocky over to her knees. "Lower your chest to the bed, baby." With Rocky lying on her chest, her ass was in the air, giving Sin the perfect angle to send Rocky over the edge. It also provided him the view her ass. Sin stroked his mate's core with long, deep thrusts, quickening his pace with each roll of his hips. Rocky had risen onto her forearms and was rocking her head side to side. "Sin, oh God, harder," she begged. In the position she was in, Rocky could push back against him, taking what she wanted. His mate was so fucking sexy when she went after what she craved. Sin slammed into her core over and over, his cock filling her up. "Sin... I'm... bite me again... please," she begged. Sin knew the mate bond had already taken effect.

"Baby, we are mated," he said between grunts. "I don't need to... fuck, bite you, unh, again."

"I want you to. It feels... oh God Sin, bite me..." Rocky's eyes were wild as she looked over her shoulder at him. He couldn't say no to her. Would never be able to deny her anything.

Sin pulled her up against his chest and dropped his fangs once more as Rocky reached behind his head grabbing onto his hair. Her pussy tightened around his dick, and Sin bit his mate's neck, making sure he marked a different spot. Her blood tasted like honey as he sucked it into his mouth. There was no trace of the foul drugs she'd been given, and Sin thanked the gods for that. He pulled his fangs back as his own release shook his body. His back arched, shoving his cock as far into her as physically possible. He held it there as his seed filled her up. Rocky panted with him as she

300

came down from the high the release offered. Sin knew this because he was experiencing the same thing. He had heard bonding with one's mate was intense, but he never realized it would be this explosive.

Rocky fell forward to the bed, and Sin followed, dropping to his side. He brushed the damp hair off Rocky's face and placed soft kisses on her lips. When she opened her eyes, they were back to their beautiful sapphire. "Wow," she purred against his mouth. "Will it always be that intense? I mean, we had sex before and it was amazing, but what just happened between us was... crazy."

"It is because we were designed for each other. Everything between us going forward will be amplified. You and I will be able to sense one another's emotions. When you are upset, I will know it. When you are happy, I will feel that too. I hope to only feel the happiness flowing through you from now own. I have already vowed to spend my life giving you everything you desire, and I promise you, today and always, to make all your dreams come true." Sin's eyes misted over when a lone tear rolled down Rocky's cheek. During the last hour, their souls had combined, and Sin could feel how deeply Rocky loved him. Words weren't needed between them.

"Thank you," Rocky whispered.

"You never have to thank me for anything, sweetheart. All I have is yours."

"Even the Lambo?"

"Even the Lambo."

"What are you saying when you call me Bella Ragazza?"

"It's Italian for beautiful girl."

"It's nice," Rocky said softly. Sin rolled to his back pulling Rocky to his side. She draped her body across his, and he breathed in the scent that was hers alone. He let if fill his senses completely, allowing the peace that came with it to lull him to sleep.

When Rocky opened her eyes, the first thing she noticed was the empty space beside her on the bed. The second thing was the glorious ache between her legs. She stretched out and pulled Sin's pillow to her nose, inhaling deeply. "Are you sniffing my pillow?" his deep voice asked from the bathroom door.

"Maybe," she said as she inhaled again. "I'll never get my fill of you."

The bed dipped down as Sin sat next to her. He placed his hand on her bare leg, but kept it from roaming along her skin. "Speaking of, how are you feeling?"

"I'll admit I'm a little sore. But I'm ready to go again." And she was. Rocky hoped at some point her libido would slacken, because they couldn't stay in bed forever. Sin had business to tend to, and she... Rocky had absolutely nothing to do other than enjoy this newfound happiness. She wouldn't dwell on the fact her mind might never recover. She wouldn't worry about becoming a nurse. She would concentrate on getting better, and that started with food. "I'm hungry. I hope Ingrid didn't throw out the leftover soup from last night. It was really good."

"If she did, she will make you more."

"I can cook for myself. She doesn't have to wait on me."

"She does, because I pay her an exorbitant amount of money to take care of us. If you want to cook something, feel free. The kitchen, the house, everything here is now yours. I want you to decorate however you want. If you prefer new furniture, we'll get it. The only thing I ask you not change is the garden. It was designed to replicate the garden Rafael has at the manor, and I really love the layout."

"Speaking of your brother, when do I get to meet him and the rest of your family?"

302

"Well, we do have to travel to Greece and try to locate my mother. After that, I thought we could spend some time in Italy, and on our way home, we can stop off in New Atlanta. How does that sound?"

"You're taking me with you?"

"Yes." Sin pulled Rocky into his lap. At some point, he had taken a shower because his hair was damp. "I will not leave you behind again. I have asked several of the Clan to come along with us. Flying fifteen hours in an airplane isn't most male's idea of a good time, but they are not opposed to the beautiful islands we'll be visiting."

"Why don't you like to fly?"

"Oh, we love to fly, but we prefer to use our own wings."

Rocky hadn't thought about that. When Sin unfurled his massive wings the night before, Rocky had been in awe of how big they were. The softness of the leathery hide was as much a dichotomy as Sin's cock with its velvety skin covering his hardness inside. Just thinking about it had Rocky wet and ready. She turned to straddle Sin's lap and rubbed against his erection. "Rocky, there is nothing I would like more than to take you again, but I need to feed you. You have to keep your strength up if you're going to get better."

Rocky knew this, and she was hungry, but she needed him filling her up more than she needed to eat. She leaned in and licked his shoulder where she'd bit him the night before. "Why are there no teeth marks?" she asked.

"Our kind has special skin. It is virtually impenetrable."

That was convenient for her. As much as she liked biting him, she wouldn't leave a mark. "Do you think it's weird I like biting you?"

"Not any weirder than me biting you. I'm of the mindset if something feels good, do it. There is nothing you can do to my body I will not enjoy."

303

Rocky ran her thumbs across both his nipples, letting her nails scrape the tips. Sin growled, and Rocky found herself on her back with her knees pushed back against her chest. Sin lowered his head between her legs and began torturing her clit. It didn't take Rocky long for orgasm number one to rock her body, and Sin filled her up the way she needed for orgasm number two. Number three came when he made love to her against the shower wall before washing her body and shampooing her hair. Rocky had never been pampered, nor had she ever felt loved as much as she did when Sin was taking care of her. When he whispered, "I love you," against her lips while he was drying her off, Rocky knew she'd made the right choice in giving their relationship a chance.

Vivian had asked her to be careful the night before when she'd come to stay with Rocky while Sin was out doing whatever it was he had to do. Rocky assured her best friend she knew what she was doing. Sitting on the patio enjoying brunch felt domestic, but it also felt like home. Sin's plate was piled high with various meats and cheeses while Rocky was enjoying a bowl of soup with a slice of Ingrid's homemade bread. Rocky's appetite was coming back quickly, but she wasn't going to push her body with rich, filling foods yet.

Sin had been on the phone nonstop ever since they'd made their way downstairs. Ingrid had prepared their food then made herself scarce, but not until she'd given them both a motherly hug. Rocky hadn't realized how much she'd missed having a mother. It had been so long since she lost her parents. Rocky clung to the older woman, and Ingrid had held on just as tightly. Ingrid had pushed Rocky's hair behind her ear and whispered, "Welcome home, child."

While they were eating, Sin explained how some humans were aware of the Gargoyles, and how their families had been serving the Clans for centuries. Ingrid's family was one of those. It did Rocky's heart good to know someone had been looking out for Sin until she came along. Granted, she could barely take care of herself, but Rocky vowed to do whatever it took to keep Sin from regretting his decision to mate with her.

The next few days were spent in much the same way. During the day, Sin worked in his office when it was necessary. He took Rocky shopping for the clothes she would need on their trip. Since her wardrobe consisted of jeans and T-shirts, Sin spared no expense buying her whatever she wanted. When she couldn't decide between two bathing suits, Sin bought them both and added one to the mix he wanted to see her in. Rocky didn't remember owning a dress, but Sin's eyes lit up whenever she tried one on, so she decided wearing something other than jeans wouldn't be a hardship. Shopping tired Rocky out easily, so Sin took her home and let her order more items online. He paid for overnight shipping so her things would arrive before they left for Greece.

It surprised Rocky how quickly Sin obtained a passport for her. When she asked how he managed, he said, "I know people," and grinned. Her man knew lots of "people", and she was quickly figuring out most of them were Gargoyles. The more of them she met, the more she realized how lucky she was to be surrounded by so many honorable males who vowed to protect her. When she thought back to meeting Remy at the gym, Rocky remembered the good vibe she'd gotten from him. She had that same vibe with every new Goyle she encountered.

Sin still wouldn't allow Ingrid into their bedroom, so mundane chores such as cleaning and changing the sheets were left up to them. Rocky didn't mind, though. Sin had stripped the sheets and together they put clean ones on the bed. As much sex as they were having, this had become a daily ritual. The first time Sin opened a closet door and tossed the soiled bedding in without looking, Rocky thought he was crazy. The second day he did it, she asked, "Aren't we going to wash those?"

Sin grinned and tugged her toward the door. When he opened it, he pointed. "Laundry chute. There's a bin in the laundry room downstairs that catches whatever we throw in." Rocky had been amazed at the enormity of the house. She was still getting used to the amenities it offered, but a laundry chute was over-the-top crazy, and she loved it. Rocky couldn't believe all this was actually hers, and the idea of being able to do whatever she wanted was going to take some getting used to. Having lived a harsh life with her aunt and cousin made her appreciate everything she now had. Everything Sin was giving her.

Rocky was tired since it was well past the time she'd been going to bed recently. Still, she filled her new suitcases with the clothes Sin had bought. His own suitcase was packed and ready to go. When she was satisfied she had everything she needed, Sin carried the bags downstairs and deposited them in the waiting SUV. Since Finley was traveling with them, he had driven the larger vehicle so all their luggage would fit. The other Clan members had left that afternoon on a commercial flight so the jet wouldn't be crowded. Ingrid had waited up in case they needed anything. She hugged the three of them before they headed out and made Sin promise to bring Rocky back home to her. Rocky teared up at the love she felt from her new friend.

Instead of driving his own vehicle, Finley climbed into the backseat while Sin drove and Rocky rode shotgun. She was nervous and excited about flying. Sin assured her numerous times she would love it, and it wasn't until she was twenty thousand feet in the air that she agreed wholeheartedly. The flight was long, and after the initial thrill of being in such a luxurious jet wore off, Rocky slept for most of the trip. The bed in the rear of the plane wasn't nearly as large as the one she'd been sharing with Sin, but it was large enough for them both to spread out. When she asked where

306

Finley was going to sleep, Sin let her know Gargoyles didn't require as much sleep as humans did, but if he got tired, he would stretch out on the leather sofa. Or the floor. Fin could sleep anywhere.

Rocky still tired easily, but Sin didn't seem to mind when she needed to nap. It was close to noon, and she curled up on the leather sofa with her head in Sin's lap while he and Finley talked about everything from sports to family business. The one thing they didn't talk about was the reason they were going to Greece in the first place. Rocky caught the name Alistair a couple of times, but neither male would say much about him around her.

The food on the jet was comparable to Ingrid's cooking, and that was saying something, especially for it to have been prepared on an airplane. Rocky had joined Andre, the flight attendant, in the galley when she'd gotten up to use the restroom. She enjoyed his company as he talked about his wife and kids. As possessive and protective as Sin was around the other Goyles, he didn't seem to mind Rocky spending time with this human.

When they were close to their destination, Rocky's breath caught in her chest as she gazed out the window at the blue waters of the Ionian Sea. Sin had given her a little background about the islands they were going to visit, but he'd failed to mention how beautiful they would be. Rocky definitely wanted to visit the islands when they weren't on business and Sin could show her around.

When their plane touched down, two Goyles she recognized exited a blacked out SUV and boarded the plane. After the initial hellos, the pilot joined them in the cabin, and Thane filled them in on what they'd been able to surmise up to that point. "We made contact with Carter. No one has heard any more from Donovan since he managed to get his message to Xavier. Unfortunately, we don't know any more than we did before we arrived. Alistair hasn't been sighted leaving his villa, but there are several vehicles coming and going. Hunter has a boat waiting to take you over to the island." There was no airport on the small island where Alistair was holed up. Sin didn't want to take the ferry, so Hunter was providing transportation for him.

"When I spoke to the King earlier, he made it clear this is a get in-get out mission. I am not to engage, so this will hopefully not take too long. Thane, you will drive me to the harbor. Finley, you and Remy will stay aboard the plane with Rocky. When I am satisfied enough people have seen my face, I will return, and we will be on our way to Italia." Sin's deep voice slipped in and out of his accent when he became serious. One day soon, Rocky was going to ask him to teach her his native language.

"Are you sure I can't come with you?" Rocky asked. It wasn't she didn't trust the other Gargoyles, but she was scared for Sin.

Sin placed his hand under her chin and tipped it up. "I am sure, Tesorina. I don't want my uncle to know I've found my mate, and I sure as hell don't want him anywhere near you. I am not going to take a chance on this being the one day he leaves the security of his villa." Sin pulled Rocky to him and slanted his mouth across hers. This was a possessive kiss for the males to see. Sinclair had told her he trusted the others with Rocky's life, but he still had to piss a circle around her since he was leaving her in their care. Sin and Thane strode out of the plane and over to the SUV, leaving Rocky with nothing to do but wait.

Chapter Twenty-Nine

Sin hated leaving Rocky, but he had a duty to the Clan, to his King, and he intended to fulfill it quickly. The sooner he showed "Rafael's" face around the island, the sooner he and Rocky could get on with the fun part of their trip. Sin was in awe of his mate. She'd not once complained about the amount of time he spent on the phone or the computer. She was becoming fast friends with Ingrid, and that warmed Sin's heart for both women. Ingrid never had children of her own. Not because she didn't want them, but because her husband couldn't have them. He'd died soon after they were married, and Ingrid never found love again. Instead, she devoted her life to caring for Sin. Rocky had been without her mother for fourteen years, and Sin could see the way Rocky clung to the affection Ingrid offered.

Thane dropped Sin off at the harbor and waited for him to return. Hunter greeted Sin, and the two shook hands. Hunter had helped Dante and Isabelle get their son back when Isabelle's supposedly dead husband had kidnapped the boy. After they boarded the small boat, Hunter gave Sin a list of establishments he had mapped. Hunter Thomason and his twin, Carter, had been born Greek, but once they realized what a dickhead their king was, they had pledged their loyalty to Xavier Montagnon, King of Italy. The two of them had recruited several of their own clan and were now spies for Xavier and Rafael. At one point, Carter had lived at Alistair's villa, but when Dante's mate had been kidnapped and held prisoner by Alistair and his adopted daughter, Kallisto, Carter had helped with Isabelle's release. Having blown his cover, Carter had to lie low after that. Now, Donovan had taken Carter's place and was currently on the inside with Alistair. If they could only get word to him regarding Sin's mother.

Hunter was a male of few words, and his broody disposition suited Sin just fine. Hunter dropped Sin off on the small island of Ithaca and handed him the keys to a car. "It's the black BMW parked in the first row."

"Thank you. I appreciate your help, Hunter."

Hunter simply inclined his head. Whatever was going on in the male's life was eating away at him. Sin didn't want to pry, but damn if he didn't want to help the Goyle. Leaving Hunter alone, Sin found the sports car and made quick work of visiting the establishments on the list. He had just entered the last one when a voice he recognized caught his attention. It had been a long time since Sin had heard the voice or seen the face, but it was one he'd never forget. Sin headed straight to the bar and ordered a double shot of ouzo while his uncle conducted business across the room. And by business, Sin meant Alistair watched while several women paraded in front of him. He pointed at two of them while the others disappeared into the back of the bar. Alistair pushed the young women in front of him toward the door. When he finally noticed Sin sitting there, Sin raised his glass and took a sip of the clear liquid.

Alistair narrowed his eyes and asked, "Rafael, what are you doing on my island?"

Sin shrugged. "I was in the neighborhood. Thought I would stop by and say hello to my mother. You wouldn't by chance know where I could find her, would you?"

One corner of Alistair's mouth curled into a snarl. "I'm sorry. It's not my day to watch after her. Besides, last I heard she was nowhere near Ithaca."

Sin ran the tip of his index finger around the rim of his glass, letting his uncle get a good look. "If you do run into her, tell her to call me."

"Where are you staying?" Alistair asked.

"Around. She knows how to get in touch with me." Sin tossed back the rest of the ouzo and returned the empty glass to the bar. When he stood from the stool and pulled out his wallet, his uncle waved him off.

"Put that on my tab, Dennis. It's the least I can do for *family*." Alistair sneered at Sin and walked out the door. Sin gave his uncle a five-minute head start before making his way back to the marina. He called Rafael while he drove around the island making sure he wasn't being followed.

"Sin, was your mission successful?"

"You could say that. I saw the bastard with my own eyes. He thought I was you, and we exchanged *pleasantries*."

"I don't suppose he gave up Mother's location."

"No, he didn't. But I would be willing to bet he has her. What do you want me to do?"

"Nothing. You did your job; now go spend some time with your mate. When you get here, we'll pull together a plan of action."

"If you are sure."

"I'm sure. I'll see you when you get here." Rafael disconnected, and Sin drove around another hour before heading back to the harbor. He parked the BMW in the same spot he'd pulled it out of and strolled back to Hunter's boat. When he stepped over the side, Hunter raised his eyebrows.

"Your heartrate's elevated. Is everything okay?"

"I ran into my uncle, but I am fine. Now, please take me back across the sea. I need to see my mate."

Hunter did as asked. While they were skimming across the water, Sin started to ask the male about his life, but Hunter's body language kept him from it. When they pulled into the slip, Sin shook Hunter's hand. "Thank you again. I hope whatever is bothering you finds a favorable solution."

Ever since Stavros Sarantos had been hauled off to jail, Alistair had kept his human partners much longer than he was used to. He preferred to rotate them out after fucking them a few times, but now he didn't have that luxury. He had more urgent matters to tend than vetting whores. Still, he'd taken the time out of his day to visit the local pub master who Alistair knew rotated new girls in and out. Color him surprised when his nephew had been sitting in the pub, sipping ouzo like he owned the place. Alistair knew that wasn't true, because *he* owned the godsdamned pub.

Kidnapping Athena had been a brilliant idea, and it worked like a charm in bringing Rafael into Alistair's territory. There was no way the bastard could bring his whole army with him, and he wouldn't dare chance leaving the mates at home without protection. Alistair needed Achilles to keep a line on where Rafael was. Kallisto had promised she was close to finding a replacement, but he knew he was going to have to take matters into his own hands. He had given his daughter a week, and she had failed him. Alistair called Achilles and left a voice message, making him an offer he couldn't refuse. Now, he had to sit back and wait for the fucker to return his call. While he was waiting, he decided to see if he'd gotten his money's worth of the two new girls he'd procured that afternoon.

Alistair's dick was hard just thinking about inflicting a little pain. He slashed a flogger over both bare asses at one time. Neither girl made a sound, not even a whimper. He hit them harder, and they remained quiet. He had hoped to get a rise out of them, but they'd been trained to accept the pain quietly. He hated training bitches, but if he was going to keep these two, he'd have to reprogram them.

"Get on your knees," he commanded. Both women scrambled off the bed and knelt in front of him, heads bowed. He tilted the blonde's chin up using the handle of his toy. "Suck my cock," he instructed. She immediately swallowed his erection all the way down, no gag reflex to be found. "Play with her pussy, but don't make her come," he instructed the brunette. She moved in behind the other girl and slid her hand between the blonde's legs, stroking her clit while kissing on her shoulder and neck.

The blonde moaned around his dick as the brunette stroked her clit and played with her breasts. She gave head better than any he'd ever had, sucking hard and taking him deep. Alistair was close to getting his nut when a knock on the door interrupted. "What?" he yelled.

"Sir, we have a problem."

"What kind of problem?" he gritted through his teeth. The blonde worked his cock harder and faster.

"It's the prisoner. She's... Sir, your sister is dead."

Alistair jerked, and the blonde's teeth scraped his dick. He slapped her hard across the face, knocking her to the floor. No, no, no! Athena couldn't be dead. He wasn't finished using the bitch. Alistair pulled his pants up and fastened them as he stepped toward the door. He threw it open, shouldering past the Goyle who had been assigned to watch his sister. Alistair strode across the compound and down the stairs to the room where he was keeping Athena prisoner. Her body was stone still. He reached out with this shifter senses and found nothing. No breath, no movement, no life essence at all. The bitch had willed herself to cross over. "Godsdamn you!" he screamed and kicked her lifeless body.

Sin made his way to the waiting SUV and told Thane what had transpired. As badly as Sin wanted to drive straight back to the airstrip, he had Thane circle around the city to be sure they weren't followed. When they arrived, Sin jumped out of the SUV and ran up the steps, taking them two at a time. He needed to see his mate and make sure she was safe. He held his breath until Rocky's beautiful smile greeted him.

Bryce had been seated with the others until Sin and

Thane were on board. "By the way your heart's beating out of your chest, I'd say we need to get in the air?"

"Yes."

Finley said, "I can feel your unease from over here. What happened?" Rocky linked their fingers together and leaned into his body, offering her support silently.

Sin inhaled Rocky's scent, allowing it to help calm him. "I saw Alistair," Sin said. The males all spoke at the same time, and Rocky pulled back, looking at his face. "I am okay, Tesorina. My uncle was in the last bar I went to. He was purchasing girls to add to his stable. He mistook me for my brother, which was what we wanted. I asked him if he knew where Athena was, and of course he said no. He left, and here we are. Rafael and I are going to decide what to do when I go visit him next week."

"Are you sure he didn't follow you?" Fin asked.

"Pretty damn sure. I drove around for over an hour before I returned to the boat, and Thane and I took our time getting back here. Bryce, please get us in the air."

"Ten-four," the Goyle said as he returned to his spot in the cockpit. The flight to Italy wasn't a long one, but Sin still wanted to relax with his mate. Thane and Remy left the plane and loaded up in the SUV. They were taking another commercial flight so the jet wouldn't be so crowded. As nice as it was, there wasn't enough room for four large males, Rocky, and Andre.

It didn't surprise Sin to see Andre was paying special attention to Rocky. Whenever she was awake, the human made sure she was well fed and had whatever she wanted to drink. Her appetite had come back full force, and Sin wanted her to have her favorite foods, even on the jet, so he had called ahead and told Andre what those foods were. Rocky had spent time talking to the flight attendant on the trip over, and he was happy to see her comfortable around another human male. Since it was so late, Andre had fed the others but had kept a plate warm for Sin. Rocky sat close by his side while he ate a late dinner. It amazed him how content she was to sit for long stretches without talking. She was nothing like her best friend, and Sin thanked the fates they hadn't stuck him with the loud redhead.

After he ate, Sin took Rocky to the bedroom and lay down with her. His mind wouldn't stop thinking about his uncle, but his mate needed to sleep. Rocky changed into shorts and a T-shirt and curled up next to Sin. The turbulence didn't seem to bother her while she was awake, but if the plane dipped while she was sleeping, Rocky snuggled closer to him. Sin didn't sleep, but he also didn't move for fear of waking Rocky. He wanted her to have every opportunity to heal.

When they landed, Finley was bouncing off the walls. He hated flying and was ready to hit the beach, where he could run and swim in the waters of the sea by the villa. Fin had never been there, but Sin had described his old homestead, and Finley was ready to partake of everything it had to offer. Sin was as well. He wanted to show Rocky where he'd been born and where he and his brothers had been taught the ways of their kind by their father. Next to sharing his homeland with Rocky, Sin was most looking forward to visiting his father's grave after two hundred years.

They were greeted by Penelope, her husband, and three children. Penelope was Priscilla's sister and equally as devoted to the Clan as Priscilla and Jonathan. Fin, Remy, and Thane were privileged with the knowledge of where the villa was located as well as to whom it belonged, an honor few Gargoyles had been afforded. Rafael had bought their childhood home from their father before he was slain, and Rafe had kept its ownership hidden from everyone, including their mother. Athena helped rescue Isabelle and had been somewhat welcomed back into their lives. With the news that Rafael and Kaya were going to have a baby, Athena had become more involved with her family. Sin had hoped one day he would also give her a grandchild, but for now, he'd have to leave that to his brothers.

Sin and Rocky spent the next three days basking in the sun by the Ionian Sea. They toured the grounds while Sin recounted tale after tale of growing up with his three brothers. He visited his father's tomb alone while Rocky stayed in the kitchen with Penelope, learning to make cannoli. Their time flew by, but Rocky had been able to see a side of Sinclair no one else did. For a little while, he was the carefree boy running over the family home, laughing at everything and worrying about nothing. The three Goyles who were with them gave them space, but they all ate together in the large family dining room with Penelope and her family every evening. It did Sin's heart good to have them all together and to see his mate flourishing among his Clan.

When their time was up, they all bid goodbye and rode together to the airport. Finley was returning to California with Thane and Remy, while Sin took Rocky to meet his brothers and their families. Other than Bryce and Andre, Sin and Rocky had the jet all to themselves. Sin could tell Rocky was tired, but she was happy. He hoped meeting the other mates would continue adding to her joy. He needed to keep an eye on her and make sure she got enough rest. He had noticed her frowning on occasion, but when he asked what was wrong, Rocky would perk back up and assure him nothing. Sin didn't believe her, but he wanted her to come to him freely. He didn't want to continuously badger her. Maybe one of the mates could get her to open up.

The Clan's jet landed at the New Atlanta airport shortly after noon on April second. The weather was perfect for that time of year on the East Coast, because it was akin to the weather in California. As Rafael walked toward them, Sin had to rein in his beast and not hit his brother. The fact he'd asked Sin to go to Greece so soon after he met his mate

316

hadn't sat well with him, even though Rafael had no way of knowing Rocky would be in trouble. Even though Sin had told Rocky that Rafael and Kaya were picking them up when the jet landed, she still stared in shock when she saw Rafael. Rocky looked back and forth between them. "I can tell you apart, but I can see why your uncle couldn't. You look like twins."

Rafael and Kaya laughed, and after official introductions were made, Kaya took Rocky and hugged her tightly. "Welcome to the family," she whispered. Rocky hugged her back and smiled her beautiful smile.

"Thanks. It's good to finally meet another woman. All that testosterone gets to be too much after a while," Rocky admitted. She had never said anything to Sin about feeling overwhelmed being in the presence of the other males. He would make sure that didn't happen again anytime soon.

"I totally understand. We have family day at our house every Sunday, and sometimes I feel like I'm the coach of a football team instead of Queen to Gargoyles."

"Oh my God. You're the Queen! Shit, and you're... Am I supposed to bow? Do the fist thing? Sin?"

"Baby, everything is fine," he assured her, pulling her into his arms.

"No, you don't have to do anything like that, Raquel. I'm just Kaya. Think of me as your sister-in-law, because that's basically what I am. Rafael, even though he is Clan leader, is now your brother-in-law. We're your family, nothing more. Okay?" Kaya grabbed Rocky's hands and squeezed.

"Okay. Sorry I freaked. I'm not used to all this. I went from being nobody with two friends to his mate with all these superheroes hanging around. I'm still trying to figure it out."

"Superheroes?" Rafael asked.

Sin shrugged. "Let's get out of here. I am ready for

317

Priscilla's cookies."

"She made some fresh this morning," Kaya said as they walked toward a waiting sedan.

"And Rafe didn't eat them all?" Sin asked.

"Nope. She hid them from me."

Everyone laughed except Rocky. She smiled, and Sin twined their fingers together. When they were seated in the backseat, he reached out and checked on her internally. Her heartrate was slightly elevated, and her mood was a little on the sad side. He couldn't ask her what was wrong with Rafe and Kaya sitting up front, so he kissed her on the temple and poured as much love into the kiss as he could. Rafael and Kaya chatted on the drive home, making sure to include Rocky in the conversation. When Rafe asked her what she thought about the villa, her mood lightened, and she excitedly told them about Penelope and her family. "She taught me how to make cannoli, but I've already forgotten how."

"Don't worry about that. Between Ingrid and Priscilla, they'll have you cooking like an Italian in no time," Rafael beamed. When he pulled up to the security box, he rolled the window down and said, "Bella Mia." Kaya's face lit up, and Sin was no longer jealous of the love shared between the two of them. He had his own love, and Sin vowed they would be as strong as his brother and his mate were. The gate rolled open, and Rafe pulled the car down the long, winding drive. Several cars were lined up in front of the massive garage.

"Brother, you didn't tell me you were having a party." Sin would be glad to see his Brothers, but Rocky might not be ready for such a large crowd. She had just commented on being overwhelmed.

"I'm not, but when the mates found out Rocky was coming by to visit, they made a point of being here to welcome her to the family."

"Yes, we need to tell her the truth about you badass

Gargoyles."

"What truth?" Sin asked Kaya, worried about what exactly the females had planned.

"You know, things like how possessive you are. How we can't go anywhere by ourselves. How you want to lock us up in our bedrooms and never let us leave."

"What is wrong with that?" Sin asked.

"My sentiments exactly," Rafael chimed in.

Sin helped Rocky out of the backseat and took her hand. While Rafe and Kaya walked ahead, Sin told his mate, "I am sorry if this is overwhelming. At any time you need a break, you let me know, and we will disappear for a while. Okay?"

"Thank you, Sin. But I'm looking forward to meeting the others. Not to learn your secrets, exactly, but they will have a different perspective where you all are concerned, and I think I need to hear what they have to say."

"Remember, sweetheart, we are already mated, so you can't run from me now."

Rocky grinned. "If I run, it will be so you can chase me." She winked at him and laced their fingers together, pulling him toward the manor.

Chapter Thirty

Rocky was indeed overwhelmed at first, but not in a bad way. All of Sin's brothers and a couple of his cousins were inside the house or on the back deck. Their wives were there along with some of their children. It made her feel special that they'd all taken the time to come meet her. When the conversations started, it was clear they were excited to see Sin, too. It had been several years since they'd all been together, and it was evident they'd missed him, and he them.

As soon as Rocky was introduced to everyone, the women stole her away and shooed the men outside. For some alpha badass Gargoyles, as Kaya put it, they did as their females asked. Sin whispered in her ear before he left her alone, "Remember what I said," and kissed her softly. When she turned around, all the women, whose names she had already forgotten, were smiling.

"That never changes," the redhead said. She looked like a cross between Lara Croft and a biker chick.

"I'm sorry. I've already forgotten your names. My brain's still a little foggy, so if I don't remember everything, please forgive me." Rocky hadn't admitted her issue to Sin, because she didn't want him to worry.

"Heck, I'm still calling roll when we're all together," a pretty blonde said. The graceful way she moved reminded Rocky of a dancer, only not a pole dancer like her. "Come on in the den. We'll get comfortable, and you can hear our stories."

"She's not going anywhere until she's had a cookie," an older version of Penelope said.

"You must be Priscilla," Rocky said as she grabbed a couple of cookies from the tub the woman was holding.

"I am, indeed. Welcome to our family." Priscilla

lovingly patted her on the cheek before she disappeared back into the kitchen.

Rocky followed the women into a den even more spacious than Sin's. Finley had mentioned about Rafael having the family over. She could see why he would need a house so big if there were more people than the handful who had shown up that day. Once they were seated, Kaya said, "I'll start since I was the first of us to mate with our men." Rocky ate her cookies while Kaya told her how she'd met Rafael and how she'd been taken prisoner by Isabelle's brother. Rocky had plenty of questions, and Kaya answered every one of them patiently.

Next was the biker chick, Tessa. It shocked Rocky that Tessa was a half-blood. When she asked the woman about her fangs, Tessa happily popped them out like they were discussing lipstick instead of sharp canines. Tessa's story took longer because not only was she a half-blood, but she was also the infamous baby who had been cloned back when the world fell apart. "Yep, Jonas is her father," Tessa said, indicating the pretty brunette sitting next to her on the sofa.

Isabelle, another half-blood and daughter of the doctor who caused the apocalypse, took that as her cue to take over the conversation. Rocky couldn't believe these women had been through as much shit as she had. Isabelle had been coerced into traveling to Greece by the daughter of the same man Sin had gone to see. Rocky hoped she never ran into that Kallisto bitch, or she'd claw her eyeballs out. How dare she kidnap a child? As if Connor knew they were speaking about him, the boy entered the den quietly. His mother stopped talking when he approached Rocky.

"I drew this for you." He handed her a piece of paper, and on it was a beautiful park. Rocky had never seen the place before, but it was somewhere she would like to visit.

"Thank you," she told him as he exited the room

321

without another word.

"Do you mind?" Isabelle asked.

"No, of course not. Your son is very talented," Rocky said as she handed the picture over.

Tessa leaned over Isabelle so she could see the drawing. "These are usually premonitions. Thank the gods he didn't draw you with Alistair."

When Isabelle showed the drawing to the other women, they all smiled. "Do you recognize the park?" Isabelle asked, handing the paper back.

"No, but it's beautiful. He has premonitions?"

Isabelle smiled. "Yes. He can also communicate with Dante mentally. When Kallisto kidnapped him, Connor would draw images giving Dante clues to where he was. He's an amazing child."

"Wow. I'm so glad you got him back." Rocky would never have a child of her own, but it didn't mean she wouldn't love the other ones. She would be the best aunt all these babies had ever seen whenever she was around. Since she and Sin lived on the West Coast, Rocky didn't guess she'd be seeing them often. "Okay, who's next?"

The pretty blonde spoke up. "That'd be me." Abbi had been married when Frey figured out they were mates. She and her brother were tormented at the hands of her husband up until the time Jasper's mate, Trevor, shot him. Rocky had been right about Abbi; she was a dancer. Abbi had been dead when Frey caught her going over the bridge, but his bite had brought her back. There was a sadness about Abbi, but it left anytime she mentioned Frey. Rocky could understand that. She was sad, too, but one thought of Sin had her mood swinging back toward happy.

"Sophia, you're up," Tessa said when Abbi was finished. Sophia was also a half-blood, and she had traveled to Egypt when Kallisto kidnapped her parents. Rocky was really beginning to hate that bitch. Even though Sophia's story had its really bad parts, there was lots of laughter when she recounted wearing prosthetics and pretending to be an old woman. "You should have seen the look on Nik's face when I kissed him and called him 'sonny'." Rocky didn't miss the way Sophia guarded her small belly the same way Kaya did.

"Hey, are you okay?" Isabelle asked, taking Rocky's hand in hers.

"Yeah, it's just..." Rocky didn't want to tell them why she was sad, but they had all opened up to her. "I guess you want to know about me." Rocky took a deep breath and started at the beginning with her parents' deaths. She didn't leave anything out. If these women were going to be her sisters, as they all claimed to be, she thought maybe they could help her get over the sadness she felt. Help her squash the notion she was inadequate because she couldn't have kids. When she got to the part about Tommy, Tessa flew off the couch and started cursing.

"That motherfucker. Where is he? I'll rip his dick off and..."

Rocky interrupted her. "He's dead."

"Oh. Well I hope it was painful." Tessa sat back down, but the anger on Rocky's behalf was still coming off the woman in waves. It flowed through Rocky, but she didn't feel the anger; it was Tessa's concern for her surrounding Rocky, and she welcomed it.

Rocky smiled, and continued. When she got to where she was currently, she admitted, "I think being that close to death did something to me. I get confused. I feel off-balanced. I look at all you amazing women. You're what a mate should be. I'm not whole. I wasn't when Sin met me, and now, I'm even less of a woman. I can't remember stuff. I can't give him babies. I..." Rocky was pulled off the sofa into Abbi's arms, and the rest of the women were right there with her.

"Stop it," Abbi said through her tears. "If anyone knows how you feel, it's me. But let me tell you something."

Abbi wiped Rocky's tears she didn't realize were falling while Abbi's own continued down her face. "None of us are whole, sweetie. You've heard our stories. Yes, some are worse than others, and I'd dare say you've been through the worst of it, but Sin loves you. For whatever reason, you were chosen for him, and if there's one thing we've all figured out in the last few months is there's a reason for it. You might not think you're good enough for Sin, but we've all felt that way about our own mates. Well, everyone except Tessa." The women laughed, and Tessa grinned.

"If Sin is like the other males, and being a Stone, I'd bet any amount of money on it, he's strong, and he has so much love to give you. Let him wash away your past. Let your strong male do his job and make you whole again. Give him a chance." Abbi pulled Rocky into a tight embrace, and the others joined in a huge group hug.

"I need my girl, now," Sin's deep voice boomed through the house, warning them he was coming. The women didn't back away though. If anything, they tightened the hug. Rocky had never felt such love coming from another woman, not even Vivian. And now she had several friends – sisters – to pull strength from.

Sin wasn't alone. The other men were right behind him, and they each went to their mate. The love between each couple was tangible. Rocky knew if she looked hard enough, she'd see it floating across the room from couple to couple. Sin grabbed her hand, and when she felt a tug, she looked up into his face. His eyes were full of worry. She brushed her free hand down his arm to reassure him she was okay. Another couple entered the room – Jasper and Trevor. Why she could remember their names and no one else's was a mystery, but Trevor stepped up in front of Sin and said, "If I may, there's something I want Rocky to see."

Surprisingly, Sin let her go without a fuss. Maybe it was because Trevor was gay, or he was already mated. Either way, Sin kissed her softly on the lips before telling

Trevor, "Don't take too long."

Rocky looked at each of the women and smiled before she and the young man who looked to be about her age left the room.

"I know the other mates told you their stories, and I wanted you to hear mine." Trevor, with his inked arms and purple streaked hair, led Rocky to Rafael's garden. She was amazed at how the air changed as soon as they stepped onto the walkway which meandered through Rafael's sanctuary. The only way she could describe it was magical. Much like Sin's smaller garden, the area Trevor led Rocky through felt as though Buddhist Monks had blessed the place themselves. A sense of peace washed over her.

Trevor stopped at a bench a short distance in and asked her to sit with him. He was silent for a moment, sitting with his eyes closed. Either he was basking in the same feeling she was, or he was gathering up the words to say. She didn't bother him in either case. When he opened his eyes, Trevor slipped his hand into hers and held it like a brother would. She liked him already.

"I'm a clone," Trevor blurted. "I was made because my brother was sick, and my parents wanted there to be spare parts. All my life I've felt like a freak. Like my parents didn't want another child, only a thing to keep their *real* child alive. Don't get me wrong; I love Travis, and he loves me. But if anyone feels unworthy to be a mate, it's me."

"How... how did you know?"

"All the mates have felt the same way, with the exception of Tessa. That broad's crazy, but I love her. She's a badass in her own right, and I'd take her at my back any day." Rocky didn't miss the admiration in Trevor's voice when he spoke of the redhead. "When a new mate meets the rest of us, we tell our stories so the new person doesn't feel alone, and so they, *you*, know we understand how you're feeling. When I met Jasper, I was in heaven. Not because I thought he was interested in me romantically, but because

325

he liked the same kind of music I do. When he asked me to a concert, I accused Dante of putting him up to it. When my boss assured me that wasn't the case, I thought to myself 'finally, I have a friend.' I had made friends in college. Most of them were clones, too. But after college they all drifted away, and I was alone. Travis was living in New Athens, and even though we talked on the phone, I rarely saw him.

"Jasper and I hung out, playing video games. Of course I was attracted to him, and it wasn't just the mate bond. Have you seen him? I still can't wrap my head around why he would want to be with someone like me, bond or not. Anyway, his ex-lover, Theron, came to town. The scary bastard followed me, but when he couldn't get to me, Theron hurt Travis and killed his girlfriend. Then he targeted Jasper. Him and his crazy human sister, Kallisto, poisoned Jasper, leaving him to die."

"Alistair's daughter, Kallisto?"

"Yep. Bitch gets around. She's had her hand in several of the mate's troubles. Anyway, Dante was the one to tell me about the Gargoyles and what being a mate meant. That explained everything. The mate bond was the only reason Jasper wanted me. Long story short, Jasper beheaded Theron and has spent every moment since then convincing me I am worthy to be his mate and that he loves me because I'm me."

"I appreciate you sharing, Trevor, but that doesn't change the fact I'm not whole."

"In what way?"

"I can't give Sinclair babies. My cousin Tommy..." Rocky choked back a sob, and Trevor pulled her into a hug.

"Let me tell you something. I can't give Jasper babies, either." Rocky laughed at his silliness, but he was speaking the truth. "Don't laugh; you know it's true. But that doesn't mean we can't adopt or find a surrogate. Just because he's Gargoyle doesn't mean our child has to be. Now, I know your situation is different. I don't have the equipment for making babies. Your cousin – who I hope is rotting six feet under – took the ability away from you. Sin isn't going to love you any less because of it. For whatever reason, you and he were thrown together by the cosmos, or the fates, or gods, or whatever. You were chosen for Sin, so there is something about you he needs. And vice versa. I'm still not convinced the fates got it right in putting me with Jasper, but I'm sure glad they did. While he tries to convince me we belong together, I bask in the love he shows me every day. I no longer identify as Trevor the clone. Now, I'm Jasper's mate and best friend. I like that title a whole lot more. Let Sin do that for you. Let him heal you."

Rocky leaned her head against Trevor's shoulder as she let the words sink in. Was it that easy? Nothing else in her life had ever come easy, but maybe this would if she let it.

"We better get back. I have a feeling Sin is standing at the back door listening in to make sure I'm not trying to corrupt you."

"He can hear us all the way out here?"

"Oh, yeah. Can't you Sinclair?"

A shrill whistle rent the air, and Trevor laughed. "I hear you, buddy. Come on, beautiful. Let's get you back to your man."

Rocky didn't like the fact Sin had listened in on their conversation, but she did appreciate his protectiveness. When she and Trevor walked out of the garden, Sin was standing on the back deck with his forearms leaning on the railing. Jasper was next to him, grinning like a fool at his mate. Jasper took Trevor's hand and led him inside, leaving Rocky and Sin alone.

"He is right you know." Sin placed his hands on Rocky's face and held her. "You are worthy, and like Jasper, I am going to spend every second proving it to you. I love you, Raquel. No matter what the future brings, I will always love you."

Sin angled his mouth over Rocky's, and the love coming from her man flowed through the kiss. Like he was sharing his life force with her. She still had doubts about what she had to offer him, but they were mates, so it wasn't like she was going anywhere. Maybe with enough time, Rocky would find something positive to offer Sin besides her body. She would spend her days making him happy, however he wanted.

They stayed at the manor for a couple of days, and Rocky spent a lot of time with Kaya. Seeing her hold her belly kept the ache in Rocky's heart churning right below the surface, but she admired the Queen and wanted nothing but the best for her and Rafael. For all her new family. When it was time to leave, Sin promised to bring Rocky back soon, but he also promised to introduce her to Sixx and his family. Rocky would have new friends in Desirae and Simone, if she so desired. And she did. The more she was around the others, the more she would learn how to deal with having an alpha Gargoyle in her life.

As soon as they were home, Rocky called Vivian so they could get together and chat. Rocky also visited RC's with Sin by her side. It was weird walking into the place she'd called home for so long, but seeing it put back together and thriving warmed her heart. She'd done right by Uncle Ray in selling the place to Banyan. Bridget was happy with her new boss. Not only did he run a tight ship, but he was extremely easy on the eyes.

Rocky and Sin got into a routine. He worked from his home office, and Ingrid taught Rocky to cook. Rocky had to write everything down, because she tended to forget some of the most basic day to day things, and when she tried to cook, she always left ingredients out. When she would get frustrated, either Sin or Ingrid would pull her into a sweet hug and tell her it was okay. Their patience never wavered, and Rocky began to get used to the fact she would never be the woman she once was.

A couple of weeks after they returned from Greece, Rocky and Sin were relaxing in the hammock he'd put up for her in the garden. Her thoughts turned to children as they often did, and Rocky said, "Something's bothering me."

"Tell me, Bella Ragazza."

"I showed you the picture Connor drew for me. Isabelle said his drawings were usually premonitions. I wonder if the one he drew for me was merely a pretty picture, or if it has a hidden meaning."

"I was going to wait, but I can see it is time."

"Time for what?"

"For us to take a ride. Let's get our shoes on, and maybe I can ease your mind."

After they found their shoes, Sin put Rocky in the Lambo, and they set out on a little drive. When she saw the direction they were headed, she said, "I'm not sure I want to go this way, Sin."

"Trust me, baby." Sin linked their fingers together and did what he always did when she was nervous or upset. Somehow, he pushed his happiness into her through nothing more than a touch. As they neared the area where the strip club was, Rocky sat up in the seat and looked around. "It's gone," she muttered.

"It is," Sin said as he parked the car in the lot in front of where the club used to be. In its place was a beautiful park. The landscaping rivaled anything she'd seen in a magazine or on television, but the best part about it was it was almost identical to the drawing Connor had given her.

"How did he know?" Rocky asked as she got out of the car.

"I honestly have no idea. Before I... before Blake went missing, he signed over the club to me. I knew then I would put something beautiful in its place, but until I saw Connor's picture, I had no idea how beautiful. Come on, let's take a look around."

They walked the path circling the park. Benches were nestled between trees and plants. A children's play area had been constructed in the middle. Rocky's heart clenched, but Sin pulled her closer to his side as they continued on around. When they came to a fountain, Sin stopped. He dropped to one knee and took Rocky's hands. "Raquel, you and I are already mated and as such, you are stuck with me, but I wanted to give you something else. Something more." He pulled a box out of the pocket of his cargo shorts and opened it. The ring wasn't huge, but it was larger than any diamond Rocky had ever seen. The setting was simple, like her. "I love you, Bella Ragazza, and I want you to have my last name. Will you do me the honor of marrying me?"

"Yes," Rocky whispered through her tears. Ever since she was little, Rocky dreamed of a man like her father. Fate had smiled on her and given her what she asked for. She wasn't worthy of him, but she was getting there. Sin slipped the ring on her finger and said, "Let's go to the courthouse. I want this done today. Then, if you want, we can have a huge wedding with all our family present."

Rocky didn't need anything extravagant, she just needed Sin.

Epilogue

Three Years Later

"Rocky, are you ready to go?" Sin asked as he snugged his tie around the top button of his white dress shirt. It wasn't necessary to dress up for the trip they were about to take, but Sin felt it appropriate to look his best for the occasion. When his mate didn't answer, Sin walked down the newly reconstructed hallway outside their bedroom. He found Rocky in the baby's room, holding a new teddy bear.

"I can't do this," she whispered as she clasped the bear to her chest. She didn't have to look at Sin for him to know she was scared shitless.

"You can, beautiful girl. You're going to be a wonderful mother, and I'm going to be there with you every step of the way. So are Ingrid, Desirae, and Simone."

Rocky had only recently graduated from nursing school. It had taken her three years and a lot of help from Sin, but she had completed her LPN course. He tried to convince her it wasn't necessary for her to get a job, but after a while and some advice from the other mates, Sin realized it wasn't about the job. Rocky needed to feel like she had accomplished something, especially after her near-death experience made it hard for her to complete thoughts at times. She often got frustrated when she forgot things, and her mood swings had worsened instead of improved.

Both Desirae and Simone had given birth four months after Sin and Rocky had gotten married. The two women spent as much time with Rocky as she would allow. She loved Rae and Simone, but the babies were a reminder of what Rocky would never have or never be able to give Sin. If he could go back and kill Tommy Cartwright all over

331

again, he would. Only this time, the torture would last much longer. He had not only taken away Rocky's ability to have children, but also something deep inside her heart that kept her from feeling whole. When Sin saw the longing in his mate's eyes each time she was around the babies, he decided they needed a child of their own.

Sin looked into the adoption process. He convinced Rocky it was something he needed in his life, even though he was doing it as much for her as for himself. She agreed but only if they slept downstairs with the child. Since Sin didn't want to change bedrooms, he had workers come in and modify the upstairs, making it into two bedrooms instead of one large one. One night while patrolling for Unholy, Rett mentioned an infant whose parents had been killed in a car wreck, leaving the child an orphan. She had been placed with children's services because no family could be located. Sin petitioned the court to adopt the baby, and he and Rocky had been approved. This was the day they were picking her up, and Sin was ready to go.

Pushing off the door frame, Sin went to Rocky and held out his hands. Rocky allowed him to pull her to her feet and wrap her in his strong arms. Over the last three years, Sin had done his best to show Rocky how much he loved her, because the gods knew he did. And he knew she loved him just as much. The sex between them had gotten even more intense. Rocky couldn't get enough of Sin when they were in the bedroom. She wouldn't admit it, but he was pretty sure she was still trying to erase the memories of her past. Whatever the reason, Sin met her thrust for thrust, bite for bite. Orgasm for blindingly powerful orgasm. But something died inside Rocky the day she almost lost her life, and he was still trying to resurrect that part of his mate. Sin vowed to make his mate whole again, no matter how long it took.

"Let's go get our girl," he whispered against her ear. Rocky didn't reply. She let him lead her to their bedroom where he helped her get dressed. When they were ready to go, Sin and Rocky climbed in their new SUV. They still had the sedan, but Sin insisted Rocky and the baby have the safest ride possible. He would have stuffed it full of bubble wrap if others wouldn't have thought him crazy.

When they arrived at the brick building downtown, Rocky's heart rate kicked up several notches, but Sin didn't let her have that moment to freak out. He rushed her into the building so she could meet her new baby. Their baby. Sin had already met with the case worker, Mrs. Pritchett, but when Rocky met the woman who reminded him of Ingrid, his mate began to calm down. The woman praised Rocky for being strong, loving, and selfless to take someone else's child into her home and love it as her own. Sin had told her the same thing, but hearing it from someone else made a difference. Mrs. Pritchett didn't make them wait. She led them down a hallway and into a room that served as a temporary nursery. Sin stood back and allowed the woman to hand the baby to Rocky.

The change that overcame his mate was instantaneous. As soon as Rocky had the sweet little baby girl in her arms, she melted, and her resolve strengthened. The love Rocky had for the baby filled the room. It was so strong it almost knocked Sin down. He knew then he'd made the right decision in convincing Rocky to adopt. He stepped closer so he could get a good look at his daughter. A sob caught in his throat. Sin had a daughter. No, she wasn't biologically his, but the instant he saw her tiny hands and her bright blue eyes, he was gone. He understood why Rocky reacted the way she had. This tiny little person was now his responsibility to love and protect. Not caring who was in the room, Sin placed his fist over his heart and bowed to the baby in his mate's arms. "On my honor," he whispered.

"Are you going to change her name?" Mrs. Pritchett asked. Sin and Rocky had discussed this already. Since the baby was so young, she wouldn't be confused if they gave her a name of their choosing. As she got older, they would tell her about her birth parents and the name they had chosen, but Sin and Rocky wanted her to have a different name. Something that was special to them.

"Yes. We've decided on Athena Michelle, after both our mothers. We're going to call her Chelle," Rocky said. "Here, Daddy. Your turn." Rocky held the small bundle out to Sin, but he hesitated. Being only one month old, Chelle was tiny. He'd held Desirae and Simone's children, but they were older. And they hadn't been his.

Rocky gently pushed the baby into his arms, and the same love Rocky had exuded rushed through Sin. It was love at first sight. "Il mio bambina bella. I'm your papa, and I'm going to be the best papa in the world. I vow this to you on all that is holy." Sin was barely able to speak the words as they caught in his throat. Chelle's tiny hand reached for Sin's face. He slid his finger in her fist, and the bond began right there. Mrs. Pritchett left the room, giving them time alone with their new daughter.

"She's beautiful," Rocky said as she ran a finger down Chelle's cheek.

"Just as beautiful as her mother." Sin tipped Rocky's face up and kissed her. Never in his long life had Sin experienced more love than in that moment. Not only the love he had for someone else, but the love his mate had for him and their baby girl. It was a living entity, and he would carry it with him throughout eternity. Sin tried daily to fill the void in Rocky's life, and now, the baby in his arms would help fill in the gap. Sin had no doubt his mate was well on her way to being complete.

Coming Soon

Julian
Stone Society Book 9

Finding Me
The Music Within Book 3

Cast of Characters

http://www.faithgibsonauthor.com/stone-society-family-tree.html

Dear Reader: The best way you can help an author is to leave a review where you bought the book. It doesn't have to be long, just honest and heartfelt. If you liked this story, please consider leaving a review.

About the Author

Faith Gibson is a multi-genre author who lives outside Nashville, Tennessee with the love of her life, and her four-legged best friends. She strongly believes that love is love, and there's not enough love in the world.

She began writing in high school and over the years, penned many stories and poems. When her dreams continued to get crazier than the one before, she decided to keep a dream journal. Many of these night-time escapades have led to a line, a chapter, and even a complete story. You won't find her books in only one genre, but they will all have one thing in common: a happy ending.

When asked what her purpose in life is, she will say to entertain the masses. Even if it's one person at a time. When Faith isn't hard at work on her next story, she can be found playing trivia while enjoying craft beer, reading, or riding her Harley.

Connect with Faith via the following social media sites:

https://www.facebook.com/faithgibsonauthor

https://www.twitter.com/authorfgibson

Sign up for her newsletter:

http://www.faithgibsonauthor.com/newsletter.html

Other Works by Faith Gibson

The Stone Society Series

Rafael

Gregor

Dante

Frey

Nikolas

Jasper

Sixx

The Music Within Series

Deliver Me

Release Me

The Sweet Things Series

Candy Hearts – A Short Story

Troubled Hearts

Spirits Anthology

Voodoo Lovin' – A Short Story

DOMESTIC VIOLENCE HOTLINE

1-800-799-7233 OR 1-800-787-3224 (TTY)

If you or someone you know is a victim of domestic violence, I urge you to call the number above. Please, say NO MORE.

Made in the USA
San Bernardino, CA
15 July 2018